The Freiburg Cabinet

a novel by

Thomas Charrington

.. for Siobhan

Acknowledgements

My heartfelt thanks to Adrian House for the considerable time and effort he spent injecting some order and decorum into the very crude initial manuscripts, and for his invaluable advice on shaping the general landscape of the book.

Huge thanks also to Kevin Fox-Slater and Fee Combe, for their numerous sharp observations and key suggestions, and for helping me mould my characters into living, breathing human beings - all from an isolated farm in the Australian outback.

My gratitude must also extend to Paul Martin of Robin Martin Antiques in Notting Hill, for allowing me access to his extensive library, and for his golden nuggets of information regarding 18th century French furniture.

Finally I must thank Ara for providing the initial spark, Fi for giving me an outlandish book by a master forger, and Philip for his artistic grip on the graphics and presentation.

PROLOGUE

Oliver Clasper had just shut Titus in the kitchen for the night and was wandering down the flagstone passage to the hall when the telephone rang. He stopped dead and looked at his watch—it was 11.48pm. A flutter of worry rippled through him; calls at this time of night were rarely good news. Turning round, he retraced his footsteps back into the dark kitchen and plucked the handset from its illuminated cradle on the wall

"Strupe Hall," he said tentatively.

There was no answer at the other end of the line, but he could sense the presence of someone very clearly.

"Hello …can I help?" he said, firmly.

A further hesitation followed, and then he heard some guttural sounds as though the caller was being strangled. Suddenly Fabien's quavering voice came through, low and urgent.

"Oliver … Oliver. I'm sorry," he began, the words coagulating in his throat, "I … I know it is late … but … oh merde, I needed to tell you something … something important." He hesitated, and Oliver heard a muffled sob. "She's … she's leaving me, Oliver. *Elle voulais me quitter!*"

"Who is?" Oliver said, momentarily confused.

"*Cecile!* Cecile … she has 'ad enough … wants to end it. Mon Dieu, I've just been speaking with her! Oliver, she says the situation is 'opeless … that I have never got any money or time … that I never *will* have any in my present job. I have told her to be patient, but she won't listen. I feel I have let her down … *failed her. Je n'en peux plus!*"

Oliver stayed silent as the young Frenchman wept uncontrollably for a few seconds, before regaining a semblance of control.

"I am calling to … to agree with your plan; let's just make the cabinet … copy the damn thing and sell it, or I 'ave lost her forever!" He choked up and fell silent again, whilst Oliver took a deep breath.

"Fabien … Fabien, now listen to me," he said authoritatively. "I'm terribly sorry to hear this … I really am. But my dear fellow, you're obviously in a highly emotional state at the moment. This is a big decision—it needs to be made with a cool mind. I don't want …"

"*Oliver … I don't care!*" the young man shouted in a high-pitched outburst. "*Tu ne comprends pas? I just don't care about consequences anymore. I am finished without your 'elp!*"

The line went dead, and Oliver was left gazing into the gloom at the glowing eyes of Titus in his basket. Contrary to his expectations, this phone call had brought some very good news indeed. The project could now begin. Carefully, he replaced the handset onto its cradle and left the room.

"Peoples do not judge in the same way as courts of law; they do not hand down sentences, they throw thunderbolts; they do not condemn Kings, they drop them back into the void; and this justice is worth just as much as that of the courts."

- Maximilien de Robespierre –
1791

Thomas Charrington

Chapter 1

Three and a half years later

Two blazing shafts of sunlight stabbed through the cobwebbed windows of Melvyn's workshop, like a pair of vigilant prefects in a chaotic and turbulent classroom. Swirling eddies of dust and steam drifted skittishly across their piercing gaze, before once again disappearing into the shadows beyond. On the other side of the cluttered space, Melvyn stood back from the grinding machine for a few moments and wiped the sweat from his brow with an old towel. Short and muscular, with a heavy boned face and dark inset eyes, his rounded shoulders and powerful stained fingers were testament to a life of hard physical work.

Blowing the dust from his watch, he glanced at the time and sighed—nine twenty am, and the air was already too warm. It was going to be one of those relentlessly hot summers, where the pitch on his roof dribbled like black treacle and the grass was crisp underfoot. Kneeling down, he reached to the back of a low shelf and pulled out a dusty fan. After giving it a few vigorous puffs, he plugged it in and pressed 'on', anticipating an orgasmic blast of cool air. Nothing happened.

"For fuck's sake!" he shouted, yanking the plug out and throwing the fan back on the shelf. "Does anything bloody work around here!"

He flexed his cramped fingers and took a long swig of water from a green canvas flask on the workbench. Belching loudly, he swept a lank rope of black hair away from his face and again picked up the chisel. Bracing himself and anchoring his feet once more, he leaned forward and carefully forced the blade against the vicious wheel, causing an angry stream of sparks to rain down on his hands.

Ignoring the hideous racket, his eyes watched the fiery spitting edge between metal and stone with intense concentration. To overheat the blade would ruin it, so every few seconds he whipped the tip of the tool into a vessel of cold water where it hissed briefly and coughed out a small cloud of steam.

After a while he switched the machine off, and grabbing a thick oily cloth, gave the shaft a few deft wipes. He then turned to face the window. The blade glittered in a thoroughly pleasing way as he rotated it slowly, close to his face, searching for any imperfections in the newly honed metal. Behind him, the grinder slowly wound to a stop and the workshop filled with a heavy silence.

As he put the chisel down, he became aware of a telephone ringing in the main house, and shortly after, his wife Mary called him distantly from the kitchen door. He muttered to himself, remembering the line to his workshop was faulty again; it was bound to be Oliver, his long-time employer. Oliver's impatience had always been a source of irritation to Melvyn, and on this particular morning, for no identifiable reason, even more so. It seemed that so often when he felt in a perfectly focused state— when his own mind was vibrating as it were, in complete sympathy with the items surrounding him—Oliver was there to interrupt.

He moved lithely across the planked floor in a well-rehearsed pattern, flicking off the power to the glue pot and iron, and then pulling the blinds down on the windows. Sometimes the conversation was short and other times lengthy, but he liked to play it safe. He briefly allowed his eyes to rove over the masterpiece in the centre—the eighteenth century Freiburg Cabinet twin, with its chequered purpleheart marquetry and intricately carved ormolu mounts. Instinctively he scanned the carcase for deviations from parallel and the entire structure for squareness. It was firmly glued now and there was precious little he could do to correct it, but checking and rechecking was an itch he could never shake off.

"Call me, I need an update, Melvyn," Oliver's voice said charmlessly on the messaging service a few minutes later.

It was a manner he had become accustomed to and reminded him that, although trained at the bench, Oliver was more a sharp businessman than cabinetmaker. But Melvyn needed him. His audacity, his ability to treat the unthinkable as just another step, was a marvel and had made him into a rich though secretive man.

He pressed a button on the keypad and waited. His Neanderthal hand looked incongruous against the high-tech black of the phone—like two separate eras on Earth, momentarily brought together.

"Melvyn?" Oliver answered gruffly.

"Yeah," he replied quietly.

"Just wanted an update—how's she coming along, my old friend," Oliver said, trying to inject some bonhomie into his tone.

"Good, Oliver, the secret compartment is finished. I'm not entirely happy with the retaining moulding though; it's going to need some work to get the colouring absolutely perfect and ..."

"Listen, that's no problem to a master like you!" Oliver interrupted, trying to disguise his impatience with flattery. "So when will she be ready—we're into June now, and I'm itching to get our creation across the channel."

"It'll be ready when it's ready, Oliver," Melvyn said flatly. *For God's sake, just leave me to get on with it.*

"Come on, you miserable old bugger, is that the best you can do!" Oliver chortled loudly down the wire, trying to humour him. "You'll be the death of me, Mel—always keeping me on tenterhooks right to the last! Between us, we're going to give the 'Antiques' trade something to talk about for the next decade— we're making history here, Mel, giving back to the world something it lost a long time ago!"

"Yeah, I know," Melvyn replied peevishly, *such grand bloody statements.* "Look, I'll call you tomorrow, when I know exactly where we are."

"You do that, old fellow," Oliver said heartily as he put the phone down.

Oliver Clasper slumped back on his Chesterfield and lit a cigar. He then stuck a finger under his glasses and rubbed the bridge of his nose. Nudging fifty-two years, plump, and with a receding hairline, he still exuded an unmistakably rakish look—a quality which seemed to emanate from the brown and silver curls that flowed back from his temples and bunched thickly at the back of his tanned cranium. He gazed through the open sash on to the beautifully manicured lawn, and allowed himself to drift in neutral for a few minutes, as the lazy sounds of early summer and the sweet scent of philadelphus mingled around him. The copper beeches lining the drive shimmered majestically in the morning heat, little twirls of wind ruffling the rusty leaves in chosen places, making them twist and glitter frivolously. The whole world was busy—kind of languidly busy—and this gave his relaxation a most satisfying backdrop.

Presently he leaned over and picked up a telephone on a small side table. Pressing a speed dial, he waited.

"Morning, Tim, all okay?" he said with a yawn as the call was answered.

"Oh hi, Oliver … yes, nothing to report, it's quiet this morning. I'm just trying to sort out the window display—a couple of bulbs have blown and it's looking a bit sad. I need to get in there with a brush, I think … it gets so blooming dusty."

Tim was Oliver's nephew and manned his antique shop in London. This was situated in that small but strategic street which runs between the northern ends of Battersea and Albert Bridge Roads. Not a grand affair, the shop was never intended to attract random visitors. It was rather a place for colleagues in the trade to pop in and peek at any new pieces Oliver had acquired, and to flaunt their own. After a brief discussion, Oliver brought the conversation to a close.

"Well, that all sounds good, Tim, well done. Speak tomorrow … oh, and let me know when Des is planning to drop by. Be in touch."

He replaced the receiver without waiting for a reply. Titus, his deep-chested boxer, jumped up and stretched noisily, hoping to cajole his master into some physical activity. Oliver ignored him and flicked through a paisley patterned address book, perched on his knee. He stopped suddenly, and again picked up the receiver whilst Titus slumped back on the carpet with a loud sigh.

"Lily?" he said in a gentle voice. There was a long pause.

"Well, well … hello, Oliver," the voice at the other end replied lazily, "what a nice surprise."

"And what are you doing on this lovely morning … soaking up the Gloucestershire sun? You sound frightfully busy."

"Sarcastic, uh? Well, I'm lying by the pool, if you must know, and wondering why I married a man who was already betrothed to a golf course," Lily said, with a tinge of bitterness.

"Once that game sinks its teeth into you, you're as good as finished," Oliver chuckled. "I've known many a good man change into a golf-obsessed fanatic overnight. I must say I'm surprised at Giles—I imagined he'd think twice about leaving his beautiful wife alone on a glorious 'Garden of Eden' day."

"You can be quite poetic when the fancy takes you, Oliver," Lily mused. "Never imagined you as the romantic sort! Is there a serpent and an irresistible fruit in this fairy tale of yours?"

"So let me guess … a blue G-string and matching top?" Oliver said evasively, sensing a trap.

"Yuk! What do you take me for—bloody uncomfortable things and so vulgar with it! I don't want everyone to see my bottom," Lily said with a little giggle.

"Everyone? Anyway, I'm told it's in great shape," Oliver said with a faint tremor in his voice.

"And who exactly has passed on that information, Mr Clasper?"

"Perfection always finds a way of revealing itself, Lily," he crooned, "and it should be entitled to an audience, if I may be so bold."

He briefly moved his head away from the phone and wiped a silk handkerchief across his brow—the morning had heated up suddenly.

"You're in a devilish mood today, Darling," she said laughing. "Come over and swim later—I could do with some company, and bring those amazing new clippers, I'm fed up with clearing leaves from the pool."

"Could do with a dip, actually," he said with a phony yawn. "I'll see you around noon … just got a couple of things to sort out."

"Looking forward Darling," she replied breezily.

Replacing the receiver, he wandered over to the window where he extended both hands onto the sash. He felt excited and, in equal measure, nervous. There was an undeniable frisson between Lily and him—a relentless current which at times he felt powerless to resist. They just got on so damn well—always had. But although she flirted—teased him with the cool cadence of her voice—he knew she was out of bounds; Lily was a married woman, and married to a man he knew well.

A bee wobbled clumsily over the window ledge and fell on the polished parquet floor at his feet. He stepped on it without a thought and, plucking a tissue from his pocket, threw the remains in a bin. The phone unexpectedly leapt into life and made him jump.

"Hello," he said softly, fully expecting it to be Lily with another trivial request.

"Good morning, Oliver," a familiar Russian voice said down the line. "It's been some time, hasn't it, but I'm back."

Oliver's mind shuddered.

"Z … Z … Zoltan?" he stuttered, a surge of adrenaline entering his blood stream. "Well … well, what a surprise … what brings you back to little old England?"

"Things change. The bitch left me … stripped me clean, or should I say, *is* stripping me clean … and I needed to get out before I went crazy. But this is not what I'm calling about, Oliver. I'm calling to give you chance to square up with me and face your obligations."

"My obligations?" Oliver said, his stomach tightening.

"That's what I said. You see … I had unexpected encounter two months ago, when I came over to see Viktor."

"Your father Viktor?"

"I believe that's his name," Zoltan said coldly. "And … well … let's say I had little time off, so I thought I'd go to one of my old haunts … okay, *our* old haunts … the Wallace Collection. And of course I just seemed to find myself on first floor, wandering into the 'Study,' just like we used to do all those years ago. Yes, just to check that Marie Antoinette's furniture was still there … you know, for old time's sake. And then woah! Who should I see? Who of all people should I bump into, except he didn't notice me … with notebook and camera no doubt, checking just how faded the purpleheart is after two hundred and twenty years. Yes, I thought you'd go quiet. I just watched him for a while and satisfied myself that he was doing what I suspected he was doing. Oh Oliver … that guy was concentrating … oh yes … the sort of concentration generated by need to copy flawlessly!"

"What are you talking about?" Oliver challenged, but with a growing sense of dread.

"I wonder," Zoltan said sarcastically, "now who could I be referring to … oh yes, it's just come back to me! *Melvyn is who I saw, Oliver, now stop playing games!*"

"You saw Melvyn?" Oliver croaked through a dry throat.

"That's right, I saw *Melvyn* … by particular cabinet … taking notes, making little sketches, sniffing for all the detailing he could, without causing suspicion, of course."

"Now … now look, Zoltan, we split up twelve years ago—twelve bloody years—and you're trying to muscle in on my affairs now?"

"You don't get it, do you? I'm at the end of my tether, Oliver, really, really close to going completely *nutty*, and I find that you're going for big one, behind my back! It was my *bloody idea*! I developed it … and you just stole it. Do you think I would just sit on sidelines whilst you make cool eight million? I even found the guy to make it, and guess what … you stole him first!"

"What … what the hell are you talking about?" Oliver said forcefully. "Let's look at the bloody facts, Zoltan; Melvyn had the choice to go either way when we ended the partnership, and he came with me … that's all! He found you difficult. And you know damn well the impossibility of copying furniture of that era … you couldn't justify its existence, let alone the technical problems; it's out of the question and you *bloody well know it*!"

"Well, you've found way, Oliver … I can smell it on your breath … and I *will* have my *cut*!" he said, almost spitting down the phone line.

"Cool down, Zoltan, just … just cool down," Oliver stuttered, desperately trying to hide the fear in his voice. "We can meet and discuss your problems when we're both in a better frame of mind; this is not the time."

"Oh, but it *is* the *time*," the Russian said venomously. "It is exactly the *time* … and I want fifty percent or you're off to Belmarsh for holiday!"

"Have you been drinking?" Oliver said angrily, "because it certainly seems like it! What the hell business have you got coming back into my life making crazy demands out of the blue; are you out of your mind? Do what you bloody well want … *as you always have*!"

He slammed the phone down, his face contorted with fury. Slumping down heavily on an elegantly carved side chair, he gazed through the open sash pondering his situation. The garden had suddenly lost its beauty, or perhaps its beauty had turned sour; a malevolent quality had descended on his day, and he felt deeply worried.

He picked up the phone.

"Lily, it's Oliver," he said flatly.

"Ooh … you do sound different, darling. Quite different and rather tense!"

"Well, I am … a bit. I've just had a rather difficult business call and—"

"You need a soothing neck rub, Olly," she said happily. "Just come on over—not forgetting the clippers—and I'll make sure you relax. C'mon!" she beckoned.

"Look, I need to …"

"Olly, you're going to feel a different man afterwards. You *need* it. Stress is a killer."

"Okay, see you later," he said charmlessly, putting the phone down.

∗   ∗   ∗

Melvyn sat on an old stained chair in his workshop, gazing intently at a photograph and then at the cabinet in front of him. He drew deeply on his pipe and let the smoke coil in soothing wreathes around him. The magnificent piece in front of him was a copy of the famous Freiburg Cabinet, which stood alone, bereft of its younger twin, in the sumptuous surroundings of the Wallace Collection in Manchester Square, London.

Made by the little-known eighteenth century cabinetmaker Johann Schafer, it stood as one of only two pieces he contributed to the court of Louis XVI of France. This most gifted of designers—a colleague of the great David Roentgen, the then "Ebeniste-Mecanicien du Roi"—was one of the highly prized German cabinetmakers whose furniture at that time was considered the most sophisticated in Europe.

Unfortunately for him, however, his entrée into the Royal Household was a little too late. The revolution was sniffing at the heels of the ruling classes by the time Schafer's moment came in 1784, and unlike the nimble-footed Roentgen, who sensed approaching mayhem and crossed the border back to Germany, Schafer lingered too long in Paris … enjoyed the fruits of royal favour just a little too much, and was murdered in a street brawl in 1788. But not before he had made the two defining pieces of his short life.

The pair of cabinets, of which the remaining one came to be known as the "Freiburg Cabinet" due to the location of Schafer's workshop in that German town, were structures of startling artistry. In fact, so thrilled was the French queen with her new piece, that she had it placed in the antechamber of her bedroom, in the Palace of Versailles. She then demanded a second be made for her Austrian childhood friend, Princesse Amalie, as a wedding present on her marriage to the Compte de Zaragon in 1786. Sadly, however, Amalie was to die in childbirth a year later. In 1789 her husband, the Compte, followed suit, murdered by thugs at the family chateau near Troyes, as France descended into political chaos. That same night, the second Schafer cabinet, the twin, also met its fate in a great fire outside the house, with other priceless artefacts.

But two hundred years later, the twin was about to be reborn … was about to rise like the Phoenix in a small workshop in southern England. Standing eighty-five centimetres high and one hundred and twenty centimetres wide, its ponderous size and weight were deflected by an impeccable lightness and delicacy of design.

Underneath the lattice work marquetry of sycamore and holly, lay a solid oak carcase, the iron hard skeleton of the piece. Onto this was laid an ormolu plumage of delicately entwined roses, narcissi, dahlias, and lilies-of-the-valley, forming an exquisite frieze across the front. Nestled delicately into the centre of this was Marie Antoinette's personal cipher of the superimposed letters "M" and "A."

Above sat a piece of cool verde alpi marble with white spiderweb veins, mirroring the sweeping curves of the structure beneath. Lower down, three doors again with lattice work marquetry panels and ormolu borders, formed the face of the cabinet and opened onto a series of sycamore-lined drawers and trays. And of course, tucked discreetly into a shadowy back panel, there was the secret compartment—the one designed by Schafer's masterful ally, David Roentgen.

Melvyn sat silently in front of his cabinet, as though eking out time with a daughter who's soon to depart. She had been part of his life for over three years now, the very focus of his existence. Sometimes he would close the workshop door behind him and just stare at her with an overwhelming pride. All his expertise, his very essence, had been lavished on her creation, and she had not been easy. Oh no … she had had her moods, her little sulks … and her big sulks. Sometimes she had been a stubborn little bitch and caused him late nights, sleepless nights even. But all the while, an empathetic energy crackled between them. Despite her petulant, teenage nonchalance to his attentiveness, there was always that certainty that he would groom and caress her until she was perfect. And now she *was* perfect, or very nearly perfect. Just a few more brushstrokes and he'd have to release her from his domain—his garden workshop—and take her to her resting place in France.

Melvyn let his eyes glide idly over the fine contours of his masterpiece for a time longer in the quietness of his workshop, and then as the bowl of his pipe offered up the last few puffs of smoke, he reluctantly got to his feet and wandered out into the sunshine.

Thomas Charrington

Chapter 2

Oliver grunted as he hauled himself out of his large Volvo estate and stepped onto the crunching gravel. He watched Lily come skipping through a gate from the garden, her sunny blond tresses damp from swimming, a bright kaftan flowing behind her. Everything seemed brighter when he looked into those glowing hazel eyes, and as usual when he hadn't seen her for a time, he felt a dull ache in the pit of his stomach.

"Oliver, darling, how lovely to see you," she said happily, throwing her arms around his neck and kissing him affectionately. "You've been bloody ages! What took you so long?"

"Oh, just this and that," he said, gazing awkwardly into her lightly tanned oval face with its peppering of tiny freckles.

"Just this and that? You call that an answer?" she said with a giggle. "I've been all of a dither for the past couple of hours!"

"I'm sorry, Lil."

"Now before you tell me about this horrible telephone call, I want you to come through to the garden, jump into your bathers, and go for a deliciously cool dip. Nothing's better to change your mood than a bit of old-fashioned exercise. You did bring your kit with you, Olly, didn't you?" she said, noticing his reticence.

"Well, actually … I didn't really feel like a swim, so I just brought the—"

"The clippers!" she interrupted. "Well, that's something at least, but I absolutely insist you take the bull by the horns and get into the pool; it's heavenly, about seventy-four degrees, and you'll feel a different man afterwards. Don't worry, Giles has about six pairs hanging around and you're pretty similar sizes, I'd say."

"Okay, matron!" Oliver said, trying to sound lighthearted. "Whatever you say."

They walked around the corner of the house, a typical Elizabethan manor with tall sculpted windows and an orgy of exotic plants wrestling for light around its walls. The lawns dropped down in a series of terraces to a tennis court at the bottom, and a glittering swimming pool, surrounded by a low privet hedge. A weeping willow stood at the northern end of the pool, its long fronds swaying languorously in the warm southerly breeze. Beyond these, cornfields stretched out like rippling green carpets to a dense wood in the background. They chatted as they made their way down, and then she stopped and pointed to the miniature romanesque building by the pool.

"There … you know the routine. Towels are in the cupboard and loads of trunks … but best avoid the red paisleys, they're his favourite."

"Thanks. See you in a moment," he said, wandering over.

Stepping inside he felt a fierce heat. There was a strong smell of cedarwood, cleaning chemicals, and the hysterical buzzing of countless flies. Along a rack he saw an array of variously coloured swimming trunks. "Christ, Giles, you're a dapper fellow," he muttered loudly, as though his friend was standing next to him.

"Are you all right?" Lily shouted from the bar, whilst popping some mint into a large jug of Pimm's.

"Oh … fine, Lil, won't be long."

"Sounded like you'd met a friend in there," Lily said, laying her slim brown body onto a deck chair as Oliver self-consciously wandered over a few minutes later. He felt the oppressive presence of her sexuality—the suggestive mound beneath her cherry bikini briefs, her small freckled cleavage. She smiled mischievously in the shadow of her wide brimmed sun hat and took a long cool sip from her glass. "Go on … in you go. No drink until you've done four lengths."

"Okay, Sergeant Major … whatever you say," he shouted, doing a flabby flop into the sparkling water and creating a mountainous wash. A few moments later he surfaced.

"God …this is superb!"

"Thought you'd like it! Now four lengths, please, and then you can join me."

"You're so harsh!" he said, as he launched up the pool doing a noisy breaststroke.

"So you did six lengths just to impress me!" Lily said, handing him a large towel a short time later. "And impressed I was. Giles hardly uses the pool. Says it gives him earache. But you know, I think he simply prefers to meet his friends up at the clubhouse and play bloody golf all day."

"I know, it's amazing how that game sucks them in. So why all the swimming trunks?"

"Giles doesn't know what frugal is. He just has to double up, treble up and on it goes."

"A bit like his salary, eh?" Oliver said with a wry smile.

"Probably," Lily said in a lacklustre way. "He's always telling me to go up and join them, but why? Why would I want to go and sit in a clubhouse with a heap of boring people when I've got this?"

She poured him a glass.

"Listen, I completely agree with you, Lil, but some people love the buzz of club rooms, the gossip, the cut and thrust of political debate and that other tempting little morsel."

"What, the chance of an affair?"

"No! I was going to say the possibility of 'that' business deal. Isn't that what golf's all about?" Oliver said, sweeping his wet hair back and giving himself a rather sinister appearance.

"Oh I suppose so, but you know, he's never mentioned clinching a deal in the clubhouse. I think he's got a girlfriend up there."

"Lily, don't be silly," Oliver said, touching her arm lightly. "I can't imagine he's the type."

"Perhaps I should use you as a weapon, Olly; make him think a bit. He's quite complacent, you know; he won't question why there are some plates and glasses on the draining board when he gets back. He'll presume in a sort of vague way that I gave Jim lunch or had a girlfriend over."

"Jim?"

"The gardener … my dear gardener … with four children and a lovely wife."

"Oh … I see." Oliver hesitated for a moment. "Any luck with …"

"Olly, let's not go there, I just don't think we work in that department, or so I've come to believe. All the tests show that we're both capable, but it just never seems to happen. I know that things can suddenly change, but when?"

Oliver took a long gulp of Pimm's and fixed his gaze on a collared dove, rinsing its head in a stone birdbath.

"It's difficult, Lil," he said awkwardly. "For some people it happens so easily; people with dreadful diets, who drink like fish and take no exercise to speak of, seem to produce children so … well, easily."

"I know … I know," Lily said quietly. "Now tell me about this 'business call,' which put you in such a horrible mood," she said, trying to shake off a growing melancholia.

"Oh, it was nothing that important, just someone calling me out of the blue; someone I used to be in business with some twelve years ago, who's going through a very rough patch and thinks that I can pull him through it."

"And can you?"

"Err … well … not really in the way that he intends me to," Oliver said, shifting slightly.

"Riiight. That sounded a bit cryptic, darling," Lily said, sensing tension. "Can I be very blunt and ask you what he's after?"

"Well, in a nutshell, Lil … money."

"Okay. Do you owe him this money or is he after a loan?"

"Good heavens! You're very to the point, sweetie," Oliver said with false jollity. "No! I do not owe him anything."

"Well, you have nothing to worry about—game, set, and match."

"If only it were that simple, Lil. But we both know life is not black and white. There are shades … and shades of shades."

"And shady shades!" Lily said, getting up and strolling towards the bar. "Another drink, you Caesar you?"

"You've got to understand, he's a—"

"I said, another Pimm's?"

"Oh, er sure, that sounds lovely … as I was saying, he's a pushy sod and thinks he can squeeze me."

"Oliver, it all sounds a bit … *shady*!" Lily said, bursting into laughter as she refilled his glass. "All a bit shady and underhand!"

Oliver suddenly felt a cold shiver of criminality slide down his back. He'd always felt sort of innocently criminal or harmlessly criminal, but somehow Lily using the word "shady" brought the truth home to him. He was a criminal … or a fraudster. Perhaps, like himself, all criminals justified their crimes by a weird process of personalization—*it's my dear little homely crime … my happy little pastime … not like those wicked deeds out there which are proper nasty crimes committed by horrible people.*

"I'm going to pop up to the house and make us up a salad, darling … not that you'd notice," she remarked, finishing the sentence quietly.

Oliver snapped from his reverie.

"I certainly *will* notice, Lil. I was, er, just watching the birdbath."

"Can I be awfully rude?" she said.

"Shoot!" he said with passion.

"It's time your equipment was put to good use."

Oliver gulped. "I'm sorry?" he said in astonishment, swivelling round to look at her.

"Clippers, Olly, you brought some clippers. Could you … please? You can see which branches need the chop."

"Oh … er … of course I can, darling," he said loudly,

standing up. "Was away for a moment … I'll get them. They're in the pool house."

"Really, Oliver!" she said, throwing him a naughty smile as she disappeared through a gap in the hedge.

He stood motionless for a few seconds, gazing out over the Gloucestershire fields. The wind was racing through the young green corn in great waves, creating a tremendous sense of purpose and festivity. But his world was the opposite of light and frivolous; behind the verdant beauty that surrounded him, he now felt the stealthy tread of approaching trouble.

Chapter 3

Zoltan Spirovich swung into Beauchamp Place, Knightsbridge, and shortly after parked by a stylish boutique. Having switched off the engine, he sat staring through the windscreen for a minute or two but without seeing a thing. Slim, Slavic featured, and armed with piercing pale blue eyes, he was a striking man, but one with a cluttered mind. His girlfriend was accusing him of disloyalty, his wife was playing mind games, and his father's respect for him was on the wane. He sighed and glanced dull eyed in the mirror. *This was going to be hard.*

Having adjusted his shirt collar and run his fingers through his blond curls, he exited his black four by four with an agile movement and strode to a nearby door. After ringing the bell, he again tweaked his collar and straightened his fawn Armani jacket—needlessly; he was already immaculate. After a few moments the door opened, and a pair of milky arms gestured passionately for a few seconds, before allowing Zoltan to step inside.

A short while later and Sasha was surveying him reproachfully as he perched himself on the suede seat of one of her chic chrome stools. Framed by a cascade of dark pre-Raphaelite curls, her pale face with its high cheekbones, strong jawline, and wide rouge lips gave her displeasure an added menace.

"I don't give a screw whether you saw her at lunch or at dinner," she said, fixing him with angry grey eyes. "The fact is, Zoltan, you told me you'd avoid a face to face meeting!"

He stood up and hugged her hard, before she could resist.

"Kitten, just let it go," he said softly. "You know I went over there to sort out the terms of our separation. Sometimes face to face meeting is the best way, the only way. Emails and phone calls always carry that possibility of misunderstanding."

"Misunderstanding … my arse! You think you can understand that crazy woman?" she said pulling away. "She's a mind fuck and you know it!"

"She was my wife … so yes, I do understand her."

"She *hates* me, Zoltan. *She* doesn't want you, and she doesn't want *me* to want you either. For Christ's sake … she still thinks she owns you!"

"Enough, Sasha, okay … enough!" he said, taking hold of her shoulders. "It's all over … it's signed! It's just for the lawyers to finalise paperwork. I'm with *you* now, Kitten, and that's the way it's going to be. And I have some more good news," he said, changing tack.

Her sulky eyelids lifted.

"I called Oliver Clasper earlier. I gave him an ultimatum. He now knows we're on to his game."

"And?"

"He tried to deny it at first … then tried to sweet talk me … and then … well, he got angry … very angry, and hung up."

"Oh … so you got round to doing it at last! Look, if he wants to act stroppy, let him. He'll come to his senses soon enough," she said, thawing. "But … do you really *know* what he's doing yet?"

"I … I think so," he said unconvincingly.

"But the point is, he now *thinks* you know … yes?"

"Well, exactly … it's the only way to scare the bastard into giving me payoff."

"And the only way to make you more popular with your father," she added, giving him a sharp look.

"Well … of course. Father thinks Oliver took me for fool … made me into idiot. The son of a bitch owes me … and he knows it!" Zoltan said passionately. "When I met that guy, he had nothing!"

"You keep saying that, Zoltan ... but where *did* you meet him?"

"At a college on the south coast ... one of the best. It must be ... must be, sixteen years ago now," he said, staring blankly across the room. "It was one of those English stately homes ... in Sussex ... West Dean College. It became part of the Arts and Crafts Movement. Viktor wanted to get me into the antique scene. Said there was big money in old furniture."

*　　　*　　　*

And that's where it all began. Under the guidance of his father, Zoltan had enrolled at that institution to learn about the "Trade"—the history, the periods and styles, the woods, the construction techniques and, of course, its restoration. Oliver Clasper had arrived some months later to do a short course in woodturning. They stumbled into each other in the grand, oak-panelled bar one evening and immediately hit it off.

Oliver *was* short of funds in those days, and it wasn't long before he realized the young Russian came from a wealthy family and was looking for business opportunities. If he could entice him on board, his fledgling antiques business could move up a gear and start trading at a higher end of the market. For his part, Zoltan was intrigued to meet an Englishman of an entirely different type to those in his usual London circle, and quickly smelt an opportunity. Oliver seemed the typical "old-fashioned" gentleman ... the type from traditional British films he'd seen, and he was eager to tap into his new acquaintance's social network.

Within a year they had gone into partnership and opened a shop in Henley. With Oliver's social skills and contacts, combined with Zoltan's substantial funding and keen business acumen, they began to get noticed in the trade. Business was brisk. Melvyn then joined the partnership and brought his formidable experience to bear. Before long, he had gently introduced his two employers into a new, more lucrative "modus operandi"—the art of deception; in short, the tweaking and remodelling of old pieces so as to allow them an entirely different provenance. This, he assured them, was commonplace in the trade.

Zoltan was keen from the start, but Oliver had hesitated, at least at the beginning. Then the money started to roll in and the business really began to flourish. Oliver felt the wind under his wings for the first time and was filled with a devil may care confidence. Life was sweet, and the delicacies of right and wrong were soon lost from his lexicon.

But as time went by, the young Russian became increasingly headstrong and volatile and was apt to remind Oliver that it was *his* ideas thât really brought in the cash. Oliver felt trapped; he was the tart to the ambitious Russian pimps. The partnership began to strain at the seams and it wasn't long before Oliver wanted rid of him … of the shared decisions … of the split profits, and of course, the looming figure of Viktor just behind the scenes.

He had learned what he needed by then, and with that confidence that springs from financial success, he wanted to go it alone. The Russian wasn't really his cup of tea anymore—not quite his sort of fellow—so he moved on and took Melvyn with him. Little did he know, however, that twelve years later, at the apex of his powers and abilities, the Russian would return to seek vengeance.

*   *   *

It was late morning in early April. One of those cold spring days when the pavements are still damp from an overnight shower and a watery sun is trying to flex its adolescent muscles. Zoltan had arrived at the main entrance of the Wallace Collection, stopped briefly to scrutinize details of a new exhibition, and then carried on in.

Reaching the first floor, he had taken a sharp left, wandered through the Damsel Gallery and on into the "Study." As he had entered the quiet space, his eyes flicked briefly over the other milling visitors whose heals clicked noisily over the polished wooden floor. Suddenly a jolt stopped him dead. Crouched by the Freiburg Cabinet on the far side of the room near the window … was the unmistakable figure of Melvyn. *Melvyn! Scribbling notes into a small book … Melvyn, who now worked for the most hated man in Zoltan's universe, Oliver Clasper.*

His heart thumping fast, Zoltan watched … and watched a little more. Then he quietly turned and left. Two hours later he was breaking the news to his father.

"Are you absolutely sure, Zoltan?" Viktor had said, staring hard at his son.

"Of course I'm sure. He was in the 'Study,' eyeballing one of Marie Antoinette's pieces. It was obvious to me what the son of a bitch was doing," Zoltan had replied. "He had that look of someone searching for very specific information … little details. But now I'm wondering if it was that particular cabinet he wanted to copy, or if he was just moving round the room. No, it couldn't be the Freiburg … that would be impossible. In hindsight, I should have stayed longer … but he could have turned so easily."

"No question it was him?"

"Father, please! I know Melvyn when I see him," Zoltan had said in exasperated tones. "Even if he's wearing glasses and is looking thinner. The man has distinctive 'way' about him, not to say personal aroma."

"He smells?"

"Yes, he smells, but not in the way you're thinking. You've got to remember, that man has lived and breathed old furniture all his life, so of course he smells … of button polish, of lacquer, of glues and stains … of years of grafting and making money for that leech Oliver. But listen, I didn't get that close this time."

"Ah ha! I understand," his father had said with a rasping chuckle, showing a row of gravestone teeth. "Ha, ha … yes, that makes sense. Those chemicals absorb into the skin and stay forever! So that's his eau de cologne, is it ... ha ha ha!"

"Probably," Zoltan had said, silently wishing his father would cut the humour.

"Right, Zol, the joke's over. We need to deal with our friend Oliver in the only language he might understand. He has insulted my family once, and it seems he now thinks he can do it again by using our ideas and strategies to make himself even richer. But I think you must make contact with him first and give him an option; either he pays you half of the expected proceeds, or you 'shop him'!"

"I will ... I will—but not yet. Too much on my mind," Zoltan had said warily.

"You've got the man by the balls, Zoltan. What's the matter with you?"

"But have I, Father? This is the problem ... I need to be sure. When I return from Munich, I'll do it ... believe me! But I need to give it more thought ... and the divorce is taking my time. When are you leaving for St Petersburg?"

"On the seventeenth."

"Are you staying for a couple of weeks or more this time?"

"Questions, questions!" Viktor had replied irritably. "I'm not sure, it depends on a lot of things. We've just bought an even better press, and I want to be around to see the quality of the results. Scanning procedures at customs are getting more sophisticated by the year; we have to be ahead."

Sensing his father's mood beginning to change, Zoltan had stood up. He was lighter than him, more boyish; he didn't have the same solidity of frame and heavy face. Viktor was a bear of a man with heavy dark eyebrows, rouge complexion, and a thick intolerant mouth. His huge chest strained at the buttons on his loud checked shirt as he observed his son indifferently through hooded eyes.

"Well, do your thinking, Zoltan," he had growled, looking up from his armchair. "If he is copying something from that place, then there's a lot at stake—those things are worth millions. It's your chance to take back what the bastard took from us."

"You don't need to tell me, Father! I'm shocked that he's going for copy of this magnitude. When I suggested we copy piece of French royal furniture all those years ago, he said … he said it was impossible. *But something has changed*—they've found an opening … I'm sure they have!"

"Mm, it would seem so," Viktor had said, getting impatient. "Now Zoltan, go and deal with that woman, do what you have to do, but when you get back … *make that call*."

And with that clear directive, Zoltan had left.

Thomas Charrington

Chapter 4

"That was delicious, darling," Oliver said, stretching after a long lazy lunch. He ground the remains of his cigar into the pewter ashtray and made a perfunctory attempt to move the plates.

"Leave those … you off already?" Lily said sadly, resting her chin on her folded knees.

"Well, this issue we touched on earlier is rather on my mind, to be honest. I can't relax right now. I need to have a chat with Melvyn and get his take on the whole thing," he said, sliding his feet into a pair of scuffed deck shoes.

"Melvyn … your workman?"

"Believe it or not, he's quite a shrewd old bugger. Not just a simple artisan."

"Oh I'm sure, I wasn't meaning to demean him … just wish you could be here a bit longer, that's all."

"Believe me, so would I, darling," Oliver said, leaning toward Lily and laying his hand on hers. "It's gorgeous here … I would stay if I could."

"Go and sort it out then," she said, getting up. "And make sure you don't disappear for weeks again. I enjoy your company, Olly, and it would be *so* nice to see more of you this summer."

She gave a shy smile and threw her arms around his neck.

"I'll call you," he said, stroking her back and immediately sensing the heat of her skin through the gossamer fabric.

"You had better," she replied, gently pulling away. "It can get quite lonely here on my own."

"I can imagine," he said quietly … and then hesitated. He

allowed his eyes to meet hers for several more seconds before dropping very deliberately onto her slender lips. She stared at him unblinking … surprised, clocking a sudden change. Again he met her gaze, but this time with a look of steely determination. Stepping forwards, he took her temples in his open palms and kissed her urgently and passionately on the mouth. A sudden gust of warm wind coiled around them and then hissed noisily through the undulating seaweed fronds of the willow. She moaned quietly, one delicate hand curled behind his head, drawing him forwards and into a domain he had long resisted. After a minute or two, he gently pulled away.

"I'd better be going, Lil," he whispered, meeting her intense gaze. "I'll … I'll be in touch soon … promise." Then he turned and headed back up the lawns to his car.

*   *   *

The driveway to Melvyn's house was shabby. The wooden fence on the right was rotten and falling to pieces, and to the left, a rusting tractor and other pieces of disintegrating machinery gave a general stamp of squalor. This was contrived, however, and gave a deceptive impression. Once through the gate at the other end of the drive, and inside the high wall that surrounded the property, a very different picture emerged.

A Victorian red-bricked building with wisteria in abundance around its walls stood, well-groomed and pretty, overlooking an expansive lawn. A flagstone path led from the patio, across a corner of the lawn to a low out building, which was Melvyn's workshop.

Oliver had long since stopped registering the trip to the workshop. The bumpy, potholed drive with its huge winter puddles went completely unnoticed and his conscious mind only seemed to start functioning again when his nostrils smelt the unmistakable aroma of furniture chemicals. Mary waved cheerily from the kitchen window as the two men disappeared into the workshop.

"So what's all this about, Oliver?" Melvyn said with his usual bluntness, whilst pulling out a pair of chairs.

"My God, Melvyn, this looks quite superb!" Oliver said with a raised voice, tapping the top of the Freiburg Cabinet fondly. "You've excelled yourself, man. It gets better every time I see it; the mirror image of its sister in the Wallace!"

"Blimey, you're in a good mood, for someone who's got some bad news," Melvyn said, eying Oliver.

"Am I not allowed to express my delight, Mel?"

"Thank you. It's getting colder, I suppose," Melvyn said distractedly. "So?"

"Well … after I spoke with you this morning, I was just organizing a few things back at the Hall, when the phone went. It was Zoltan!"

"Zoltan?" Melvyn said, raising his tangled eyebrows, a shadow moving over his face. "What the hell is *he* calling you for? He doesn't like you."

"Sure he doesn't, and that hasn't changed. His wife's divorcing him, though, and he's in a hell of a state."

"Too bad, that's his problem. He's a tricky bastard and probably deserves it," Melvyn said with feeling.

"My thoughts exactly, Melvyn. But there's another problem which is much more serious and which is why I'm here. During the course of our conversation, he told me that he'd been in London some two months back … April sometime, to see Viktor … and, well, I'm sorry, Mel, but he said he saw you at the Wallace … purely by coincidence. Yes, I'm afraid he watched you taking notes on this"—Oliver tapped the cabinet—"and then put two and two together."

Melvyn looked at him speechless, his mouth open.

"It's not your fault, Mel. It's just as I said … appalling bad luck," Oliver resumed in a conciliatory tone.

"But … but … surely I'd have seen him. I never forget a face," Melvyn stammered.

"Think about it; you're concentrating on the cabinet in front of you …"

"No! I always stand to the side. I don't want to make it obvious."

"The point is, you're concentrating hard; he was probably only there for a couple of minutes, at most three, and then gone! He saw what you were doing ... it's obvious ... but it isn't your fault, Melvyn. We just have to decide how to proceed."

"Oh God!" Melvyn moaned, putting his hands up to his temples. "So what's the situation at the moment, then?"

"Well, he said he wants half the proceeds."

"Half the proceeds!" Melvyn said in a high-pitched outburst, colour growing in his cheeks. "That's crazy! That's just plain bloody mad! Anyway, he can't be sure I was copying, for Christ's sake!"

"Mel," Oliver said, staring at him, "he does know. He's no fool. We all discussed this type of copy many times, if you remember, but there was no way we could authenticate it back then."

"But we haven't even made any money yet!"

"I know. He means he wants an agreement at this stage as to what his cut will be."

"Why the hell should we give that Russian bastard a cut, for Christ's sake? He hasn't done anything to deserve it. He may have *wanted* to make a cabinet of this standard, but he didn't have the rat's ass sense of how to do it! He's done fuck all! You worked out the history, and I built the bloody thing ... simple," Melvyn implored.

"Unfortunately, my friend, right and wrong have no bearing in this. He knows something extremely destructive. There was bad blood after we split—you know that—plus he thinks this copy was his idea in the first place. The guy's always wanted revenge, and now ... let's face it ... he's got us over a barrel."

"Christ's sake!" Melvyn muttered. "That was the last bloody visit ... the last one. There was just one little thing I had to check ..."

"I know, Mel, but we have to look at the options. Close the project right now, or carry on and give him a cut, but much less than he's demanding."

"We can't close it now, Oliver, not after all this time and effort," Melvyn pleaded.

In a rare moment of physical expression, Oliver put his hand on Melvyn's shoulder and patted him affectionately.

"We'll sort it out, Mel, don't worry."

Twisting a cigar through his fingers, he sat down on one of the chairs, deep in thought, whilst Melvyn absentmindedly tidied some tools.

"Right," he said at last, "we're going to have to include him. He's much better connected in the underworld than me or you, and we're going to get hurt otherwise. Of course, he won't get half … or anything like half, but he'll have to be paid off somehow. His father, as you may remember, is not to be crossed. Sorry to break such bad news, Mel … but keep going as though this never happened. Either way we're going to make a shed load of money and put the antiques trade on the front pages!"

"Bastard!" Melvyn said in exasperation.

"But what I *can* do is play dumb for the moment and wait and see how serious he is. Where are we … four or five weeks from completion, and then our baby goes into incubation in France. Let's hold tight for the moment and see if he contacts me again. For all we know he may be bluffing."

"I don't think so," Melvyn sighed. "That guy means business, Oliver, and once his jaws are locked, there's no getting rid of him."

"You're probably right, and anyway, we can't stop now, Fabien's whole life depends on this. I think he'd throw himself off a cliff if we called it off."

"Guess so," Melvyn agreed.

Oliver deliberated for a few moments, looking out on to the garden.

"Good God," he said suddenly, "do you realize it's well over three years now?"

"What is?"

"My meeting with Fabien. Remember? In Piccadilly … when

I broached the whole idea of copying the cabinet—everything was gearing up for the millennium."

"Oh yeah, I do. It was a bit touch and go, if I remember right," Melvyn said with a small chuckle.

"It was, Mel. It certainly was. In the end, he just couldn't let Cecile go."

Chapter 5

London was pulsating with energy. Building sites with cranes and ground-shuddering trucks had erupted like open sores across the capital, as contractors struggled to meet the demands of the impending millennium celebrations. There were the iconic structures like the Dome, the Wheel, and of course the Millennium Footbridge, but also a plethora of other nail-biting projects, all of which had to be completed on time. And this excitement was reflected within Oliver. He also was about to engage in a new and dangerous enterprise—one which depended wholly on the compliance of the young man he was about to meet.

Turning into Prince Street, Piccadilly, he found a parking bay some fifty yards from the entrance to that hallowed auction house, Hardy's. He glanced at his watch and pressed a speed dial on his mobile; it was six forty-five pm.

"Fabien, it's Oliver," he said. "I'm parked up the street on the left; I know I'm a bit early, so come out when you're ready."

"Oh … okay, Oliver, just give me ten minutes," Fabien said from his office which was no more than a tatty cubicle, filled to bursting point with all manner of chunky books.

A young Frenchman in his late twenties, Fabien was being groomed to take over from the resident expert on the Dutch Masters. This was his area of primary expertise, but he also had an abiding love of eighteenth century French furniture, and this was where Oliver's interest in him was seated.

From a distinguished family in Paris, he had started out

running an art gallery in the Rue de Fourcy, but this had proved to be a cul-de-sac and the chances of promotion extremely limited. So he had made a career move to London to join an institution with scope for upward mobility. Hardy's was now his kingdom, and though his salary was still modest, he adored his job with a passion.

Idly scanning the buildings around him, Oliver rehearsed the conversation he was shortly to have with the young Frenchman for the final time. He was about to take a very risky gamble and needed to tread a delicate and carefully planned path. He jumped involuntarily as Fabien gave a light tap on the car roof. Slim, with an open, friendly face, he had a dark cotton jacket slung over his shoulder with a pretty floral tie tucked into a pale blue shirt. The beige trousers seemed a size too big, Oliver thought, as he climbed out and shook the young man's hand warmly.

"Bonsoir, Fabien!"

"Salut, Oliver, comment vas-tu?"

"Je vais bien, merci." Oliver replied in his wooden French.

"It has been some time since you've needed to pick my brain … Christmas, was it not?"

"Yes … don't you remember … that chiffonier."

"Yes, I do. So you have nothing with you this time?" Fabien said, stooping down to peer into the back of the Volvo.

"No, not this time. I … er … wanted to discuss a project with you this time, Fabien.

Ideas are easier to carry than furniture!"

"Well, of course," the Frenchman replied with a friendly smile.

"Right," Oliver said with authority, "I hope you're hungry. I've booked a table for seven thirty at Stafford's, so we've got time for a couple of sharpeners first. They've got a rather appealing bar and some pretty Russian waitresses to give you a good appetite."

"You are splashing out!" Fabien exclaimed. "I went there once only, for a drink, three years ago when I joined Hardy's. It is too expensive for me."

"Well relax, this is my call," Oliver beamed.

"I am curious as to what this is about, Oliver … you have a slightly mysterious way about you this evening."

"I do?" Oliver said, surprised. "Are you still with that gorgeous Cecile?"

"Why, of course!" Fabien said passionately. "I love that girl, and I have to see her every other weekend. She keeps me sane!"

"Good, very good. True love is a rare thing these days," Oliver said, with a skip in his voice.

They turned into Old Bond Street and entered the grand marble porch of the restaurant which in its earlier life had been a bank. Hugely spacious, it suited Oliver's temperament and allowed a degree of seclusion from fellow diners.

"On second thought, we'll give the bar a miss," Oliver said distractedly. "It looks a bit busy, and I see our table is free."

They sat down and ordered their drinks. Oliver casually scanned his nearest neighbours, satisfying himself that their conversation could be private.

"Now Fabien," he began, whilst pulling a cigar from a silver case. "I'm going to get straight to the point. I had an idea some months ago, or should I say, you created an idea in my mind that evening we went to the Festival Hall with your delightful Cecile … by telling me the story of your ancestor at the time of the French Revolution."

"You mean my aristocratic origins!" Fabien said with a shy chuckle. "My ancestor the Comte de Zaragon, who had the estate near Troyes."

"Yes, him. But perhaps more importantly, his wife, or should we say concubine?" he said, drawing the flame into the tobacco. "You told us a lot that evening, no doubt the result of my endless questions. Do you mind if we delve into that a little more tonight?"

"What is this, a history class?" Fabien chortled. "Of course not, go ahead. It will take some of the today's annoying problems from my mind."

Oliver resumed eagerly in a cloud of smoke.

"Ok, so going back to those times. Now correct me if I'm wrong, but I remember the Comte's wife Amalie died around 1787, and he took up with a maid in the house—a very beautiful girl."

"Well I didn't see her but yes, that's right. His own wife died in childbirth leaving him childless. So after a short period he formed a relationship with this maid … and she became pregnant. I believe she was called Madelaine. But she was no ordinary maid—she herself was the illegitimate daughter of an unscrupulous aristocrat and another man's wife and had been virtually thrown out."

"Oh I see; quite a tangled web," Oliver said hesitantly. "But the Comte acted honourably, if I remember correctly; he refused to push the whole matter under the carpet and took her in as his adopted wife, though they never actually married. You said that he made it his business to look after her."

"Absolutely … and especially in view of the fact that he no longer had a wife. They had a child … a son called … er … Bastien, I think, and then a daughter as well who was not born when he died. Where is this heading, I'm a little confused?"

"You probably will be for the moment," Oliver said with a chuckle, "but there is a purpose to all this! So, the revolution came in seventeen eighty-nine, and at some point that year the Comte was murdered."

"Right again, Oliver! I am impressed. Yes, he was murdered by the gangs of looters that were going to all the big houses around that time demanding food and so on. You must remember the French aristocracy were driving the ordinary people into the ground at that time."

"Yuh, I know."

"At the death of Jean-Baptiste, his brother Jacques-Jerome took over the estate. He, being unmarried, took on the two children, although the girl was not yet born, and he and Madelaine ran the place together. But within two years, Jacques-Jerome also met his end when his coach lost a wheel and careered into a ditch near Aperts."

"My God, it goes from bad to worse!"

"He wasn't killed outright—sustained a terrible injury and died a few months later. But not before he recognized her as the natural heir and signed everything over to her. Or perhaps, to be accurate, he signed it over to Bastien, being male, with her in control until he came to the right age. But the title was lost, partly because the children were born out of wedlock, but also because the new constitution swept titles away. Otherwise, I might be the Comte de Zaragon!" Fabien said laughing.

"What a shame. And it has remained in the family ever since, has it not?" Oliver pressed eagerly.

"Yes it has … and it now belongs to my grandmother who is living there today; that is, when she is not in 'ospital in Troyes. She has terrible arthritis, poor Agnes."

"And am I right in saying that she is leaving this property to you?" Oliver said leaning back as a waitress appeared at the table with a tray of drinks.

"Wow…you *were* paying attention that night!" Fabien said good-heartedly. "Yes, I will inherit it. But Oliver, this is no place to live! Once it was a grand chateau, but now … phu… it is in a terrible state. The roof is not great, the whole place needs a total overhaul; in fact, that is one of the reasons my father has not the slightest interest in the chateau.

Anyway, he made money of his own in the wine trade and has a big apartment in Paris. He suggested it be made directly over to me. My aunt was similarly uninspired by the place, and although there are a few bits and pieces on her sentimental list, she is married to a rich American and is not interested. So it is all mine as they say over here, lock, stock, and barrel!"

"Completely yours?" Oliver said, giving Fabien a beady look and taking a gulp of gin. "Or are there strings attached?"

"Non! The house and all its contents … well, apart from a few odd pieces. There are no strings. I am the sole beneficiary. But why does this concern you? The chateau in its present state is not worth a huge amount, and the contents don't add up to much," Fabien said, puzzled.

"But there is something else which intrigues me, Fabien … the furniture which was left to Madelaine and which presumably was handed down through the generations involved one particular item of great value, did it not?"

Oliver wiped his brow with his napkin and took another sip from his glass.

Fabien looked at him quizzically for a few moments.

"Ahh … I am with you!" he exclaimed. "You're thinking of the Freiburg Cabinet Twin; it would be valuable by today's standards, all right, but it wasn't then. Well, not to the same degree."

"Exactly," Oliver said with a glint in his eye. "That is exactly what I am referring to."

"But Oliver, as you know, that cabinet was lost long ago. It was burned by the looters. That cabinet does not exist now— phew … if it did I would be sitting on a fortune! It had quite a history, mind you. I'm quite sure you will have seen its twin piece at the Wallace Collection."

"Yes, I remember you telling me. I do know the piece," Oliver said emphatically. "I just wanted you to remind me of how it was lost."

"Well as I said, in the year the revolution broke, violence spread out of Paris and into the countryside. People were being killed all over the place, especially people of wealth and position. Gangs of looters were going from one grand house to another, accusing them of hording grain, money, of being against the revolution and in favour of retaining the monarchy. The servants were no match for these people. They broke in and ransacked these places, throwing furniture out of windows—beautiful exquisite pieces, made by master craftsmen, thrown and broken to pieces. They were animals, hunting in packs … bent on destruction; what did they know or care about art, culture? They wanted blood!"

Fabien took a deep draught from his glass.

"And Jean-Baptiste … what was his fate?" Oliver asked.

"Oh … he was killed at the outset. He heard the commotion

and went straight out to confront the mob. He tried to reason with them, but they weren't having it; they didn't want to listen. I believe he was stabbed and then beaten in front of his household. She was spared—Madelaine—a few of the mob knew her circumstances of being a servant and let her be. Which was lucky for me, really," he said smiling, "or there would be no me!"

"And the Twin was burned! God, what a horrible thought. … along with other beautiful pieces, no doubt, paintings included."

"That's what I have read," Fabien said with a sigh. "But don't forget we're talking about events over two 'undred years ago. The facts have probably been distorted over time."

"But let's assume a mob did assault the house, Fabien. That seems quite likely at that time, no?"

"Oh yes, it was definitely ransacked, without a doubt, but the exact details of events are probably a bit cloudy now."

"Sure, but I can't help feeling that people, important people with substantial houses, estates, like the Comte would have been warned of this beforehand," Oliver said, taking a drag on his cigar and letting his eyes settle idly on the bottom of one of the waitresses clearing a nearby table. "They would have taken counter measures … like hiding money, silver, valuable paintings and furniture, before they were taken."

"I am quite sure they tried to," Fabien said, "and probably succeeded … who knows."

"Things must have survived … surely. The house is big, going by those photos," Oliver continued.

"Sure … some things, smaller items, would have been hidden, I suppose, and been overlooked. I really don't know enough about the exact circumstances, but you should remember peoples' loyalties changed with the wind at that time and, for all we know, the servants could have turned on their employers too. They may have had no choice."

"Such a pity," Oliver said, gazing across the restaurant.

"The revolution?"

"No! Well … er … yes, the revolution was a monster … I

was meaning more, the Freiburg Twin being burned. But I guess the story is true; it's never surfaced anywhere else."

"Oui. I believe it myself, but, just think if that thing still existed. I would potentially be very wealthy man!" Fabien said with a smile. "Except it would most probably have been sold by now."

"Yes, of course, and you would have your father and aunt to deal with. But just imagine if, when you take possession of the house, you were to discover an item of … er … great value which had been overlooked—something which had been locked away in a safe place and been forgotten about! It's not inconceivable, is it? I've seen the photographs and it looks enormous and … well … solid, shall we say. The place is intact … it's just been a bit unloved, neglected over the decades with probably only the most urgent structural repairs being attended to."

"Well, I would certainly agree with you on that!" Fabien snorted. "That's why Cecile views it with such horror. She sees the amount of money needed to just make it habitable again, and then there's the annual maintenance costs. It is out of my reach, Oliver … it is as simple as that."

Oliver gave him a long glance.

"Yesss …," he said slowly, lingering on the word for a moment. "I understand your predicament perfectly. But look on the bright side, Fabien, you're coming into a magnificent chateau with fantastic potential … now you just have to make a fortune."

"With a lifetime of repair bills and running costs to keep the place together. I simply don't have the capital to take it on, Oliver, this is the sad truth. You should see it; it needs *so* much doing to it. My grandmother's arthritis has probably been caused by the dampness of the place. Lately I've been 'aving terrible rows with Cecile over our future, and the Chateau always seems to cause them."

"Oh … that's a pity."

"She keeps asking me to go back to Paris and get a job that pays better. She's fed up with this half relationship, as she calls it, and even when she does see me, we seem to quarrel. I see trouble ahead unless I can convince the chairman to raise my salary. God knows, Hardy's is such a successful company."

"And what about your father, can he help you?" Oliver probed.

"Papa is on his third wife! He doesn't have so much money himself these days. Non, that will never happen."

"So my payments to you are useful then?" Oliver said, playing one of his cards.

He gave Fabien a meaningful look.

"Yes, certainly, Oliver, I'm very grateful," the young man replied, shifting on his chair slightly. "But we must be careful; it would be bad for my … er … prospects, as it were. I'm not sure how Hardy's would view this situation, not to mention the tax man."

"True, we must be careful."

A waiter appeared at the table and took their orders. A few minutes later a waitress brought a bottle of Chianti, and they clinked glasses.

"To you and Cecile," Oliver said with a smile. "Take my advice, never let a good girl go."

"I know," Fabien said, flexing his jaw.

"I do love this place," Oliver said, changing tack. "Such pretty waitresses and their food is always perfect. When I come into this part of town, I make it my business to eat well, and being a Frenchman, I know you appreciate good food!"

"Well, this is very true," Fabien said, taking a large gulp of wine. "But since I have lived in London I have become lazy. Buying ready made meals and pushing them into the microwave."

"Don't worry, we men are pretty much the same when there's no woman around keeping an eye."

Twenty minutes later their respective orders were wafted onto the table in a whirlwind of garlic. A gently crisped entrecote steak for Oliver with a clutch of French fries, and for Fabien, it was a pair of plump poussin in a brandy and cream sauce. The dishes steamed enticingly as the two men picked up their cutlery.

"Wow, I'm suddenly feeling very 'ungry!" Fabien said with a chuckle.

"Bon appetite!" Oliver said, slicing into the pink meat.

They chatted amiably for the next half hour, and Oliver was happy to listen to Fabien's take on the inner workings of Hardy's. The petty squabbles between the various experts, the flirtations between certain high-profile directors and their personal assistants and the gossip this generated; it was a story Oliver knew only too well, and the same pattern was probably replicated in every large institution in the land.

Having finished, he wiped his mouth, pushed his chair back from the table, and pulled another cigar from its case. He lit it with his old-fashioned lighter and disappeared momentarily in a cloud of smoke.

Oliver now ran a finger inside his shirt collar and checked his mobile (which was off); his face looked calm, but underneath the tablecloth his ankle was flexed awkwardly to one side. He looked at Fabien for a few seconds as the young man finished the last few morsels on his plate, as though deciding how to proceed. He then drew a deep breath.

"Fabien," he said uneasily, "forgive me for being … erm … a sort of social observer, but I think I understand your position very clearly. You're quite obviously from a family with an illustrious history, what one could call an enviable pedigree; you're part of an elite though rather old social network, and I would imagine you've rubbed shoulders with some important people over the years."

Fabien listened with concerned interest.

"Your family has had money and prestige over the generations, but now … and please don't think I'm being rude … in your generation, through no fault of theirs, or of yours, for that matter, because of natural events, taxes, a few bad marriages possibly, and an altering world, the wealth seems to have dried up. And here you are, cultured, urbane, well connected in an old-fashioned sense but … bluntly speaking, broke."

Fabien looked across at him uneasily.

"Don't misunderstand me, Fabien," Oliver said, lifting his palm to silence a reply. "I'm not criticising. There are others like you. You haven't been brought up with that hungry cutting edge which so often defines the wealthy of today, but you have immense charm and style. You put personal fulfilment above financial status. Foremost, you're a decent … honest … polite young man, Fabien; a quite appalling handicap in today's world!"

Oliver's face cracked into an immense grin at this point, and he chuckled whilst filling Fabien's glass. It broke through the young man's sudden surge of despondency, so he too laughed, in spite of himself.

"Wow, Oliver, you painted a sad picture of me," he said, trying to regain his composure. "But to be honest, you have a point."

"It hurts, doesn't it," Oliver said, clasping Fabien's forearm briefly. "But sometimes you need to take a good look at yourself and take stock. You have a girl who loves you, Fabien, a girl who's going to depend on you. Are you going to let her slip away?"

"Slip away? What do you mean? Do I seem defeated?" Fabien said, frowning. "I most certainly will *not* let her go. I intend to marry Cecile; she's perfect for me and I will do everything possible to make this 'appen."

He picked up a cocktail stick and twisted it through his fingers, driving the pointed ends deeply into his flesh, as though chastising himself for his impotence. Flushed, he avoided Oliver's eyes.

"Perhaps I should be more financially ambitious," he mumbled, almost to himself.

"Yes you should Fabien!" Oliver said, driving his point home. "You need to start living, breathing, thinking money, when you're awake … and asleep. You need brashness, my friend; the brashness of the east end barrow boys who migrated to the stock exchange and the property market. Yes, who used their 'go get' attitude and are now driving the latest Bmw's and

Aston Martins. Do you know why they're rich? Well I'll tell you. *Because they really wanted it! They craved it above everything!* They wanted to leave their old life in the dust behind their tail lights."

"But I am not a stockbroker, Oliver, I don't see how brashness is going to 'elp me," Fabien said, genuinely confused.

"It's a mindset … a mindset which will help you to look at possibilities within your own business. Brush away the good, patient, well-mannered Fabien; you don't have time to be patient. You need money and you need it now! How long will Cecile wait?"

Oliver sat back and sucked deeply on his cigar as a waitress removed their plates and dishes. Coffee was ordered.

"I now get to the crux of our conversation," he continued. "Everything we've discussed to this point has been leading to this. Tonight, Fabien, I'm offering you the chance to sweep away your money troubles in a relatively short amount of time."

He held up his hand again to stop interruption. "Please wait until I've finished."

Fabien looked at him with surprise and wiped his mouth with the napkin.

"Ever since that evening at the Festival Hall when you introduced me to Cecile and told me your wonderful story, I've been thinking about a possibility. You didn't realize it at the time, but when you informed me that the twin of the Freiburg Cabinet once belonged to your family, I very nearly fell off my chair! I simply couldn't believe it!"

"You did? Is this so fantastic?" Fabien said, perplexed.

"Let me explain. As you know, I'm an 'antique dealer'— someone who buys and sells antiques and hopefully makes some money along the way. My knowledge of antique furniture is my power; my skill is using that knowledge cleverly. I may not have all the information I need in my head, but I sure as hell know where I can find it … and pretty darn quickly! You're one source, and there are others as well, plus a substantial library of books I've collected over the years. But there's a problem. Antique furniture is running out. It's been disappearing abroad in alarming quantities, leaving a scarcity here. There simply isn't enough to go round. So I've had to keep my wits about me and improvise."

Oliver leant forwards to make his point.

"Fabien, have you ever stopped to consider how many so called 'antiques' are actually fakes?"

Fabien raised his eyebrows and fiddled with the cocktail stick without speaking.

"Well, let me assure you, there are a lot of fake antiques around—an awful lot. Some are detected, and others … well, let's just say they are just too good. Or they are good enough to convince certain 'officials' that they can accept them. Now, my intention tonight is to run a simple idea past you. We've been through your family history around the time of the French Revolution; it's been a sad little sortie into a time of desperation for your forbears, a time when their world was suddenly shattered. Your family lost things at that time, Fabien, things they should rightfully still possess now. Particularly poignant for me is the loss of the Freiburg Twin, a piece very close to the heart of your dear forebear Madelaine and made by a quite brilliant cabinetmaker. Now we come to a point in our conversation where you will need to rein in your natural reaction and hear me out before passing judgment."

Oliver took a long pull on his cigar and exhaled in a masterful display of nonchalance.

"Are you prepared to enable me," he hesitated for a few seconds, "to bring the lost twin of the Freiburg Cabinet back to life…. yes, to make a copy … and … in so doing, secure a very bright future for you and your beautiful Cecile?"

Fabien sat dumbstruck for at least five seconds.

"Did you say make a … make a copy … a fake, that is pretending to be the lost cabinet?"

"Yes, that's exactly what I mean," Oliver said, staring at him.

"Putain! Are you crazy? M … make a copy of the Freiburg Cabinet? Are you out of your mind, Oliver? Me, help a forger, a criminal?" he whispered incredulously, fixing Oliver with a hot gaze. "I would lose my career, my credibility at a stroke … I couldn't do this in a million years! Please, Oliver, you misunderstand me … or is this an English joke?"

"Fabien, calm down, we're discussing an idea," Oliver said firmly. "The most difficult aspect of any forgery of this magnitude is trying to slot it authentically into a historical context. Cabinets like this don't just 'pitch up' out of the blue. If they did, they may as well have a flashing neon sign attached to them saying, "*Fake*"!

"Exactly, exactly!" Fabien said in outraged tones.

"But Fabien, the beauty of this situation is that there is a perfect historical pocket to place our cabinet into. A pocket which has been opened up, as it were, by the weird circumstances surrounding the original's demise!"

"Demise?"

"I mean disappearance, loss. Don't you see, this almost insurmountable hurdle is already overcome. Documents prove that two Freiburg Cabinets left the workshops of Schafer in 1784 and 1786; that they were both commissioned by the Royal Household. That one was retained for the royal apartments and found its way to the Wallace Collection … that the other was given as a wedding gift to the Comtesse de Zaragon. It disappeared from the historical record in about 1791 when Jean-Jacques had his will drawn up shortly before his death. The cabinet was burned, so of course it has been deleted. I don't doubt the real story. But I have an *alternative history* for this cabinet."

"An alternative history? Please, Oliver, this scares me … I couldn't contemplate such a thing," Fabien said, glancing nervously around the restaurant.

"As I was saying, I have an alternative history," Oliver persisted. "As a previous member of the staff, Madelaine was in touch with ordinary people. She was able to talk to the locals on a level which was denied the aristocrats she mixed with. She knew what was happening in the local villages and was given ample warning that bad things were heading their way. She knew an attack on the house was very possible, since such events were spreading out from Paris like wildfire. She decided to take evasive action.

To begin with she implored Jean-Baptiste to leave whilst there was still time. To make his way to Austria and wait for the turbulence to subside. Yes, to join the already large numbers of émigrés escaping the country. But he refused … and his fate, sadly, is history. But she took action of her own behind his back, prior to his death. She told the estate carpenter, a man of great loyalty, to make up a chest in a rough but thorough way, which could house the Twin. This chest was then taken into the roof space and hidden amongst the rafters in as discreet a manner as possible until some time in the future."

"Oliver! What are you saying? I don't feel you are the person I know any more!" the young Frenchman said, staring aghast at Oliver.

"Just listen, Fabien, don't pass judgement," Oliver said firmly before resuming. "She told no one. She was falling into the hands of her brother-in-law, Jacques-Jerome. She wasn't sure how things would turn out for her, so she kept the secret of the cabinet to herself in case her life took a plunge. Then Jacques-Jerome had his accident in the coach and later died. This might have been the time to reveal it to her children … but why? It wasn't gold. Its value then would have been negligible; a piece of furniture made by a discredited cabinetmaker, a slave of the royalists. So it remained hidden and only she, the old carpenter, and a couple of his loyal friends knew. Eventually they passed on, and then in 1836 so did she. The cabinet was alone, and it stayed that way in the garret of Chateau Clery for the next 160 years. Agnes never discovered it in the roof space, and it wasn't until you and Cecile moved in to assess the work needed to repair the roof that it was discovered."

"Oliver, *this is madness*! You really are giving this serious thought! It would mean prison. Mon dieu! How could you make another Freiburg Cabinet … and get away with it!"

"This may come as a shock to you, but I have someone who

is very capable of making a copy—exquisitely."

"This is not *possible*, Oliver! You don't understand the … the difficulties are huge. We would be discovered and thrown behind bars. I hardly believe we are having this conversation. The wine, this restaurant … I feel I am losing my mind!"

"You need courage, Fabien; you live only once. When you inherit the house—which with great respect to your grandmother may not be so long—you're standing on the threshold of a momentous opportunity in your life. You have the key; you just have to turn it."

"Mon Dieu, mon Dieu!" Fabien whispered to himself.

"Do you believe Madelaine would hate you for such a thing?" Oliver continued. "On the contrary, I think she would look down with pride that you were sanctioning the rebuilding of a cabinet she adored, and at the same time financing the restoration of the house, and more importantly than anything, securing a future for you and Cecile. She was a maid, Fabien, she knew the hardships of life and what it is to struggle; she had no airs or graces. She wasn't bourgeois; if she saw a chance, she grabbed it with both hands!"

"But how could you possibly make such a thing, Oliver, and fool the experts? I don't believe it can be done. They would find a flaw; it only takes one tiny oversight."

"Fabien," Oliver said with deadly assurance, "the Freiburg Cabinet can be made flawlessly, believe me. I've made … well, one or two other pieces, and I'll show you. Understandably you doubt the ability of someone to make such a piece; you are becoming an expert yourself and therefore it lies with me to prove you wrong, before you commit to anything. I understand that. But what I'm asking you now, is whether you will agree to the idea; that takes courage. Crossing that boundary is not easy … but the rewards for those who have the guts are stupendous!"

"Oliver … this is *madness!*" Fabien muttered, gazing at him hotly across the table.

"The most dangerous part of this operation, or should I say one of the most dangerous," Oliver continued undeterred, "is getting the cabinet across the channel. Customs are not focused on furniture in the same way as drugs, firearms, etcetera, so I'm prepared to take the risk. My biggest problem is if they suspect me of carrying cash; it's highly unlikely, but if they did, they might do a search, which would not be a good thing.

Of course, I'll have a couple of tricks up my sleeve, but the risk is there if they went to town on me. The other thing, of course, and one that you're very familiar with, is that once the cabinet is revealed in France, it will shortly become a Monument Historique. This will prohibit it from export and therefore deter wealthy foreign buyers. This depresses its value comparatively speaking. But Fabien," Oliver said, leaning forward and looking at him intensely, "let's make no mistake … the cabinet will still sell for a *phenomenal* amount of money. Its discovery in France makes its authenticity that much more believable! Also, there are a few extremely wealthy individuals over there who keep a sharp eye on the top auctions. The artefacts of Marie Antoinette are very sought after amongst the French elite."

He stopped for a moment, letting his words sink in.

"Mon Dieu … mon Dieu!" Fabien muttered again to himself, whilst staring at the ceiling. "Merde … you are *crazy,* Oliver!"

"Listen, Fabien, I know it's come as a complete surprise to you … this whole concept; of course your immediate reaction is negative. You've probably never done anything wrong in your whole life, apart from ignoring some parking tickets in the Rue de Lion; you've been a good citizen. But I implore you to think hard, think about Cecile and your future; good honest people, Fabien, get left behind in the world of today, and lord forbid Cecile should leave you for someone … well … with a bit more to offer."

With the final card played, Oliver stubbed out his cigar very thoroughly in the porcelain ashtray and stood up. He took a last gulp of coffee and then gestured for the bill. Cigar smoke eddied around him, giving him the aspect of a magician who had emerged miraculously from beneath the stage. Flexing his elbows backwards, he stretched briefly, and then placed his hand heavily on the young man's shoulder.

"Fabien, I've thoroughly enjoyed our evening, but there's nothing further to say on this particular matter. You need to think. We'll carry on our other business as per normal, of course, but this subject won't come up again unless you instigate it."

Without waiting for a reply, he turned and walked towards the bar.

Chapter 6

'Sometimes, the treacherous wind of Fate, can blow the arrow of suspicion into the flesh of an innocent man'

It was early evening in Battersea, and July was well underway. A black Mercedes Sprinter was taking up position in a quiet nook of Wandsworth called Warriner Avenue, which lies in that network of streets just south of the park. When the engine stopped, the two burly occupants remained seated in the vehicle, listening to the radio and casting furtive glances towards the door of number nine.

This was the home of Tarquin Stanhope—a man in his late forties of good honest character, but perhaps one, who through a blessing or curse of birth, was given to a life of little unnecessary effort and a good deal of leisure. Standing six foot two inches tall, broad shouldered, and with a shock of sandy hair, his facial features might well have been equally pronounced.

But Tarquin was charmed with oddly fine features. A short and chiselled aquiline nose arched out below a pair of well-placed clear blue eyes and terminated above a small thin-lipped mouth. Above the eyes sat a heavy brow and a wide, furrowed forehead—not unlike an imposing frieze on a piece of Roman architecture. The overall effect was of a man who could have been a brute, but one whose brutishness had been hobbled by a perceptive and empathetic nature. There was, of course, one other defining feature of Tarquin Stanhope; he was hopelessly vain.

Wrapped in a colourful bathrobe, he stood in his dressing

room sifting through a small box of cuff links. Percy, his border terrier, lay curled up asleep on a thick jersey by the foot of his heavy bateau bed. After a few moments he closed the lid and strode purposefully towards a large antique mirror. He viewed himself briefly, and after running his fingers through his damp hair, went to the door to switch off the overhead light. The room with its curtains closed was now lit only by the reddish glow of a small table lamp, but the subdued effect seemed to satisfy him.

Turning his head, first this way and then that, he eventually settled into an angled position as though posing for Caravaggio, the master of chiaroscuro. He studied himself gravely and then, imagining himself on stage, took a deep breath and said in a loud, pompous voice …

"All the world's a stage … and all the men and women merely players … they have their exits and their entrances, and one man in his time plays …"

Tarquin was stepping back from the mirror for full dramatic effect when his mobile phone gave vent to a piercing ring. Snapping to his senses, he took hold of the plastic lump.

"I'm on my way, darling," he shouted guiltily, closing the phone as quickly as he'd opened it. Without hesitation, he now dashed around the small room, plucking various items of clothing from drawers and hanging rails, and then throwing them on, in a frenzy of arms and legs. Finally, he slipped into a pair of tan loafers, grabbed his coat, and launched himself down the stairs (three at a time).

A short time later his car slid to a halt at a mansion block in the Prince of Wales Drive. This was where his longtime girlfriend Diana lived—an ambitious and somewhat bossy estate agent. Behind him, and at a discreet distance, the black Sprinter also pulled in and waited.

"You never seem to learn, Tarquin," Diana began, having folded herself into the low-slung seat of Tarquin's ageing Mercedes. Short, curvaceous, and amply endowed, she was pretty, in a pink and milky complexioned English way (though Tarquin had long since stopped noticing).

"I was reorganizing some photographs, darling, and the time just seemed to …"

"Just seemed to what, Tarquin?" she said sourly.

"Well, you know, darling. When one's concentrating … time just … just seems to …"

"Tarquin, how often have I heard the same old patter of you being so engrossed in something that you lose track of time!" she said hotly.

"But it's true, I do lose track …"

"Tarquin, you have more spare time than anyone I know, and yet you're still always late!"

"Look, you don't seem to appreciate that I'm really quite busy and …"

But before he had finished his sentence, her derisory laughter exploded all over him like a shower of acid.

A short while later they were standing at the bar of the Garrick Theatre in Covent Garden. Thankfully Diana's mood had lightened and she smiled politely as he handed her a cold glass of champagne. Studying him over the rim, she took a long cool sip.

"Now … darling," she began, fixing him with her dark eyes, "have you rung Freddie and at least shown some interest in the gallery? He really likes you, and you could find a nice little niche for yourself there; the art world's quite racy, you know … I can see you taking to it like a duck to water."

Tarquin shifted uneasily and took a huge gulp of champagne.

"I know. I should," he mumbled, "but I've been sort of busy really."

"What … still plugging on with your ideas of amateur dramatics," she said with a whiff of sarcasm.

"It's something I'm really into, darling. I've been talking to various people," he replied, avoiding her eyes.

"*Talking* about doing something, darling, is very different to actually *doing something*!" she said, adjusting her hair band. "We've been through all this. Freddie has a fat wallet and he wants *you* in his gallery. He thinks you're exquisitely mannered, well dressed, and perfect for the place. His clients will adore you, and before you know it, you'll have started a new chapter in your life and be wondering why … why …"

She trailed off, staring fixedly at a group in the corner.

"My God!" she exclaimed. "There's Christopher Bentham!"

Tarquin felt a fist grab his guts. Glancing over his shoulder, he was able to confirm in one millionth of a millisecond that it was indeed Mr Bentham—the glamorous god of estate. A man whose knowledge of the property market combined with an unerring ability to sniff out the 'in people' had transformed him into a celebrity in his own right.

"Do you mind … I'll be back in a moment," she said urgently.

Tarquin felt sick as she pushed past him. He wouldn't follow—no, that was out of the question. Memories of dinner at the Chelsea Arts Club the previous Christmas came flooding back and filled him with an overwhelming sense of inadequacy. Bentham was everything he was not. Successful, sophisticated, and revered by his business peers. He didn't belong to anything so pedestrian as an established company. No, Bentham was an independent property specialist and acted for a small but elite clutch of wealthy clients.

A few long minutes passed, during which he heard loud spurts of synthetic laughter coming from Diana. Then the bell rang. Tarquin hastily poured himself a large glass of water and a moment or two later she joined him, flushed and agitated.

"Christopher's well … is he," Tarquin said, making clear by his expression this was a dig, not a question. Diana bristled.

"C'mon, for God's sake … we need to shift," she said, plunging ahead brusquely.

They took their seats. Although touching at the shoulders, it was obvious there was now an invisible barrier between them—an emotional disconnect. Her demeanour had changed and the blood-red nails on her fingers fumbled nervously with the programme.

"What an extraordinary thing to bump into Christopher," she said in a loud, formal voice. "He's looking well … I must say."

Tarquin twisted his lips downwards by way of an answer but said nothing.

"Looks like he's just come back from the Maldives!" she continued. "He's a very smart operator, Tarquin … we could both learn a lot from him."

Tarquin mumbled something and scrutinized his mobile phone.

When the curtain eventually rose, he struggled to concentrate. He was all too aware of Diana's attraction to Bentham—he'd witnessed it before. Yes, he had got drunk that night at the Club all those months ago. Good God, who wouldn't have? Was he to watch the ugly spectacle of Diana's flirtatious behaviour towards Bentham sober? The evening had been a disaster from start to finish and had very nearly ended in a brawl.

Gradually, as the play proceeded, Tarquin succumbed to the warmth and semidarkness of his surroundings, and his eyelids fell. He entered a fitful daydream. No longer was he sitting in the Garrick Theatre surrounded by people … he was approaching a dimly lit bedroom. Diana and Christopher were entwined at a ridiculous angle on a bed, sheets tangled erotically around their bodies. Clothes were scattered across the floor, whilst Bentham's trademark bow tie hung limply from a lampshade. He was whispering breathlessly into her tousled hair whilst she giggled beneath him. Unseen, Tarquin approached and viewed with disgust the damp tanned neck of Christopher Bentham.

This guy needed to be taught a lesson. How dare he think that his status could allow him to snatch any bit of pretty fluff which drifted his way. He may be a property mogul with a house or three on every continent, but so what? So bloody what?

Tarquin, now hopelessly lost in fantasy, was just considering how to deal with Bentham when, in the real world, his phone suddenly leapt into life and peeled shrilly across the breadth of the theatre. Electrified, he jumped awake, and in a blind panic his knee flexed upwards, dislodging the water glass in its holder and hurling the contents in a great arc of liquid, over his neighbour.

"*Oh my God! Oh my God!*" the woman sitting next to him shouted in strangled tones, whilst jumping up. "You bloody fool …what on earth are you doing? I'm … I'm soaked!"

Tarquin, dazed, looked at her aghast.

"Oh no … no … no, I am so sorry," he stuttered, squirming with embarrassment and pulling out a handkerchief. "Can I help?"

"No, get away from me! Go away!" she sobbed, moving along the row with her husband. "You've ruined my evening, you bloody oaf!"

"What in the hell are you playing at, Tarquin?" Diana whispered sharply in his ear, whilst grabbing the phone and switching it off. "For Christ's sake!"

The lead was fluffing her lines. There was an awkwardness on stage which took a couple of minutes to smooth over. Tarquin's mind was scrambled. Should he stay … or go?

All around, people's heads were swivelling round to give him disapproving looks. Sweat trickled between his shoulder blades as his head dithered through the options. Then, a few minutes later, as if by magic, his legs threw him into an upright position and transported him with a determined stride to the emergency exit. He didn't even glance back.

At the crowded bar of the Nags Head, in a street nearby, Tarquin ordered two double whiskeys as though in a dream. He drained the first glass in two gulps and then paused to look around him and reflect on his predicament. How had he fallen asleep and made such a fool of himself? Yes, Christopher was a threat, a sort of walking insult to his own shortcomings, but to let this happen, to have to leave his favourite theatre by the emergency exit—this was beyond appalling. He shuddered at the memory, and picking up the second glass, drained it in a similar fashion to the first.

"Blimey, you was thirsty," the big-bosomed girl now wedging

herself against him said, having watched him down the two shots in close succession. Tarquin squinted down at the cheeky stranger for a second or two, taking in her fleshy rouge lips, blue eye shadow, and short pink skirt.

"I'm terribly sorry," he said loudly, a small trickle at the corner of his mouth, "but sometimes a man needs a drink, and he needs it fast!"

"I'm Shirley, by the way," she said chirpily. "Nice to meet you. I like a man who's tall. I only seem to know short arses—fat short arses at that! What do you do then?"

"What, when I'm not throwing drinks over my neighbours in the theatre?" Tarquin replied, dissolving into a fit of hysterical laughter.

"Throwing drinks over your neighbours?" Shirley said, puzzled. "Oh well, whatever! It's nice to meet a bloke who's in a good mood with a happy-go-lucky nature. My boyfriend Terry is so bloomin' bad tempered. Like this evenin', I told him I wanted to go out with Claudia—that's her there with the bald geezer—and he flies into one and starts screamin' and hollerin', over what? Aren't I allowed to have some fun for a change? I told him he drinks too much Coke and eats too many burgers and it ain't doing him no good. I mean, he can't work it off 'cos he's a lorry driver, sitting on his fat arse all day!"

"Deary me," Tarquin replied obligingly. "Seems we're both in the same boat. What's your tipple, Shirley?"

"You better tell me your name before you get me a drink," she giggled wheezily.

"Tarquin," he said, gazing down at her.

"What?"

"Tarquin!"

"Tarquin? Cor blimey ... you're the first geezer I've ever met with a name like that!" she said with a shrill giggle. "Sounds right poncy ... are you a toff?"

"Well ... I didn't choose it," Tarquin said resignedly. "And I probably am a toff!"

"Let's drink to that, Tarquin!" she said, clashing her glass clumsily against his.

She turned towards a group behind Tarquin and screeched, "Claudia, come over 'ere and meet my new friend Tarquin!"

The tall blond girl broke away from her group and sauntered up to Tarquin. She looked him straight in the eye and he felt her measured scrutiny.

"Hello," she said coolly, extending her hand. "I am Claudia."

"He already knows that, love … you can forget the formalities. His name's Tarquin, and before you say it, he already knows he's a toff!" Shirley said, cackling raucously and slapping Tarquin on the shoulder.

"It is nice to meet a tall Englishman," Claudia said in a familiar accent, "and a well-dressed one!"

He liked her style immediately. She was confident and wore a strongly waisted black leather jacket over a white T-shirt. The line of brass buttons up the centre and small epaulettes gave her a military flavour. Below her black jeans he noticed a pair of quality leather shoes; classic, bordering on old fashioned.

"Thank you," he said, returning her gaze. "I was beginning to feel a little out of place in here."

"Well, of course … you need to dress like a gypsy to fit in here," she said, clutching the bald head of the man next to her, like a hawk might grab an egg. "Isn't this right, Cliff!"

"Might be," her overweight sidekick replied, whilst bobbing his head to the rhythm of the music.

"Are you here alone?" Claudia said, turning to Tarquin with a searching look.

"Jesus Christ, girl … show some tact!" Shirley hissed at her shoulder. "Don't be too obvious!"

Tarquin made the connection … the Russian cleaner he used to have.

"Well, at the moment I am; I was in the … erm … theatre and left early. Are you Eastern European?"

"Sure. I been here some time now … like five years. Actually I am Romanian. But my accent is obviously not very good yet!" she said with a small smile.

"Come on! All this serious chitchat!" Shirley said, thrusting her large bust into the conversation. "We're here to 'ave some fun, not discover each other's bloody life histories!"

"Are you ready for that drink now, Shirley?" Tarquin said loudly, like he was talking to an old friend.

"Yes, I bloody am … a black velvet, please … me mouth's bloomin' parched!"

"And you, Claudia?" he said, pulling his wallet from an inside pocket.

"Err … okay, I will. I don't usually have more than two … but on this occasion … a gin and tonic, please."

"A gin and bloody tonic?" Shirley screeched. "You haven't had one of those since I've known you, girl. Jesus, you're turning poncy as well, Clauds!"

Claudia smiled warmly and revealed a set of perfect teeth. Tarquin strolled to the bar.

*   *   *

"Well, what a nice surprise!" Christopher said to Diana at the bar during the interval. "I really didn't imagine we would ever meet again; such are the ways of this impersonal town."

He handed a bottle of champagne and some glasses to the outstretched arms of one of his friends.

"Come and have a sharpener with us until Tarquin gets back. What on earth was that all about? He very nearly brought the whole thing to a close!"

"God, don't remind me!" Diana said in an exasperated tone. "I think he fell asleep and that bloody mobile of his went off!"

"Rather an extreme reaction," Christopher said, giving Diana a searching look.

"He spilt an entire glass of water over the woman next to him, Christopher … I don't blame her! God knows what he's up to now, probably getting sloshed somewhere. He hates scenes … and come to think of it, I hate driving that car of his; and guess who's going to be chauffeur tonight!"

Christopher put his hand softly on Diana's arm and very gently stroked her with his thumb.

"Don't worry," he said soothingly, looking into her eyes. "I'll look after you until he gets back."

*　　　*　　　*

Meanwhile, across the street from the Garrick and tucked discreetly into a narrow passage, the black Sprinter sat unnoticed by the swirling crowds. Inside, the two men viewed the entrance to the theatre with watchful eyes. Reg Guston, better known as Gus, and his trusty henchman, Robert 'Bob' Stiles, were both west London men and worked for Viktor and Zoltan.

"Look, G, I'm not being funny or nothin', but I still don't think we're on to the right geezer," Bob said, turning to Gus. "Zoltan said—and I heard 'im clear as day—that Oliver drove one of those Volvo estates, and that he was about five-eleven, and on the porky side. This guy is big, about six-three, and he drives an old Merx!"

"Shut it, B," Gus said cuttingly. "You know as well as me that Zol is prone to a few errors of detail every now and then. We both saw him come out of number nine, and that's the address he give us, okay? Regarding his car … he's probably got the Merx as well as the Volvo … as his lady puller. For romantic nights at the theatre! Something you know nothing about, my friend, 'cos you only has romantic feelings for fancy tools, mobile phones, and all things with buttons, lights, and batteries."

He elbowed Bob with a wink and revealed a row of stained teeth.

"And what about the dog?" Bob said, ignoring Gus's rudeness.

Gus lowered his head and peered at Christopher and Diana through the spy hole. They were still talking at the door of the theatre, people milling around them.

"Look, I'm trying to do a job here. What about the mongrel? We both saw the bloody thing being walked a couple of days ago. Have you forgotten already?"

"That's where you're wrong, mate," Bob continued. "We saw a dog being walked, all right, but it wasn't the animal that Zol described. He said it was a boxer dog."

"A what?"

"A *boxer*—a big dog with long legs and can run like the frigging clappers," Bob persisted.

"And?" Gus said irritably.

"This guy has a terrier, not a boxer! A boxer is three times the size of that thing."

"Okay, *you* ring Zoltan, and tell 'im the good news, but I'm telling you, my friend, this is our man, and no amount of irrelevant details from you is going to change my mind."

Bob clicked his tongue and rolled his stool back to one of the spy holes.

"We should have nailed him back in Battersea, mate, like we planned to do. This place is teeming with people," he said, gazing through the spy hole.

"Of course we should have, but you know as well as me that he come out of his front door at a gallop and jumped straight into his motor! We was caught on the hop, okay. We have to be strategic my friend … just be patient."

"Balls to patient, mate … this is getting untidy," Bob said sullenly. He sat silently for a minute and then felt the need to break the silence.

"I wonder if he's armed?" he said, changing tack.

"Eh?" Gus said absently, whilst scrutinising Bentham and Diana through the tinted glass. "Armed? Are you crazy, mate? These aren't yer east end gangster types, for Christ's sake … these are gentlemen crooks. They use brains, not fuckin' guns!"

"S'pose so," Bob mumbled.

"Now for fuck's sake, we need to concentrate. What the hell is going on? Our man goes into the theatre with his squeeze, and a couple of hours later, she comes out with a bald gnome, and our man is nowhere to be seen. Something's going on 'ere. I bet you he's given us the slip. From what Zol was saying, he's very slimy. This time *pay attentionee!*"

"But he doesn't know we're here, G!" Bob said, puzzled.

"You finished? Now listen up … I'm going round the back of the theatre to see if I can spot Oliver whilst you keep a hawk eye on these two. Follow them wherever. Keep your phone handy and any probs call me. Now, you got that? *Comprende, comrade?*"

"Yeah."

Gus emerged from the side of the black van and strode off in the direction of the Garrick.

Three minutes later Bob was "discreetly" shadowing Christopher and Diana. They were evidently in quite a hurry, and he had to strike a brisk pace to stay in touch.

*　　　*　　　*

"I really am getting worried now," Diana said to Christopher as they passed the Coliseum and headed up St Martins Lane. "It's just not like him to ignore my calls continuously. Where on earth is the idiot? I can tell you, if I wasn't worried something had happened, I'd be leaving him to his own devices!"

"Well, frankly, he's behaved appallingly," Christopher agreed. "You don't leave a woman on her own in a theatre without an explanation."

"Well, I know! So he embarrassed himself, but what about me?" she said shrilly. "I mean, what on earth was he thinking?"

"Well, precisely."

"This *would* have to happen to Tarquin. *Tarquin,* of all people … he's so damn proper!"

"Does he fall asleep in the theatre as a rule?"

"Yes, he does. Says the warm atmosphere knocks him out. But he's *never* caused a problem like that. He didn't even tell me he was going, just got up and left. He's in a dream most of the time."

Christopher sighed sympathetically.

"I really don't know what to say, darling."

"Right. We've tried Flannagans, the Brasserie; he wouldn't be seen dead in the Fighting Cock. Oh for God's sake, we could be here all night!" she said in exasperated tones.

She tripped suddenly on a raised paving stone and Christopher's hand closed reassuringly on her arm. It felt good and she turned towards him and smiled.

"Thank you, Christopher, for being here," she said quietly. "It's really not your problem. I feel terrible that you're marching around the streets with me when you could be at dinner with your friends. It really is too bad!"

"Diana, I'm very happy to be roaming the streets with you," he said huskily whilst letting his hand rest softly in the small of her back. "Very happy indeed."

She glanced at him and smiled. "I guess we could try the Nags Head as a last resort …"

*   *   *

Tarquin returned from the bar with yet another round of drinks. Shirley, who had been dominating the conversation with gossip about their kitchen job in a busy city office, fell silent for a few moments. Claudia took her opportunity.

"So who was with you at the theatre?" she said to him above the din of music and drunken voices.

"Oh … er … my girlfriend," he replied shiftily.

"You have a girlfriend—but no wife?"

"No … no … long-term girlfriend," Tarquin floundered.

"And you left her in there?" she said, raising her eyebrows.

"Well … er …"

"Clauds, get with it. He had a barney and he's come here to drown his sorrows!" Shirley said with an evil twinkle. "Am I right or am I right?"

Tarquin hesitated and then clutched the opportunity.

"Yes, you've got it in one, Shirley. We met … well, *she* met an old boyfriend."

"Say no more, Tarq," Shirley said, holding up an

admonishing index finger and pushing herself against him cosily. "Been there, walked the plank, written the bloody book! Best thing to do … just get away. You did the right thing, mate. You don't need to be a spectator to their canoodlings!"

"This is true?" Claudia said, looking hard at Tarquin.

"Yes … yes, it's true. He's a bloody property developer. She's got the hots for him," he said, embracing his new status as a cuckold.

"Right, that's it!" Shirley shouted. "You're going to have fun with us tonight, Tarquin. Sod the lot of 'em!!"

Claudia gave Tarquin a conspiratorial wink as she brushed past to get to the bar.

"You forgot Cliff, Shirley," she said, putting a hand on Shirley's shoulder. "He's on the lime and lager."

"Oh blimey! Sorry, Cliff!" Shirley shouted. "You keep disappearing into the crowd, love."

A minute or two later Tarquin took the lager from Claudia and stretched over Shirley into Cliff's gang.

"Gawd help me!" Shirley giggled as Tarquin leaned over her. "You've got arms like a gorilla, Tarq!"

They carried on in this vein for the next hour, but Tarquin had lost all track of time. In his mind, Diana was still in the theatre and the play was still in full flood.

As the liquor flowed, so too did Tarquin's inhibitions ebb. Shirley, who was by far the more oiled of the two girls, was taking every opportunity to touch, rub, and scrape against him, and he was enjoying the escapism.

"Tarquin," she said at a certain point, "do you think I'm a bit chubby, if you know what I mean?"

"You're a hefalump!" Tarquin replied with a brazen lack of tact, which in the circumstances was well received.

"Why?" said Shirley with a leery grin.

"You're top heavy, girl … and I'm not complaining!" he said with a huge laugh, whilst throwing his arm around her shoulders.

"How much do you think I weigh, Tarq?" she challenged, disentangling herself from his grip.

He stroked his chin and took another slurp of whiskey.

"I would say … I would say … as a man who's not unfamiliar with the weighing of sheep … a hundred weight!"

Claudia kicked him, and Cliff burst out laughing.

"You're a rude man … and a toff!" Shirley giggled drunkenly. "Now pick me up and tell me what I weigh!" she demanded.

"Pick you up? Are you sure?" he said laughing.

"That's exactly what I mean, you bloomin' ponce … are you a man or a mouse?"

Tarquin put his glass down and got behind her. He locked his arms around her waist, which meant he had to bend his knees and press his pelvis against her in a rather obscene pose. She wriggled suggestively and her pink skirt rose even higher as Cliff clapped enthusiastically.

He was about to flex upwards, when a screech ripped the air like a scalpel.

"Taaaarquin!!"

"Ooh! I think your missus has just turned up, Tarq!" Shirley giggled loudly, looking at the auburn woman who had just walked in.

Tarquin spun round to face Diana, as though he'd been stabbed by a cattle prod.

"Daaarling! Daaarling! I … er … I … what …" he stammered.

His facial features now seemed to lose all allegiance to each other and went in strange directions quite independently. One eye was fixed in terror on Diana whilst the other seemed ready to make a dash for the street. Meanwhile, his lips had twisted upwards into a grotesquely synthetic grin, making him look like a deceitful politician.

"This nice man has been entertaining us ladies for the last two hours," Shirley said boldly as Diana approached, "and he has behaved like a true gentleman. You're a very lucky lady, and you need to appreciate him more!"

"Yes, he's the best-looking boy in here," Claudia added, curling her hand over Tarquin's shoulder. "You could do a lot worse."

"Thank you," Diana said icily, before turning back to Tarquin. "It's time to go … we've been looking all over for you."

"I'm sorry, darling … seems I—"

"Shut up!" Diana hissed.

"Bye, Tarquin!" Shirley said, kissing him on the lips. "Thanks for the drinks, darling. You're a lovely fellow. Take care!"

Claudia then embraced him and gave him a peck on the cheek.

"Good-bye, nice man," she whispered intimately with a wink, and then raising her glass, "until we meet again!"

"Come *on,* Tarquin," Diana snapped. "Christopher's bloody waiting."

"See you, Tarq," splurged Cliff in the background, dribbling beer onto his trainers and hanging on to another customer for support.

Christopher was standing at the back of the bar with his arms crossed firmly over his chest. His head seemed shinier than ever, and his neck looked like it had frozen solid. Even his bow tie had lost the self-confidence of earlier and was drooping forlornly at the tips. A rough-looking man with a ponytail and forearms emblazoned with tattoos was watching him like a hungover celebrity chef might watch a cockroach which had strolled casually onto his chopping board.

"Let's go!" Christopher said anxiously, wiping a handkerchief across his forehead. "This place has got a malignant feel."

He catapulted out of the door followed by Diana and then Tarquin.

"Don't you … ever … *ever* … *ever* do that to me again," Diana said, seething with indignation. "I've *never* felt so humiliated. What a pair of *witches*!"

"They meant no harm, d … darling," Tarquin blustered drunkenly. "Bethides, I needed some company."

He extended his arm in Diana's direction, but she twisted out of reach and moved in close to Christopher, who was walking like a man possessed.

"Blimey! Thlow down, folks," Tarquin said as he stumbled behind. "What's the big rush?"

"We're being followed," Christopher said, his voice trembling and looking furtively over his shoulder. "The bloke in the baseball cap—the *big* bloke in the baseball cap—has been behind us for some time."

"What? Being thollowed? Are you paranoid or something, Christopher?" Tarquin slurred whilst gazing blurry eyed behind them.

Suddenly Bentham broke into a run, waving his arms frantically.

"Taxi! Taxi!" he shouted.

The vehicle came to a halt.

"Who's coming with me?" he said breathlessly, whilst holding the cab door open.

"I am!" Diana replied, climbing in without so much as a glance in Tarquin's direction. "He can sort himself out!"

"But my car! I can't drive it like thith, darling. I can't leave it. It'th bloody Friday tomorrow!" Tarquin whimpered pathetically.

The cab door slammed shut, then opened briefly for Bentham to shout, "*Call Scooterman. Good night!!*"

Tarquin stood drunkenly watching the red taillights merge into the traffic.

"Thuck!" he said loudly. "Thuck, fuck, fuck!"

He turned round, and a fist like a sledge hammer slammed into his solar plexus. Then, as he doubled up, a knee whipped into his chin. Completely winded, he fell to the pavement groaning.

Next he felt a hefty boot in his groin, which mercifully hit his bunched fists and missed its main target. Tarquin yelled as his little finger snapped.

"Read this, Oliver, an' you'll make your life an' ours a whole lot easier!" a gruff voice above him said. Another kick from behind caught him in the lower back and he heard another voice. "That'll teach 'im."

An envelope was shoved in his pocket, and he was dimly

aware of two men walking casually away.

Tarquin groaned and fought for breath. With his cheek on the cold, callous pavement, he felt scared—scared like he hadn't been scared in years. There was no reassuring hand, no sympathetic, "That was a tough tackle, old fellow. You okay?" He was down where the lowlife lives, viewing the world from a low dangerous perspective; the perspective of a rat.

Gradually his focus moved from his pain to his predicament. How quickly he'd changed from a respectable, charming human being, to something animal and alone—something quite unclean. He rolled over and stood shakily on his feet. He felt stickiness around his cheek. People were crossing the street to avoid him; he didn't care. He was dislocated from "them" now. He was marked, dubious, of suspect nature—in short, he was an outsider.

He reached into his inside pocket and checked his wallet; strange … still there. Next he groped for his mobile and cried out as the broken finger on his left hand gave him a sharp stab of pain. But the mobile was there. Again he felt puzzled. And then he remembered his assailant's words, "*Read this, Oliver.*"

"Oliver? Who the hell is Oliver?" Tarquin glanced down and very nearly lost his balance. His head felt raw, inside and out. With one arm steadying him against the wall, he squatted down and picked up a clean white envelope by his feet. The name OLIVER was written on the front. It was good quality and well sealed. He put it in his pocket for later; he'd had enough pain for the moment.

Removing his jacket, he tried to brush off the street grime. It was horribly scuffed, but being dark, it would pass. His knee too was torn and showed his white skin beneath. Suddenly he remembered his car—shit! It would be towed in the morning.

As he began dialling directory enquiries, he heard some drunken voices and high-pitched laughter approaching. Two women and a bloke were teetering towards him, engrossed in conversation.

Suddenly the conversation stopped, and he heard Claudia's

voice.

"Jesus! It's Tarquin!!"

They clustered around him as he told them what happened.

"You say your woman just left you and went off with that geezer? The bitch!" Shirley said, putting her arm around his waist.

"And they took nothing?" Claudia said, the only vaguely sober one of the trio.

"Nothing at all. Just wanted to give me a good kicking and called me Oliver," Tarquin said in confusion.

"And you wasn't mouthy or nothing with them, Tarquin?" Shirley said.

"You poor shod," Cliff mumbled.

"I hadn't said a word to them," Tarquin said in a faltering voice. "I just turned round and wham! Punched straight in the belly."

"Look, you're in a bad way, Tarquin, and I'm gonna make sure you get home tonight," Claudia said with authority. "You said earlier you've got a car here, so can we leave it till the morning?"

"*No!*" Tarquin groaned. "It's on a yellow line. It'll be clamped or towed in the morning. It's in Shelton Street … About a five-minute walk in that direction. Use my phone and call 'Scooterman.'"

"Who?"

"It's a company which drives your car home when you've drunk too much," he said, steadying himself against the wall.

"So we go as passengers?" Claudia queried, getting it straight in her mind.

"That's right. But it's small. Mercedes sports. Won't take us all."

"Did you get that, Shirl? We could call the police, but they're gonna ask a heap of unnecessary questions and keep us up all night. I'm going to call these people and get them to drive his car back to Battersea where he lives … and you know what," she added, thinking aloud. "I'm going to go with him to make sure he gets back."

"Oh yeah!" Cliff said sarcastically.

"Look, Cliff, he's in a bad way. He's a bit dazed, and we won't all fit in. Get real!"

"Sure, okay," Cliff mumbled.

"So Shirl, you and Cliff go on back and I'll call you a bit later!"

Shirley beckoned Claudia aside.

"Are you sure about this, Clauds," she whispered. "You don't know this guy, and it's a bit odd, this whole thing about being beaten up for no reason. Perhaps he's done something?"

"Shirl, I'm going on instinct here. I know what you're saying, but you know I can look after myself."

"Okay, darlin' … just be careful. Those kicks you was showing me might be comin' in handy. And what do I tell them in the kitchen tomorrow if you're late?"

"I'll call you," Claudia said with a wink. She turned back to Tarquin.

"Now come on, Tarquin. Let's get on to those people."

"Bye, Clauds," Cliff said, drifting away with Shirley.

"Speak later, darlin'."

Chapter 7

Forty-five minutes later, Tarquin's car came to a halt in Warriner Avenue, Battersea. They clambered out and Tarquin fumbled for his keys.

"Wow! This is fantastic!" Claudia said as she stood in the richly decorated hallway of Tarquin's house. Percy came rushing up to greet the new visitor.

"Hello, little dog," she said, bending down and giving him a cursory stroke. Percy lay on his back, his tail wagging deliriously.

"Well, it's home," Tarquin said wearily. "Come and have some coffee, or something stronger if you want. You've been an angel tonight, and I don't really know how to thank you." He wandered into the kitchen and opened the door to the garden.

"I'll have a tea, if it's all the same to you. Is this really your place then?" she said, her eyes roving over the colourful bird paintings and running a finger along the top of the lime-green dado rail.

"Certainly is," Tarquin replied.

"You mean you own this whole place?"

"Yes ... now let's get the kettle on."

"No. We better get you properly cleaned up first," Claudia said, fixing Tarquin with a beady look. "Where's the bathroom? I'll need some disinfectant, cotton wool, and some plasters. You've got a nasty cut on your cheek and a graze on your chin, and we don't want any infection. We really should get you to hospital with that finger, but I'll bind it up for tonight and you must go first thing in the morning."

"Oh … er … no, look, Claudia, it's been very kind of you, but …"

"Tarquin, shut up and let's get you sorted out. I know you're going to crawl into your bed as soon as I'm gone. You men are all the same," she said with amusement in her eyes.

"Oh, all right, but you really should be getting back. This is beyond the call of duty," Tarquin said awkwardly. "Come up to the bathroom."

"I knew it!" she said, chuckling at the top of the stairs. "Look at the state of this. Looks like you're a very tidy man, Mr Tarquin. Were we in a bit of a hurry when we left this evening?" she said, picking a coat hanger off the floor by the door of the bathroom.

"To be honest, yes," Tarquin said resignedly. "My girlfriend was getting a bit hysterical, so I had to leave quickly."

"I'm not surprised. Something tells me you're not big on punctuality!" she said sternly. "Are you really called Tarquin, or is that a nickname?"

"Yuh … that's my name, all right," he said.

"Weird! Sounds a bit old fashioned or something … it's all right, though. Don't get me wrong," she said. "So where are the plasters and things?"

"There … in that cabinet … everything we need, I hope," Tarquin said, gesturing to a mirror-fronted wall cabinet.

Claudia searched amongst the bottles and packets and then sat next to him on a large blanket chest with split cane panels. First she wiped the dried blood from his chin and cheek with a wet flannel and then dabbed the wounds with cotton wool soaked in surgical spirit.

Tarquin winced as the cool liquid stung his flesh, whilst also taking in the close proximity of her striking features. The irises of her pale eyes were an exotic cocktail of marbled blues and yellows embedded in the purest glass. It gave her pupils a hawklike intensity, as sharp as the spirit itself. They instilled wariness and attraction in Tarquin in equal measure and eventually forced him to move his eyes away.

Detecting his sudden shyness, she began to chat.

"Well, my name isn't really Claudia," she said.

"Really?"

"It's Constanta."

"Constanta?" he said, brows raised.

"That's right. I changed it because it was too Eastern European, and I wanted to fit in … you know, to disguise myself."

"Well, I noticed you had an accent … thought it was Russian."

"Well, as I told you, I'm Romanian. I came over here five years ago to make my fortune in rich western country. I was trained as a gymnast at home, and I mean trained. I didn't have normal upbringing. I was talent spotted and as a result my whole existence was dominated by exercise routines, strict diets, early nights. I was a mechanical doll designed to impress audiences with my gymnastic skills. But I grew too tall and was dropped."

"Well, you're certainly tall, Claudia … I mean Constanta," Tarquin said smiling.

"I'll tell you about that another time," she said firmly. "There's a more urgent issue which we need to clear up … and with that guy talking the whole way back, it wasn't easy in the car."

"Urgent issue?" Tarquin said quizzically.

"Darling, you've just been beaten by a pair of guys on a London street who referred to you as 'Oliver' and that doesn't strike you as weird? And what about that envelope you mentioned they gave you? You've got it in your head that you were mugged, but I'm telling you, there's more to it than that. What did they take? Absolutely nothing! Now that really adds up, doesn't it!" she said with a cynical glint.

"Well … I suppose you're right," Tarquin said hesitatingly.

"I know I'm right. Now, this isn't going to make you look beautiful, but it's got to be done," she said, applying a large plaster to Tarquin's chin.

"Oh no!" she giggled, leaning back to get a better view of his face. "You look like the Gaboar just got hold of you."

"The what?"

"The Romanian police, darling, the Gaboar!"

"Oh Christ!" Tarquin muttered with a sense of horror at his reflection. "I need a drink."

"Oh no you don't! You need to show me the envelope, and then get yourself off to bed and sleep."

"It's in my coat pocket, I think, down in the hall."

Constanta sprang to her feet and disappeared downstairs, leaving Tarquin to scrutinise his reflection sadly. He heard her having a small conversation with Percy, which pleased him, and filled him with guilt at his earlier petulance.

"Have you fed him?" she shouted up. "He looks hungry."

"I … er … left in a bit of a hurry. Please give him the remains of the shepherd's pie in the fridge," Tarquin shouted down sheepishly.

"You are a *bad* man, not looking after your little doggy. I'm getting to know your ways, Tarquin, so watch out!" Constanta shouted up reproachfully.

Tarquin sat on the blanket chest listening to the muted noises from the kitchen below, and pondered as to how on earth he had arrived at this most unlikely of situations.

*   *   *

Gus brought the Sprinter to a halt at the entrance to Bob's housing estate in Fulham. Although it was late, lights showed brightly in the numerous windows of the imposing tower blocks.

"Okay, mate, job done. Now we just wait for the arsehole to call Zoltan and plead his case," Gus said, arching his back in the driving seat.

"Sure thing … bastard got off lightly in my opinion," Bob said without feeling. "If I had it my way he'd be in hospital now!"

"Listen, mate, I gave 'im a good whack in the goolies … there's a broken bone in there somewhere, I bet you!" Gus said with a smirk. "But Z told me to go steady on this occasion."

"S'pose so," Bob conceded. "I got 'im good as well, with me first punch to the guts followed by the old knee in the chin … nice combination that works every time!"

"Funny, innit, how these guys take the piss and just think that it's all going to be fine. Nobody, like nobody, gets one over Zoltan," Gus said with an element of reverence. "And Oliver needs to get this into his thick skull or the guy will be in the fucking cemetery."

"Yeah, too right, mate," Bob said unbuckling. "Right … well, give us a buzz in the morning and tell me what the big man says."

He climbed out of the van and stood holding the door.

"Get yer head down, okay?" Gus said, starting the engine.

"Sure."

*   *   *

Tarquin sat in the kitchen staring at the letter. It made no sense to his dulled senses, and it was getting late.

> *Oliver,*
> *Since my phone call 6 weeks ago I have not received any communication from you.*
> *You have my mobile number, email address, and a land number.*
> *This was unwise. You have had ample opportunity to honour your obligations and suggest an amount you intend to pay me for my idea of the French cabinet.*
> *Unfortunately, you did not take me seriously, which is why my father, a man you should be careful of, decided to teach you a small lesson. I say 'small' lesson in order to assure you that 'bigger' lessons will follow if you do not come round to our way of thinking. It is dangerous to play with Russians, my friend, you should know this by now.*
> *Call me.*
> *Z.*

Constanta came in from the sitting room.

"Do you understand what is happening, Mr Tarquin?" she said as though cajoling a child through an elementary exam sheet.

"Well … er … not really. It seems to be addressed to this mysterious man Oliver."

"Exactly, so what does that tell you?"

"Well, I suppose … they—the two blokes—thought I was him," Tarquin stuttered in disbelief.

"Well done, well done. We're getting there!"

"Look, I'm tired," Tarquin said irritably. "I don't need this right now. You've been wonderful tonight, Constanta, and I can't thank you enough."

"Oh shut up, you silly Englishman. Always so polite! Now I must ask you a serious question, which you must answer honestly."

"What's that?" Tarquin said defensively. "Is your name really Tarquin … or is it Oliver?"

"What!" Tarquin said incredulously. "Of course it's not bloody Oliver. Do you think

I'm lying to you?"

Constanta looked hard at him and then smiled. "No, I don't think you are lying. I just wanted to be quite sure."

"Well, thanks very much," Tarquin mumbled. "That's a relief. Feel free to look at any letters or magazines in this house which have a name and address on. Do you want my passport?"

"Later, darling," Constanta chuckled. "So we can think that this Oliver man has done something rather bad and is being given a lesson, can't we?" she said. "It would seem that the letter is written by someone, a Russian, who has been ripped off … had piece of furniture stolen or something like that. You see, it mentions 'the cabinet'; 'the cabinet was our idea and you stole it.' Does that mean the idea or the cabinet was stolen?"

She looked up expectantly.

Tarquin groaned whilst clutching his head between his hands. "I just don't know. It's bloody double Dutch to me. What time is it, anyway?"

"Okay, I get the message. You want me to go."

Tarquin was quiet for a moment.

"Look, Constanta, this is silly. It's 1.20am. There's a bed on the top floor, all made up with its own bathroom, towel, and so on."

"Are you crazy … me stay here?" she said, raising her eyebrows into a pair of beautiful arches. "I need to be up early to get to work. I start at 7.30am!"

"Constanta," he said with sudden determination, "don't be stupid …"

"You think I am stupid?"

"It's a manner of speaking, sweetie, don't take it literally. Just go upstairs and sleep. Let yourself out in the morning and don't wake me up. There's money in that bowl there for a taxi. Order one now; the number's on that board."

She hesitated.

"Go on … I don't bite," he said. "This house is number nine Warriner Avenue. There's a phone by your bed. You're in Battersea, by the way, in case you didn't realize."

"Can I take Percy for protection then?" she said.

"Please do. He likes girls. Oh, and be sure to leave your telephone number."

"Okay."

She sidled off and had taken two steps up the stairs when she suddenly stopped and leaned over the banister.

"Tarquin," she said. "Do you know anybody called Oliver?"

Tarquin clasped his forehead.

"Well … of course … it's a familiar name. Let me think. Oh of course, my godson, Olly, and there are some others, I'm sure, but this means nothing … they're hardly going to be criminals."

"Mmm … okay. Good night."

"Good night, Constanta."

With that, she went lightly up the stairs, chatting to Percy as though to a child.

Thomas Charrington

Chapter 8

Melvyn couldn't sleep. He sat on his favourite garden bench viewing the great orange moon rise above the cedars, whilst the cool night air nipped at his ankles. He could sense the three-dimensional bulk of that huge ball of rock on nights like this … its ponderous presence in space. In its paler, smaller guise it was just a flat nebulous disc, a gossamer decoration somehow lacking in solidity.

Sucking hungrily on his pipe, he thought of Zoltan watching him at Hertford House, the seat of the precious Wallace Collection, and it was a thought that made him squirm. Zoltan knew what he was doing, oh yes, no question of that—it would have been as clear as day. And the thought of being watched … ugh! That didn't sit well at all. It made him feel extremely threatened and at the same time stupid. He'd been caught out at a time when he felt he was being supremely vigilant. Why in God's name did this have to happen? Agreed, he had been to the Wallace for regular, intense sessions of scrutiny, but why did a man who was living in Germany have to appear at one of these precise moments? It was blatantly unfair.

He often felt his life was being handled by others. He sometimes imagined the whole world was in some sort of weird collusion against him, and that he had to jump through a series of hoops for some higher and entirely unfathomable purpose. Like the people around him were actors, taunting him to just the right pitch so as to strengthen but not break him.

And yet … sometimes, he had to concede that things worked

in his favour. Within a few months of that restaurant meeting between Oliver and Fabien near Hardy's, the young Frenchman's life had literally fallen apart. Cecile had decided to leave him. She could see no future with him living in London on a limited salary and wanted to cut her losses. Her man was never around and her friends in Paris were talking. And yes, Fabien had become desperate, desperate to get her back at any cost and by any means, even if this meant doing the unthinkable. And this had provided the spark to launch the project.

Melvyn came back to his senses and his immediate predicament. The thought of having to give Zoltan a payoff for doing absolutely nothing was monstrous. Yes, it *had* been the Russian's idea … he had to admit that; but the idea was just the beginning of a long arduous road, and it was he and Oliver who had walked it, not Zoltan.

But perhaps it was all working out okay after all. There had been no word from the Russian for weeks. Had he and his wife made up, and he'd simply shelved the whole idea of blackmail? Or was there something that Zoltan feared, that was holding him back? Did he and Oliver hold an ace without realizing it? Come what may, he would call Oliver in the morning and let him know the cabinet was now ready.

With that thought in mind, he got to his feet, and after tapping the remaining embers of his pipe on the side of the bench, he went back to bed.

*   *   *

Constanta too was restless. She lay in the semidarkness of Tarquin's top bedroom, gently threading her fingers through the soft fur of Percy's neck. The evening had been a crazy one, to be sure, and here she was, sleeping in the house of this guy she'd met only hours earlier. Who was he and what was he into? Something, for certain; people were after him. And yet he swore he didn't know what it was all about, and she felt compelled to believe him.

She considered what type of guy Tarquin was, but soon realized, *he wasn't like any guy she'd met*. For one, he was rich, and yes … that was appealing. He also had good manners as she'd observed throughout the course of the evening, and dressed in a way she liked. His clothes were undoubtedly good quality. He wasn't one of those smooth modern guys, there was something old fashioned about him, and she could relate to that.

But he also seemed vulnerable in a weird way; kind of unstreetwise and a little foolish. Yes, he was big in a purely physical sense, but there was something about his … his unguarded honesty that was unusual. He had no lines, no bullshit, and this made her feel strangely protective of him. Sure, he was a little cagey about his girlfriend, but that was normal. There had been a row and he obviously wasn't in love with her…no, definitely not.

She lay for a while longer in the quiet room considering the events of the evening, until, with a loud sigh, she reached over and pressed a button on her mobile. The screen glowed 3.05am. With her hand resting on Percy's warm coat, she adjusted her pillow and soon fell asleep.

Thomas Charrington

Chapter 9

Tarquin's eyes flicked open with unusual alertness and focused on the customary crack of daylight at the top of the curtains. For a few minutes he lay absolutely motionless in the warmth of his bed and played the film of the previous evening through his visual mind with great speed and clarity. He squirmed and flushed with shame at certain scenes, and at the point where Constanta applied the plaster to his chin, his hand whipped up to his face to verify that this wholly unbelievable series of events had actually taken place.

Fully booted up, he hauled himself out of bed and stumbled rather raggedly down the stairs to the kitchen, almost tripping over Percy on the way. A note lay on the kitchen table in very neat writing.

> *Thank you, Tarkin, here is my number …There is a card on your board from Oliver Clasper Antiques?? He lives two doors away at no. 5—Coincidence? Call me please, Constanta x*

He bent down, wincing with pain, and picked up Percy who immediately began sniffing the cuts on his face. He then plucked the card from the board and gazed at it for a few moments.

"Percy, it's been a very strange night, my boy, but it turned out okay, didn't it?" he said with affection. "And I see you even got breakfast!"

Percy looked away with embarrassment and pretended to be interested in the fridge.

Next he went to the top of the house to check the bedroom, more out of curiosity than purpose, and found the bed neat and made. Apart from some water around the basin, the room looked unused.

Having washed and dressed, Tarquin began to carry out the actions he had decided to take. One was to call Diana and apologise for his appalling behaviour, and then to ask her out to dinner the following night. This would be a "special" dinner— the sort of dinner that only men who are madly in love, or those who sense they are in a very precarious position, would consider with any enthusiasm. Secondly he would call Constanta and thank her for her unbridled kindness in helping him. Thirdly he would call the police. Lastly, he would go to Casualty and get his finger dealt with.

As he gulped back the last sweet mouthful of coffee, the telephone rang.

"Tarquin?"

"Er … yes … speaking?" he said hesitantly.

"It's Patience, dearest. I just wanted to see how you were. We haven't spoken for so long and it is so *gorgeous* down here at the moment."

Patience was Tarquin's godmother, who lived in a small village in Wiltshire.

"How lovely to hear you, Patience. Well, I'm fine actually. Doing this and that, as per usual. I … er …went to Covent Garden last night to see a rather raunchy play that's just started. You probably won't have heard about it. *Sir Neville and the …*"

"Oh but I *have* heard. One of my new friends at the life drawing class in Salisbury saw it and said the ending was too rude for words!"

"Well, it is fairly fruity, shall we say, Patience. As you can imagine, Diana's choice!"

"But *do* they, Tarquin?"

"What?"

"At the end …*do* they?"

"Sorry, I'm not quite with you, Patience."

"Tarquin … are you being coy? I want to know … *do* they or don't they?"

"Oh … well … er … it certainly looked like it … but you can never tell, Patience, what with clever lighting and large cushions and … er …" Tarquin stumbled.

"You're not very observant, my dear Tarquin," Patience said with a chuckle.

"Look, sweetie, I am sorry, but I'm going to have to call you back later. I have someone at the door who wants … er … information about understreet cabling."

"Call me, promise."

"I will later, I promise."

Tarquin put the phone down and sighed heavily. Percy sat looking at him expectantly, wagging his tail.

"I know, Percy, I know. Give me twenty minutes."

Next he dialed Diana, feeling distinctly nervous. She didn't answer, and he was subjected to her rather brusque message, which didn't sound like her at all. He hung up; this was no situation for a voice mail.

He hesitated for a moment then called Constanta.

"Hello, it's Tarquin," he said sheepishly.

"So you didn't die in the night, Mr Tarquin!" she answered, in a mocking hurried voice surrounded by the sounds of clinking china.

"Did you sleep okay?"

"No. I couldn't sleep very well … drink, strange bed, but that's not your fault. Percy looked after me," she said with a little giggle.

"Oh, I'm sorry. I just wanted to say—"

"Tarquin, sorry, I can't speak now … very busy. Call me around four o'clock, please. Bye."

She put the phone down and he was left considering whether to call the police now or wait until he'd spoken with Constanta. He decided to wait.

Thomas Charrington

Chapter 10

Zoltan's father, Viktor, looking grey and unhealthy, gripped the greasy receiver of his bakelite telephone so tightly that his knuckles were white. His ample frame was slumped back in the huge scuffed leather chair in his office in St Petersburg, giving an appearance of relaxation—but Viktor was far from relaxed. His thick fingers agitated with the frayed phone cord, which intermittently flicked ash from an overloaded ashtray.

"So he's been given the treatment, uh?" he said, in a deep, intolerant voice down the telephone wire.

"Yes, Father, last night in Piccadilly. He was enjoying an outing at the theatre with one of his girlfriends!" Zoltan said with a sense of accomplishment.

"Was he now! Our man is enjoying the good things in life and thinking he can ignore us, like we don't exist!" Viktor said with a snort.

"Well, he won't be thinking this now; he'll be in shock, wondering how we found him in London!" Zoltan replied. "In fact, the boys tell me he's in town all the time at the moment. They've been monitoring his activities."

"Let's hope so, Zoltan. Oliver seems to be sleepwalking these days. He got the letter?"

"Yes, they put it in his jacket pocket and told him to get in contact or things will turn nasty."

"And they will turn nasty, Zoltan, very nasty!" his father said, his voice lowering to a growl. "Oliver got started on our capital, our ideas. Then he got rich and decided to ditch us. Bad move.

Without us, he'd be in a small shop dealing in low-grade tatt! He used to be a man who knew when to look after his skin," he continued, "when to be smart and avoid trouble. He knows what I'm capable of. He must have got very confident and very stupid with it!"

"Well, they put him on the floor and gave him a good kicking. Left him in the street. You know they don't mess around; they enjoy it too much."

"Sure," Viktor said flatly.

"I think we can be certain of getting a call in a day or two, perhaps a week, when he's come to his senses."

"Look, Zoltan," Viktor said, suddenly flaring up. "Forget the days, the bloody weeks! We want the son of a bitch to respond *now* and make us an offer, or he's going to spend long time in hospital. Stop being so bloody soft, boy, and get your hands around the man's throat. I *will not* be treated like idiot! You're going to lose a fortune with that bitch of a wife of yours running rings around you, so you need this money and you need it soon. For the love of Lenin, Zoltan, toughen up and stop relying on the company to sort your problems out."

"But I am not expecting …"

"Cut the crap, Zoltan, and remember who you are and where you come from. Our family is strong, and it will remain strong, but only as long as we act brutally against people like Oliver—people who think they can muscle in on our affairs, our ideas … and make themselves rich on our backs. Do you understand?"

"Yes, Father."

"I told you that woman would screw you over. I saw it in her crafty little eyes, but you didn't listen. Now stop expecting me to keep helping you out. I've had enough, okay! Do something dynamic, Zoltan … *impress* me, for God's sake!"

Zoltan heard the phone being slammed down and looked at his mobile dejectedly. When in Russia, his father was always in a bad mood; it never changed.

Chapter 11

At ten past four, Tarquin called Constanta.

"Hello Constanta?" he said hesitantly.

"Hi," a sleepy cracked voice said, very different to the sharp delivery he'd grown used to.

"Oh … I'm sorry. Have I woken you up? I'll call again—"

"Shut up, Tarquin! Stop being so polite. I said call at four and I meant it. It's just last night made me tired and I been sleeping for the last hour. Some of us have to work, you know." She laughed sleepily. "So what's been happening in your crazy life, Mr Tarquin? More fighting in the street, uh? A bit of midafternoon fisticuffs before theatre?"

"Look, that's unfair. I am not a common yob," Tarquin snorted. "Last night was an exception, which has me even more puzzled than I was earlier."

"Well, that's no surprise. It doesn't take much to puzzle you, Tarquin …or should I say Oliver!!"

"Now come on, this is plain silly. I need to talk with you properly. I'm about to call the police, but I thought I'd wait until I'd spoken to you first."

"The police? You really are crazy, aren't you? Rule one, leave the police out of it and take control of the situation yourself. You need to find out who is this Oliver and find out why you were mistaken for him. You may look like him. You may have taken his seat in the theatre after he cancelled."

"But I wasn't attacked in the theatre!" Tarquin replied, his voice rising.

"Tarquin, do you really think they would take you in the theatre with loads of people around … they probably followed you."

"Well, now you say it, the fellow my girlfriend went off with did say something about being followed."

"You see, I am not so stupid, am I? Check at the theatre if your seats were someone else's who cancelled, and you may even get a name."

"This is mad. I feel I'm in a gangster movie."

"Perhaps this Oliver stole the cabinet and in some way left your details—you know, identity fraud—to try and put you in the way."

"But I wasn't at my house, my address, I was attacked in the west end, which has nothing whatsoever to do with my address," Tarquin said loudly.

"Calm down, Tarquin. I was just giving you some suggestions, that's all; perhaps they followed you from your house in the first place."

"What? To the west end for more privacy! Come on, this is just silly. Next you'll—"

"Psssssssst," she said, stifling his flow. "Who is Oliver Clasping? You have his card on your board."

"Oliver Clasping?"

"Yes, his card is on your wall board with the taxi numbers."

"Oh, yes him. I know who you mean. Clasper, actually. He's a fellow I met on the street who's just moved in to number five, and our dogs had a bit of a ding dong. He's an antique dealer but lives mostly in Gloucestershire. He's got a shop in Parkgate Street, I think, near the river. Look, I don't know the fellow; just met him once and he gave me his card. You're right though, he is called Oliver." Tarquin chortled.

"Gloucestershire?"

"Yuh, a county in the west … Bristol direction."

"And he is involved with furniture and possibly cabinets," Constanta said teasingly.

"Oh come on, Constanta, you sound like Miss Marple!"

"Who?"

"Never mind; just a silly English joke."

"Tarquin, please don't call the police yet. I want to discuss something with you, so why don't you take me out tomorrow night and we can talk it through?"

There was a pause.

"Erm … well … it's certainly a possibility that we could meet and … and have a little talk." he stammered.

"Good. Then I'll see you at Marble Arch tube station at seven o'clock. Bye bye, I must sleep."

"Err … good-bye, Constanta," Tarquin said, putting the phone down like a man in a trance.

He sat staring out onto the street for a few moments, when there was a vibrating sound from his mobile. Picking it up, he saw that Diana had called and left a message.

He felt a tension in his stomach as he listened.

"Tarquin," her voice said hesitantly, "I hope you got back all right. I'm sorry, but I'd had enough. I really had; was at my wits' end, and … well, the taxi was there." She hesitated. Tarquin heard her swallow. "Look, this isn't easy at all; in fact, it's hellish, but …well … Christopher's asked me to join him in Sri Lanka. They're flying out on Thursday for a three-week break on the south coast, a property he wants to look at. I'm going to go, Tarquin. I'm sorry, I've just sort of had enough. I need some time out, I really do. I can't get through, Tarquin. I just cannot get through to you. I'm sorry, but I've tried; I really have. We'll talk properly later. Be grown up about it. I'm not in the mood right now. I'm fragile. Please don't call at the moment. I know it's horrible …"

Tarquin closed the phone. He felt sick, scared, and shocked. Percy jumped up next to him and stared at him expectantly. He sat, blindly watching the street for a further five minutes, not moving a muscle, oblivious to his surroundings.

He reflected on his life and his failings. He hadn't achieved very much, it was true. He was prone to start things and never really finish them. He had never really had a proper job; he'd inherited enough money to make him lazy, or perhaps unfocused. Yes, Diana was right; he probably wasn't worth staying with. He had never really tried hard enough, never made a concrete commitment; and then there was that other realization. He simply wasn't, and never really had been, in love with her.

Suddenly he got up and grabbed the lead. "C'mon, Percy, let's go for a walk."

Chapter 12

Oliver sat in the "Friends Room" of the Royal Academy with a black coffee and a copy of the *Times*. He had arranged to meet Fabien here so they could talk through the forthcoming trip to France with the cabinet, but he had forgotten how quiet this place could be. People sat in furtive silence on deep leather sofas, hidden behind their newspapers. Any communication was conducted in muffled tones, as though conversation was a dirty habit.

He quickly realized that this was no place to discuss the forgery of the decade. He'd buy Fabien a takeaway cappuccino at Pret a Manger and they'd have a "street" discussion … possibly find an appropriate bench somewhere. They'd already agreed never to discuss such matters over a landline or email, with all necessary communication being conducted on a "non-personal" mobile. Twenty minutes later, the two men were strolling along Piccadilly.

"She's a different person now," Fabien replied to Oliver's questions about Cecile. "Thanks to your help! She just keeps saying that these unexpected windfalls from the old fellow in Morocco are incredible … unbelievable … and that it means we were meant to be! I feel terrible. I must create this great story to back it up. I can't just be vague and change the subject—it's too obvious. I feel like the fraud; forget the cabinet!"

"You won't ever tell her though, will you, Fabien?" Oliver said, searching the young man's face. "It's important I'm out of the picture. And if it makes you feel any better, these advances are for my benefit as well. I needed you in that house. The whole project rests on that."

"Sure … I realize this—non, this is our secret, believe me. But Oliver, I am so incredibly grateful to you, it's made all the difference. The Moroccan millionaire is perfect! It even has a certain mystery, and when you think about it, there are plenty of old lonely people sitting on fortunes, who don't have relatives. I don't need to go into details with my family; they took it at face value. They know I spent a year out, travelling around North Africa, so why shouldn't I have struck up a friendship with a fellow traveller with a passion for antiques?"

"Quite right Fabien, why the hell not!"

"They just warn me about the tax side of things and to be careful."

"Well, quite right too! Now to get to the main point of our little meeting," Oliver said, as Fabien prised the lid off his cappuccino and took a frothy gulp. "I want to meet in Troyes, so there's no chance of us being connected. This is important to you too. I'll be using a friend's trusty van on this occasion. It's quite roomy for longish trips, and we need the space. Remember it will need to take the three of us from the Troyes train station to the chateau."

"Of course," Fabien agreed.

"The outer chest, which will conceal the cabinet at the chateau, will be in pieces in the van and will simply look like a pile of rather scruffy planks. Your average customs man won't concern himself about that. The assembling of this 'chest' will be done at the house by Melvyn, who has a meticulous knowledge of how it most likely would have been made. Of course, it's already been assembled, and now it's dismantled again."

"Sounds good to me."

"I will make arrangements to visit a French dealer whilst over there, to give our trip an independent reason. I'm planning to leave on an overnight ferry from Portsmouth to St Malo, drop in on this fellow in the morning, and then we'll make our way to Troyes. We then pick you up and head on to the chateau. You'll be taking the train, of course. The most dangerous part of this operation, or should I say one of the most dangerous, is getting the cabinet across the channel."

"Exactly, Oliver! You have to be really careful," Fabien said anxiously.

"Well … yes," Oliver resumed, "but customs are not really focused on furniture in the same way as drugs, firearms, etcetera, and it's French customs we're really concerned with here. If we were coming into the UK, it would be a whole different ball game. Of course, I'll have a couple of tricks up my sleeve, but the risk is there if they do a really thorough search."

"What sort of tricks?" Fabien probed.

"Well … the cabinet will be traveling in a softwood and plywood crate for the bulk of the journey, wedged against the bulkhead of the van. You know, the metal division between the front and back."

"Okay."

"However, Melvyn has arranged it so that anyone opening the sliding door only has to push the plywood to one side, and the underlying cabinet will be open for anyone to inspect. The reason for this is that we don't want a large disguised object in the van if someone *does* want to take a look. We need to reveal the object inside, as well as imply that it doesn't need much packaging or protection."

"But I don't understand," Fabien said frowning. "The cabinet in full view?"

"Yes, because customs won't be looking at the real cabinet, they'll be looking at a scruffy, cheap-looking pine shell which Melvyn made months ago, and which fits snugly over our piece. And this battered shell will match other pine artefacts in the van, giving the appearance of a job lot."

"Oh, je comprends," Fabien said, shaking his shoulders in an affected shiver. "This scares me!"

"Don't worry, Fabien. Have faith!" Oliver said, smiling. "Now another thing, of course, is that once the cabinet is revealed in France, it will quickly become a Monument

Historique and will be restricted for export. Let's face it, it's a highly prized piece of French royal furniture … one that has incredible provenance."

"Well, I know this, I've been doing some investigation on these things."

"Good, and therefore you realize the downside is that it'll have a reduced value compared to the same cabinet being auctioned in, say, New York."

"But of course."

"Fine. We understand each other. But Fabien, rest assured, it will still be worth a fortune!"

"I know," the young man said quietly, casting a furtive glance over his shoulder.

"Okay … now let's talk about travel details." Oliver continued, "What was it to Troyes from Paris by train … about an hour and a half, I seem to remember?"

"About this."

"So if we collect you at, say, six pm, we can be at Clery at around seven. On Saturday morning we all go up to the garret and decide where to place the cabinet. Exciting, eh? Which reminds me … is everything arranged for Bernard and his wife to move in?"

"Oh yes. He's packed up what he needs … made arrangements. He's delighted, actually. Work is thin on the ground. As I said, the chateau has a strong connection with his family, especially his grandfather who used to garden there full time. Even Bernard himself worked one summer there, as a very young man. They could do with the money, I think, and that cottage of theirs in Geraudot is tiny. His dogs will love it as well … all that space! If he's good we'll keep him on and possibly do up one of the out buildings for them to live in more permanently." Fabien said with a growing sense of pride.

"Great … everything seems to be falling into place. So while the cabinet incubates for a year, it'll be guarded in our absence by a trustworthy local."

"But … they won't realize they're guarding it, surely?" Fabien said, raising his brows.

"Of course not!" Oliver chortled. "Only you, me, and Melvyn know of its whereabouts in the chateau—this is crucial."

"Sure … it is what I thought."

"Good. We can't afford to make some blunder. This chest has been here for two hundred and thirteen years, don't forget! We need to block access to the top floor once it's been planted, though. You were going to call the carpenters, remember."

"I already did … don't worry. But remember it's going to be very heavy, Oliver!" Fabien said with concern. "There are a lot of stairs to climb."

"I know … it won't be easy. Melvyn has to assemble the chest first. He'll then need some help to put the cabinet into it … on the top floor, I hasten to add. Before all that, though, he'll be doing what he does best—giving it the illusion of age … little puffs of dust here and there and all the other clever little ploys he has, which frankly are beyond me. He thinks these things through, you know; imagines the carpenter making the crate and almost becomes him … like an actor really. He lives the moment."

"You make him sound like a wizard!" Fabien said in awe.

"Well, he is really," Oliver resumed. "He'll have thought about the cabinet in its protective shell. Would insects have got in … would moisture have stained the box in any way …. how would the floor of the crate look where the feet rested on it for all those years. He goes through it all like a forensics man. And he knows! He's seen so much old furniture, he knows how it behaves over time."

Fabien took a gulp of coffee.

"I can feel the nerves in my stomach already … this is like a strange dream!" he said, his eyes flickering over the passing traffic.

"And then there's your part in the whole thing. Your discovery of the box. You have to become an actor as well, Fabien! We need to think through the exact circumstances which bring our baby into the big wide world, approximately a year from now."

"Jesus Christ, this is so crazy!" Fabien said in a forced whisper.

"Are you and Cecile going to discover it together as you are clearing the garret one day?"

"Non, I like your idea of the roofer being with us," Fabien said forcefully. "I think it's important that there's someone else."

"True. It will add to the authenticity. As you all stumble around up there at the top of the house, you suddenly spot this chest. He will then become a witness to the 'moment critique,' so it will be important that you play your part well. You'll need to be mildly curious to begin with, and then ratchet up the excitement level as you get him to take a peek inside. We need to pray that Melvyn doesn't leave his boat ticket on top of the cabinet!!" Oliver grinned, giving the young man a light slap on the back.

Fabien looked at his watch.

"Yes, you'd better be going … was getting carried away," Oliver chuckled. "We don't want you losing your job!"

"Okay, Oliver, this is sounding fantastic and scary at the same time. I'm shaking just at the thought of it. I feel like a man who's about to enter the last game to win a tennis tournament … it all rests on me!"

"You'll be fine, Fabien … you have a quiet confidence."

They shook hands, and the young Frenchman disappeared into the bustling crowds.

Chapter 13

Tarquin was late for his rendezvous on Saturday; seven minutes, to be precise. He looked at the milling crowds on the pavement and was just wondering how impossible it would be to meet Constanta at such a location, when the car door flew open and she was suddenly beside him.

"You are late, Tarquin," she said sternly. "I like punctuality."

"I'm sorry," he said sheepishly, pulling out into the maelstrom around Marble Arch. "Would you like to eat something now or have a drink or—"

"I'm famished," she interrupted. "Let's go to McDonald's up the street here, I fancy a Big Mac."

"A what?" Tarquin said.

"A Big Mac burger, Tarquin! Is this difficult to understand? Do you not eat burgers?"

"Well … I … er … have had hamburgers from time to time, but certainly not at McDonald's; wouldn't occur to me frankly."

"Oh I'm *so* sorry," she said theatrically. "We can go to one of your *expensive* restaurants if you prefer, but if I have to wait, I will get very bad tempered."

"No, look, we'll go to the hamburger place, just tell me where to go," he said firmly.

"Tarquin, why the suitcase?" she said, looking into the backseat. "Are you leaving the country?"

"Oh … no, I'm going down to Wiltshire tonight to stay with a friend for a few days."

"A friend, uh?" she said, angling for an answer.

"My godmother, if you really must know. She's getting on, and—"

"Getting on? On where? What are you talking about, Tarquin?"

"Oh, of course … 'getting on' means getting older. Just another silly English way of speaking," he smiled.

Constanta pushed some air through her pursed lips.

"Anyway, she enjoys my company and needs little jobs doing around the garden. Besides, I need to get out of London for a few days; Thursday night shook me up a bit, to be frank."

"You'll be fine, darling … just play it cool, and mind that finger. Don't get the binding covered in mud," she said, gazing at the shop windows. Constanta wasn't good at sympathy; it was an emotion that had been starved of oxygen throughout her life.

Three quarters of an hour later they were parked in the centre of Hyde Park and walking towards the Serpentine like a pair of promenaders from the nineteenth century. Whilst they'd been eating, Tarquin had had to endure a lengthy blow by blow account of Constanta's day at the kitchen and a seeming rivalry she was having with another member of the staff. He had raised his eyebrows and nodded attentively as she described her frustrations with this person, but had found it nigh on impossible to follow the convoluted repartee between them.

"Now we need to make a plan, Tarquin," Constanta said, at last managing to disengage herself from the gossip of the day. "I think you need some help. You seem to have some crazy ideas about calling the police when this isn't going to help you at all; it's just going to waste a whole lot of time."

"Well, I'm not sure about that, Constanta," Tarquin said solemnly. "I would naturally call the police. It's what they're there for, and they have the authority to make enquiries where I have not."

"Sure they have, and where do you think they will start with their enquiries?"

"Well … I don't know how important they would consider this," Tarquin said defensively.

"The first thing they'll do, Tarquin, is make you fill out forms—lots of forms—and then, if they can be bothered, they'll want to look into your affairs and see if you have been up to something that would cause this to happen. You see? It's you they'll be looking at—at least to start with—and you have to decide if this is what you want."

"But I've done nothing wrong!" he said in exasperation.

"You know that, but they don't! To them it looks like you might have been doing things you should not have. Don't forget you had nothing stolen. This is your problem. And the letter to Oliver, this will only make them more suspicious."

She looked at Tarquin for a reaction, but he just stared at the path in front of him, his brow heavily wrinkled.

"Oh hell!" he said loudly. "Why me? Why bloody me?"

Constanta moved closer to him and threaded her arm through his.

"I have a friend," she said quietly, "someone who might be able to help. He's not good like you, Tarquin. He's done some things in the past; not really bad like hurting people, but stealing, yes. He had a tough upbringing back in Iassi, my hometown; it was difficult … I would never judge him."

"And?" Tarquin said resignedly.

"He would help you. He can watch people … he's good with computers and getting into houses. Yes, he can do this very well."

"What, burgle people?" Tarquin said, beginning to feel this was going in the wrong direction. "Why on earth would I need him to do that?"

"Burgle? What is this?"

"To steal stuff; take things from their house."

"No! Not burgle! Just take a look inside. Stealing was before. He now sells bagels on the south bank for a friend of his … he's clean now. He's proud to be out of that bad scene!"

"So he's a burglar who sells bagels!" Tarquin said with a sarcastic snort.

"This is serious, Tarquin, I feel you have been set up."

"Listen, sweetie," Tarquin said, suddenly stopping and looking straight at her. "I think this whole thing is getting blown out of all proportion. It's just some funny mistake; some oddity with no rhyme or reason, which doesn't mean anything. I don't think anyone's after me, or has mistaken me for anybody else. I don't belong in that world. I think those guys just didn't like the look of me, it's as simple as that. They just wanted to give someone a good bruising, that's all."

It was Constanta's turn to look defensive.

"Wow! Moments ago you were all worried!" she said with surprise.

"I know I was," he said smiling, "but I've just suddenly realized how ridiculous this whole thing is. We're creating drama out of nothing!"

"I think you're wrong," she said quietly. "Why the letter about a cabinet? That makes no sense at all."

"Okay, then, perhaps they did think I was someone else last night … and … and now they'll have realized their mistake, won't they!" he said with a show of confidence.

"Will they? What makes you so sure?" she said, searching his face.

"As I said, sweetie, that isn't my world. I don't belong amongst street thugs and hobos. Their disputes are between members of their own tribe, not with people like me. Admittedly, Oliver is an unusual name for a yob; next there'll be hobos called Horatio!" He snorted with amusement.

"Okay, have it your way," she said with a concerned expression, "but I think you're wrong."

"Look, let's forget that whole business for the moment and have a drink at the restaurant there," he said, studying her. "You can tell me all about life in Romania after Ceausescu. I really enjoy your company and … and … well, I'm not feeling great about myself at the moment. My girlfriend called yesterday and basically said she wanted to finish with me. You know, wants space and all that caper. I probably deserved it. She just wants a break, wants to be spoilt. So you being here is a real bonus; you have a positive energy which is very attractive."

Constanta hesitated for a few seconds.

"Oh, I'm sorry," she said slowly, "shit happens. But you seem happy enough?"

Tarquin looked at her tenderly for a moment. "It's just a show," he said quietly.

With that they moved on, walking closely and chatting incessantly.

*   *   *

Zoltan looked out on Beauchamp Place through the dusty window of Sasha's flat. He liked this street—the smart boutiques, the stylish girls, and the proximity to Knightsbridge, one of London's prime shopping areas. But Oliver still hadn't called, and this irritated him intensely. The complete lack of respect gnawed at his insides and made him feel murderous. How dare the insect treat him in this way. Even his own father was losing respect for him. He wouldn't demean himself with another call; no, he would simply set the boys on him after one further warning. This would be the last warning, and if ignored, would mean more than a scuffle on the pavement, Next time, Oliver would be spending a month or two in hospital.

Sasha quietly pushed the stool away from her PC and came up behind him. She put one arm softly around his shoulder and slid her other hand down his arm, spreading her fingers through his and squeezing tightly. He inclined his head towards her face as she placed some feathery kisses down the side of his neck, seducing him with soft nasal sighs. He turned, and pulling her towards him, took a deep draught of her scented skin.

She leaned over and flicked a cord, allowing the slatted blind to fall. The room became twilight. Pressing her pelvis against him, she kissed him strongly on the mouth, undulating gently and coaxing a spark to ignite in his groin. He stared unsmiling into her eyes for a few moments, then, lifting her short skirt, he hooked his thumbs into her knickers and slowly squatted, pulling the little band of cotton to her ankles and out from under her feet.

Her hands played through his blond locks as he slowly rose, drawing his fingertips languidly up the backs of her legs and into a series of sensual loops over the firm, cool curves of her buttocks. He kissed her again … across her parted lips, her cheek, and into the scented cleft below her seashell ear.

She pulled him closer, breathing heavily, as his hand moved onto the silky skin of her inner thighs, where it lingered tentatively for a few moments, as though teasing. Her heartbeat was quickening and blood gathered in hot ruddy pools in her cheeks. Enveloped in her animal musk, he kissed her again, harder this time, whilst pushing her firmly back onto the desk.

She gazed up defiantly for a few moments as he stopped and surveyed the sheer rudeness of her pose. She was leaning back with her weight on her elbows and her small skirt pushed clumsily up around her tummy. One long leg stretched to the floor, whilst the other knee was bent and angled to the side provocatively, revealing her gently split fruit.

"Would the Sultan like a sweet ripe fig?" she said, tilting her head slightly and mustering an innocent expression. Zoltan smiled whilst staring hard into her eyes. He flexed his jaw muscle.

"Yes … yes, the Sultan has a taste for something pink and fleshy … right now."

With that he unbuckled himself, stepped forwards and curled his hands around her buttocks. Then, pulling her pelvis towards him roughly, he pressed himself slowly but forcefully into the damp tangled curls between her legs. She tilted her head back, gasping softly, her fabulous silver eyes reflecting in miniature the brilliance of the slatted sunlight through the blind.

Chapter 14

"Okay, it's Monday now and you delivered it on Saturday, is this correct?" Zoltan said to the man at the other end.

"That's right, Z. Popped it straight through his door at nine thirty Saturday night. Wasn't no one there, though. House was dark and his motor was gone," Gus said respectfully.

"Okay. Okay. Sweep by the house every now and then, and tell me if he comes in. Could be he's back in Gloucestershire, in which case you know where to go."

"Completely right, Z, we know exactly where to find him. But you give him five days, didn't yer—that's till Thursday night, in it?"

"I did. So if we hear nothing by 6pm Thursday, we're going to act," Zoltan said with quiet fury.

"Quite bloody right, Z. I don't blame yer! He needs his arse walloping right good and proper—the man's taking the piss," Gus said passionately. "It's unbelievable, we floor him in Piccadilly and give him a good going over, and yet the guy's back on his feet as though it's business as normal, a few days later. But Z, there's kicking arse and there's kicking arse! This time we'll give him the grown-up treatment! We'll kick him to hell and back and rearrange his features a bit. I'm thinking a Marlon Brando nose would suit him nice, along with a Vincent van Goth ear, if yer know what I mean."

"Yesss, we will kick his bottom and carry on kicking it until he wakes up from his cosy little sleep," Zoltan said, forming a satisfying image in his mind. "I want Oliver to plead with me …

to beg me, to admit that he's been extremely stupid and disrespectful, behaved in very bad ways towards me and my family, and that he stole my idea. I want him to squeal like pig, okay, Gus?"

"Exactly right, Z," Gus said with approval.

"Okay, I want you in state of vigilance as of Wednesday. I want to know his every move. Do what you're good at, my friend, and keep me in the loop."

"Sure thing, Z. Nice to speak to yer. We're on the case," Gus said, closing off.

*　　　*　　　*

Tarquin fumbled for his keys outside his house, whilst gripping a box of various handpicked vegetables under his arm. After a week with Patience in Wiltshire, he felt a new man. The plaster was off his chin, and once again he'd had some amusing exchanges over cocktails in the social stream which gurgled and eddied around her little cottage. Patience loved having Tarquin to stay. She had never married, and he was useful; plus it was an excuse to have her friends over, using him as suitable bait.

Diana had a strong dislike of Patience, who had made it perfectly plain that she felt they were a bad match and, therefore, it would be preferable for Tarquin to come and stay alone. The icebox and spirits were all in a state of constant readiness, and of course there was that "list" that always seemed to appear when he stayed. To clean the gutters, to trim the untamable hedge, to build the bonfire. Yes, Tarquin had his uses, and he enjoyed his tasks with a passion; they made him feel manly.

Stooping to pick up a substantial pile of post, he spotted an envelope which changed his mood in the crack of a whip. It had a horribly familiar look. Again that ominous name "Oliver."

Suddenly scared all over again, he dropped the vegetables and felt a cold shiver sweep through his body. Panicking, he fumbled for the paper knife in the silver tray, whilst looking furtively out onto the street. He hesitated, then inserted the knife under the flap and sliced it open. Shaking violently and feeling a sense of intense pressure, he pulled the contents out …

> *Oliver,*
> *I am very disappointed.*
> *You are not the sensible man you used to be. You have become complacent and thinking nothing can do you harm. Well, what you experienced ten days ago is nothing to what is going to happen to you very very soon.*
> *I will not be treated like fool, Oliver. Please understand most clearly that you will be badly hurt if you do not contact us within five days.*
> *Be assured we know where you are, in London or in Glostershire. You cannot hide, we are watching you.*
> *CALL ME!*
> *Z.*

Tarquin gazed at the letter, blood pumping through his temples. He felt sick. He really was being hunted, and the hunter knew where he was.

Was there something in his past which was coming back to haunt him? Had he snubbed someone without realizing it? Had he said or done something terribly serious and simply not recognized the gravity of what he'd done? No! Why would this person refer to him as Oliver? It had to be a mistaken identity. He felt his brain was going to explode. This wasn't a "random" attack in the west end; this was home. They knew where he lived; Constanta was right!

He went through it for the seventh time, and then leapt to his feet. "Gloucestershire!"

That was where his neighbour lived, Oliver Clasper! But … but … that didn't mean anything, did it? He wrestled with his reasoning. It *could* be that guy, but there again he could be completely innocent. Just because he lived in Gloucestershire wasn't proof of his guilt; that would be a ludicrous deduction. Tarquin felt so scared he just wanted to tell someone. He strode out of his door and knocked at number five. He waited and knocked again. He wasn't even quite sure what to say when Clasper opened the door.

'I'm … er … sorry to trouble you, Oliver, but you wouldn't … er … be in a spot of bother, old fellow, with anybody, would you? It's just I've got this strange letter.'

No! That sounded crazy, and Clasper would rightly consider him to be a bit odd, or worse, rather suspect. He quickly retreated, but it was obvious the house was empty anyway. He made himself a cup of coffee and tried to think rationally. Should he call Constanta or the police? He decided to call her first, and say that it was time to involve the police.

"Tarquin, you should know by now this is a bad time to call," she said assertively. "Always text me in the mornings … there is no …"

"I had to call, I've had another letter for Oliver delivered through my door," Tarquin interrupted desperately. "This is really serious now. I must call the police!"

"*No!* Tarquin, *do not* call the police; believe me, it won't help you, darling. Call me at four. I have a plan," she said decisively.

"Look, I just …" he hesitated. "Okay, at four."

He gulped back the remaining half cup of coffee without even noticing it.

Percy looked up at him expectantly; the two-hour car journey up from Wiltshire had primed him for a walk.

"Okay, Percy, let's go," Tarquin said as he grabbed the lead. After locking the door, he glanced nervously up and down the street. He felt vulnerable; his sense of security was ebbing away. In the park, he decided to call a lawyer friend and run it past him. He'd been reluctant to reveal the strange happenings in his life to his friends, for fear of ridicule. But the pressure was mounting, and he felt the need for some solid English advice.

"Toby?" he said hesitantly.

"Speaking," came the clipped reply.

"It's Tarquin here."

"Who?"

"Tarquin," he said, amping up. There was a long pause.

"Well I'm damned, nice to hear you, Tarquin!" Toby said, sounding both surprised and pleased.

"Hope all's well with you, and Susan," Tarquin said awkwardly.

"Yes, she is actually, fine old boy! Must be a good six months since we saw you. Everything okay in your world? Diana keeping you on the straight and narrow, eh?"

"Well, no, er … she's actually … uh … well … you know, gone on a little hol to Sri Lanka and seems to be having a fantastic time," Tarquin blurted.

"Good stuff. So you've got a pink ticket, you lucky bugger. Wish my other half would have the decency to go on a little holiday. Truth is, she won't let me out of her sight! Says I have a gilded tongue that can't be trusted! But you lead a charmed life, old chap. Life for you appears to be a stroll in the park. Nothing seems to ruffle you, Tarquin. You should come and watch me in court one day, and then you'll see the tarnished side of the coin."

Tarquin laughed thinly.

"Well, I think I already have, to be frank, Toby. Life has thrown an odd one at me of late, and I need your opinion on something. I think I've been caught up in a sort of mistaken identity fiasco, and … well, it's turned a bit nasty. I was decked in Soho by a pair of thugs a couple of weeks back, broke my finger, bruised ribs, but thought nothing more of it."

"Mugged?"

"Well … that's what I thought at the time, but it seems to be a bit more sinister than that. I had nothing stolen and … well …these people are now pressuring me at home."

"For what?"

"I don't know, but they address me as Oliver and keep telling me to make contact with a mysterious person called Z. And as you can imagine, I don't have a clue what they're talking about!"

"Sounds unpleasant," Toby mumbled, and then paused. "I'm sorry, old fellow … but are you absolutely sure there isn't something … erm … well, something you are involved with which might have caused this to happen?"

"Completely and utterly, Toby. I'm not one for dabbling in dickie business," Tarquin said, beginning to sound faintly hysterical.

"Police involved?"

"Not yet."

"Bring them in, they'll sort you out. Horrible for you; I sympathise. Sounds odd to say the least. Look, I'm sorry, Tarquin, but I must dash. Got to be in court at two, and I need to get back to chambers. Let me know what happens, and meanwhile I'll speak to Sue and we'll get a date in the diary for dinner … when Diana's back. Good to hear you, old fellow. Chin up!"

He closed off, and Tarquin was left watching Percy humping another dog, and wondering if he was any closer to a course of action.

* * *

He was waiting this time as Constanta came out of the tube at Marble Arch. She jumped into the car and demanded to eat immediately. Tarquin didn't need to ask. As they drove, he handed her the letter which she read intently three times before folding it and laying it on the dashboard.

"Well, it seems they have known each other for a long time," she said, gazing out on Oxford Street.

"Really?"

"Tarquin, did you read it properly? He says … this Z guy … you are not 'careful' man you *used* to be."

"Oh, yuh … it … it does imply that, I agree," Tarquin muttered. "I was just so shocked to get the damn letter, I wasn't looking at the details."

Constanta clicked her tongue and studied the passing windows of Jigsaw.

Sitting opposite each other at McDonald's twenty minutes later, she chomped into her hamburger with a very unladylike gusto. He smiled, which she immediately picked up on.

"What's your problem?" she said, with ketchup smeared on her chin.

"There's no problem. Just thought how pretty you look, even when you eat like an animal."

"Oh, I'm *so* flattered," she said, giving her face a thorough wipe with a tissue. "Now Tarquin, this is getting very serious. It seems I know what's going on more than you, don't you agree?"

"Well, it does seem you have a keener grasp of the situation than me, Constanta. My mind just refuses to acknowledge that this could be happening to me! I just don't have things like this going on in my life, and it's difficult to take it on board. I keep thinking it's just a mistake. Perhaps you're just more used to this sort of ... er ..."

"Of what?"

"Well, perhaps you've seen the rougher side of life, and you look at things more clearly. You don't suffer from reality blockages."

"Exactly, Tarquin! You've lived a pampered life, and even when things jump out at you, you refuse to see them. Well, I'm telling you to be very careful. This is not the time to have one of these blockages, because you will end up getting badly hurt. This people mean business, and at the moment you are the target. Yes, I have had it tougher than you, darling. Can you imagine what it's like to be brought up in a house with no toilet? Where you have to crap against the side of the house at night, 'cos you don't want to freeze to death going to the hut, and you know by the morning it'll be like a lump of stone, so you can throw it in the bushes? Where you clean your arse with a corn cob 'cos there's no paper ..."

"I don't understand," Tarquin said, looking completely puzzled. "A corn on the cob to—"

"No ... not a corn on the cob! Are you crazy? I said a corn cob—the thing that's left when you've eaten the corn, stupid. Yes, it has its uses; it's quite soft."

"Good God," Tarquin muttered incredulously.

"You see, you're shocked, aren't you! Doesn't fit in with your world view, does it? Well, what I've just described is not unusual back home. We were often four of us crammed into a freezing bed, in a room with black mould all over the walls. The winters in Romania are really bad, and the summers are the other way. The fields are like ovens. It can be forty-two degrees sometimes, and in the winter it can get to twenty below. And my grandmother would be out in those fields in that heat, bent double using her bare hands to gather the crop day after day. She didn't have sun cream … we couldn't even afford toilet paper, darling! That's why she looks ninety when she's only sixty-five!"

She looked at Tarquin for a few moments as though gauging his reaction. He looked back at her speechless.

"Now, I have a plan," she continued. "I've called Petru, my friend I mentioned a few days ago …"

"What, the fellow who can … er … get into people's houses?" Tarquin said quietly.

"Yes, the boy you wanted to take the piss out of."

"I certainly did not," Tarquin said defensively. "I was just being a little humorous, that's all …"

"Well, don't laugh too hard, time is running out, darling. Petru is going to help you, though."

"How?"

"I've told him to get into Oliver Clasping's house and have a little look around."

"What? Snoop about my neighbour's house? What if he's there, for God's sake. He comes and goes without any pattern … and the house is probably alarmed as well."

"Do you think Petru's stupid? He'll check all this out."

"And what's to say there's anything to find? The guy's more than likely completely innocent. Just because he lives in my street and happens to be involved with antiques."

"And lives in Gloucestershire, and is two doors away from you, and also—which is something Petru picked up on—is at number five and you are number nine."

"And? What's that supposed to mean?" Tarquin said, raising

his eyebrows.

"Think about it. The numbers five and nine sound quite similar. don't they? They are the only two numbers under ten which can be mistaken for each other quite easily."

"This is ridiculous!" Tarquin said, shaking his head. "What on earth would that have to do with anything?"

"A lot, Tarquin. I have a problem with a person who owes me money, so I ring someone up to go and frighten this person. I tell him he lives at number five bla bla street and guess what, he rocks up at number nine because he misheard me on a bad line and scares the shit out of the wrong guy."

"Oh, come on, Constanta, this is—"

"Pssssst. You're doing it again, Tarquin, blocking things that are easily possible. Have you not heard of the charging light brigade in the Crimean War? I think there was a small mistake there which led to a big problem."

"Oh, we are knowledgeable," Tarquin said sarcastically.

"You think I am stupid, don't have any education? Well, I'm sorry to disappoint you, but the education system in Romania is very good," she said fiercely.

"No … look, I'm sorry," Tarquin said quickly. "I … I suppose you saying that, just seemed … Well, a bit out of character."

"The character you've built for me, more like. You don't know me yet, Tarquin!"

"Very true. Sorry … look, I'm a bit uptight. I shouldn't have said that," he said, squeezing her forearm softly.

"Petru is coming at nine thirty tonight with some stuff to … well, get into the house," she continued. "We just need to see that Clasping's not there, and call him with the green light. Okay?"

"Okay," Tarquin said obediently.

Inside he felt he was losing control, involving himself in things which went against all his instincts.

"Don't worry, darling," she said, putting a hand on his shoulder. "It'll be okay. Petru is good."

Thomas Charrington

Chapter 15

"Good evening, Melvyn," Oliver said, stepping into the workshop and adopting a rather formal tone. He felt like the general in a forthcoming campaign who has to reinforce a sense of authority, having become slightly too familiar with his soldiers.

"Hi mate," Melvyn replied softly.

"Well, it's Tuesday and she's ready for the off! Well done, you! I've dreamt of this day, and you know, Melvyn, I feel certain that when you say it's ready, it really is ready. I have a lot of faith in you."

"It's taken its time, but it had to be right," Melvyn mumbled shyly.

"It most certainly did. We don't want this thing going off half cock. Now, have you got a pen and paper handy, as I want to give you the boat times and all the details of our trip?"

Melvyn fumbled in his heavily stained apron for a pencil and picked up a scruffy notepad.

"Okay, I'm ready."

"We're leaving Portsmouth at eight thirty pm on Thursday, which means we will have to leave here no later than three to be safe. I'd like to have the van ready as far as possible by tomorrow night, but we can't load the cabinet until Thursday morning. There's no way we're going to risk it overnight anywhere except here in the workshop. That means we spend Thursday morning packing it up in the van, nice and discreetly, and making sure everything is ultra-secure. Do you need more foam rubber or blankets?"

"Nope, got plenty."

"Okay, so we arrive at St Malo at seven am on Friday after a good night's sleep and a hearty breakfast, I hope. Don't worry, you'll have your own cabin. From there we go and visit Frederic in Laval. Do you remember him? The guy who sold us the Austrian table."

"Oh yes, him."

"Well, he's about two hours away, so we'll have a coffee with him and see if he's got anything of interest. Then it's a straight run to Troyes, arriving somewhere around six, all things being equal. We'll each have to do a bit of driving, I'm afraid, but we'll have a couple of stops as well. By the way, when Frederic asks us what we've got planned with the van, we tell him we're picking up a piece near Paris from a relation and delivering another. I'll handle it; don't worry yourself about that. But we mustn't let him look in the back of the van at any cost! He's an inquisitive fellow, as you know."

"Yeah, best keep him away from the van, I think," Melvyn agreed.

"Good, so going back to our plan, we get to Troyes and then pick up Fabien at the train station around six. Apparently there's a hotel opposite with a nice bar so he'll be in there if we're late. Pretty town, Troyes. You'll like it; very medieval. The house, though, is about half an hour outside, near a village called Lusigny sur Barse; it's called Chateau Clery. You'll love it, surrounded by a wall and plenty of trees, so no prying eyes. It's even got its own orangery. The whole area is magical; it's called La Foret d'Orient. How evocative is that?"

"Sounds very nice," Melvyn said matter-of-factly.

"We're leaving the cabinet downstairs for the night, and in the morning we'll get up into the roof so you can see for yourself how suitable it is for our purposes. I don't think you'll be disappointed. And then, my friend, we have a well-earned drink!"

"Sounds good."

"Fabien's girlfriend is working in Paris, and they normally spend the weekends down there, so the poor bugger has had to concoct some reason for keeping her away! I believe he's told her he's meeting an architect to discuss building something in the garden; you know … a big surprise!"

"He'd better be careful. My Mary knows straight away if I'm telling a porky!" Melvyn said with a chuckle.

"Well, I know, but he had to get her out of the way somehow."

"Sure."

"Anyway," Oliver continued, "there's a huge staircase leading up to the garret with these massive oak timbers forming the framework for the roof. Doesn't look like anyone's been up there for decades, which suits us perfectly. Cobwebs everywhere! Once you've looked at the spot I have in mind and agreed it'll work, you can start assembling the crate. When you want help, Mel, we'll be there."

"Blimey, sounds quite a place. Straight out of a Dracula movie!" Melvyn said with a snort.

"When you've finished doing that part, we'll bring the cabinet up, and then you can work your magic. I've bought some walkie-talkies for our stay over there. It's a hell of a way from the top of the house to the ground floor, so anything you need, just call me up. Prefer you turn your mobile off once we leave Frederic. You know, less traces of us there the better. I'll make sure Mary has a contact number."

"Mmm, sounds like fun," Melvyn said, not sounding in the least bit excited.

"Okay, so there you are, Mel. You've got more of an idea of our plan now; I'll leave you to get yourself organized."

"Okay … speak tomorrow," Melvyn mumbled.

With that, Oliver wandered out and left.

Thomas Charrington

Chapter 16

"Right, he's in," Constanta said, coming into the kitchen as Tarquin pulled a tray of ice out of the freezer.

"In? Already? How in the hell did he do that?" Tarquin said, utterly perplexed.

"It's called experience, darling," Constanta said, smiling cheekily. "To you it probably seems like magic, but when you've had a lot of experience in something, you learn a lot of tricks. Locks have their weaknesses, and if you have the right tools, you can take advantage of that."

"Bloody hell, this makes me very nervous. It's just not me. I mean, the poor guy doesn't deserve this. He's more than likely completely innocent and here he is with a bloke sneaking around in his house because of me!"

"Let's wait before we feel sorry for Clasping; he may not be so innocent. And if he is, no harm done. Petru is careful; I told him to keep his urges under control, if you get my drift!"

"I most certainly do," Tarquin said, giving her a direct look.

"Relax ... relax ... it won't take long. He's taking photos of anything which looks suspicious, and yes, he'll be closing the curtains; flashes going off in a dark room may attract attention."

"Too bloody right it might! I just want him out of there as fast as possible."

"Okay, I'm going back out to keep an eye on things; I don't like sitting in your car in the dark, it looks a bit odd, but I can have the radio on and make some calls. See you in a while."

"Lock the doors from the inside and call me if there's a

problem," Tarquin said, pouring himself a powerful whisky and slumping down on the sofa to watch the news.

Petru moved like a cat through the house. His slight, wiry frame was perfect for sliding through small spaces and his movements were sharp and precise. The alarm system wasn't active, which made the whole operation much easier, and it was just light enough to see around inside, whilst also remaining discreet. It was obvious that Clasper had left in a hurry as there was a half-finished cup of coffee on the kitchen table with some leathery toast and a jam called marmalade. A dribble of water coming from the cold tap irritated him, so he turned it off.

A notepad had fallen on the floor by a kitchen chair, possibly suggesting Clasper had suddenly jumped to his feet. He picked it up and flicked it onto the most recent page. The tight surgical gloves he was wearing made the paper very obedient. There was a series of dates, times, and days written down in a very rough way as though he had been holding the phone and writing, whilst the pad skidded around on the polished surface.

He pulled out his camera and took a close-up of the writing; he then flicked to the page behind. It was much neater here and he could easily make out the words. *Paris, ferries,* and some place called *Portsmouth* and another called *Troyes*. There was some more writing at the bottom, but this was very scribbled and he couldn't make it out. The word at the top of the page, "*Itinerary,*" he didn't recognize. So he photographed this page as well and looked at the one behind. Here, it just had in large writing: *Parking Permit and Cleaner.* He nudged the pad over the edge of the table, where it took up something like its original pose on the floor.

He was just about to leave the kitchen when he noticed a large book underneath a copy of the *Financial Times*. Lifting the paper he looked intently at the cover for a moment or two and then felt a little prick of curiosity. The book was called *Drawn to Trouble* by someone called Eric Hebborn. But what caught his eye was the word "*fake*" in the top right-hand corner with a little question mark after it.

Petru was well accustomed to the word "fake" as it had a warm connection in his mind with his large collection of watches. He took out his camera and took a quick photo of the cover before glancing proudly at his own "Rolex." He had to hurry now; his thirty minutes was almost up.

Springing up the stairs, he went straight to the bedrooms. One had just a bed and mattress, and the other was obviously the man's room. It smelt stale and unused and empty apart from some jackets hanging in one of the wardrobes and a pair of dusty black shoes with wooden stretchers. A large lorry suddenly appeared in the street below throwing a fan of unwelcome light into the room. He crouched for a few moments to let it pass. As he left the room, his eyes fell hungrily on a pair of silver foxes and a silver cigar case on a chest of drawers: He picked up one of the foxes and bounced it in the palm of his hand; it was reliably heavy. He replaced it with a sigh.

Back in the kitchen he stopped and scanned the room very carefully to make sure all was in order. He then let the blinds up and left as he arrived, through the lavatory window.

Petru and Constanta came back into the house together to find Tarquin glassy eyed in front of the TV, and Percy curled up beside him. He growled as they approached.

"All done," Constanta said. "He's taken shots of anything important."

"Did anyone see you?" Tarquin asked the diminutive Romanian anxiously.

"No, it's been quiet out there. The people in house opposite are out and nobody's been taking any interest," he said shyly.

"Thank you, Petru," Tarquin said, looking down at him in an avuncular way. "I really appreciate this. I cannot believe there's anything to find in there, but ... well, Constanta seemed to think it was important."

Constanta leaned toward Petru and said something in Romanian. They both smiled.

"Right. So what have you discovered in Mr Clasper's house, Petru … anything of any interest?" Tarquin said to the young man whilst glancing at Constanta in a slightly mocking way.

"The man left his house in a hurry, I think. There was a half-eaten meal on the table: a cup of coffee not much touched; a tap running; uneaten toast," Petru said hesitantly.

"And?" Tarquin said with a false yawn.

"There was a notepad on the floor by the table with some writing in it, so I took some photos so you could see for yourself," Petru said awkwardly.

"Show him," Constanta said.

Petru shuffled through his backpack and brought out a camera. He flicked it on and they all peered at the screen.

"Okay, so this is the last picture, of a book I found on the kitchen table under a newspaper. It's called *Drawn to Trouble*. You see it had word 'fake' at the top there, and I thought this may be interesting to you."

Tarquin craned forward, frowning.

"Can you get closer, get the image bigger?" he said, suddenly more interested.

Petru pressed a button and the image zoomed in.

"In the centre there, please … underneath the main title," Tarquin mumbled as he squinted intently at the screen.

"It says 'The Forging of an Artist'" Constanta said loudly. "So our friend is into fakes and forgeries. This is getting interesting."

Tarquin blanked her.

"Right, let's see the other ones," he said tetchily.

Petru flicked back to the first of the notebook images.

"Okay, so this notebook was on the floor by the table, where he had his meal," he said.

"Sounds like he was having breakfast," Tarquin mumbled. "Coffee, toast …"

"Yes. I believe so. Now, you see the writing is here very bad, like he was on the phone and trying to write."

"Was there a phone on the table, Petru?" Constanta asked.

"Yes."

Tarquin leaned forward again squinting at the screen.

"These are just ferry times from Portsmouth to St Malo," he said, "and the trip is—is quite soon," he glanced at his watch. "In fact, this Thursday!"

"Next one, Petru," Constanta commanded.

"Itinerary," Tarquin mumbled as he soaked up the words. "He's making a trip to France on Thursday, the first of August, going from Portsmouth to St Malo at 20.30 and heading to a place called Troyes on the second, which I've never heard of. Meet Fabien at train station at 6.30pm."

"You know the other places though?" Constanta asked.

"What, Portsmouth and St Malo? Of course I do ... they're major ports. One on the south coast of England and the other in France. Look, there's more writing at the bottom, can you zoom that as well, please? It's like a scribbled footnote," he said, pressing against Petru's shoulder in his eagerness to see the screen.

"That's as good as you'll get, Mr Tarquin," Petru said. "I'm sorry, I didn't think it was so important. Did you see he is meeting with someone—Fabien—at 6.30 at train station?"

Tarquin didn't hear him; he was just able to make out the words in the footnote. "*The cabinet must be concealed from Frederic. Tell* something *to bring sufficient blankets.* Something *he stays away from van.*"

He stood up, shocked, and realized his back ached.

"Can you see what that said?" Constanta asked, her eyebrows raised.

"It says ..." Tarquin hesitated. "It says the cabinet must be concealed from Frederic."

"The cabinet!" she said, giving him a piercing stare. "*Must be concealed!* I told you, Tarquin. I fucking told you! He's trying to hide it!"

"There's more, but I couldn't make it out," he said. "I ... I really think we need to see that. It's vital."

"You're going back in, Petru," Constanta said sternly, turning to him. "You'll get more money, but we have to see that notebook page with the … the 'tinery' word at the top really clearly. Sorry."

Petru swore vehemently in Romanian and picked up his rucksack. Constanta handed him his camera.

"Just get a good close-up of that page, darling," she said, pulling him towards her and hugging him warmly. "When you've finished, Tarquin's going to take us both for a megaburger!"

Tarquin looked momentarily irritated and then smiled in acknowledgement that this was all being done for his sake.

"Do you like Chinese or Thai food?" he said. "I really can't drive, so we'll order in."

"Thai is good," Petru said as he slipped out of the door.

*   *   *

Gus and Bob sat in their black van in Fulham drinking tea from a flask. The vehicle exuded a menacing quality which even made the police uneasy. With its cluster of aerials, they seemed to suspect it as a shadowy member of their own pack, and preferred to give it a wide berth. The wheels were fat racing alloys and there were only three windows, the windscreen and the two side windows, which were darkened glass. There were none in the rear at all, just the discreet spy holes with their telescopic lenses custom built. The van glittered like Darth Vader's helmet in the cold orange streetlight.

"All right, now listen up," Gus commanded, having been subjected to a ten minute rant about Bob's niece who, at sixteen, was running three boyfriends at once. "Zoltan has got the hump big time with our man in Battersea, and we need to be right on the pulse, okay? We fuck this one up, B, and we're going through the slicer. As you remember, they used to be in business together years ago, and it seems Oliver is doing some fancy footwork, which is pissing Z off. Bad move. So he's given 'im till Thursday night to get in contact and do a deal. What it's all about, I don't know and I don't bloody care. As yer know, our man has a house in Battersea and a place out of town, like towards Bristol way, and he seems to go from one to the other on a regular basis. Now, if our man doesn't do the sensible thing and call Z, we're gonna give 'im a right going over … kick 'im to hell and back, and he's gonna wish he was never born! Comprende, comrade?"

"Yeah….yeah all right then, G, if it's got to be done, let's do it. We're the pros, aren't we!" Bob replied, chuckling sadistically.

"Right mate, I'll drop you off; get some clothes together and washing stuff as per normal on a job like this, and get some big time shut-eye, because I need you sharp, yeah? Real sharp. That means not watching films or playing games till four in the morning - it means tucked up in yer bed by twelve, all right?"

"Okay, okay. Yer made yer point," Bob said, staring out onto the street.

"We know what our man drives—an old Merx—so we're going to park up in his street tomorrow morning at eight and we're going to watch what's going on and stick to 'im like glue. Wherever he goes, we follow, unless of course he's just taking his yapper for a stroll in the park. If we see 'im getting into his motor, we need to act fast."

"Sure…no problem."

"Right, let's get you home, and I'll be round at seven-thirty. Remember, we could be away for a couple of days or more, so get yourself ready," Gus said, trying hard to get the information through Bob's skull.

"Okay, got it," Bob said blankly.

Gus started the engine and revved it as though bolstering his words. The van moved away, and the orange streetlight slid silently over its black shiny skin..

*   *   *

Petru came urgently through the door behind Constanta and quickly shut the door. Exchanging a few jokes on the pavement before coming in, they'd been startled by a car which had suddenly entered the street and driven quickly to a parking spot opposite Oliver's house. Petru hurried to the curtains and scanned the street outside through a tiny crack.

"Shit! It's the man, I think. Yes, he's going into the house," he said in a loud whisper.

"Wow, that was close! Ten minutes before, and I would had to hide in a cupboard!"

"Are you sure?" Tarquin said, his brow furrowed with concern.

"I don't know what the man looks like, but someone certainly went in," Petru said.

"Has it arrived?" Constanta interrupted, sniffing the air like a dog. "I'm hungry."

Tarquin paced around the kitchen ignoring Constanta and wondering whether to confront Oliver.

"Look, it's all a bit suspicious," he said, trying to work it out in his own head, "but we don't know anything for certain yet. I need to be sure before I … well, bang on his door and spill the beans."

"He'll deny it, Tarquin," Constanta said, "and it'll leave you feeling stupid. I even think you might start apologizing to him in that stupid English way, and then I'm gonna puke. Let's eat."

"Mmmm. Guess we could leave it till the morning, then I can nail him. It's in the oven."

Tarquin and Petru sat at the table nibbling crackers as Constanta noisily gathered some plates and cutlery and began pulling the lids off the array of silver foil containers.

"Right!" Tarquin said, wiping his mouth with a paper napkin. "Let's take a look at the spoils."

"Petru!" Constanta said, giving him a friendly slap on the back as he drained the last drops of beer from the bottle. He leaned over and unzipped his bag.

"As you told me, I made some more photos of the notepad, especially that page. Some close-ups, so you can see the writing much better, I think. Oh, and I took a better look at that book. There was a card inside it which I also photographed."

"Great. Well, let's take a look," Tarquin said impatiently.

Petru pulled out the camera and switched it on. They both peered over his shoulder at the screen.

"This is the last one I took, of the card in the book."

Tarquin stared unblinkingly at the words.

> *"What this man did in two dimensions, with paper, ink, and paint, Melvyn, we are about to do in three dimensions with wood and sheer audacity!! Do you realize this man's 'work' adorns some of the most celebrated museums and galleries in the world?! Onwards and upwards, my old friend. Enjoy! We are in good company."*

"Good God!" Tarquin said, stepping shakily back from the camera. "I just don't believe it! I just don't bloody believe it! He's obviously giving this book to someone called Melvyn as a present and … and … well, he's basically implying he's creating his own forgery, isn't he? 'With wood and sheer audacity.' I just can't believe what I'm seeing."

"Tarquin!" Constanta said, giving him a hot look. "Don't start that."

"I'm not, I'm not. I'm just completely and utterly amazed … that … that … my neighbour is a crooked bloody antique dealer!"

"Petru!" Constanta said, trying to smother Tarquin's indulging. "Let's see the other pictures."

"I'm getting a copy of that book tomorrow. Waterstone's will have it," Tarquin said to himself.

"This is the page in the notepad with that … er … 'Itinery' word at the top. This is for you to look at, Mr Tarquin, and see what it means. I have not looked very much. I just wanted to get out."

Tarquin came up and peered over his shoulder once again.

"Here, take it," Petru said, handing him the camera and stepping away.

Tarquin squinted at the screen.

"Ah yes. That's a lot better," he said absently.

"*The cabinet must be concealed from Frederic. Tell Melvyn to bring sufficient blankets. Imperative he stays away from van,*" he muttered softly, almost to himself.

He let his arms drop and looked expectantly at Constanta.

"Look, he's got his cabinet in the van," she said assertively. "His *fake* cabinet worth *a lot* of money, and he doesn't want this man Frederic to see it! Simple. So where is he going to see Frederic?"

"Well … I think this Frederic character is probably in France. It's a continental name; not definitely, but it certainly suggests it, especially as we know he's heading in that direction," he said, gazing vacantly through the window onto the garden.

"How long before those guys are coming to see you, darling?" Constanta said, forcing Tarquin to focus.

He froze for a second, and then spun round to look at Constanta.

"Christ, I'd forgotten about them. Was thinking that now we know Oliver's the criminal here, that they'd be off my back."

"Yeah, right!" Constanta said sarcastically. "They think you *are* Oliver, darling, so they're coming for you, make no mistake, and soon … five days, remember."

A shadow of fear passed across Tarquin's face and for a second he looked scared.

"Right. That's it! I'm going over to Oliver right now and I'm going to tell him what I know and …"

"Hang on!" Constanta said, holding her hand up like a traffic policeman. "And what do you think he'll say? Well, I'll tell you exactly what—'*Nu stiu nimic!*'"

"Uh?" Tarquin said. "What's that supposed to mean?"

"*Nu stiu nimic!* I … don't … know … anything. I don't know what you're talking about!"

"Well, then I'll show him the photos … and writing … and …"

"And before any of that he'll have slammed the door in your face, darling."

"And then ... well, I'll call the police and tell them the story—"

"Wow! And you think that'll solve your problems? By the time the police have decided that you're not just another crazy guy who hates his neighbour, you're going to be in hospital, Tarquin, in a very bad way! This is not a clever way to proceed. The police won't save your arse in time! Don't you understand? You have a couple of days only. You're not the prime minister!"

"She's right, Mr Tarquin," Petru said with a look of grave concern. "You needs to get away from here for a bit until you have a plan. It is not safe. I think this people are dangerous."

"Bloody fucking hell!" Tarquin exploded, slumping back onto the sofa and causing Percy to spring to his feet.

"Are you saying I have to leave my own house because of these bloody criminals? I have to hide because my bloody neighbour is being chased by some Russians? What the hell is *going on* next door?"

There was quiet in the room for a moment or two.

"He is two doors away, Mr Tarquin," Petru said.

"I know, I know, but it's close enough! And what's with the hasty retreat, leaving taps running and breakfast on the table? Perhaps they've realized Oliver lives at number five after all, and he had to leave quickly before they got hold of him?" Tarquin suggested.

"Possibly, darling, but I would not risk it," Constanta said. "He may have left for another reason, who knows. And anyway, why is he back now?"

"But he left the book, the notepad with the ferry times; the fellow was in a serious hurry!"

"He may be picking them up now," she said.

"It may be more simple," Petru offered, "It may be that he sat eating breakfast and suddenly saw a traffic warden in the street by his car ready to write ticket ..."

"Oh come on!" Tarquin said angrily. "Then he comes back in and tidies up."

"Yes, it's possible," Constanta agreed, ignoring Tarquin's

protestations. "Those people make everyone jumpy. He could have got into an argument, lost his temper, was told to move his car immediately … perhaps it was a tow truck even, so he quickly locks and leaves, thinking he's got everything—and perhaps he did—he may not have needed those things right then."

"And don't forget in his notepad," Petru added, "he mentions 'parking permit,' so he needs one, I think!"

"It's all fucking crazy," Tarquin said, smoothing Percy's coat. "I honestly think I'm going mad."

"Going mad is not a luxury you can afford right now, darling. You need to think carefully," Constanta said sternly.

She stood staring at Tarquin for a few moments, deep in thought. Suddenly, she pointed an admonishing finger in his direction.

"My God! I just realized what you've got to do!" she said excitedly. "You've got to catch Oliver with the cabinet. I mean follow him, and see the cabinet, or at least see where it's being taken to, and then you have him properly. You need to photograph it so that the authorities can establish what it is; it must be very luxurious to be so … well … expensive."

"That goes without saying," he said sullenly.

"Someone, an expert perhaps, would know from a photo what it is, and then you can nail him. In fact, I think you need many detailed pictures of it. Your plan to knock on his door is crazy; might just give him warning, make him deny any involvement and change all his plans. Are you really prepared to tell the police that you asked someone to break into a house to get evidence because you had suspicions? How do you think that sounds?"

Tarquin stared at her angrily, taking in her words.

"Listen to me!" Constanta said urgently. "You have to follow Oliver, you know where he's going and what time! Then you can get him properly. You have no real stuff to convince the police right now, and you have some guys ready to kill you if you stay here. They're coming Thursday … the day after tomorrow!"

Tarquin suddenly looked drained of energy.

"But he may have changed his boat times, his plans," he said listlessly.

"He might have done this, and he might do that, Tarquin, but since you can't stay here, what have you to lose?"

"What are you saying, Constanta," Tarquin said in a low voice, "that I book onto the same ferry as him—that's presuming I can get a reservation—and follow him James Bond-style across France? Do you know how difficult it is to follow a car for a long period? It's almost impossible unless you're prepared to run red lights, shunt other cars out of the way, and stick out like a sore thumb. Don't you think he might get a little suspicious if the same Mercedes car is behind him from London to this place in France?"

"Mr Tarquin, excuse me," Petru said deferentially, "but I think there is a time on the notepad, when Oliver is meeting his friend at Troyes train station on Friday, so why do you need follow him? You can go straight there?"

"Perfecto, Petru!" Constanta said, looking at Tarquin triumphantly. "That is the best to do, just catch up with him there."

"And how will I find him?" Tarquin said quietly. "I've only met the man once; I'm not sure I'd recognize him. Besides, how do we know he's not doing something with the bloody cabinet before he gets to Troyes?"

"We don't, but there's no mention in his schedule of another stop, so let's assume he's taking it there," Constanta said.

"Okay, okay, but how do I recognize the man?"

"Do you know his car?" Constanta said.

"No. I don't recall what he drives," Tarquin said.

"Well, look across the street, stupid," Constanta said. "He's parked outside!"

"No," Petru said waving his finger. "He's in van, remember, and that is car out there."

Constanta went over and peered through the curtains.

"Shit, he's gone. The car's already gone," she said.

Tarquin got up and went out onto the street. Oliver's house

was completely dark.

"Well, that settles that, he's buggered off!" he said, coming back in.

Constanta went into the kitchen and poured herself a large glass of water. Percy joined her as she noisily put things into the fridge.

"I've got it!" she shouted suddenly. "I'll ring the ferry company in the morning and pretend to be Oliver's secretary and say I want to check the booking and … and also that I want to check the van details are correct … you know, because Oliver can be a bit stupid about the …"

"Registration details?" Petru interjected.

"Yes. That's the number, isn't it?"

"Sure. And then you check the other details like car type, and model and colour," Petru said excitedly.

"And if they ask why you need these details?" Tarquin said.

"Well, because Oliver has a number of vans, that's why," Constanta riposted. "And he can get confused, and me his secretary am looking after him!"

"Well, all I can say, Constanta," Tarquin said, holding his face in his hands, "is that you remember he's called Clasper, not Clasping."

"Okay, okay, grumpy old man!" she said, squeezing his shoulder. "And I hope you are appreciating you have two very intelligent people helping to save your arse!"

"I certainly do, my friends," Tarquin said, straightening himself into a more relaxed position. "It's just this is very foreign territory to me, that's all. I'm sorry to be negative."

"Petru, can you hear some violins?" she said mischievously.

Tarquin mustered a weak smile.

She continued. "So hopefully we'll soon have all the details of Oliver's van, and if the station in Troyes is small, then you should be able to find him and follow him! Easy, eh?" she said grinning. "Have you got a camera? And shit, yes … what ferry company am I ringing?"

Chapter 17

Gus and Bob arrived in Warriner Avenue at eight thirty exactly and found a parking spot on the opposite side of the street to Tarquin, but several houses up. It afforded a good view of his house.

"What the hell is so frigging funny?" Gus said, turning to look at Bob as he wrenched the handbrake up. "You've been sniggering to yourself for the last couple of minutes."

"Don't you remember the last time we used these magnetic plates, G?"

"Eh?"

"Don't you remember the last time when we was pretending to be satellite TV experts, and that old lady come up and asked you to look at her dish because it wasn't working proper. And you said you was busy, and she said you didn't look very busy because she'd been watching you for two hours, and all you did was sit in the van and listen to the radio!"

"Oh, her!" Gus said with a toothy grin. "Yeah, the stupid old bag. Jesus, she wouldn't leave me alone, kept asking all those bloody questions about her TV and the channels she couldn't get! What the 'ell was I meant to say? 'Of course I've got time to come into your 'ouse, madam, and sort your TV out. Just let me grab me toolbox!"

"Well, we 'ave got 'Magnum Satellite Services and TV Maintenance' stamped all over our motor, G. So what do you expect?" Bob said with a rasping chuckle.

"Look, mate, as you know, we have to have something on the frigging motor when we're doing a stakeout, or we look like a pair of villains."

"Which is what we are, G!" Bob said, chuckling again.

"Okay, you got a better idea? Shall I change it to 'Sanitary Services, Lavatory Blockages our Speciality?' I'm sure I can get some nice brown overalls for you and a pole with a brush on the end to give you the authentic look!" Gus said, throwing his head back and laughing loudly. Bob laughed as well whilst quickly sticking his head out of the window.

"And what about the time when you was mending the floorboards at Frank's gaff?" Gus said, with a view to getting his own back.

"Floorboards?" Bob said, bringing his head back into the cab.

"Yeah, when you was doing a bit of carpentry for him so you could get a good ogle at his daughter."

"Okay, okay," Bob said, vaguely recollecting.

"Don't you remember? His dog … you know, that bloody rottweiler called Major took a fancy to you—you being down on the floor an' all—and got his paws round your neck and started getting well fruity!"

"Fuck me, yes! I remember now," Bob said sheepishly. "Bloody animal was well attached to me with his filthy breath all over me neck. And then he had the bare faced cheek to growl when I tried to push him off. Frank shouted at me to let him be or he'd get the ache! Luckily he had a bone in the fridge and managed to remind Major that his stomach came before a ride. God knows what would have happened otherwise … but he seemed to think it was well funny, I remember that."

Gus threw his head back, laughing again, whilst Bob wiped the wing mirror with an old tissue.

*   *   *

Tarquin answered the phone; it was Constanta.

"Hi, partner, how are you today?" she said, sounding excited.

"Partner?" Tarquin answered, bemused.

"That's right, 'partner'!" she said again, revelling in Tarquin's unease. "You see, Petru and me had a long chat last night after we left and we made a big decision, a really big decision."

"Okay?" Tarquin said guardedly.

"We decided …," She paused for effect.

"Yes? What?"

"We decided, darling, that we're coming with you on this trip to France!"

"What? Aren't you working? And isn't Petru doing his bagels?"

"Yes, we both have jobs, Tarquin, but I am owed a lot of holidays, and Petru can take some time off without a problem as well! We are worried for you."

"Look … sweetie. I really don't know about this whole French trip thing," Tarquin stuttered. "It just seems a crazy idea with … with very odd goals."

"Tarquin! When are you going to wake up? You are in a very dangerous place right now and you need help … *real* help. You're out of your depth, darling. You do not understand what this Russian mafia can do to you. You talk about calling the police when this will only give you the feeling of safety. We've been through this before. The police will not react fast enough. They'll be suspicious of you. By the time they're up to speed, you will be in hospital … if you're lucky! We *know* what these people can do, Tarquin, believe me," she implored.

Tarquin held the phone against his chest for a few seconds, his face a mask of worry.

"Right! Okay! Let's bloody do it!" he said with sudden determination. "I need to think about a few things before."

"I already did the thinking for you. Number one you need to decide who can look after Percy …"

"He can come with us," Tarquin interrupted. "He has a passport, he's been vaccinated, and France is … well, dog friendly when it comes to hotels."

"Really?" she said, sounding dubious. "Do you need to check this?"

"No."

"Okay then, next you need to hire a vehicle; the Mercedes

will be too small for this trip."

"Err … shit, you're right! Perhaps I can borrow something from …"

"Tarquin! You don't have *time!* Do you want to be half killed by this people? There will be questions and delays if you ask one of your friends. There are hire companies everywhere, and they'll do you a deal over a week."

"Okay, okay. Leave it to me."

"They are coming for you, darling … *please* understand! It's Wednesday today, and we need to leave tomorrow. The letter gave you till Thursday. Don't you remember?"

"Constanta, I understand! I'm on the case."

"Oliver is meeting his friend at Troyes railway station on Friday. He's getting the ferry tomorrow evening with the cabinet."

"Yes, I know."

"Petru thought something like a Ford Focus—sort of low-profile car—would be best."

"Yuh. I'll check what's on offer," Tarquin said, feeling like he was being propelled down a tunnel.

"Don't forget you have to book us on this ferry or tunnel thing. If we arrive over there in the evening, we can drive towards Troyes and find a place to stay on the way."

"I'm going to sort it all out, Constanta. Stop worrying!"

"Look, darling, there will be expenses for you to pay, but we'll help you to sort this problem out. Petru is good with a camera, and I have some skills as well! I can think on my feet, and think of ways to turn this to your advantage. This adventure might have an interesting conclusion."

"That's a big word for a Romanian," Tarquin said, trying to lighten the mood.

"Wow, you're a funny man," she said without a trace of amusement. "Now I got to go, but you know what you have to do, organise a car and book a ferry, or whatever, but make sure we are over in France by tomorrow in the evening at the latest, perhaps even earlier. We'll be over at your place by eleven o'clock in the morning unless you call. Oh, and don't forget some food for Percy and some water."

"Have you got … are both your passports up to date?" he asked tentatively.

"What's that supposed to mean? Of course they are. See you tomorrow."

"Okay. Oh, hang on! Just one other thing," he said hastily. "Did you get hold of the ferry company and manage to find out the details of Oliver's van?"

"I'm a professional, darling, what do you think! It's a red Toyota."

She put the phone down without waiting for a reply.

Thomas Charrington

Chapter 18

"That's perfect, Melvyn," Oliver said, looking at the casing around the chest. "That'll throw them off the scent … and keep Frederic at bay, for sure! He's a nosy bugger, and we don't need to get tripped up by him, not at this stage in the proceedings. As you know, it's all in the detail, and one silly oversight could scupper us and send three years of work up in flames."

"God forbid," Melvyn mumbled quietly.

"Okay, that's it till tomorrow at nine. Please just double-check you have all the tools you'll need, and of course all the things for your 'magic box of tricks.' I trust you've cleared it all with Mary?"

"Yep, she's happy. Just thinks we're off to do some deals in France, that's all; not really that concerned. As you know, she's only really interested in the garden."

"How sweet. You have a lovely wife there, Mel. Some women would be asking a thousand questions. And it's kind of her to keep an eye on the 'Hall.' I always hate to leave the house unattended for any length of time, and besides, she's good with Titus. He's grown fond of chasing hares recently and she can bring him to heel immediately with that voice of hers!"

"Don't I know it," Melvyn said with a smile.

"Oh, and please don't forget your passport, Mel," Oliver said with a wink as he stepped out of the workshop door.

Shortly after turning out of Melvyn's drive, Oliver suddenly remembered he must put a final call through to Fabian. He pulled over and reached for the dedicated handset in the glove compartment.

"Hi, Fabien, everything okay?" he said anxiously.

"Oh, hi, Oliver, that was lucky, I was about to go down the steps to the underground! Yes, everything is fine this end, and I've said my good-byes to the team for the next two weeks. They're fine about it, and I think a little envious that I have a big house to go and sort out in France."

"Yes, of course," Oliver said without any interest. "Now I just want to check what time you arrive in Troyes. I know you told me, but I didn't write it down. Was it six eighteen?"

"Six twenty-eight, Oliver … five twenty-eight English time. I'll be leaving Cecile's flat in the mid afternoon and the train should take about an hour and a half. I'm taking her for a spectacular dinner tomorrow night at a seafood restaurant near the Place de la Republic."

"Lucky her! Careful what you say. Right, I'm reckoning we'll be there somewhere between five and six, or rather six and seven French time, so just wait in that hotel if we're not there. Are you packed, got your passport, ticket, and so on?"

"Please don't worry. Oliver. I'm very organized, I can assure you. Just a few little things to do in the morning and that's it. I will meet you in Troyes definitely … unless something unexpected happens. My life would be in ruins if I didn't make it!"

"Sorry, Fabien, just last minute jitters, I suppose," Oliver said with a loud laugh. "See you on Friday evening, and keep your mobile to hand."

"Okay, see you then. Good-bye, Oliver.

Chapter 19

On Thursday morning, Bob was slumped on one of the observation seats as Gus stirred in his sleeping bag.

"You know what, G, I'd forgotten how stiff me muscles get doing these stakeouts," he said to the barely conscious Gus.

"Well, you seemed to think you was in a five-star hotel by the way you was sleeping earlier," Gus croaked drily as he unzipped the bag. "Took a few good kicks to get you into the land of the living. I thought you was the one that could survive on three hours a night! Now pass us the cold box and let me get a cool cup of orange down me throat. I'm fucking parched here. What bloody time is it, anyway?"

"Six twenty-five."

Gus clumsily rummaged around in the box, and having found a plastic cup, poured himself an orange juice. His Adam's apple bounced up and down to the inhuman grunts he emitted as he swallowed two cupfuls in quick succession. He smacked his lips.

"Right, I'm going up to the park to sort myself out in a proper toilet, okay, so you're in charge for the next twenty-five minutes. I've got me dog, make sure yours is up and running, and for Christ's sake, call me if there's any change in status."

"Okay, G. I'm on it," Bob said, looking keenly through the spy hole at Tarquin's house.

The street was quiet and empty apart from a noisy band of starlings, flitting between the small trees dotted along the pavement. Ten minutes later, a milk float appeared, and the sound of clinking glass added to the steadily rising tempo of distant traffic.

Gus reappeared a bit later looking fresh and purposeful. His thinning hair had been gelled and was swept back, accentuating the bony contours of his skull and sharp cheekbones. With his black shades, black sweatshirt, and powerful athletic build, he looked entirely wrong in this leafy haven of suburbia. In fact, the only thing in the vicinity which chimed in sympathy with Gus was the brooding dark vehicle he now climbed into.

"Magnum Satellite Services, my arse!" he said with utter disdain to Bob as he took up his position behind the wheel. "Ruins the lines of our girl, and the sooner we rip 'em off the better."

"Serves a purpose, G," Bob said with a yawn. "You didn't forget to put the false plates on, did you? I forgot to look."

"For fuck's sake, B. Stop asking stupid questions, will you? Of course I bloody didn't!"

"Right. I'm going for a scrub as well, mate. I'll be back in a tick. It's by the first gate, innit?" Bob said. climbing out.

"Yeah. Hurry."

Tarquin, who'd been up since six, pulled the zip around his suitcase for the last time, stood up and took a slurp of cold tea. It was now seven twenty. Percy stood looking at him forlornly, having shadowed his every move.

"Look, Percy," Tarquin said, looking down tenderly at the white and tan creature at his feet. "You're coming with me, so stop worrying. No kennels for you this time, you're coming to France."

The small dogs' ears pricked up and his head tilted to one side, desperate to read his master's intentions.

"C'mon, boy, it's time for a good walk before we leave," he added, as though the animal was perfectly conversant in English. "I don't want to have to stop for you."

As they left the house, a pair of yellow eyes in a nearby black van studied them intensely, and a heartbeat moved up a gear. Gus watched them until they disappeared from his field of vision and then groped nervously for his cigarettes. He needed to calm himself; it wasn't time for any action. Oliver was simply taking his dog for a walk.

"Blimey, G. There's a friggin' fog of smoke in 'ere," Bob said a while later as he climbed in beside Gus. "You want to go easy on those or they'll nail you."

"You're not me doctor, B, but I appreciate your concern. Now, did you see him? He's gone off to the park with his mutt."

"Who? Oh … er … you mean our man. No, I didn't, as it 'appens; must've just missed him."

"Wakey, wakey, B. I need you sharp, real sharp. Get a coffee down your gullet and give us that bag of sandwiches. I'm fucking starving."

Twenty minutes went by as Capital radio washed over them, and Gus munched his way through some sandwiches.

"Oh, he's back!" Bob said in a loud whisper, looking in Gus's wing mirror as Tarquin sauntered back up the street with Percy. "He's a big bastard, isn't he? And he looks all dressy, like he's off somewhere."

"Well, he probably is, and he's gonna have company, isn't he!" Gus said with a leer.

Under the malevolent gaze of the two men, Tarquin let himself back into the house and all was quiet again. The two men settled more comfortably into their seats and let the early morning minutes roll gently on.

"Right, B. I want you to look the part of a satellite TV expert," Gus said suddenly, yawning. "We've been sat here for twenty-four hours and we 'avn't done very much, have we, apart from strolling up and down the street with a clipboard taking photos! So open up the back and grab that coil of cable I put there and lay it along the pavement for say ten metres, then grab that satellite dish and stick it at the end. Then grab that toolbox and lay out some frigging tools like you know what you're doing. Anyone says anything, just say we're doing a survey for the council and you don't know nothing, okay? If you want to know what to do, just pull the different wires out the cable and start cutting them. You know, take the plastic sheath off the wires. Start looking technical, B. We don't need someone getting suspicious and calling the cops."

"You gonna help, G?" Bob said. looking at Gus.

"Someone's got to keep an eye out, as you know. Oh, go on then, I'll grab the cable," he said suddenly, jumping out and going round to the back. "I'll take a tape measure and a book and start taking measures."

At 10.15, a vehicle pulled up outside Tarquin's house and hooted. Tarquin came out and talked to the driver for a few minutes before directing him into a parking spot nearby. Gus and Bob watched intently as Tarquin was shown round the exterior of the vehicle and was then given a demonstration of the interior workings. He then signed a pad of paper held by the driver and received some keys. They continued to chat for a further five minutes before another car appeared and the driver was taken away, leaving Tarquin and what was obviously a rental vehicle.

"Right, mate, it looks like it's green for go," Gus said urgently. "Pack up the kit quickly and let's get ready. Our man is heading somewhere, and for some reason he doesn't want to take his Merx."

"He's not necessarily going now. Could be going later on."

"I've got a feeling in me bones our man is on the move, my friend, so snap to. Make sure that cable and toolbox are secured proper. I don't want things skidding around."

"Sure thing."

Bob began clearing the various items from the pavement and noisily loaded them into the van. A curtain hung towards the back, which hid the main body from prying eyes when the back doors were opened.

"Okay, all done," Bob said, slumping in his seat slightly out of breath. He idly flexed his fingers and arm muscles and studied his tattoos fondly.

A few minutes passed by.

"Okay, Okay," Gus said quietly, almost to himself, whilst scrutinizing his wing mirror. "Seems we really do have a party going on here this morning."

"What's up now?"

"Right, I want you in the back in full observation mode, B, and let me know exactly what's happening. Two more bods have just pitched up at his door as we speak. A tall blond woman, I think, and a bloke … on the smallish side."

Bob swivelled the front seat and moved quickly into position at the spy hole in the main body of the van.

"Yep, you're right, G. Oliver's talking to them now; she's got a suitcase and he's got a rucksack. Hey, Oliver's pointing at the rental and handing her the keys. They're loading up. Perhaps they're going to take it and leave our man?"

"Just watch, B, just watch," Gus said, drawing heavily on his cigarette.

"Blimey, his dog's just run out and jumped into the motor," Bob said excitedly.

"It's looking like he's on the move like you said, G. He ain't going to let his precious mutt go off and leave him, is he!"

A minute or two passed in silence as the two men watched.

"And here comes the main man with his suitcase," Bob said urgently in a low voice. "He's locking up … real proper lock up … double-checking, and now he's taking a gander up and down the street. She's also taking a look. Okay, okay. Oliver's getting into the driving seat. It's showtime, G!"

Gus turned the key, and the Sprinter roared into life.

"Fuck, they're facing in the other direction, you're going to have to hurry."

"Relax, they're going into a one-way system and will be coming right past my snout when I take a right here," Gus said with supreme confidence.

They turned at the bottom of the street and waited.

"You smart bastard," Bob said with feeling, as they tucked in behind the Voyager leaving a car in between.

*   *   *

"This is a nice car, Tarquin," Constanta said, settling Percy into her lap and tickling his ears. "Why such a big one?"

"If we're travelling across France, we need some space, don't you think? I can't bear being cramped."

"I agree, Mr Tarquin," Petru said from the backseat. "I can stretch out and go to sleep!"

"Petru, don't get silly ideas," Constanta said curtly. "This isn't a holidays."

He can sleep if he wants," Tarquin interjected. "It'll be a boring drive to Dover … about two hours or so. As long as you are awake, sweetie, we'll be fine."

"Thank you. Mr Tarquin," Petru purred, whilst lying back and sighing.

"So what exactly is the plan?" Constanta asked, giving Tarquin a sharp look.

"Right. We're catching the three-thirty ferry to Calais, arriving at about six o'clock local time, as France is an hour ahead of us."

"Okay."

"So the actual boat journey is an hour and a half. We then drive out of Calais and take the motorway to Reims, a city on the way to Troyes, arriving there … say about nine o'clock. Then we find our hotel, which I've booked, drop our bags, and go and have a well-earned supper! Sound all right?"

"Wow! You have been doing your homework, darling. Congratulations!" Constanta said, grinning.

"Thank you, I'm glad Madam approves!"

"Well, I certainly approve. Mr Tarquin," came a voice from the rear.

"Is this Reims place close to Troyes, or do we have a long drive tomorrow too?" she asked.

"No, probably an hour and a quarter … something like that," Tarquin replied with a growing sense of control.

*   *   *

"Now he'll be heading to Gloucestershire, according to Z, and then we'll catch 'im in the act. Catch 'im playing with his little cabinet, and then we give him the fright of his life," Gus said, as they moved up the Latchmere Road.

"Too right, G!" Bob smirked, whilst stretching his arms out and flexing his fingers so they cracked one by one. "I'm looking forward to this."

They arrived at Clapham Common and took a left into the one-way system.

"Should 'ave fucking guessed," Gus said with annoyance. "He's going in to fuel up. Look, I'm taking a dive down this street for a second, and we're going to jump out and get these bloody TV plates off! I'm sick of the things."

They came to a quick stop and both jumped out and removed the various magnetic plates advertising their satellite communications expertise. They threw them in the back with a loud clatter.

"Done!" Gus said, slamming the doors. "Now we can follow him a bit more discreet." The Voyager edged out of the petrol station, mirrored a short distance away by the Sprinter with its black nose and bull bars.

They headed east along the top of the common and then took a turn towards Clapham South. Shortly after, they headed east on the south circular.

"What the fuck is he up to?" Gus said, more to himself than Bob, whose sense of direction didn't exist. "He's heading southeast, for Christ's sake!"

"Not good?" Bob answered, trying to sound concerned.

"No, it's definitely not good; he's either got a crazy route to his gaff in the country, or he's got another plan. I was thinking that if we lost him we could catch up with the roach at his other house, but we haven't got that option if he's heading somewhere else. We're going to have to stick with him like shit to a blanket."

"Bloody 'ell," Bob said absently, whilst ogling a buxom

coloured girl at the lights.

"Perhaps he's got a lockup in this direction or something."

They carried on through the various neighbourhoods and on past Dulwich College.

Every now and then they lost sight of the Voyager, and Gus fretted and swore at every vehicle around him. Eventually they moved out onto the motorway

"Where in the hell is this geezer going?" he said in frustration. "At least we can keep a good distance back from him on these big roads. I bloody nearly rammed him a couple of times earlier!"

"We're doing good, mate, we're still with the arsehole," Bob said soothingly.

*   *   *

As Gus and Bob passed under the M25 and out onto the M20 in determined pursuit of their quarry, Fabien glanced up briefly from his newspaper as his train was swallowed by the gaping mouth of the channel tunnel. He'd made this journey countless times, but he always liked to witness the transition from the open air of Kent, to the tight sleeve of concrete he now plunged into.

He felt strange … even to himself. Who was this man, Fabien, who was about to carry out this audacious act? The grief-crazed state he was in, those three years ago, were a distant memory now—a time when the world suddenly turned as cold and solitary as a drafty winter platform on the journey to school; a time when it took every grain of his will to haul himself from his bed. Cecile was his sun … and she had gone out.

But someone had pointed to an escape hatch in his cell; a hatch which would change his life forever. What previously had seemed so repulsive and dangerous to contemplate had suddenly become a blessed release from the leaden twilight that surrounded him. He had reached for it, yes, in desperation to get out into the sunshine and find Cecile; and Oliver had been there to grab his hand and pull him through.

He had embraced Oliver's ethos as a drowning man claws buoyancy from the rowing partner he despises. But that was then. He felt stronger now, in control of his life, and a part of him baulked at the enormity of what he was about to do. But Oliver's words that fateful night in the restaurant still reverberated in his mind …

"*… that takes courage, Fabien. Crossing that boundary is not easy, but the rewards for those who have the guts are stupendous.*"

And it was true … it did take guts; guts, imagination, and unbelievable skill. He had seen the cabinet with his very eyes; had absolutely insisted. And it was a masterpiece of authenticity. Something already smouldering with a perceived provenance, ready to burst out into the world from the womb of Melvyn's workshop and be feted.

The man, Melvyn, was a master. Well, he should be. He had a history … a fascinating history of innocence corrupted by the guile and greed of others. Yes, like so many, Melvyn had entered the restoration business all doe eyed and keen, and then, as his talent became noticed, he was gently nudged into another world … a world where things happened that shouldn't happen.

A place where his pay had suddenly bloomed, where he was taught the subtle science of subterfuge. Where it was not just about *restoring* old bona fide pieces, it was about building *new* "antique" pieces. A place where he learnt about old glues, varnishes, polishes, and waxes. A place where there seemed to be a reservoir of aged timbers, metals, and veneers for particular regions and centuries, and where the construction techniques of these workshops was well documented.

He also had contacts—people who were specialists in very particular disciplines, ready to jump to his command. Yes, by the time he came to Oliver, Melvyn had already been forged in the crucible of chicanery … and eighteenth century French furniture was his speciality.

And with him on board, Fabien really did believe the ship could sail. After all, he deserved this—of course he did—for Cecile and for his family; Oliver was right. He'd been kept down for too long. Her attitude towards him had changed lately. She laughed a lot, teased him … was more the joyous creature she had been when they first met.

At last she sensed the foundations of a stable future. Yes, he was joining a different fraternity now … he was crossing over to the other side. Rolling his newspaper, he stood up, stretched his limbs, and then made his way purposefully to the bar

Chapter 20

"Sorry, Mel. I meant to call you an hour ago, but bloody Titus has decided to take himself off on a hare hunt," Oliver said breathlessly on his mobile. "Damn animal! Dogs always do this when they know you're about to go away; you know, play up like spoilt children!"

"Oh, not to worry then ... just wondered if you'd like some lunch; Mary's got some sausage rolls lined up and salad. Everything's ready and packed and I've got some drinks in a cold box."

"That's great, Mel, and it's a long run tomorrow, too ... six or so hours to Troyes. He glanced at his watch. "Twelve thirty. Look, just go ahead and I'll be over as soon as I've found the dog. I think I know where he might be, and I've got a couple of things to sort out for Frederic. Would you mind if I snatch a bite with you ... say at two, and then I can have a chat with Mary about Titus's new habits in case he goes off again! You go ahead though."

A short while later, with Titus locked securely in his kennel, Oliver stuffed some papers into a drawer in his desk, locked it, and picked up the telephone.

"Lily?" he said gently.

"Hello," she replied coolly.

"Just wondered how you were, and to say thanks for dinner the other night."

"Glad you enjoyed it," she replied matter of factly.

"It was a fun evening, beautifully organized, as usual. You're a fabulous cook, darling."

"Thank you … I try."

"They were an interesting bunch, and good to see Giles in such cracking form. The city seems to be treating him well."

"Does it ever not?" she said curtly.

"Well … uh … I haven't seen him for a while so I wouldn't really know," Oliver said, aware that Lily's mood could be better.

"Just wish he didn't talk about it so much … it's soo boring," she said irritably. "As we both know, the city's a bloody casino, and the gambler in Giles just can't get enough of it. But it's a man's playground, you know, and any woman that ventures into it has to grow a leathery skin pretty quickly, or she'll become a mere ornament."

"My dear Lily, aren't we being just a little cynical," Oliver said chuckling. "I presume you're referring to Sabrina?"

"Oddly enough I am, and no, Oliver, I am not being cynical. Giles is a man's man, you know. Doesn't really get women; they're play things to be humoured and shepherded. I mean, he's perfectly 'het' but we just don't interest him."

"Oh? He seemed to be sparking with Sabrina."

"Sparking! Oh Lord, yes, he can spark, all right, if the girl's got the right plumage. But that's acting, and I can assure you it's his own performance he's really watching. Besides, Sabrina's more of a man than Giles will ever be. I'm sure I saw some balls under that ridiculous little pelmet she was wearing. She's ambitious, you know, keenly aware of her career path in the square mile, and she knows how to flatter!"

"Really?" Oliver said uneasily.

"Come on! I'm sure she took Geoffrey's cottage for the summer in order to wriggle her way into a rich social set down here. I can tell you, I saw through her in seconds. It was Giles who asked her to dinner; said it seemed sad not to introduce her to some locals. Men are soo stupid! She's deceptive—the parasitic pilot fish waiting for the sharks to make the kill before helping herself to some juicy leftovers."

Oliver burst out laughing.

"Well … can I say I thought you were looking absolutely ravishing, darling; the glowing hostess in slinky peach! David couldn't keep away from you."

"Exactly … so where were you?" she said tetchily. "Pretending to be interested in the badgers on Botcombe Farm?"

"Were you eavesdropping?"

"No. I just know what Fiona's favourite subject is, and I know that it wouldn't interest you. You were a bit distant, that's all," she said sighing. "I'm terribly fond of you, Oliver, don't you understand? I'm confused."

" I … er … I'm sorry, darling, but … you … well … seemed quite busy. Look, when I'm back from France, I'll come over and do some serious pruning and … and bring you a couple of bottles of something delicious and some gorgeous French cheese!"

"You charmer," Lily said sadly. "Go on, off you go."

"Call you when I'm back," he said, closing off.

Thomas Charrington

Chapter 21

As the tarmac river of the M20 raced under his wheels, Tarquin was already looking completely at ease in the driving seat of his new machine. Clear of London, he was feeling the first flutters of excitement at what bizarre experiences lay in wait for him across the channel.

This would be something to lift a few eyebrows in his social circle. Heading off to the continent to catch an antiques fraudster with a Romanian girl he'd met in a pub; a woman he barely knew and who seemed to become more obscure the closer he got to her. A woman whom, he had to admit, had an uncanny knack of seeing what he was blind to.

"He can sleep anywhere, that boy," she said, glancing over her shoulder at the stretched out body of Petru. "He works hard, though, so it's not surprising. They open the bagel stall at six thirty in the morning, so he has to be up at five, which is early even by my standards. He does the first three hours alone."

"Cooer, that's a time of the morning I rarely see," Tarquin said, feeling vaguely ashamed. "How did he manage to get away for this trip if he has to do the early shift?"

"Oh, Zavasta, who owns the business, has a cousin who just came over to England, and he's going to do the early bit until he gets back. He doesn't pay him much, so he deserves it. As I told you, Petru had bad life before. He was with some bad people and they used to do organized robbery of shops and things like that around London. Petru is good boy at heart … it wasn't what he wanted. He didn't want to be a criminal, but he saw no other way. His real interest is in electronical things … you know, computers and stuff. His older sister was my best friend at school in Iassi, though. She called me one day completely unexpected from home."

"What … from Romania?" Tarquin asked.

"Yes. She gave me his number and asked me to get in touch with him and try and help. And I did, and that's how he came to be working for Zavasta."

"Okay … that was good of you," Tarquin said, looking absently in the rearview mirror. "I can see he's a smart cookie. The way he got into Oliver's house was a marvel, and then all that information he uncovered; he'd be an asset to our secret services."

"He sure would … that's why I insisted he came with us. I think he's going to show you what else he can do on this trip. The other tricks he has in his box!"

"Well, if it ever comes to it. To be frank, I'm really not so sure that we're going to catch up with Oliver. It just seems a bit of a long shot, but what the hell, we're going to have a fun little road trip, that's for sure!"

"Oh Tarquin … you're such a pessimist. We're going to find the bastard, I'm telling you," she said, gazing ahead. "By the way, just so you know, it will only be us two on the way back. Petru will be going straight back home for a bit; his mother's ill and she needs help."

"Oh, okay … that's sad," Tarquin said, as a green sign with "Dover 22 miles" hurtled past. "I hope she's not too unwell."

"Shit happens," she said, "but I don't think it's so bad."

$$*\qquad*\qquad*$$

Six seconds later and the same sign registered in the muddled head of Bob.

"Oh … the white cliffs of Dover … we'll be seein' France shortly, G!" he mumbled.

Bob's words slowly trickled into Gus's mind. Suddenly the

blood began to drain from the folds and gullies of his face, as a tsunami started building in his brain. *Dover … Calais … France … Freedom …* There was a long pause and then it rushed back, red and turbulent, and his eyes turned hot.

"Oh my *fuuuck*!!" he shouted, causing Bob to almost jump out of his seat. "Bloody idiots! Of course … of fucking course! He's going across the channel; the bastard's going to France!"

"Eh? What? Where? Well, we just follow 'im, don't we, G?" Bob said, startled.

"No, we can't, you clown! Unless you've got you're fuckin' passport!" Gus said panicking.

"Oh … yer … well … the thing is you never said nothing about a passport, G," Bob said, looking at Gus nervously.

"Exactly, Bob! I didn't, and now we're fucked!" Gus said desperately. "Just shut it, B … don't say nothing, okay? Just … just let me think!"

They sat in silence for two minutes, Gus's fingers white on the wheel, his jaw muscle flexing uncontrollably.

Suddenly he broke the silence.

"Right, I've got it!" he said quickly. "Worked out what we're going to do, okay. Now listen up, Bob, listen up careful. Our man is heading to the tunnel, or he's going to catch a ferry. Either way it's going to be a disaster for us 'cos we haven't got passports. So we're going have to stop him going, okay … we've got to act *now,* Bob, or we are seriously fucked. So what we're going do, is wait till we get off the motorway … yer know … outside Dover and onto a smaller road, and ram him from behind."

"Ram him?" Bob said, looking worried.

"That's right. Ram him and force him to stop. Then we're going to give him what he deserves, and force the bastard to tell us exactly where the cabinet is and what he's planning to do with it."

"But, G, that's going to be tricky, innit? How you going to make him stop, and what about the other traffic? We'll be seen."

"Of course we'll be seen, but we don't have a choice, do we!

We have to stop him, and this should work. You get clunked from behind and you slam on the anchors … reflex action. Then we block him. He doesn't know who we are; he'll think it's a mistake! And then wham! We let him have it! Besides, we have false plates on, so anyone who calls the cops can give the bloody reg, for all we care! Anyways, we'll swop 'em over shortly and put the mag plates back on."

"Bloody 'ell, I hope you're right. G," Bob said, staring at the Voyager a couple of hundred meters ahead. "How long we got?"

"About five minutes, so get yourself in gear, and no hurting the dolly unless she asks for it. Get in the back so it looks like it's just me in here, or they might get suspicious and do a runner."

Bob swivelled his seat and disappeared into the back. Gus lit a cigarette and sucked on it hungrily.

"I'll give you the word, okay, so don't move till then. You might want to get a hold of something; it's going to get bumpy."

"Okay, mate, I'm ready," came a muffled voice from the back.

A few minutes later and the Sprinter slowed down for the first of a number of roundabouts. Bob peered through a spy hole in the front and watched the Voyager getting close and then farther away and then closer again.

"Get ready, B!" came the tense command from the front. "After this one."

Bob felt the Sprinter slow down, take the bend, and then accelerate angrily as it straightened out. His heart raced. Suddenly there was a sickening thud, and he was thrown to his left as it lurched violently.

Regaining his balance, he saw the Voyager weaving erratically just in front of them, its brake lights glowing. As predicted, it moved towards the side of the road, and the Sprinter took up a commanding position on the outside as the two vehicles came to a stop.

"Go!" Gus yelled.

Tarquin felt the shock from behind and the subsequent flex

of his head backwards onto the headrest as though in a dream. He found it difficult to regain control of the car, which weaved dangerously for a few seconds. Gradually he slowed down and then moved onto the hard shoulder, his heart racing. Some idiot had made a mistake.

A black van screeched to a halt menacingly on his right. He heard Constanta's voice beside him shouting something in Romanian, and then he heard Petru telling him to keep driving. Completely disorientated, Tarquin imagined they were blocking the traffic, so he quickly moved the vehicle forward fifty meters. Two men had appeared from the van behind them and were running towards them as he stopped and got out.

Constanta was already out shouting something in Romanian to Petru. Percy was barking wildly and would have followed Tarquin had Petru not managed to grab his collar in time and hold him back.

As Tarquin walked shakily towards them, vaguely thinking he should have a notepad and pen, Constanta yelled at him to get back in the car. It was too late. Tarquin turned his head towards her as Gus's fist crunched against it in a glancing blow which was aimed at his throat. He groaned, a deep, low, animal sound, and as he fell he heard a piercing scream like an enraged raptor whose nest was being raided.

Thudding onto the tarmac, he looked up and saw Constanta in slow motion, her bare foot silhouetted against the blue sky slamming into the side of Gus's head, throwing it sideways. A spray of saliva gleamed briefly as it burst from his open mouth. She landed like a cat and momentarily watched Gus fall, then a hand like a vice closed on her arm. She spun round and found herself gazing into the sadistic eyes of Bob. As his other hand began to tighten around her neck, she let herself drop, and then with another shriek, whipped her foot viciously into his groin. His hand loosened on her arm and he doubled up moaning.

Tarquin stood shakily to his feet. Petru was in the driving seat revving the engine yelling at him to get in. Constanta was also yelling.

"*Get in, Tarquin … they're gonna kill you!*"

She pushed him forcefully into the back and slammed the door.

"*Go, Petru, go … go … go!*" she yelled, falling headlong into the passenger seat.

The door swung open for a few seconds and then slammed shut with a loud bang as Petru put his foot down and careered into the traffic, swerving erratically.

"*Petru, shift as fast as you can, they gonna follow, believe me. Move it! Now do you understand, Tarquin!*" she yelled at him. "*You don't fuck with this people!*"

"I … I … didn't realize … I thought …"

"*I know what you thought … now tell him where to go!*" she yelled.

"Okay. Okay. Just follow signs to ferries … cross-channel ferries … you can't miss them; they're clearly marked," he blurted.

Constanta glanced repeatedly through the back window as they crossed a series of roundabouts on the route to the terminal. Tarquin noticed Dover Castle on the left and then a towering white cliff which dwarfed the houses below.

Suddenly she shouted, "*Here the bastards are!!*"

Tarquin looked painfully through the rear window and saw the unmistakable black Sprinter powering towards them in the distance, gaining by the second. Percy couldn't be held back and, sensing the tension, jumped from the front seat to the back repeatedly in a state of high anxiety.

"*C'mon, c'mon,*" she said frantically, "*where is this place!*"

"There!" shouted Tarquin. "Take that exit!"

They straightened out and looking back saw the Sprinter closing in rapidly. A car in its way was clipped and weaved violently as the black van thundered forwards in a headlong rush.

"Here we go … just go straight across there … and … and down there!" he shouted as the Voyager hurtled down a road with high walls on either side. "We go through to the right there and there's the custom point where we show passports!"

As they came to an abrupt halt at customs, they all peered

back anxiously. The Sprinter came to a screeching stop at the top of the incline, its shiny skin glinting eerily in the afternoon sun. It waited there for forty-five seconds, engine revving as though panting—a hungry dark predator watching the prey it so nearly caught, slip away.

Thomas Charrington

Chapter 22

Oliver brushed some flakes of pastry from his shirt and pushed his plate to one side.

"Thank you, Mary, that was perfect," he said. "I sometimes forget to eat, and then I'm suddenly famished!"

"You bachelors are all the same, Oliver, you don't look after yourselves properly," Mary said, taking his plate to the sink. "It's always slap dash meals at odd hours, and then you wonder why you get ill."

"True, I can be rather lazy in that direction," Oliver conceded. "A slice of toast and some cheese is just so easy, I suppose."

"Easy, but not wholesome, Oliver … you need a good woman to look after you," she said in a matronly way. "Now where's Melvyn with that map?"

Suddenly the door flew open and Melvyn came in looking flustered.

"Sorry, I thought I'd put the map in the holdall with the other papers, but it was behind the driver's seat in that pocket," he said, handing it to Oliver.

"Okay then, I'll leave you two men to finish your business," Mary said, putting on a pair of gardening gloves. "I'm at the far end of the garden by the shrubbery if you need me."

"Thanks again, Mary. If I don't see you, have a very peaceful few days with only yourself to worry about!" Oliver said warmly as he spread the map open. "Oh, and don't get fooled by that dog of mine … he's always hungry, however much he's eaten."

"Don't think for one moment that Titus will get the better of me!" she said, disappearing out of the door.

Oliver fumbled for some glasses and then peered down at the map with Melvyn by his side.

"Right, Mel, here's Paris," he said, pointing with a biro, "and down to the southeast a little is our destination, Troyes. And you pronounce it like the French three. 'Trois,' not Troy!"

"Oh, okay," Melvyn said, stroking his chin.

"So we arrive right over here at St Malo at seven tomorrow morning, having come from Portsmouth. We then drive over to here, Laval, and just outside is a little village called Argentre … which is where Frederic lives. You've been there before, so you'll recognize it. I reckon we'll be there around ten, and that gives us an hour or so to check out his stock and have a cup of coffee before heading on. We then take this road east and head towards Troyes, and as you can see, it's a fair old way, so you'll have to take the wheel for a bit. I've got you insured."

"Right, that's no problem," Melvyn mumbled.

"Good!" Oliver said, standing up and folding the map. "We then pick up Fabien from the train station and take you to that most wonderful house which I briefly mentioned before … Chateau Clery. And then, my friend, we go about the business of altering history!"

He looked at his watch.

"Okay, it's five to four, so we have five minutes. I'll go out to the van and wait for you. Oh, and do please check you've got your passport, Mel."

*   *   *

Tarquin and his companions sat in a secluded part of the main refreshments lounge on the *Dover Princess* as she ploughed her way towards Calais. Percy stayed in the car with a large bowl of water and some treats to calm him down. Constanta and Petru sat opposite each other, chatting incessantly in Romanian whilst gazing out of the windows in awe at the glittering sea.

Tarquin sat a little apart, seemingly engrossed in a copy of the *Telegraph*. But he was not reading. He was in fact reliving again and again the recent events on the road and the ghastly humiliation of being saved by a beautiful young woman, half his strength, from a pair of thugs, and then being virtually thrown into the backseat of the vehicle he had been so thoroughly in command of moments before.

Absently turning the leaves of the paper, he pondered his situation with an increasing sense of panic. Who exactly *was* Constanta? Obviously a woman fully conversant in hand-to-hand combat, that was for sure; and why was it that her appearance in his life dovetailed so neatly with his rude introduction to two men who seemed intent on killing or maiming him? Were they linked, or was this just the weird coincidence he had presumed it to be all along? Perhaps they were all actors working in cahoots to lure him abroad for some dark reason, and he had fallen, hook, line, and sinker, into their trap?

But for what purpose? He wasn't excessively rich, or a diplomat, or a member of parliament, or in MI5, or a scientist, or even a powerful businessman with international interests. He was just a normal guy with a fairly normal life and a dog. What possible reason could there be to make him a target?

He lifted his eyes discreetly over the newspaper and watched Constanta for a few moments as though trying to find some sign on her that would give credence to his newly hatched suspicions; like a barely visible gesture or subtle signal to Petru that might indicate a hidden game … a tacit alliance. But there was none; just a girl having fun and intrigued by her trip on the sea. She was the arch opposite of furtive or underhand; everything about her was genuine.

In his shame, Tarquin now felt an overwhelming desire to sulk or cry or unleash an act of extreme violence on somebody or something. He felt like storming the bridge, wresting the wheel from the captain whilst punching anyone who tried to stop him, and then ramming the bloody *Dover Princess* at full speed into the nearest super tanker. His head throbbed, one of his ears was badly cut, and he boiled with rage at himself and his pathetic antics in front of these two young people. Folding the newspaper noisily, he thumped it down next to his coffee cup, livid blotches showing on both cheeks.

Constanta turned towards him with a look of concern.

"Are you all right, darling, or are we annoying you with our chatting?" she said affectionately. Her words acted like a lightning conductor under a crackling thunder cloud, pulling the negative energy out of him and earthing it in an instant.

"Oh … I'm okay … I think … just a bit hyped up," he said, managing a tight smile. "Just annoyed with myself, I suppose. I'm always being caught on the fucking hop!"

"Don't be hard on yourself, Mr Tarquin," Petru said earnestly. "You are not used to these things … you have no experience of it, whereas me and Constanta grew up with it and know the signs of trouble. That's why we are here … to protect you!"

"He's right, Tarquin," she said. "Don't kick yourself. I know I was a bit angry back there, but you have to act quickly in those situations, so don't take it the wrong way. In England the girls are expected to be girlie and the men expect to take charge in physical situations. But Romanian women are tough bitches … they can't afford to be girlie, and if they've been put through what I have in my training, they're tough bitches with attitude and moves!"

She leant forward laughing and gave Petru a high five.

"But that doesn't mean I don't like being treated 'girlie' sometimes," she said, turning to Tarquin, putting a finger on her chin and fluttering her eyelashes. She cocked her head teasingly. "I'm young … helpless … I need a daddy!"

Against his wishes, Tarquin was forced to laugh out loud at her histrionics and the residue of his anger evaporated.

*   *   *

"Slow down, Gus," Zoltan said down the telephone as he sat

reading a legal document on Sasha's sofa. "Just calmly tell me what has happened."

Gus resumed.

"As I said, we followed them out of town, expecting them to be heading west, yer know, towards his country place Bristol way, and he seemed to be going in the opposite direction ... yer know ... towards the southeast ... along the south circular. I couldn't work out what the geezer was playing at. There was three of them in the motor. but we thought no problem, we could handle it," Gus said nervously. "There was Oliver, a blond girl ... possibly his bit of fluff, and another huge geezer. We thought we had to go for it once we realized where they was heading.

"We just put two and two together and realised they was heading for Dover and a cross-channel ferry. We decided to stop 'em before they reached the terminal. I didn't think the bastard was going abroad, so we didn't have our passports."

"Mmm ... okay," Zoltan said, sounding displeased.

"I mean, yer said he'd be heading to his gaff in the countryside, so no way did I expect this," Gus said imploringly.

"So what did you do?" Zoltan said coldly.

"Well ... we ... er. decided to ram their motor once we got off the motorway; you know, once we was on a smaller road, and force them to stop. And that's what we done. We gave them a right could shunt from the back—no damage to our motor so don't worry—and as I thought, they pulled onto the hard shoulder. So me and Bob jumped out to take control.

"I handled Oliver no problem ... flattened him straight away, but then," he hesitated, "the tall blond girl who I told Bob to go easy on, did a sort of ... well, judo kick at me and caught me bloody head. I went down, Zoltan ... simple as that. Bob then grabbed the bitch, and fuck me she does a number on him 'n all, and kicks him like a frigging donkey in the nuts!"

"This was woman?" Zoltan said sarcastically.

"Was she and some, Z!" Gus said, reddening. "I reckon she was Eastern European ... I know the accent; no offence ... and she was tall, well tall. We wasn't expecting it, Z, not from a woman."

"Okay."

"When I got me senses back, they was already back in their vehicle and driving off. We chased them like the bloody clappers all the way to the ferry terminal, and then we had to stop or it would have been suicide. I'm not a pretty sight, though. Bloody great bruise on me left cheek. Bob's knee took a nasty hit n' all. I'm real sorry."

"Mmmm … I see," Zoltan said slowly. "This is bad news … but it is also good news."

There was a pause.

"It is?" Gus said tentatively.

"Think about it, my friend. The amount of protection a man hires is in direct balance to the value of his business. What your little adventure has told me is that Oliver's business is very valuable indeed! This is not so bad … and though I do not like my men being, well, outgunned, I can handle this little humiliation for what will be rich rewards at a later date!"

"Er … well … yes … yes … I like your way of thinking, Z. I hadn't thought of it like that," Gus said with a great sense of relief.

"As you know, my friend, Viktor has very considerable resources, very considerable indeed, but he doesn't want to use these with every encounter. In other words, we don't use a grenade to kill a fly!"

"Of course not, Z … that would be stupid," Gus agreed eagerly.

"But now that Oliver has chosen to pull out his pop gun … it seems only sensible that we … that we … *bring out our cannon and show him just who is in charge here*!" Zoltan said, raising his voice to a hysterical level suddenly, and causing Gus to jump.

"Q … Quite true, Z … I'm right with yer there!" he said placatingly. "We've got to show him the difference between the … the pussies and the proper bad cats in the jungle, and you and Viktor are the ones to do it!"

"Good … we're on the same page. Now take a few days off, rest up, and I will be in touch," Zoltan said impatiently.

"Sure thing, Z … nice speaking to yer," Gus said, waiting for Zoltan to hang up before snapping his own phone shut and letting out a huge sigh of relief.

Thomas Charrington

Chapter 23

Safely on board the ferry to St Malo, Oliver closed the door of his small cabin with a flex of his shoulder and threw his overnight bag onto the bed. Unzipping it, he pulled out his wash bag and pyjamas, some fresh underwear, and an alarm clock. He then rezipped it and placed it in a corner before taking off his shoes, plucking a book from his briefcase, and slumping back on the pillow.

He read and dozed for the first hour in a state of euphoric relaxation. They had made it at last, left the shores of England with their precious cargo without so much as an anxious moment. The plan was working with almost perfect precision. The only shadow in his mind was passing through French customs in the morning. Never in his long career as an antique dealer had he ever had more than a cursory glance in his vehicle during these crossings, and it was this which imbued him with confidence. But was this going to be the moment when everything changed?

By a horrible fluke, was there a new customs regime at the port, headed by a thrusting ambitious upstart, eager to prove himself? As he considered the scenario in the darkness of his cabin, his calmness began to evaporate. Images of the cabinet being confiscated by armed officers with him and Melvyn in handcuffs plumed up in his mind. His career would be over, his life really. Absolute humiliation.

The alarm beeped suddenly and snapped him from this wave of uncertainty. After a quick shower and freshen up, he made his way as prearranged to the carvery, where Melvyn was already waiting for him.

Oliver was completely at ease with Melvyn in virtually every respect, having known him for so long, but there were some settings where he felt as though Melvyn was almost a stranger. Seeing him sitting there at the starched linen tablecloth in a tweed jacket and tie was just such a moment. He felt uneasy, shy almost, as though Melvyn had morphed into someone unfamiliar. He'd seen him in a jacket and tie on many occasions, but these tended to be antiques trade fairs where the hustle and bustle around them diluted the effect. Perhaps it was simply that Melvyn suddenly had the appearance of his equal as opposed to his scruffy artisan employee, and at some deep psychological level this jarred. In addition to this, Melvyn himself felt oddly transformed as though he was now expected to make conversation on more lofty affairs than the mere curve of a cabriole leg, or the book matching on a pair of doors. Arriving at the table, he pulled out his chair and sat down.

"Well, we're here at last, Mel," he said with a jaunty spin. "I've been so looking forward to this moment, knowing that when we reached it, everything would be in place. Did you have a doze? It's been quite a hectic day, hasn't it?"

"No," Melvyn replied, gazing out on the sea. "I was doing some reading on the French Revolution and trying to get my head round why it all happened. My Mary gave me a book about it."

"Oh, really, Mel, that was very studious of you!" Oliver said, sounding faintly patronizing.

"It's all about the 'haves' and the 'have nots' to my way of thinking," Melvyn said with a very stern expression. "And that Mary Antoinette was a spoilt little madam, if you want my opinion. She thought she could do what she darn well pleased whilst half the population was starving; and the king was no better either, hunting crazy … didn't give a monkey's … so it's no surprise that that Robbis Pier took charge … you know … took control of the situation."

"Sorry, who, Melvyn?"

"That Robbis Pier man … who …who had the aristocrats' heads off by the bucketful."

Oliver looked at Melvyn for a few moments with a blank expression and then twigged.

"Oh … you mean Robespierre! Yes, he was a repulsive creature if ever there was one. Now, Mel, let's get the waiter's attention or we'll be here all night," he said looking over his shoulder and sticking his hand up.

"And that Mary Antoinette just spent her days in the palace, with her lady friends having fun," Melvyn continued. "You know … in all those fancy clothes and …"

"Ah, good," Oliver said to the newly arrived waiter. "We'll have a bottle of that red, please. Oh, Mel, sorry, would you like wine … or prefer beer?"

"No, as it happens I like wine at certain times," Melvyn said, looking extremely stiff.

"Okay, that's the one," Oliver said, closing the wine list. The waiter sloped off.

"But as I was saying," Melvyn persisted, "Mary Antoinette was just a good time girl, no sense of responsibilities. Lord knows, the French king and all his cronies were just take, take, take, and when you tax people too much, they eventually get fed up and revolt."

Melvyn carried on in this vein for a further ten minutes, divulging snippets from his new book and failing to spot the emptiness of Oliver's terse replies. "Yes, quite true, Melvyn" or "Really?" and "How interesting."

At last the waiter reappeared.

"Like to try this first, sir?" he said with a bored expression.

"No, just pour it, if you would," Oliver said with barely concealed urgency.

The waiter filled the two glasses and ambled off.

"It's something I need to learn more about, wine," Melvyn said, studying the liquid like it was a specimen in a test tube.

"Well, we're heading to the land of wine, my friend!" Oliver said, swilling the wine around his glass in a most accomplished manner before draining it in one protracted gulp. He smacked his lips and let out a long sigh of satisfaction. "Not bad, not bad at all," he muttered. "But these glasses are tiny!" With that he took hold of the bottle and sloshed more in. "Now, Mel, what are you having to eat? Steak and chips like me, or grilled sole?"

Melvyn hesitated for a moment.

"All right then … the steak please," he said closing the menu carefully.

"Great … makes it easy. God bless, old fellow! To a fruitful trip."

Oliver struck Melvyn's glass and took another long gulp whilst adopting the manner of an over-enthused bon viveur who isn't remotely interested in serious conversation. He wanted to unwind, have a loosely coiled conversation about nothing in particular … have a damn good laugh.

The day had had its tensions, its worries, and this was the moment to just sit back and savour their success so far. He needed to humour Melvyn and make him abandon his urge to speculate on the French Revolution as this could make for a dull dinner indeed. And to this end, he began trawling his mind for some amusing anecdotes to put a firm cork in that possibility.

*   *   *

Tarquin and his three companions had arrived in Reims at about nine pm. Having parked the car and deposited their bags and Percy in the Hotel Bristol, they were sitting down to some French cuisine in one of the small noisy restaurants which cluster along the Rue de Talleyrand. Dishevelled and blatantly nonlocal, they looked to the sharp-eyed waiter as rather untrustworthy guests … possibly of gypsy stock. Tarquin's left ear was a bloody congealed mess despite a cursory cleanup in the hotel, and crimson spots speckled his collar. The cuts on Constanta's hand and arm were also evident, and a turquoise bruise was beginning to manifest itself around her neck where Bob's arm had tightened earlier. They were all aware of being scrutinised by the other diners as they settled into their seats.

"So what's their fucking problem?" Constanta said under her breath, whilst scanning the other tables with a scowl.

"Guess we look a bit strange or something," Petru suggested as he took the menu from the waiter. "We don't fit in with this French people out for regular evening meal, do we! Look at us!"

Constanta looked at him for a few seconds. Then she erupted in a loud cackle and broke into fits of hysterical giggles. Tarquin broke away from his menu.

"Are you feeling all right, Constanta?" he said with a hint of disapproval.

"Don't worry, she always been like this, crazy and laughing for no reason," Petru said, grinning.

"No wonder they're looking at us, Tarquin," she stuttered through spurts of giggling. "We …We come in here speaking half in Romanian, half in English. I look like shit, like I just escaped from the hangman's noose, and you look like Sherlock Holmes after the hound of the Baskervilles grabbed his ear …" She trailed off with tears rolling down her face.

"What on earth are you jabbering about?" Tarquin said, peering over his menu at her and casting a furtive glance at the other diners. "And what's this about Sherlock Holmes?"

"You look like him, darling, so serious, and with that … that big tweed coat with the tartan design," she said, giggling uncontrollably and wiping her eyes with a tissue.

Tarquin shook his head and continued with the menu.

"You know … I don't get you," he said suddenly, staring at her again. "You've just kicked the living daylights out of a pair of bruisers in a scary life and death struggle on the road, and here you are, giggling like a fifteen-year-old schoolgirl who hasn't a care in the world. It just doesn't add up!"

"Oh come on, old man … loosen up! I just letting out some bad energy. You English … so fucking stiff!" With that, she burst out laughing again at the indignant expression on Tarquin's face.

An hour and a carafe of red wine later, they sat back from the table, replete and relaxed. Tarquin went ahead and collected Percy for his evening walk, and the trio then drifted back onto the street. Not ready for bed, they took a stroll to see the famous Cathedral of Notre-Dame in all its floodlit splendour. Late as it was, the streets were pulsing with life. Young couples in their best clothes meandered tipsily along the pavements exchanging noisy insults with each other, laughing and shrieking in the balmy night air.

Eventually they reached the Rue du Tresor, and turning a corner were confronted by the walls of the Cathedral rearing up before them—a gargantuan edifice of sculpted stone. The dark gargoyles, both hideous and magnificent, stretched out from their bleached stone anchorings above them with a demonic ferocity to defend their bastion. In his elevated mood, Tarquin gazed up in awe at these loyal guards and fancied he had two such entities of his own, red in tooth and claw, ready to spring into mortal combat to protect him.

Reims was alive, vibrant, and Tarquin felt a rush of exuberance at wandering so far from his cosy London life. He was on an adventure, a mad road trip with an even madder purpose; to discover whether his seemingly respectable neighbour was in fact an antiques fraudster. Diana would have scoffed at such an absurd course of action, and this made him smile. He realized he wasn't missing her much … if at all. He had other priorities. More acutely engaging to him now was his predicament. Someone was hunting him, and the creatures this puppet master employed were dangerous and driven.

*　　　*　　　*

Viktor stood in a warehouse in St Petersburg with a small group of men looking at a printing press when he felt his mobile vibrate in his pocket.

"Zoltan, why so late? I'm in the plant; I can't hear you in here! Wait a minute."

Barging through some swing doors into an office, he slumped down in an easy chair.

"You still there?" he shouted.

"Yes, Father, I can hear you fine, you don't need to shout now," Zoltan replied with trepidation. "I ... er ... wanted to let you know how things were shaping up regarding Oliver and the cabinet ... there's been a bit of trouble ... not serious."

"What trouble?" Viktor said, his face hardening.

Zoltan described how Oliver had taken an unexpected route out of London and it wasn't until the last moment that they realized he was heading across the channel.

"So you are idiot as well?"

"Why should I expect him to go in that direction?" Zoltan said nervously.

"Zoltan, *never* presume to know what people are going to do! If he's gone to France, he's gone for a reason, and we should be following him to find out what that reason is. But the two idiots you are controlling ... or supposed to be controlling ... did not have their passports, so they stood on quayside and waved them good-bye!"

"No, Father. Because they are dedicated men and prepared to take risk, they decided to ram them before the port ... force Oliver off the road and confront him," Zoltan said, swallowing, "which they did."

"And ruined my vehicle!"

"No, it is unharmed. But we think Oliver had some protection."

"What do you mean?"

"He was not alone in that car. He had two other people. One was a tall blond woman and the other was a guy. The boys said she was a Russian, and a martial arts expert."

Viktor remained silent, so he felt compelled to continue.

"She took out Gus, and ... and then she did the same to Bob. They weren't expecting it, Father ... our boys are not used to fighting women. She had surprise on her side ... they could do nothing. They managed to get away this time."

There was a long pause, and then Viktor's voice came back quieter, more measured and infinitely more menacing.

"Zoltan, am I hearing you correctly? You just said that Oliver … that Oliver had protection?"

"Yes, Father."

"And they got better of our boys?"

"Yes … so it seems … this time."

"Are they all right?"

"Yes, just superficial … bad bruising, cuts. They chased them all the way to the ferry terminal after that, but … but …" Zoltan said quietly.

"So Oliver and his protection are in France, and we don't know where or why they're there?" Viktor said, thinking aloud. There was another long pause.

"Right, Zoltan, it's obvious to me that Oliver has something big up his sleeve."

"Exactly what I thought," Zoltan agreed, with a sense of relief.

"Something that he needs to protect. Oliver is becoming more of a man these days … coming up through the ranks. Good. He must get ready to fight like an officer. If he's away, then we will pay his 'empty' house in Gloucestershire a little visit and see what we can find. Sammy is unfortunately our best man for discreet break-ins, and I need him elsewhere … and those two idiots will go and get themselves caught."

He went silent for a moment, and Zoltan heard him thinking.

"All right, I'm going to send him with them, but just for twenty-four hours," he said at last. "He's got a flight on Sunday evening, so let them know they'll pay a heavy price if he misses it. Let's just hope Oliver is away for a week or so; it'll make our lives a bit easier."

"Okay, Father. Sorry to bring you bad news. I'll tell the boys."

"Zoltan," Viktor said firmly, "whatever Oliver is doing … it is big; I can feel it in my bones. I'll call you when I have done some thinking."

Without waiting for a reply, he closed off.

Chapter 24

The next morning, as planned, Oliver and Melvyn arrived at Frederic's house in a small village outside Laval a little before ten o'clock. Melvyn had never seen Oliver in such high spirits, his normally taciturn nature having given way to a torrent of conversation from the moment they left the port. Customs hadn't so much as given them a second glance, and with this hurdle behind them, another worry had evaporated. They parked the van behind a high hedge on the street outside Frederic's house to try and stifle his urge to inspect their cargo.

"Just let me do the talking, Mel," Oliver said quietly to Melvyn as they approached the front door. "We've got to be a little careful here."

They knocked, and there was the muffled shout of a woman inside. A few moments later the door flew open and Frederic stood there grinning.

"Bonjour, Oliver!" he said, embracing him warmly on the doorstep. "And bonjour to you too, Melvyn. I don't often have the pleasure of seeing you; Oliver likes to keep you hidden!"

"Hi, Frederic," Melvyn replied awkwardly.

"Come in and have some coffee and something to eat. Where are you parked?" he said, looking quizzically over Oliver's shoulder towards the road.

"We're just down there behind that hedge. I didn't want to block the drive," Oliver said in a carefree way.

Frederic moved across the grass to get a peek.

"Oh yes, I see … a Toyota, mmm … reliable, very good."

They wandered through his front door.

"So you have nothing to show me this time, how disappointing!" Frederic said, taking a good look at Oliver.

"I'm sorry, Frederic. Perhaps on the way back from Paris," he said apologetically.

"No problem … let's get the coffee going."

Isabelle started gathering some cups and saucers noisily.

"But you've brought a van, my friend, so you intend to use it for something, I presume?"

"You're quite right there!" Oliver said, looking furtive. "As I mentioned on the phone, a friend has bought a largish house near Chavenay—you know, just this side of Paris—and wants me to collect some of the pieces she doesn't want. A couple of wardrobes, I believe, and a side table. She wasn't very specific. Nothing of great value, but I should be able to make it worth my while plus have a little break. And Melvyn here needs a bit of time off, don't you, Mel?"

"Yeah, sort of," Melvyn said, looking out of the window. "I like France."

"You English are buying up all our beautiful 'ouses, Oliver!" Frederic said with a chuckle. "But I don't blame you; property is so expensive over there, especially in London. It's gone crazy, uh? All those people crammed into such a small space! Whereas 'ere in France we still 'ave empty roads!"

"Unfortunately, Frederic, we have a very generous welfare system over the channel which draws people from all over the world like moths to a flame," Oliver said with a sigh. "But I think there's a storm brewing on the horizon."

"Possibly," Frederic agreed. "Let's 'ope it doesn't affect us too badly. Anyway, your trip sounds good … wish I was coming with you," he said wistfully. "Nothing I like more than sifting through old 'ouses. Come on, let's go through to my showroom and sit down. Isabelle will bring the coffee soon." He led the way through a broad doorway.

"And you can give me your opinion on these pieces I just bought," he said, pulling open a drawer on a small dresser.

They stayed with Frederic for a further hour discussing his latest purchases and the state of the antiques trade in France in general, and then bade their farewells.

By twelve o' clock they were back on the road and heading for their true destination, which was certainly not Chavenay. It was Troyes.

*   *   *

A few hours earlier, Fabien had awoken with a start and noticed his heart was pumping fast. He'd had a night of fitful dreams, even though he and Cecile had enjoyed a romantic evening in the Place de Republique at her favourite fish restaurant. She lay asleep in a maelstrom of crumpled sheets and pillows, breathing deeply, her auburn hair tousled like a rag doll. Her petite white bottom displayed itself cheekily in the dim morning light and made him smile as he headed quietly to the kitchen.

But as he waited for the coffee to brew, the full enormity of his decision to aid Oliver in this, his most brazen of forgeries, flooded his mind like an electric current. This was it! The day had dawned, at the end of which he would be irrevocably involved in a crime of monstrous proportions. He looked at his hands and noticed they were trembling.

Cecile loved him because he was an honest, upstanding man; a decent human being with a good job, who by sheer chance was the recipient of an unexpected windfall. To be blunt, Cecile loved him for someone he was not.

She had no idea he was in cahoots with a fraudster who could at any moment get caught and ruin her future husband's life and, by default, her own, and her children's. Yes, *he, Fabien,* was the fraud! The real test must surely be whether her love for him would remain true once she was furnished with all the facts, and he doubted that. There would be no gasp of admiration followed by smouldering passion from Cecile; there would be a blazing row and a hasty farewell. No, he couldn't tell her … not yet. That would be suicide.

He just had to pray that Oliver knew what he was doing. At some point in the future, he would probably confess. By that time she would have grown used to the lifestyle and would be more inclined to accept his motivations; besides, she would have to admit that it had been an outstanding success and all risk of exposure was now minimal. But was it? Sometimes fraud took years to be uncovered. He looked out over the grey Parisian dawn, his face furrowed with concern as these contradictions once again raged inside his brain.

Suddenly some slender fingers slid through the curls at the back of his head and made him jump. The sleepy, smiling face of Cecile greeted him as he turned guiltily, like a child caught doing something he shouldn't. Standing in a short silk negligee, she looked up at him with innocent, loving eyes.

"Bonjour, mon cheri," she said giggling softly. "Mon tigre! The bed is chaos … what did you *do* to me last night!"

"Ah, cherie! You gave me a fright! Was thinking about work; didn't hear you sneaking up on me," Fabien said, wrapping his arms around her and trying to appear carefree. "Yes, it was a good evening. I hope you enjoyed yourself as much as me."

"Enjoy myself, Fabien? What's happened to you suddenly … so formal? Have you become all English with an iron post up your bottom! I haven't seen you let go like that since we first started dating. You were a wild animal … and I loved every minute of it!" she said, slapping his backside.

Fabien pulled away and began to pour the coffee.

"Now, cherie, you're heading to work now, aren't you?"

"Yes, I suppose so," she said with a sigh. "They've been so good to me at work and didn't mind when I mentioned I'd be a little late. What time are you meeting the architect, bad boy?" she said, wriggling up against him and gazing adoringly into his face.

"Who?" Fabien said without thinking. "Oh, the architect! Thought you said something else," he said quickly. "Er … between ten and eleven tomorrow morning."

"Don't know why I couldn't have been there … you're only *discussing* things with him at this stage. I could have got on with measuring curtains and other things. I certainly wouldn't have eavesdropped … I want this garden house to be a surprise!"

"I know you wouldn't, Cherie, but … but something may have slipped out by mistake and given the game away. Besides, how often have I given you my card to go and buy some beautiful shoes, uh? Isn't that more exciting than measuring some silly old curtains?"

"Fabien," Cecile said sternly, "you need to realize that curtains as well as shoes are very close to a woman's heart and should not be treated flippantly!"

She burst out laughing at the look on his face, and turning like a ballerina on her bare toes, disappeared back to the bedroom.

*   *   *

Tarquin felt ghastly as he manoeuvred the Voyager onto the A4 out of Reims. His head was thick from the wine and his neck was much stiffer than the previous evening. He couldn't turn it properly and was heavily reliant on the wing mirrors. Although now clean and in a fresh set of clothes, his ear was extremely painful if he so much as brushed it by mistake.

With the time at 12.55pm, they would arrive at Troyes somewhere around 2.30, which was much too early for their rendezvous with Oliver. But they wanted to get a feel for the geography of the place prior to his arrival so that they had a better chance of tailing him when he did show up.

Constanta and Petru sat in the back chatting, so Percy had the front passenger seat all to himself. He stood with his back legs on the seat and his paws on the dashboard looking forward eagerly. A small globule of egg yolk hung on his whiskery black chin, the remnants of his master's breakfast, which had been secreted back to the hotel room earlier.

Tarquin looked ahead to the evening when they would all

converge on Troyes train station. Would the red Toyota van that Constanta's detective work had revealed show up at the right time, or had there been a change of plan since Oliver wrote his "itinerary"? Was Oliver on his own, or did he have accomplices? Who was the man, Fabien, they were meeting at the station at 6.30pm, and where had he come from? Were they getting themselves into even more danger by closing in on this gang of fraudsters? What if they were spotted? Judging by the naked brutality he witnessed only yesterday, it seemed highly probable that all these people were of the same ilk—vicious and violent. They would think nothing of dispatching a pair of Romanians and an English oaf who stuck his neck out a little too far.

He imagined the headlines in the local paper.

"Three bodies found in the Foret d'Orient, badly disfigured. Police are checking dental records with missing persons in the region."

"You okay, darling?" Constanta said from the backseat, putting her fingertips on his shoulder. "You look a bit long in the face. If you're worried about things, then that's good; we need you on your toes now. Here, take these two ibuprofen tablets. They'll make you feel a lot better and help your neck."

She handed them to him with a small bottle of water.

"Okay, thanks," he said, tossing them back without a thought and gulping some water.

"No, I was just thinking about meeting up with these people, that's all," he said. "Wondering what they'll be like … you know, whether we can carry out our plan and get photos of the cabinet and so on."

"Look, Tarquin, this was never going to be easy, but we're gonna do it and we're gonna do it well. Have faith! You have two very smart people behind you," she chuckled. "Literally … but we will not be in the backseat, darling, we're gonna be right beside you, kicking their arses!"

"Speak for yourself, Constanta," Petru chuckled. "I think I prefer backseat. You are liability!!"

"Oh yeah? Well, let me tell you both something," Constanta said fiercely. "When all this is finished, you're both going to be kissing my arse!"

She threw her head back and laughed; a deep growly laugh that seemed to demonstrate to Tarquin an innate confidence. Suddenly his mind took him back to the previous night and he saw the Cathedral of Notre Dame standing gigantically before him, the gargoyles thrusting forwards, angry and fearless against the night sky. It seemed to stand in judgement over him, like a looming intolerant member of his ancestry waiting to see if he was up to the task. He flexed his jaw and shifted slightly in his seat.

"I am thinking that it is best we don't confront them tonight, if possible," Constanta said from the backseat. "I'm a bit tired, and I think you are as well, darling. I think it would be ideal if we discovered where they are staying and then had an early night somewhere nearby."

"But this could be problem," Petru interrupted. "What if they move on when we are asleep? This whole trip would be waste of time!"

"Petru, I said ideally. If it looks like they're not hanging around, then we have to act immediately. But they probably will stay somewhere local; don't forget, Oliver has come from a long way today … you know, that place on the coast."

"St Malo," Tarquin said.

"Yes, so he's probably going to be tired himself."

"Possible," Petru said, unconvinced.

"Look, let's be honest, we simply don't know what the hell's going to happen," Tarquin said. "He may stay in Troyes tonight, or he may deliver the cabinet, if he still has it, and move on somewhere else. If that's the case, then we have to jump in right then and confront them."

"Wow! Has the dog woken up?" Constanta grinned, whilst giving his shoulder a tiny squeeze.

*   *   *

Back in London, Bob scrabbled for his vibrating mobile in the folds of an old blanket.

"Hi, mate, I've been trying to call yer!" Gus said to him gruffly.

"Sorry, mate, I had a skinful after you dropped me off, and I forgot where me phone was," Bob said defensively. "Fell asleep on the couch till five this morning … bloody freezing."

"Okay, but get with it, mate, we're on the move tomorrow. I spoke with Zoltan last night and told him the bad news."

"Oh yeah? So what did he say? Bet he was well pissed off," Bob said, doing his belt up.

"Well, as we discussed, I weren't going to tell him the truth, was I. That would have landed the pair of us in a right spot of bother. So listen careful, okay, in case he calls yer and asks any awkward questions."

"Shoot, mate," Bob said.

Gus told him what he'd said to Zoltan. That they had tried to stop Oliver leaving Dover, by shunting him off the road. That they came face to face with a pair of martial arts experts and had been out gunned, because they were gentlemen and not in the habit of hitting women.

Bob snorted.

"And what did he say to that?"

"Well, let's say he wasn't happy. It's a first for me to have me arse spanked by a frigging woman! Pussy whipped! What sort of a creature was that? A bloody gorgeous bitch with a kick like a mule! I mean, where did she come from? Didn't sound English, that's for sure. I reckon she was one of those tough Russian bitches with balls like coconuts. Me bloody face is well bruised. I just didn't see the cow coming, did you?"

"Mate, let it go. You didn't see it coming, and neither did I. Don't forget she whacked me in the goolies as well. Shit happens. We expect girls to be girls … not fucking eastern block fighting machines. Now we know, don't we. She had the element of surprise. Next time I'll crack her over the skull with me wrench and see how she likes that!" he said with a leer.

"Well, it wasn't all bad," Gus resumed. "Zoltan's sort of

excited by this whole thing and reckons Oliver is up to something big. He can smell the lolly!"

"I bet he bloody can," Bob said with feeling.

"As long as no one in the company finds out, I don't bloody care," Gus said. "Let's face it, we'd be the laughing stock of—"

He trailed off suddenly.

"Oh shit! Talk of the fucking devil; it's him on the blower now. I'll catch up with you later, mate," he said, cutting Bob off.

He stumbled to his feet and stood very erect.

"Zoltan? Can you hear me?" Gus said nervously.

"Yes, just," came the clipped reply. "I want to let you know what your instructions are. I spoke with Viktor and he came to the same conclusion as me."

"Which is ... er ... what?" Gus said.

"We want you to go to Oliver's house in Gloucestershire and do some digging. We need to find out what his game is. Look for diaries, notes, any antiques books that are lying around. We think we know, but need confirmation. Be very careful, his house is probably alarmed, and you'll have the police round very quickly ... probably have no warning. Also, he may have alerted somebody local that trouble may be coming his way, so be very vigilant. Do recon during daylight hours and make your move soon after one am. Country people go to bed early and get up early. If it looks dodgy, get out of there. Do you remember the place?"

"Er ... sort of. It was a long time ago, Z, so it's a bit hazy, to be honest," Gus replied.

"Do you have a pen?"

"Yeah," Gus said.

"It's called Strupe Hall, near Marston Meysey. I'll give you precise details shortly. Get your map out and get familiar with the area first. As I remember, the lanes are very narrow and difficult to navigate. Really check it out and remember in country you'll be noticed much more than London. Get some parcel delivery plates on the van or you'll stick out like wolf's bollocks. How are you feeling ... is the neck better?"

"A bit better, but still painful. I can drive okay. Can we leave it till tomorrow?"

"Yes, that's okay, but no later. How is Bob? He came off better than you, no?"

"Yep ... I took the big hit. He was lucky this time."

"Oliver will pay, don't have any doubts about that. But we need to act while he's away. This window may be small," Zoltan said firmly. "Call me if you need to discuss anything more, but I'll send those details later."

"Okay, Z, no problem," Gus said, waiting for Zoltan to close off before slumping back into his easy chair.

*   *   *

As the first traffic sign to Troyes glided past Tarquin, alerting him to their imminent arrival, Oliver and Melvyn were enjoying a short break at the side of a country road somewhere between Le Mans and Orleans. They sat at the entrance to a farm track on one of many blankets Melvyn had stowed in the van, eating the bread and cheese bought earlier in Laval.

"God, this is bloody gorgeous!" Oliver said as he helped himself to a chunk of Brie. "I really can't think of anywhere I'd rather be at this precise moment."

"I'm with you there, Oliver," Melvyn agreed as he broke open some French bread with his gnarled thumbs and covered his legs in crumbs. "But the truth is it scares me when things go too smooth ... it's like, well, like someone is setting us up for a fall."

"That's a bit gloomy, isn't it, Mel?" Oliver said, looking at Melvyn with slight disapproval. "Why should we have to fall? We've planned this whole thing like a military campaign, and so far it's yielded just the results you'd expect."

"Yeah, I know what you mean ... the logic of it. But all the same, it's just something in my guts which sort of resists feeling too relaxed. I mean, it's going great, really good, but my experience is that when your guard is down, that's when it strikes!"

"What, for God's sake, Mel?" Oliver said, raising his voice.

"I don't know! I suppose I sometimes think that we're being watched by a higher force, and it sort of lets you have a good time for a bit and then thinks, right, let's shake things up now; they're getting cocky."

"Oh come on, Mel!" Oliver said mockingly. "A higher force? Surely you don't really believe that. There is no higher force judging you! There's just you and the world, Mel, you, your wits, and your skills to use as best you can. You've fought for this. You've paid the price in bloody hard work over the years, and no one's going to snatch that away. Enjoy it, my friend. God knows you've earned it!"

"Yeah, I s'pose you're right!" Melvyn conceded. "There's just one thing that niggles at the back of my mind."

"What?"

"Why the hell did we never hear any more from Zoltan?"

"Because I told him in no uncertain terms that his accusations were ludicrous! That there was no way we could be doing a forgery of that calibre. I told him he was deluded."

"You've got a blooming nerve!" Melvyn snorted loudly. "He watched me at the Wallace, and like you said, he knew I was up to something. That guy's not stupid. I just think … just think he wouldn't have given up so easy. He doesn't let go; he's obstinate, he's angry, he hates us both."

"True! You can't blame the man. We've become quite successful."

"Exactly. He's going through a messy divorce, and the way you talked about him was like the guy was explosive! He'd do anything to get back at you. And this is what worries me; he's gone quiet after all those threats. But why? It just doesn't ring true, especially when you remember that bastard of a father of his … you know, Viktor. Viktor doesn't miss a trick and would be onto us if there was so much as a whisker of chance you were doing something big."

"Mel, stop being so melodramatic, for pity's sake!" Oliver said, slapping Melvyn on the shoulder. "You're getting the jitters, that's all. It's understandable. We're about to break through our boundaries. This is our biggest ever!"

"True. I'm getting soft or something," Melvyn said with a weak smile. "Guess I'm just a worrier at heart; always waiting for something to happen." *And something will happen, my friend. It's brewing … I can feel it in my blood.*

*   *   *

"This doesn't look like a medieval town to me!" Constanta said as they drove into Troyes down a long carriageway lined with dreary modern buildings and countless billboards.

"We're in the outskirts, that's why," Tarquin replied. "The old town is much farther in, and I can assure you it is medieval. I've done a spot of reading about it, and I don't think you'll be disappointed."

"Wow. I can't wait," she said, her eyes flickering over the passing scenery.

"You'll like it. It's got character and loads of history … and a McDonald's, which I'm sure will cheer you up!"

"Oh, in this case, Mr Tarquin, she will be very happy," Petru said, elbowing Constanta.

"Like you're interested in history, Petru!" Constanta said, giving him a surly glance.

"Right, children," Tarquin interrupted. "I need your full attention please, to find the train station, which in case you didn't know is called La Gare in French."

"La what?" Constanta said, leaning forward.

"La Gare! G. A. R. E," he emphasized.

Gradually the real Troyes began to appear and was met with admiring exclamations from the two Romanians.

"Jesus, these buildings look old … really old," Constanta said, gazing at a house which was leaning ominously towards its neighbour. "Why all the shutters? These people are crazy for shutters."

"The French love shutters," Tarquin said. "They're part of

the culture. Probably have their origins in keeping houses safe … deterring thieves," he continued, beginning to sound like a bona fide tourist guide.

He suddenly swung the car to the right. "Got it!" he exclaimed. "See the sign there, 'La Gare'?"

"Okay, okay … it says take a right at the end," Constanta said with her face next to Tarquin's shoulder.

They carried on for a further five minutes turning this way and that, and suddenly at the end of a short avenue of trees stood the "Gare de Troyes" in grand lettering.

"Voila!" Constanta said smiling. "It's party time."

"Is this your one word in French, Constanta," Petru said mischievously.

"At least I have one, darling," she replied sharply. "And it's actually three now, I just added La Gare."

"Quite an impressive building!" Tarquin said, driving up to the main façade of the station and gazing up at a series of high arched windows. A tricolour fluttered happily on a long white pole above a balustrade, and a big ornamental clock showed the time. It was five past three.

"There seems to be car park in front of station and also to the side … over there," Petru said, pointing through a gap to another open area of cracked tarmac.

"Right," Constanta said, surveying the scene and getting a feel for the layout. "This is the great Troyes station! So it's possible he can park in either of these two places. If they go there"—she pointed to the spaces under the trees—"we'll see them immediately, but over there in that big space it will be a bit more tricky."

"Sure, we'll take up position under the trees so we can see who comes in."

"No, that's too obvious, Tarquin. Don't forget we have English numbers like him. I think we need to be hidden … better, just a little back from the end. We don't want him to clock us in any possible way. Perhaps he's not alone. We can see very well from that position, and when he arrives, Petru and me will need to get out and see where he parks and then shadow him. It's important we see who he's meeting, you know, that guy Fabien, so we'll probably go into the station. You can stay here in the car and be ready to move. When we come out, get the fuck ready … we need to be right behind him. How's your fuel, darling?"

"Fine at the moment, but we'll fill up. Not sure how far we're driving later."

"Too right! This is getting interesting. What the fuck are these people doing? Why are   they taking the cabinet to this place?" Constanta said, close to Tarquin's ear so he felt the warmth of her breath. "They obviously have some plan up their sleeve which …"

"Wow, that's a good guess!" Petru said mockingly.

"Okay. arsehole … you explain what they're doing," she said, glancing back sourly.

"We got to wait, that's all," Petru replied.

"Look, I'm hungry," she said suddenly. "Do we need to see anything else here?"

"Perhaps check if there is a train arriving at 6.30?" Petru suggested.

"Go on then. We'll wait here!"

He jumped out.

"Let's check to see if this is the only entrance, Tarquin. Drive around that car park and make sure. It would be disaster if there was some exit we knew nothing about."

They did a circuit and confirmed it was watertight. Moving back to the train entrance, Petru appeared and jumped in.

"Well?" Constanta said.

"A train arrives 6.28 from Paris, and at 6.42 train arrives from Dijon," Petru said, looking at a small piece of paper. "And he gave me this map of the city," he said, handing Tarquin a folded tourist map.

"Good, so the plan Oliver wrote on that notepad seems to fit, you know, his … itinererarary," Constanta said self-consciously.

Tarquin burst out laughing.

"What's your fucking problem?" she said, giving him a sharp look.

"Sorry … that just sounded funny, that's all," he said, smiling.

"Oh ha ha ha! You're soo funny Tarquin!"

He gave Percy a few indulgent strokes.

"Shall we have some food now, Mr Tarquin?" Petru intervened, "We got some time to kill, I think."

"Sure … I'm starving," Constanta agreed.

They parked and went into a grand five-storey building on the corner with a red neon sign above the entrance. The restaurant was ground level, but the floors above had a series of balconies with elaborate wrought iron balustrades, giving the impression that this was once a more opulent residence. After lunch they opened up a map and huddled around it.

"This shows a ring road with eight major routes off it," Tarquin said, gazing at the road map on his knee. "And these basically head off in every conceivable direction. If he is leaving Troyes, this will probably be the road he takes; probably, not certainly. For all we know he may be staying in some swanky hotel here, in which case we just have to stick to him like glue."

"At least he's in a red van," Constanta said.

"We hope! But that's as long as nothing's changed. If he's not in a red Toyota, then we're relying on me recognizing him, which is going to be very unlikely!"

"Tarquin, relax! You will recognize the bastard," Constanta said with certainty.

"I don't think he's going to hotel, Mr Tarquin," Petru said from the backseat. "He has cabinet in his van, and I think he wants to take it somewhere first. This is valuable thing, not to leave in street."

"Mmmm … true," Tarquin said thoughtfully. "That's a good point. If he still has the cabinet on board, then he's going to drop it somewhere first … possibly a house here in Troyes or somewhere outside. Look, we don't have a clue what he's up to.

Let's face it; there are countless possibilities."

With that, he started the engine and they began their circumnavigation of the city.

*   *   *

Later, as Constanta and Petru stood in the station tourist office booking a hotel, Oliver and Melvyn had just joined the A5 motorway in the final leg of the journey towards Troyes. Coming to his senses after a light afternoon nap, Oliver realized it was time to take control again and navigate them through the streets to the station. Melvyn had done well, despite driving in that awkward hunched position he preferred—like a wax dummy wedged against the steering wheel.

Fabien had boarded the 4.56 train to Troyes at the Gare de l'Est in Paris and was flicking through a book on Classic Garden Houses. This was to underpin his alibi … give him some ideas so he could report back to Cecile with some authority.

As Troyes drew closer, Fabien, Oliver, and Melvyn all felt the approach of a life-changing event just over the horizon. For Oliver and Melvyn, this change was not so much of a financial nature; it was more the approach of a momentous milestone. They were venturing onto a rarified stage where their skills and expertise would be tested on a level well beyond their previous experience.

For Fabien, what approached was a defining moment in his life; he was saying good-bye to his old honest self. By the end of the day he would no longer be the innocent, principled man he had been all his life; he would be a willing accomplice in a very serious fraud. Metaphorically speaking, he was about to ride, with a mixture of excitement and intense foreboding, into the realms of criminality, on the back of a horse called Desperation.

"Pull in at this next layby, Mel," Oliver said, pointing ahead. "I think it's best if I take over now."

The Toyota came to a halt, and they both climbed out and

stretched.

"Gawd, am I glad that's over!" Melvyn groaned, arching his back.

"You've done a straight two and a half hours, Mel, so I dare say you need a break!" Oliver said with a chuckle.

"Yeah, feels like it. Funnily enough, I quite enjoyed a spell of driving. Don't do much at home, and the French roads are lovely and empty."

"That's true," Oliver agreed. "Well, hop in and let's get on. Only another half an hour. We'll be there, say …," he glanced at his watch, "just before six, which is fine."

Twenty-five minutes went by before they came off the ring road and headed towards the town centre.

"If I remember correctly, the station is on the west side of the old town … down this way," Oliver mumbled.

"Boulevard Delestraint … good … over the lights … Boulevard Victor Hugo. Yes, now I remember. Over the roundabout … Boulevard Carnot. This is it … and … take a left! Gare de Troyes!"

Chapter 25

"Fuck, it's them!" Constanta hissed loudly, getting lower in her seat. "They've arrived!!And guess what they're driving ... a *red Toyota!*"

She giggled excitedly.

"Bull's-eye!" Petru said, slapping her leg.

"Well done, detective!" Tarquin whispered, his head swivelling as they passed. Percy leapt from the front to the backseats repeatedly, sensing excitement, till Tarquin grabbed him and held him on his lap.

"Right, Petru. Let's go," she snapped, opening the car door. "Don't stare at them ... we just got to keep an eye on where they park and who they meet, okay?"

"Sure thing, boss."

"And Tarquin, be ready to move, for fuck's sake. I'll call to let you know when they meet him and what they're doing, okay?"

"Thanks."

"Hope there are not two red Toyota vans with English plates here today!" Petru said, trying to keep up with Constanta's long stride.

"Ha ha ... you're soo funny, Petru. I'm dying here," she said breathily over her shoulder. "There they are ... parking by that small house."

"That's a toilet."

"Whatever, let's just wait on this bench and keep watch on them."

They sat down by the station entrance, their eyes glued to the red van, people milling around them.

Presently a stocky, middle-aged man climbed out rather stiffly and stretched. Another man emerged from the passenger side and came round the van. He was slighter in build but with a mop of black hair and distinctly rounded shoulders. They both looked surprisingly respectable in checked shirts and well-cut trousers. The driver scanned the car park and then glanced at his watch. After a brief word to his partner, he disappeared into the lavatory.

The dark-haired man leaned with his back against the van and took a long thoughtful look at the station building, as though absorbing the architecture with some interest. A few minutes later the stocky man reappeared and, having taken his jacket from the driver's seat, locked the van. They both then strolled casually towards the station entrance and passed Constanta and Petru who were having an apparently animated conversation in Romanian.

"Fuck me, they were so close!" Constanta said excitedly under her breath.

"This people are not hard men," Petru muttered, looking over his shoulder. "They look smart, like businessmen."

"Sure, I know what you mean. Not like those bastards from yesterday," Constanta agreed.

"I think the driver must be Oliver," Petru offered, "and the other guy is his helper. Did you see his hands?"

"No, darling, I didn't," Constanta said, stretching out her legs and pointing her toes.

After a few minutes, the dark-haired man reappeared and walked back to the van where he took up his position as before. The time was 6.25 pm.

They kept up a casual banter in Romanian for the next few minutes and then heard the arrival of a train.

"Very good," Petru said quietly, "it is on time."

A further few minutes went by, and then Constanta put her hand briefly on Petru's shoulder and wandered into the marble-floored station. People were meandering about in all directions, reading newspapers, chatting, and gazing at the arrivals and departures' board. She spotted Oliver by the entrance to the platforms. A large number of newly arrived passengers were winding through a gate, displaying their tickets to a bored-looking official.

Suddenly a lean, fresh-faced man emerged from the bustling crowd and, having handed over his ticket, headed straight to Oliver. He greeted him warmly in English. They spoke for a moment or so, then made their way casually towards the entrance. This was Fabien, she figured; much younger than Oliver, and clearly nervous. She noticed the reserved almost awkward way they interacted and decided he was more a business colleague than a true friend; their body language was clumsy.

She moved closer in behind them, just another girl engrossed in her mobile. But her ears were straining for information. Then suddenly it came, unmistakably. In the gush of conversation, the word "cabinet" popped out like a sweet cherry. A ripple of excitement coursed through her stomach. They really had hit the target.

"No, Oliver," Fabien said firmly. "I think we leave it in the van tonight and probably most of tomorrow as the 'ouse is damp, especially the ground floor. I want to open the shutters and windows before we bring it in. We can't afford to risk it."

"Is it safe?" Oliver asked.

Fabien laughed.

"Of course it's safe! You've seen it. Don't you remember those 'uge iron gates at the entrance with that big rusty chain and lock? No vehicle can get in, and the whole estate is surrounded by a wall."

"Okay … if you're sure," Oliver agreed, nodding. "Probably not a bad idea. Melvyn can build the chest tomorrow and we'll put it straight inside. We don't want sudden changes in humidity causing problems."

"The garret is much less damp; it's drafty and the air is

clearer," Fabien said.

"Well, that's good. The house is about half an hour away, isn't it?" Oliver said, trying to dodge an incessant stream of people pushing against them.

"Approximately."

"Wonderful. It's great to see you, Fabien ... away from London. The day of reckoning has arrived!" He patted the young man's shoulder briefly as they headed out into the car park. Constanta peeled away to join Petru. It was time to move.

They strode hurriedly across the tarmac and back into the Voyager where Percy immediately leapt onto Constanta's lap and licked her face feverishly.

"This is it, Tarquin," Constanta said, holding Percy away. "Don't fuck this up, pleeeease!"

"Wait for the moment, Mr Tarquin, they are talking," Petru muttered from the backseat. "I'll tell you when they move."

After five minutes of discussion, the three men climbed into the Toyota, did a loop, and then headed towards the entrance.

"Okay, Mr Tarquin, they are moving!" Petru snapped, looking over his shoulder. "Just wait till they come past ... which is ... wait ... wait ... wait. *Okay, now!*"

Tarquin lurched forward and stalled.

"You fucking idiot, Tarquin!" Constanta shouted. "What's the matter with you!"

Tarquin fumbled with keys and gears for a few moments without saying a word and then, having restarted the engine, roared forwards, tyres squealing. Beads of sweat showed on his forehead as he accelerated towards the Toyota.

"It's okay, Mr Tarquin. Go steady," Petru said urgently. "We don't want crash into them!"

"I wouldn't put it past him!" Constanta mocked with a high-pitched cackle. "Okay, so they're turning right."

Tarquin moved in close behind them.

"Sorry about that, folks," he said sheepishly. "Haven't done that in ages!"

"Okay, roundabout coming up," Constanta said, ignoring

him. "Keep close. Keep close ... gooood!"

They carried on in this vein for the next ten minutes, and then suddenly the Toyota did a swoop to the right and they found themselves in the car park of a supermarket.

"Right, so they're getting some groceries," Constanta said. "Which ... which I suppose means they are not going to a hotel."

"Let's just see," Tarquin said as he took up a strategic though discreet position near the red van. "We don't need to jump to conclusions ... who knows what they're up to."

The young man and the fatter of the other two climbed out and disappeared inside the shop, leaving the third man in the van.

Half an hour went by and they then reemerged pushing two trolleys bursting with all manner of bags.

"Fuck me, how long are they planning to stay?" Constanta exclaimed.

"And *where* are they planning to stay," Tarquin added. "Obviously not a hotel!"

Leaving the car park, the two vehicles then headed out onto the ring road and presently turned east towards the Foret d'Orient.

"Wow, this is nice," Constanta said, looking at the unfolding countryside on either side of the road. "What a place ... guess it's good-bye, Troyes!"

"Don't get too close, Mr Tarquin," Petru warned. "We must not let them realize they are being followed!"

"Sure, quite true," Tarquin mumbled, pulling back.

"I think they are too busy chatting to notice, darling," Constanta said over her shoulder. "They're discussing how much money they're going to make!"

The landscape became increasingly wild and wooded as they left Troyes behind them, and the low light of the sun bathed everything in a soft pinkish light. Then, between the trees, lakes glittered and flashed at them intermittently.

Without warning, the Toyota took a left turn down a narrow

country lane towards a place called Lusigny sur Barse. The Voyager followed at some distance as this road was completely empty and their presence more obvious. Fifteen minutes went by as they wound left and right through thick woods, punctuated by occasional clearings and old wooden barns.

Suddenly the indicator blinked on the Toyota and the brake lights glowed. This was it … they were turning.

"Slow down, Tarquin!" Constanta hissed loudly. "For Christ's sake, keep back, they look like they're stopping."

Tarquin pulled onto the side of the road where they could observe the van from the deep shadows of some lofty oaks.

The young man got out and disappeared down a side turning or driveway. A few minutes later, the van turned off the road and disappeared. They waited a few moments.

"Go!" she said. "We need to see where they went."

"Careful," Petru said, leaning between them anxiously. "They may not have gone so far."

They moved forwards slowly.

"No, go faster … this is too obvious … just go past naturally, Tarquin, and we'll take a look. Okay, Petru, are you ready?" she said over her shoulder.

There was a high wall on the left side of the road, smothered with moss and clinging plants which rippled irregularly as they drove beside it. A short time later, the wall stopped abruptly at a large iron gate flanked by two monumental piers.

"Yes, I'm looking," he said absently.

The Voyager passed the turning at a leisurely pace without stopping.

"Well?" Tarquin said anxiously moments later.

"Fuck me! It was. It was a road, like a private road to a huge house!" Constanta stuttered. "I could only see it a bit through the gates."

"Yes, it was a very big house, Mr Tarquin … perhaps two hundred meters from the road. The young guy they picked up at the station was right there, closing the gates. The Toyota was nearly at the house, I saw a cloud of dust! I guess he wanted to get some exercise!"

"Did he see us?" Tarquin asked, concerned.

"Probably. Look, we're just a car driving by," Petru said, "but we need to move fast in case they take cabinet out now. Constanta, hand me the camera, we must get over the wall and up to the house somehow to get the shots!"

"Cool it, Petru!" she said, putting a hand on his wrist. "I heard them talking in the station, saying that the house is too damp to take it in now. They are going to leave it in the van tonight and remove it later on tomorrow when the house has been aired a bit."

"Are you sure?" Petru said, giving her a sharp look.

"Yes, darling, I am sure. They were talking about building a crate or something before bringing it in. Remember, this is a wood cabinet, a copy. It must be treated like a baby!" she said, smiling widely.

"Mmm ... okay," Petru said, putting the camera down with a sigh.

"I'll turn and we can take another look," Tarquin said, pulling in to the side.

"Not yet! Go on for five minutes and then we can turn round. Just give them a bit of time," Constanta instructed, her hand closing around his wrist.

"This must be important place ... look at this wall! It was built to protect some very rich people, I think," Petru said.

"It's in a crappy condition, that's for sure," Constanta added. "Look at all the ivy and the trees growing over it. It's creepy!"

"Even creepier when it's dark and we have to climb in!" Petru said, smiling.

"Fuck you, Petru!" Constanta said with a twisted smile.

For all her bravado, Constanta was scared of dark old places. Eventually the wall curved away from the road, and Tarquin pulled over and turned off the engine. He studied the map for a few minutes whilst the others chatted, then he turned the car around and headed back towards the entrance.

"Drive past, Tarquin, and stop fifty metres the other side,"

Constanta said. "Petru and me will walk back and get some photos of the place to show you. You go on a bit farther and we'll catch up with you by those trees."

"Yes, it is best if the car is out of way," Petru agreed.

Tarquin pulled over and they jumped out. Constanta immediately started picking some wild flowers and gathered them into a bunch. Petru watched her quizzically.

"We're going for a romantic walk in the countryside, darling … any problems with that?" she said, threading her arm through his and walking towards the gates. "We need to blend in!"

As the sound of Tarquin's engine disappeared, they became aware of the silence, broken only by the soft cooing of roosting pigeons.

"Where is everyone?" she said, looking at Petru with genuine surprise.

"What do you mean? Why are the roads so empty?"

"Well, duh! It's fucking deserted. We haven't seen another car the whole time we been on this road. Don't you think this is weird?"

"Not so much. France is less populated than the UK, and it is much bigger," Petru said matter of factly. "Besides, I think this is a National Park so there are not so many houses."

As they approached the gates, Constanta felt a prickling on the back of her neck and a tightening in her stomach.

"Keep to the side," she said in a loud whisper.

Tentatively at first and then more boldly, they moved closer until their noses were pressed against the rusty vertical railings of the gates. They gazed through in awe.

Chateau Clery, magnificent and yet strangely withdrawn, stood at the end of a long unkempt track which in previous times had presumably been the well-maintained drive to a grand house. Large weeds formed a green Mohican down the centre of the two tracks and gave the place an overwhelming sense of abandonment and neglect; like an old, dishevelled relative, forgotten and unvisited, left to face the embers of their life alone.

The years, the centuries even, had muted and intertwined the definition of the building with its surroundings, and now it seemed to be dissolving into the dense shrubs and trees which crowded around its walls, embracing its stony skin.

Chapter 26

Lily slammed the kennel door and then stuck her hand through the bars to give Titus a final stroke.

"There you are, boy, at least you got your walkies," she said as though to a child.

Walking back on to the gravel drive, she pulled out her mobile.

"All done and dusted, Mary," she said warmly, "and yes, the bugger did·try it on. Made a dash for the meadow! But I shouted and shouted, and to my surprise he came back looking guilty!"

"Oh, thank you, Lily," Mary chuckled. "How lucky is that … to meet you in the village shop just when I really needed someone! My mother doesn't call for help often, but when she does, I have to get over there fast!"

"I know what you mean; mothers are ignored at our peril! Was she okay?" Lily asked.

"It sounds so silly to be stuck in one's own bedroom, but if the handle falls off, that's what happens!" Mary said laughing.

"Well, thank God she had a telephone in there," Lily offered.

"Yes, I know. I mean, at ninety-two, you can hardly shuffle down the drain pipe, can you!"

"Your husband is with Oliver, isn't he?" Lily asked tentatively.

"Yes, they're on a trip to France … looking at some furniture, I believe. A friend of Oliver's bought a place near Paris, and there was a lot of furniture he didn't want. So he asked them to go over and pick it up. It's good stuff, mind you; Oliver wouldn't be looking at tatt, if you know what I mean!"

"No, quite. You don't end up living in a place like this, fiddling around at country fairs. How long are they away, Mary? I tried to get an answer out of him the other night, but he seemed very vague."

Mary laughed. "That's Oliver all over! Never gives a direct answer. Even my Mel doesn't know what's going on half the time, and he works with him! I've given up asking, to be honest. He's back when he's back!"

"Golly, I see. Doesn't like being tied down."

"That's about right," Mary agreed. "Not that I care, mind you: it's nice to have the place to myself for a bit and not have to run around after him. Men are just children, really."

"Yes … he must be very good at what he does, your husband? I can imagine Oliver being quite a tough task master!" Lily said.

"Yes, he is. But then, Mel has been in the trade for almost forty years now, so he knows what he's doing. Started at Malletts when he was sixteen, straight out of school, and moved on from there. Hasn't done anything else. But I stay clear of his work these days. He doesn't like me in his workshop, that's for sure. Every now and then he might ask for a spot of advice, but not very often."

"Wow, that's amazing. What a skill! I have to say, Mary, I love it that we still have some master … er … master …"

"Cabinetmakers."

"Precisely. There are so many button-pushing money people in England these days, you wonder how anything gets made at all," Lily said sadly.

"That's right. We've handed it all to China and India! And then we have the bare faced cheek to tell them they're creating too much smoke."

"What … pollution?"

"Yes, that's right. We've made our fair share of smoke in the past, and now we expect them to do all the manufacturing, because we like to sit on our backsides; but woe betide them if they make any pollution. We want it all ways."

"Mmmm, sad," Lily said, pausing. "Oh well, I must let you go. I've been holding you up far too long, Mary. Lovely speaking with you. Oh, and I put the key back under the brick."

"Great, nice talking to you, Lily. Don't hesitate to pop in and see us for a cup of tea when Melvyn gets back. I reckon you and he would have a lot to say to each other about the state of the country."

"I would love to, Mary. Bye for now."

Lily slid the phone into her pocket and stood quietly by her car for a few minutes absorbing the particular atmosphere of Strupe Hall. She thought about Oliver and the faint whiff of mystery that surrounded him. There was something about him … something she couldn't quite put her finger on. Above her, the dying rays of the sun blasted the tops of the copper beeches into a blaze of gold, whilst at ground level, swallows flitted low and fast over the long shadows of the lawns.

Presently, she climbed into her car and drove home.

*   *   *

"Is this okay?" Constanta said, looking at an exhausted Tarquin as they slumped down in the bar of the hotel.

"It's perfect!" he said, mustering a weak smile. "Let's just get a drink and fast. What a day!"

"I think it's a beer for me, a big one!" Constanta said, gesturing to the waiter.

"Mmm, good idea," Tarquin agreed. "And you, Petru?"

"Make it three beers," the young man muttered.

"So, here we are, in Troyes, with some time to relax and see things more clearly," Constanta said, trying to stimulate the men into some meaningful speculation. "We know we have tomorrow morning off, and then we cruise over there in the afternoon for 'showtime.' We would never have got this far if it had been down to you, Tarquin, would we. This might happen … that might happen … this may not happen … blah blah blah … but because I'm a stubborn bitch, we are here, and so are those bastards who caused you all this trouble."

Tarquin turned his tired eyes towards her. "You're absolutely right, Constanta. I wouldn't be here if I was left to my own devices, and … and I wouldn't have been nearly killed by a pair of nutcases on the way to Dover!"

"Oh, so it's my fault now, is it? And sure, you wouldn't have been attacked on the roadside; you'd been attacked in your fucking house!"

Tarquin smiled and put his large hand on her knee.

"You're right. They'd have caught up with me somehow. I'm pleased we're here, I really am. You've done brilliantly to get us to the house."

"Darling, don't look so serious!" Constanta said, removing his hand and placing it back on the chair arm. "I was just making a point … and anyway, you're gonna pay!"

"Well, of course you won't be out of pocket," Tarquin said, raising his glass and taking a gulp.

"Not in that way, stupid. You're gonna pay because I'm gonna make sure they—those bastards—pay you. So we're are all going to get paid off!"

"I wish I had your confidence, sweetie," Tarquin said, staring at his beer glass. "But I'm not so sure that that will be the outcome."

"There you are again with doubts. Be positive. Things will fall into place, just you wait!"

"Mr Tarquin," Petru said straightening his legs under the table. "She is most definitely a stubborn woman, and she just might make it happen!"

"Right, boys," Constanta said, sounding like a school mistress. "Let's see those photos and decide what we're gonna do. There are loads of trees and bushes around the house, which is great, and they don't have a dog, which is even better! I think we need to be over there by say … two o'clock?"

"Mmm, that should be fine if they stick to their plan,"

Tarquin agreed. "But what if they bring it in earlier? Then we miss the shots of it being unloaded. We have to remember, they've done nothing wrong in the eyes of the law at the present time. They've brought a van to France and are delivering a piece of furniture."

"A fake piece of furniture, Tarquin … a forgery," Constanta retaliated.

"Yes, but we have to prove this," he continued.

"In this case, we need to get pictures of the actual furniture itself, not just a crate with something inside it," Petru said, flicking his camera on so they could look at the house again.

"Well, duh! Of course we do. You were the one who was so keen to get in and start photographing."

"I know, but now I gave it more thought. How, if it comes out of the van in box … which it probably will … how are we going to photograph it?" Petru said, looking at her.

Constanta took a gulp of beer and gazed across the bar in thought.

"But will it be in a box?" Tarquin said.

"Think about it, Mr Tarquin, they will not have this furniture sitting in van without at least wrapping it up in protection of some sort; and in this case we cannot photograph it."

"He's right … we will need to get inside," Constanta said firmly. "I think this will not be so hard. In the station I heard the young guy saying the house needs airing, so he wanted to open the windows and shutters."

"Oh, great! And I suppose it's me who is going in first?" Petru said.

"Well, darling … you are the best; the most experienced at this! You had no trouble in the house in Battersea."

"Shit! This is different!" Petru said vehemently. "You cannot get lost in a Battersea house unless you're stupid. But this … just look at it. It's huge!"

"And probably haunted!" she said, throwing her head back and cackling softly.

"No, Constanta, this is not funny," Petru persisted. "We need to work this out carefully!"

"Perhaps we should simply confront them when they've unloaded the bloody thing," Tarquin offered. "Forget all this creeping around."

"What, and order them to unpack crate in front of us?" Petru said.

"No. I don't like the sound of that, Tarquin," Constanta interrupted. "Perhaps there are other guys in that place. It sounds untidy and risky. We need to get a better understanding of what they're planning to do. I mean, what *are* they planning to do, for fuck's sake?"

"I honestly don't have a clue," Tarquin said wearily. "They've brought a fake piece of furniture from England to a chateau in France, and now what?"

"Well, it's worth a lot of money, that's for sure," Petru said. "They've got the Russian mafia on their case!"

"Look at the place, it's derelict!" Constanta said, picking up the camera and scrutinising the shots. "It doesn't make sense. Anyone can see this house is not being used … at least not very much; it has plants on the driveway."

"I agree, it's a bloody mystery," Tarquin mumbled.

"And what about the car, we can't leave it at the side of the road," Constanta said, shifting her eyes from Tarquin to Petru. "Do we take a taxi?"

"I was thinking there is possible place," Petru replied. "When we were first coming to the house, there were some farm buildings off the road … just before where we stopped the first time. We can drive off the road and perhaps put the car behind those buildings … they didn't look used."

Constanta leaned forward and gave Petru a high five. "All right with that, Tarquin?" she said, turning to him.

"Yuh. Would prefer to have a vehicle nearby," he said, yawning. "Do you mind if we get supper now? I'm hungry."

"Good thinking," she said, standing up and grabbing her jacket. "Did you feed Percy?"

"Yuh. He's fine. Poor dog's bloody knackered with all this

excitement!"

"He has water?"

"Yes … he's fine."

*   *   *

With the van safely tucked in an overgrown courtyard on the far side of the chateau, Oliver and Fabien decided it was time for a celebratory drink. Melvyn wasn't ready to relax. He was enjoying some time to himself, exploring the rooms closest to the kitchen where the other two were chatting. But it was getting dark, and as the thickening gloom pervaded the house, he felt an instinctive need to hear their voices.

Many of the lights didn't work, had never worked, not even when the old lady lived here, and this gave his wanderings an eerie quality. At one point he ambled along a corridor a little too far and, with a jolt, felt the oppressive silence around him. Oliver and Fabien were no longer audible. Like snow on the forest floor, the wood panelling damped all sound, making the walls creep silently inwards, choking his sense of space as though to snare him. Ruffled, he hastily retraced his steps to the areas with electric light and presently returned to the kitchen to join the others.

"There you are, Mel," Oliver said, extending a welcoming arm in his direction. "Thought we were going to have to send out a search party!"

He poured him a glass of wine.

"Yeah, it's pretty dark along there, I have to say!" Melvyn said, feeling sheepish that he had felt so scared only minutes earlier.

"Is it as you expected, Melvyn?" Fabien said.

"Better! To be honest, it goes well beyond my expectations, Fabien," Melvyn replied. "It's perfect for our needs. It has such a strong atmosphere, you know, a feeling of history."

"You know, Melvyn, I love to 'ear you saying this," Fabien continued with a look of great gravity. "This place is in my blood, and yet—unbelievably—a few years ago I was planning to get rid of it. Oliver knows why. It was to do with my job, my prospects, my outlook on life, I suppose, and yes, the problems with my girlfriend."

"Oh, sorry to hear that," Melvyn mumbled shyly.

"Don't be sorry, Melvyn! It's all worked out fantastically now. That is, of course, presuming our little 'project' goes to plan," he said, smiling.

"It'll go to plan okay," Oliver said with extreme confidence. "Just look at this place; it aches to have hidden treasure, doesn't it?"

"I think so, Oliver," Fabien agreed. "It has a romance to it. An old French chateau, built before the revolution and home to the Comptes de Zaragon … buried and almost forgotten in the Foret d'Orient … has revealed an 'idden chest containing a priceless artefact—the find of the century!"

Oliver raised his glass and they all toasted, "To the Freiburg Cabinet!"

"Right," Fabien said, standing up. "Let's get the food going before it's too late. We need to be sharp tomorrow, so I think an early night all round. Are you sure you'll be all right down here, Melvyn? Cecile got both beds in the blue room aired and ready for you and Oliver; but as you wish."

"He likes his own space, does our Melvyn," Oliver said. "Besides, he can keep an eye out for any robbers!"

Melvyn smiled self-consciously.

"I like my sleeping bag and camp bed. I've sort of got used to them," he said. "Can never really sleep well in a proper bed if my Mary isn't there; feel a bit lost."

"That's absolutely fine, Melvyn, if you're comfortable. I suppose you can 'ave a cup of tea in the night if you like as well!" Fabien said.

"But no scoffing our food, Mel!" Oliver said lightheartedly.

"Oh, have you got a spare torch, Fabien? I left mine in the van," Melvyn asked.

"Yes, up there on that shelf. 'Elp yourself. That's one thing we 'ave lots of. The electrical wiring in this 'ouse is terrible, but it's a major job, and we really want to do the whole house rather than just a little bit. Cecile and I know exactly which lights work and which don't, but it is a bit confusing for guests."

"No problem," Melvyn said. "I'll keep to where the lights work till the morning. The air's very heavy tonight," he continued. "I reckon we've got a thunderstorm on the way."

"Yes, there are some storms around at the moment. I 'eard it on the radio," Fabien agreed. "Don't worry, there are no leaks in your bedroom, Oliver."

"I'm glad to hear that!" Oliver said with a chuckle.

Half an hour later they were eating a microwave supper of lasagna and green beans with a basket full of French bread. A ripe Brie and some apples were pudding.

"Wonderful!" Oliver said, pushing his chair away from the table after finishing. "Would you mind if I smoke, Fabien, or prefer I stand outside? I know Mel loves his pipe after supper too."

Melvyn grunted his approval.

"No, go ahead, it's no problem," Fabien said. "The house is so big, the smells all disappear. Besides, we're opening all the shutters tomorrow morning, or at least the ones that do open, to get some fresh air into the place. It can be a bit damp, and it's going to be a lovely sunny day, so I 'ear."

"That's good," Oliver said, puffing hard on his cigar whilst lighting it. "Do you know much about the history of the forest, Fabien? I feel sure we should have some idea of what went on here. Isn't that right, Mel?"

"Yeah, it's true, we should," he said, pulling a tuft of tobacco from a pouch.

"Well, I do know a bit about it," Fabien replied. "After all, it's a big part of my ancestry."

So he settled himself into a more comfortable position, and with a replenished glass of wine, took them through a short potted history from Roman times to the part the forest played in the crusades, and then on to the revolution of 1789 when his family lost its grand status.

"Quite a sad story, Fabien," Oliver said presently, getting to his feet and stretching. "But families come and go, I suppose. Look on the bright side though … yours is about to rise again!"

"If only," Fabien mumbled.

"Right, it's time to get some snoring in, I think," Oliver said, looking at his watch. "Eleven o'clock. Okay, what shall we say … breakfast at eightish?"

"Sounds good to me," Fabien agreed.

He and Oliver headed off chatting noisily, leaving Melvyn to assemble his bed. As the sound of their voices became fainter and then altogether unheard, a slight shiver went down his back. The silence of the house was heavy on his ears. But within half an hour he was sound asleep. In actual fact, they all fell asleep, quickly, deeply, safe within the walls of that ancient edifice, until, that is, Oliver was woken by the sound of distant voices.

They were shouting, taunting, angry voices, at first some distance away and then gradually coming closer, causing a chill to sweep through his body. He lay there rigidly, not able to move a muscle … like a deer in the darkness sensing the approach of the leopard. Louder the sounds grew, men's voices, harsh and challenging, until they were outside the gates at the end of the drive.

Then they were through, moving forward … a column of hate. They cried out angrily in the darkness, their yells like sharp blades cutting into the inky velvet cloth of the night and causing Oliver to feel an overriding terror. He saw the flicker of their torches on the black glass of his windows, heard the metallic clink of their weapons, and he knew what they wanted. It was him they sought … and he knew what he had to do.

Fighting an overwhelming heaviness, he went out and faced the mob, and they jeered at him, rebuked him, and told him he was a liar; that he was hoarding food for himself and his family … allowing them to starve. He stood there and told them he had nothing to give them, that it was a mistake, that they were misinformed and to move away and return to their villages. But they came ever closer, spitting words of fury, thrusting their sharp blades towards him and demanding satisfaction.

And then, quite suddenly, the mob dissolved and he found himself looking into the greenish pockmarked face of Robespierre, whose cold eyes fixed him with a steely stare. Surrounding them was a chanting crowd, now numbering in the thousands, and he realized with an electrifying jolt that he was elevated on a platform. Robespierre's slight frame was perched arrogantly on the precious cabinet, his heals kicking the purpleheart sides with callous disregard. And Oliver could smell the fear of the people he stood with, the people destined to share his fate. The horde was below them, a sea of crazed faces gorging on the unspeakable butchery they were witnessing.

Should he make a run for it and be hacked to pieces by the soldiers and rabble, or accept the clean, cruel surgery of the state? What would he feel? Absolutely nothing? Or would his severed head live on in the basket briefly, as his light dimmed? He was engulfed by an aching loss. The cabinet had been his main focus for years, and now, right at the last moment, the glory of its birth into the world would pass him by.

The drums were rolling. He was getting close now; he felt the evil draft of the blade as it fell, stopping with a sickening thud to an explosion of applause. He looked down. His feet were standing in pools of sticky scarlet; then, as he was roughly manhandled and bound to the plank facedown, the walls of the world crushed in on him. It was his turn now.

Oliver sat up panting, his heart racing chaotically. For a few moments he sat there rigid, staring into the darkness. And then, gradually, gradually, he felt an overwhelming gratitude. He was still alive! His life was spared! It was just a dream … a ghastly nightmare; the cabinet was safe. Suddenly a shivering light lit up the room, followed immediately by a thunderous, stone-shaking roar. Oliver cowered. The immensity of the noise and the still vivid images of the dream brushed his fleeting sense of relief away. He lay still as a statue, in a suspended state of dread, as the storm unleashed above him and the lightning played tricks with objects in the room.

Eventually the thunder rolled into the distance and rain started falling. It coursed off the roofs, down ancient gutters, and splashed into shallow pools beneath the walls. Presently, the mesmerising sound of dripping water worked its magic on Oliver's overwrought nerves and coaxed him back into a heavy sleep. The house, meanwhile, became deadly quiet; an impassive sentry spreading its dark protective cloak over him, without care or feeling.

Chapter 27

The main façade of Chateau Clery faced south, with its grand columned portico standing proudly over an expansive semicircle of what would once have been gravel. Although the shape was still discernible, the flat area was now sprouting with colourful plants which seemed to be marching with increasing density towards the monument in the centre. This was a weathered stone lion, over five meters tall on a square engraved pedestal, atop a large circular plinth. Its finer features had long since been pummelled away by decades of wind and rain, but its powerful muscular body rearing up on clawed feet, spoke of a previous era of wealth and status. Around its base, an algae choked pool of green water was being noisily replenished through the gaping mouths of four hideous bronze sea creatures.

Melvyn was enjoying a second cup of tea under this portico when Fabien came striding out to greet him.

"Bonjour, Melvyn!" he said heartily. "I 'ope you slept well!"

"Morning, Fabien. Yeah, pretty well, thanks," Melvyn mumbled. "Though the thunder woke me up for a bit."

"Oh yes. It was a dramatic storm. We tend to get them at this time of year. Beautiful out 'ere, isn't it? Superb views across the parkland!"

"Yeah, great. You've got a lot of birds around here."

"Oh yes, there's an abundance of wildlife. It's protected, being a National Park. Well, it looks like we've got the sunny weather they promised, after all. Hopefully it's a good omen."

"Yeah, would have thought so," Melvyn replied.

"I banged on Oliver's door; he sounded very groggy," Fabien continued. "Probably tired from yesterday. It was a bit of a marathon for you two, plus all the organization before leaving."

"Yeah, were a few things to be sorted out, it's true. My Mary is looking after Oliver's dog, though, which helps. He can be a bit mischievous, that Titus, when he wants to be, but my Mary knows how to handle him," Melvyn said, making polite conversation.

"Bon. Your wife sounds like a good lady," Fabien said. "Look, Melvyn, would you mind coming round the 'ouse and helping me open the windows and letting some air in? It needs it, and then I'll feel happier about bringing the cabinet inside. Also, you'll get a feel for the layout of the place."

"Yeah. Sounds like a good idea," Melvyn agreed, standing up. "I'm just going to the van to get my tape measure and notebook; need to be sure of the door and staircase widths and the vertical spaces in the attic."

"Sure. Take that passage there. See you shortly, I need a cup of coffee!" Fabien said, heading towards the kitchen.

Ten minutes later, Melvyn reappeared.

"Blimey! Got lost for a moment!" he said sheepishly. "Couldn't remember which of those doors to take back into the house. Nearly ended up in the orangery!"

"Easily done, Melvyn!" Fabien said lightheartedly. "I know this place like the back of my hand, but it is a bit of a labyrinth! Everything okay out there? Be careful the van doesn't get too hot; although, come to think of it, the sun won't be over there yet."

"No, it's cool in the courtyard at the moment."

"Right. Let's go. Bring your tea with you if you like."

They headed down a long passage chatting amiably. Somewhere above them, Oliver heaved himself out of bed and sat on the edge of it with a blank expression. The dream had shaken him and left a horrible stain on his sensibilities. The image of Robespierre sitting nonchalantly on the cabinet was difficult to dislodge.

*   *   *

"Well, mate, it's Saturday morning, and we have a drive ahead of us," Gus said to Bob on his mobile.

"Morning, mate. Yeah, I'm just getting meself sorted out. Leaving at two, aren't we?"

"Yeah, that's right. Take us about three hours to get down there, so we'll arrive around five-ish. Can't go any later or it'll look a bit odd delivering parcels, if yer know what I mean!" Gus said, chuckling.

"Yeah, that's right," Bob said, taking a large slurp of tea. "So what is the plan? Is Sammy coming to your place or to me?"

"He's coming over to my place at one thirty," Gus replied.

"We 'aven't seen him in ages; be nice to catch up," Bob agreed.

"Yeah. Zoltan keeps him very close. He's always got some sneaky little job to do, some window to climb through ... usually abroad somewhere!" Gus said, chuckling.

"Yeah. He earns his keep," Bob replied.

"Yer can't beat the ex-army boys, mate. He's off again on Sunday night ... got a seven o'clock flight. Viktor will bloody nail us if he misses it," Gus said.

"Well, he won't, will he?" Bob said emphatically.

"Right. We leave at two with the parcel delivery gear on the van as per normal. You've got the overalls, which I hope look nice and clean."

"Of course, was just getting them ready, as it happens."

"Good. Right, so we head for that place Marston Meysey, which is in the middle of bloody nowhere, and then make our way to his house which is nearby; think it's called Strupe Hall. Well, it would be, wouldn't it, a right toff's residence."

"Using the sat nav?"

"'Course I bloody am, but from what I remember, even then it's not easy. Place is like a maze and the gear starts to fry ... all those narrow country lanes with horses and dopey old geezers on tractors," Gus continued.

"Yeah," Bob said, beginning to lose concentration as a leggy girl wandered past his window.

"So we arrive at his house, and take a little peek whilst it's light. Ye know, let Sammy check out the landscape. We know Oliver's not there, but who knows? Someone may still be at the bloody place, in which case we have strict instructions not to do anything stupid," Gus said emphatically.

"Okay, okay," Bob muttered as he stretched across his kitchen counter to get a final glimpse of the girl.

"Are you following me, mate?" Gus said, detecting a vagueness in Bob.

"Yeah, course I am. We're … er … we're checkin' out the gaff before it gets dark," Bob said focusing again.

"Yeah, and then later, and I mean a lot later, like around one in the night, if it looks like it's a goer, we take Sammy round and drop him off nearby, and he can do the business."

"And where are we gonna be?" Bob said.

"Where do you think? Playing rummy in the back of the van, somewhere out the way, as per usual!" Gus said chuckling. "Yer know, in a layby with the other trucks."

"We need to be very careful here," Bob said. "Country places are a real problem. People are right nosey; always watching what their neighbours are up to. You can hear a sparrow fart half a mile away in the countryside, so let's hope there's a spot of wind. We need noise, don't want the whole place lighting up with barking dogs, etcetera."

"Calm down!" Gus said. "I don't think there are any houses nearby, not near the Hall."

"Whatever, it's still a different ball game," Bob continued. "To be honest, I don't know why we're bothering. Z knows Oliver's got something up his sleeve, he just doesn't know what … yet! But the geezer is going to come back and that's when we jump him, in London. Not out in the bloody countryside where we don't know our way around and the coppers can land on us."

"Look, I agree with yer, Bob, but the guy's impatient, wants to get the picture now, not later," Gus said.

"All right. So we roll up at Stripe 'all at five o' clock."

"Strupe Hall … get it right."

"Okay, so we drive off the main road into the private driveway of this big house pretending we're delivering a parcel. Well, we're going to get someone asking us questions, remember that, so make sure you have the spiel, okay!"

"For fuck's sake, Bob, what's the matter with yer?" Gus said, raising his voice. "I've got it covered, okay?"

"Okay. Mate. I'll see yer about two then," Bob said, keen to get off the phone.

"Sure, see yer later," Gus said, closing off.

*   *   *

"Bonjour, Oliver!" Fabien said, coming back into the kitchen with Melvyn. "You sounded a little sleepy earlier."

"Bonjour, Fabien," Oliver replied. "Yes, I'm afraid I was finding it difficult to surface this morning. Had a ghastly nightmare last night which woke me up, and then I lay awake for a bit."

"Oh, I'm sorry!" Fabien said, looking concerned. "Nothing to do with the room, I hope?"

"Absolutely not. Bed was very comfortable. I fell asleep in minutes. It happened much later on, somewhere about two thirty, I think. I dreamt I had woken up to the sound of voices outside on the drive. I was terrified. And then there was that thunderstorm!"

"Mon Dieu," Fabien said. "It sounds like you had a bad night! Like some coffee?"

"Sure, thanks," Oliver said. "It was horribly real. I felt at one point that I was about to be guillotined! Perhaps the events of the past are like vibrations trapped in the walls of the house."

"Possibly," Fabien agreed, with a downwards twist of his lips. "Now let's have breakfast. Melvyn and I have opened all the windows, or at least the ones we can open, and hopefully we'll drive the damp out. It's going to be a brilliant day."

He started getting the breakfast organized. Some croissants, jam, and more cheese.

"Yes, it looks idyllic," Oliver agreed, gazing out of the window through tired eyes. "How are you today, Melvyn?"

"Good, thanks, Oliver. Looking forward to getting the chest made up."

"Well, let's not delay. After breakfast, we'll go out to the van and get the parts. Then you can begin the assembly. Have you been into the roof space yet?"

"No. I had a brief glance up onto the third floor, but thought I'd wait till we all went up. I'm worried I'll disturb something I shouldn't, and Fabien's been a bit busy."

"Quite right, Mel, but we really need to get the exact location sorted out soon. I've been up there before, as you know, and have a couple of places in mind, but I want it to be your decision."

"Sure."

"Yes, we've been running around a bit this morning," Fabien said as he plucked some knives and teaspoons from a drawer. "But everything's ready now."

"Thanks. Sorry for being slow," Oliver said.

"No problem. You had a bad night. Tonight we'll celebrate with some delicious red wine, and you'll sleep like a baby!"

Oliver chuckled and drew his chair up to the table.

After breakfast, Oliver asked Fabien to lead them up to the garret to establish the final resting place of the chest. This was the fourth floor and was a voluminous space by virtue of the steeply slanting roof.

Three dormer windows with pretty sculpted surrounds provided fans of daylight at the front, but away from these, twilight dipped into varying degrees of darkness. It had long since become a domain for bats and swallows, the floors strewn with old sacks, broken tiles, and layers of rubble.

Huge roughly hewn oak supporting timbers with pegged joints sprouted from the planked floor and disappeared into the shadows above like the ribs of an old galleon. Here and there, sunlight pierced small apertures in the roof and white shafts of light penetrated the gloom like laser beams, creating incandescent pools on the dusty floor. Watching the dust pass lazily through one of these beams, Melvyn suddenly spotted further steps in the shadows beyond.

"Where is that leading to, Fabien?" he said, pointing.

"Oh, it's some steps to another level, or should I say to a platform," Fabien said, squinting into the gloom. "I think at some time in the past there was a much bigger floor up there, but a lot of it has fallen, or been taken down as it was probably dangerous. Perhaps when the roof was being repaired it was damaged and partly dismantled."

"Do you mind if I go and look?" Melvyn said, suddenly interested.

"Yes, but don't go up the stairs, they're dangerous. And be careful where you tread, some of the planks on the floor have huge rusty nails sticking up out of them."

"We don't want you getting tetanus, Mel!" Oliver said, stepping into one of the light pools and transforming his face into a deeply furrowed mask, like a Shakespearian actor.

Melvyn mumbled something and disappeared into the semidarkness, silhouetted against his torch beam.

"It's incredibly dry up here, Fabien," Oliver said, running his finger over a beam and blowing some chalky dust off it in a puff.

"Yes, it is. The air movement keeps it this way, I suppose. This is good, non?"

"Very much so. It is just another fortunate circumstance. Our project seems to have the blessing of the powers above!" Oliver said, chuckling.

He moved to one of the dormer windows and looked out on the landscape stretching out below him.

"My God! What a view! This is mind boggling. If only we could step back two hundred years and see it in all its glory," he said wistfully. "The Foret d'Orient is a magical place, Fabien. Just look at those lakes, and so much unspoilt woodland."

"I've got it!" Melvyn shouted from the gloom.

"Sorry, Mel?" Oliver shouted back.

"Here! This is the place; under these steps is absolutely ideal. Dry as a bone," Melvyn shouted excitedly to the others.

Fabien and Oliver moved carefully across the dusty uneven floor into the shadows where Melvyn was standing triumphantly.

"Just look at this!" he said to them, shining his torch under a thick planked platform.

"Can't see a lot, Mel!" Oliver said, squinting.

"This is the perfect place, Oliver," Melvyn persisted. "It's protected from above by this obviously old platform, in front by this staircase, and from behind … well look"—he pointed his torch—"it's a niche between these two buttresses. Perfect! Anything left here would remain untouched for … well, centuries! Even roofing repairs wouldn't have interfered with it. Plus, it's dark as hell and the floorboards are in good shape. See, there's no hint of water stains."

"Yes, it looks like an excellent place to me!" Fabien agreed. "It's beautifully protected."

"Mel, you're absolutely right … it's perfect. I'm ashamed to say I wouldn't have spotted it," Oliver conceded.

"Good, that's another thing out of the way then," Melvyn said with a pleased grin.

Oliver picked his way carefully back towards the dormer windows, followed by the others.

"Well, it's time to get this show on the road," he said, taking a last glimpse out onto the parkland below.

Back downstairs, it was as though the three men had suddenly become wired into an electric circuit. The heaviness had evaporated from Oliver's mind, and he rolled his sleeves up in preparation to help Melvyn assemble the chest. Fabien was striding around the various rooms on the ground floor checking the shutters were okay and drawing curtains to protect his furniture from the increasingly fierce sunlight.

Cool morning air, laden with fresh pungent aromas from the garden, was already beginning to flow through the open windows, expelling the listless atmosphere from panelled rooms and passageways, and breathing life once again into the stale lungs of the chateau. How changed it was after a deep gulp of garden air; the whole house seemed to be rejoicing, preparing itself for the arrival of an old friend.

Thomas Charrington

Chapter 28

Tarquin wandered into the hotel lobby with Percy and spotted Constanta tapping out a message on her mobile. It was ten forty-five.

"Hi. Had a good old 'lie in,' did we?" he said, slumping into an adjacent seat.

"Yeah. There's nothing else to do around here, so why not sleep," she said, her eyes not leaving the screen.

"Where's Petru?" he said, faintly irritated at being ignored.

"Not sure. He went out about an hour ago to take a look around. There's a photographic shop he saw on the way back last night and he wanted to get something … like some batteries or something like that."

"Oh, okay," Tarquin said, feeling unwanted. "I think I'll see if I can get hold of an English newspaper. Feeling a bit out of touch."

"C'mon, darling," Constanta said slowly, still engrossed in her screen. "The news is all the same: financial problems here, a murder there, some gossip about a celebrity. Give it a rest!"

"Well, of course. Perhaps I should just start writing some garbage on my mobile to a few of my friends," he said tetchily. "I'm sure they need to know what I had for breakfast, how I slept, what the weather's like … oh, and who I've fallen out with recently!"

Constanta broke away from her screen and looked at him hotly.

"Look, Tarquin, if it's a problem me sitting here sending texts to a friend back home, then you don't have to be here, okay? And by the way, I'm not discussing the fucking weather. I'm texting Petru's sister about her mother's health problems."

Tarquin stood up.

"Oh, sorry. Hope it's not too serious. I'm going up to my room for a bit, see if I can get an English channel."

"You know, Tarquin, that dog of yours has more sense sometimes," she said as he wandered off.

Ten minutes later Petru came in and sat where Tarquin had been.

"Did you get it?" Constanta said, still immersed in her mobile.

"Yes. Perfect. Cheap as well. Where's Tarquin?"

"He's gone upstairs, pissing me off," she said.

"Yuh? What's he done?"

"Oh, just getting bitchy 'cos I wouldn't speak to him. You know, give him my undivided attention. I'm talking with Natalia … I'm busy!" Constanta said, clicking her tongue.

"How is she?"

"She's fine, but very worried about your mum. Looking forward to seeing you, darling."

"Well, it won't be so long. France is cool, I'm enjoying myself for once, but I'll be back over there soon," he said. "Tell her 'Hi' from me."

"Sure."

Petru looked at his watch.

"Okay, it's eleven twenty. I think we should get moving, say soon after twelve. We've got to drive there, lose the car, get over the wall and into the park, and we got to find the best place to hang out."

"So soon?" Constanta said. "I thought we were leaving about one?"

"No, it's too late," Petru said firmly. "We got a lot to do. We have to find where their van is parked, to start with. Then we have to find the best place to get the shots. It might be impossible to photograph the cabinet outside the house. I might have to get the shots inside, when they remove the packaging or take it out of its box. You have to realize, Constanta, we have no idea what this thing is. How big it is."

"Well, it can't be bigger than the van, can it?" she said with a serious look.

"Well, duh ... of course it can't! But if it's small, it will probably be packed in a box, but if it's massive, then it's possible it will just be covered in sheets, in which case I might be able to get a photo when it's being unloaded. I'm the asshole taking the pictures, and it would help if I knew. I still say that we will struggle to get a picture of this thing outside the house. I can probably get shots of them unloading something—get their faces and the van—but the cabinet ... this is our problem."

"Mmm. I guess you've got a point," she said, finally putting her phone down. "We just don't have a fucking clue what they're planning to do with it. I mean, how do we know they *are* going to unpack it? Perhaps they're just going to stick it somewhere in the house and leave it as it is?"

"Look, as you said before, we have to play this as we go along," Petru said with a sigh.

Constanta didn't respond for a few moments and let her eyes focus on the bustling square outside the window. There was a merry-go-round with heaps of shouting children scampering around, eager for a ride. Suddenly, she made up her mind and stood up.

"Right, darling, the best thing we can do is get into a position where we can *listen*. We have to find out what the fuck is going on. We've got a bunch of guys with a fake cabinet in a huge weirdo house in France, and guess what? Some other guys who happen to be Russian are trying to find them. And I mean, *really trying to find them!* Why? What are they fucking doing? There's a plan here, Petru, and we're in the fucking dark; perhaps the Russians don't know either, but sure as hell we're gonna find out! Can you knock up the grumpy old man, darling, and tell him we're gonna leave earlier. I'm going to the room to get ready. Oh ... and make sure he takes Percy down to the concierge's wife with his two bowls, or he'll probably forget!"

"Sure. See you up there," he said as she walked out. "And take that thick coat in case. We might be there late tonight."

Chapter 29

In a smallish room adjacent to the kitchen, probably the old pantry, Melvyn unrolled the first of several bundles of sacking which he and Oliver had retrieved from the van a little earlier. He felt a wave of affection at the sight of his precious handiwork again; the old oak posts, rails, and grooved boards of the outer chest which would harbour the precious cabinet itself.

These had been made with equal diligence and attention to detail as the artefact they were protecting, but their finish had to be appropriately rough to reflect the skill level of the artisan who had made them. This estate carpenter would have had a much cruder style of construction to the cabinetmakers of the period, but would still have been skilled in the robust jointing techniques befitting the functional everyday objects his job entailed. To this end, Melvyn had produced a masterful piece of mimicry. There would be no glue; just a series of pegged joints holding the mortise and tenons together tightly.

He began by laying each section out methodically, according to some chalky lettering whose meaning was only known to himself. It was now splayed out on the floor in two dimensions like the bones of an animal, ready to be assembled into its three-dimensional form. A small number of oak pegs at each end were ready for insertion at the appropriate moment. To ensure these joints were tight, and to make the assembly a little easier for himself, Melvyn had brought some long sash cramps and wooden blocks to apply some serious pressure when needed; a rubber-headed hammer and some sharp chisels stood by in readiness, plus a small bag of other tools. The lid of the chest (like the base) was already made up. It would not be hinged; it would be hammered down onto the chest using some tight-fitting dowels. The floor and legs had been treated to one of Melvyn's favourite devices; contrived disfigurement, to mimic the gnawing of mice.

Melvyn, who always did his best to get inside the head of the person behind an artefact, had imagined this carpenter making the chest with some urgency. Word was out that gangs were already raiding the larger houses in the region for anything they could lay their hands on. The rule of law was faltering. The cabinet had to be secreted away into the garret … fast! As he was pondering these thoughts, the door suddenly swung open and Oliver's head popped in.

"How's it going, Mel? Wow. ready for assembly, I see, you clever bugger! Do you need a hand with anything?"

"No, I'm okay, thanks," Melvyn said, whilst giving a dowel a sharp rap with a hammer.

"Tea?"

"No, I'll be finished shortly," he said, his cheeks red with effort.

"Okay, I'll leave you in peace," Oliver said, removing himself. He knew Melvyn well enough not to hang around.

Fabien walked into the kitchen as Oliver was pouring himself another cup of coffee.

"Oh, there you are, Fabien. I did shout, but you were out of range. Want a coffee?"

"Non, not for me, thanks," the young man said, looking out onto the garden. "It's warming up out there, and the van will be catching the sun now, so we probably need to bring the cabinet in soon."

"Yes, quite true," Oliver agreed.

"Does the air in the house seem lighter and drier to you?" Fabien said.

"Very much so," Oliver said, taking a gulp of coffee. "It's a completely different place! How often were you and Cecile coming down here?"

"Not enough. We were coming every other weekend at the beginning—you know, after our 'agreement'—and cleared huge amounts of stuff from the rooms through there and burnt it. So much unnecessary clutter; it had to go. Then more recently, Cecile got interested in garden design and started doing some studies on the weekends in Paris, so we came down less. Probably once a month. It wasn't enough, and as you can see, the house gets damp."

"Well, quite."

"You see, Oliver, I had to be careful. I was always thinking about the cabinet and its placement here. I didn't want to get an army of tradesmen in here to start renovating the place until the cabinet was in its niche. The whole idea rests on the fact that the house is ... *undiscovered.* If people had been in here doing things—like electricians, carpenters, roofers, and so on—the magic would have been lost and our discovery that bit less believable."

"Yes, you're quite right, Fabien. The mystique of an old, neglected but grand house is essential for our requirements," Oliver conceded.

"Absolutely!" Fabien said emphatically. "And once the cabinet has been placed and has had enough time to accumulate a load of cobwebs and dust, that's when we get the roofer in ... to *discover* it in front of me and Cecile!" He laughed out loud as he said this, and Oliver himself couldn't resist a cheesy grin.

"My word, Fabien, you beat me at my own game, and I'm not complaining!" Oliver said, chuckling. "C'mon, let's go and get the cabinet, for God's sake, before it cooks!"

He took a final gulp of coffee, and without further ado, they went out to the courtyard where the red Toyota stood waiting.

"Blimey, it's hot out here!" Oliver said, looking skywards. "We need to get that thing inside sharpish! It's so cool in the house one forgets how quickly it heats up outside!"

"True, on a scorching summer's day, the house is always cool. It's superb."

Oliver opened the back doors of the van and a wall of hot air rushed past his head.

"Fabien, do you mind getting inside and manipulating it this way? You're younger than me; my back creaks when I have to bend down inside that thing."

"No problem," he said, jumping nimbly in and stepping over a heap of blankets. "Phew! It's so hot in here!"

He clasped the corner of the makeshift crate containing the cabinet and pulled gently, then with greater force. "Mon Dieu, it's heavy!" he said. "How did you get it in here?!"

"Melvyn's surprisingly strong," Oliver replied, "and wiry. He can bend this way and that without a problem, the lucky bugger."

Fabien pulled again and the crate moved backwards with reluctance.

"Look, I think it's better if we get Melvyn out here, Oliver, I'd hate to damage something; he put it in here, so he knows how to get it out."

"Okay, I'll go and get him," Oliver said, disappearing at a fast amble.

Fabien sat on the rear deck and wiped some sweat from his face with the sleeve of his shirt. A faint breeze was beginning to stir the tops of the beeches and higher still, cirrus clouds skidded across the blue sky on a fierce invisible wind.

Three minutes went by and then Oliver reappeared with a rather vexed-looking Melvyn.

"You'll see what I mean, Mel," Oliver was saying apologetically. "It's scorching in the van, and we were worried."

"Okay, open the side door," Melvyn said sternly. "And Fabien, if you could get in and twist the crate away from the bulkhead a bit."

Fabien jumped back in and did as he was told, whilst Oliver stood by looking anxious.

"That's it. Now push towards me … slowly … slowly. Oliver, can you give me a hand here, please."

The two men took the weight of the cabinet as it emerged from the side of the van. Then, as it came out nearly its full length, Oliver shuffled to the other end where Fabien joined him to take the strain. Finally the whole of the crate was out and being held on three pairs of hands.

"Okay, let's let her down for a moment," Melvyn said in a strained voice, "and check we have a free passage into the house. We don't want to be stopping to open doors. Let's get her to the top of the steps there, have a rest, and then do a straight run to the bottom of the main staircase."

"Okay, Mel. Sounds like a good plan to me," Oliver said slightly breathlessly.

A minute or two went by whilst Fabien checked the route. Then Melvyn crouched down whilst the other two took the opposite end.

"Okay. One … two … three … lift!" Melvyn said as he flexed upwards. The crate swayed ominously and then steadied. "Right, slowly does it to the top of the steps."

Twenty minutes later and the three men were slumped at the bottom of the main staircase enjoying a cool drink.

"Bloody hell," Oliver said, sweating profusely. "That was hard bloody work!"

"That was nothing, Oliver, we have four flights of stairs to go up next," Melvyn said with a serious look.

"God help us!" Oliver muttered.

"Merde! Pain before gain," Fabien said, chuckling and taking a glance at his watch. "Look, it's one thirty, everyone, shall we stop and have a little lunch before we do this marathon to the garret?"

"Bloody good idea Fabien!" Oliver said, wiping a hanky across his forehead. "I'm starving!"

They meandered into the kitchen and slumped down on some scruffy painted chairs, whilst Fabien busied himself getting plates, cutlery, glasses, various cheeses, and bread. Finally he plonked a jug of celery on the table.

"That's salad! No time for fancy stuff till later," he said, grinning.

They chuckled and got stuck in with the sort of macho gusto

generated by hard physical exertion.

*   *   *

Tarquin and his two companions dropped onto the cool damp earth inside the overgrown wall surrounding the parkland. The low-hanging branches of an old oak and some thick ivy stems had provided excellent support to haul their bodies over the crumbling brickwork. Tarquin opened a flap of torn cloth on his knee and dabbed some blood with his handkerchief. The air was thick with the pungent smells of rotting vegetation, fungus, and decaying wood.

They scanned their options from the thick undergrowth and bushes. The land directly in front of the house was empty of shrubs or bushes, just some magnificent cedars with their tiers of flat leafy branches scattered randomly. These wouldn't provide the protection they needed. Someone looking out of the house towards the south would see them immediately.

A route to the north of the building was their only option. Here an almost unbroken swathe of low bushes and shrubs stretched in a great arc towards the house, amalgamating with those around its walls. Their only problem here was how to get across the drive. This was the one place where they would be exposed.

"I think it has to be this way, guys," Constanta said in a low voice. "The other way is out of the question, and I don't want to climb back out and then in again farther down."

"Yuh, you're right. We don't really have a choice," Tarquin said as he eyeballed the landscape through the leaves and branches.

"I'll go first and you follow one at a time, okay?" she said, moving ahead.

"Sure," Petru said, falling in behind her.

At the edge of the bushes they waited for a few moments to work out the route. Suddenly Constanta was off, scuttling low and fast across the drive and into the undergrowth at the other side. Petru followed and then Tarquin.

"Well, we don't have a fucking clue if anyone saw us or not!" she said, laughing quietly. "The house is so far away!"

"Let's just assume not," Tarquin said, breathing heavily.

They moved on towards the house, keeping low. After twenty minutes they slid silently into the thicker bushes of the garden.

"We need to get to the back to … the other side," Constanta whispered. "I think the van is parked in there somewhere."

"Let me go first," Petru replied huskily, shouldering his way in front of Constanta. "I can see a route through there."

They followed him quietly, Tarquin taking up the rear.

After a further few minutes of ducking and weaving through the intricate web of branches, Petru suddenly gestured to Constanta to stop. He carefully moved ahead alone. She could see him through the foliage edging along a wall.

He stopped and peered round a corner. Almost immediately he turned and beckoned her to come closer. She moved quietly towards him, pushing rhododendron branches out of her way as she went.

Arriving at Petru's shoulder, she peered past him and into the courtyard. The red van stood there in the blazing sun, the back doors gaping open.

"Shit!" she hissed quietly under her breath. "They've taken the cabinet inside already!"

"Yes, we've arrived a bit too late," Petru whispered.

Tarquin arrived at her shoulder and peered round.

"Fuck!" he muttered.

"Look, Tarquin, I suggest you go back along the wall to the end and wait. It's not so thick there and you can relax. But keep hidden. Your phone's on vibrate, so I'll let you know what's going on, okay?"

He disappeared back into the green jungle, shafts of sunlight playing on his clothes as he went. She turned to Petru.

"Right, darling … who dares, wins! You're gonna take a trip into the house, okay?"

"You think?"

"It's all we can do. Like we discussed last night, just get some pictures and find out what the fuck's going on. You are our eyes and ears!"

"Shit!"

"You'll be fine; you just have to find out where they are. There are no dogs, just three guys!"

"Fuck you!"

"My pleasure, sweetheart," she said, flashing her white teeth and squeezing his shoulder.

"Okay … I'm going in, I'll call you when I can. Don't leave without me."

He glanced furtively into the courtyard, and without further ado, dashed across the entrance to another smaller patch of shrubs against the wall of the house itself. She then watched him scuttling low and fast towards the nearest open window. He stopped and listened intently for a few moments for any presence inside. Nothing. With a final glance towards Constanta, he jumped up and levered himself slowly over the ledge and disappeared inside.

*   *   *

"My God, this is tough going," Oliver said, slumping down on the stairs. "Two flights over and two more to go!"

"It'll get easier, strangely enough, Oliver," Melvyn said lightheartedly, "as your brain works out the easiest way to carry it!"

"Of course it will!" Fabien said chuckling. "Soon it will float up on its own!"

"Like it, Fabien," Oliver said, laughing. "Mel, you've got the heavy end; are you sure you're okay?"

"Yep … no problem," Melvyn mumbled breathily.

"Just think how much sweeter it'll be when we haul it up those final steps onto the top floor! Our bird will soon be in its roost!" Oliver said poetically.

*   *   *

Down on the ground floor, Petru had slithered from the window ledge onto the old Persian carpet and stopped dead. He listened intently and allowed his eyes to adjust to the gloom. Nothing, just a strong smell he couldn't pinpoint. Slowly he stood up, steadying his small rucksack. The room was like a museum—old looking with walls covered in wooden panels and countless pictures. Pieces of furniture, old used furniture, stood around in a haphazard way, including a writing desk with a chair pushed under it, held together with string.

He stood gazing around him for a minute or two and then padded his way carefully towards the half-open door. This was a huge six-panelled affair which reminded him of a computer game called "Castle of Gems." He stopped again and listened.

This time he picked up the sounds of male voices, far away. They came and went intermittently and created an overwhelming sense of dimension in his mind. He moved out of the room silently, following his shadow for a few moments before he found himself in an even darker passage with a worn stone floor. With blood pumping through his system, he edged slowly along, passing another room on his left and a small staircase adjacent to it.

A cool breeze poured through the doorway and coiled around him, urging him forwards and deeper into the house. All the time his muscles were primed to turn him in a split second and hurtle him back down the passageway, across the room, and out through the window. He crept slowly along towards another open door off the passage. A green glow emanated from it and flickered restlessly on the wood panels opposite.

As he came to it, he saw it was a lavatory with a massive sink and worn brass taps; sunlight was blinking through some thick fleshy leaves directly outside the window, and their movement was projecting onto the opposite wall. It was like a crazy dream.

Moving on, he could now see the end of the passage quite clearly—a rectangle of brightness into another space. He reached it and stopped, awestruck. He was standing looking into a cavernous hall. He listened, whilst his eyes scanned methodically around. The space unnerved him; he would be so exposed. Was there someone in that space sitting quietly, unobserved, ready to sound the alarm? Towards the far end, an imposing stone staircase with intricately sculpted wrought iron balustrades swept upwards in a great curve out of sight. A light brown piano stood cradled at its base, whilst behind this he could see farther doorways to rooms ablaze with sunshine.

In the centre, beneath the spreading arms of a brass chandelier stood an octagonal oak table badly disfigured by age. He could hear the voices now much louder and clearer. They were coming from above and seemed to alter dramatically in volume and pitch.

Plucking his rucksack off his shoulder, he pulled out his camera and, checking the flash was off, took some photographs. He cursed at his trembling fingers. He was more frightened than he realized. Before heading forwards and upwards towards the voices, he took a careful tour of the rooms off the hall.

The first was the kitchen. Spacious and light, he could see it had been used very recently. Dirty plates with cheese rinds and apple peelings sat on the rough oak table with chairs shoved dismissively away. He shuddered. It was like visiting the den of some wild beast, about to return at any moment. He took a couple of shots and then moved into the room next door, all the while keeping his ears pricked for approaching noise.

This was a small room and much darker. With a jolt, he spotted a chest on the bare floorboards and some tools scattered around it. Shit! Was this it? The cabinet they'd been searching for? He tiptoed nimbly over and scrutinized it. It was old—rough looking—and seemed to be in the process of being repaired.

This wasn't what he was expecting, but there was no time for deliberation. He hurriedly took shots from all angles, waiting for a hand to close on his shoulder at any moment. He then edged back out into the hall and listened. Nothing. What were they doing?

He scanned the rooms around him, assessing his best escape route if he became trapped. Or a temporary hiding place? Somewhere to go at a moment's notice. Suddenly he heard them again; low conversation a long way above. Underneath the staircase, a door set into the panelling caught his eye. Keeping to the perimeter of the hall and erstwhile looking upwards towards the upper landing, he crept quietly around. Reaching the door, he lifted a small circular ring handle and pulled it fractionally. There was a loud creak and something shifted inside.

He held the door hard and listened. Yes, the voices were still there, but more distant now. Opening the door more fully, he glimpsed a large table leg swinging viciously towards him. He lunged at it, stopping its fall, a hot wave rushing through him. He stayed motionless for a moment or two, his heart pounding. Then he pushed it back and adjusted its position carefully so it balanced.

Closing the door, he glanced around. He had to get on with the job. There wasn't time for this. If he ran into trouble down here, it would be a straight rush outside, simple as that. He moved round to the front of the staircase and looked up listening. After a moment or two, he heard the muffled voices some way above him. Moving quickly, his muscles supercharged with adrenaline, he sprang up the stone stairs hugging the wall. Slowing towards the top, he crept carefully onto the first floor landing. Again he marvelled at the space around him. What a house!

The main landing had a number of rooms sprouting from it with peeling paint on their faded cream panels. Some of the doors were open, and he could see at least two brightly lit bedrooms. Passageways in two directions were completely sealed off and afforded no escape route. He figured these were too dilapidated parts of the building and had been sealed to protect the better parts.

Returning to the stairs, he again inched his way upwards, aware he was closing in. The men were seemingly on the third floor.

"Thank God, we're nearly there!" a voice above him suddenly said, causing him to freeze.

"One more flight, Oliver, and the heavy lifting is over!" another voice said.

"Look ... let's get it to the top and have a break before we take it into the garret. A nice 'cup of English tea,' non?" a third voice said.

"Fabien, we were always going to stop at the top," the second voice said with a snort. "We've got to fetch the chest from downstairs yet!"

"Mon Dieu! Of course we have! I was thinking we were going to deposit this in there!" the third voice said.

"Now, Fabien, I think this would be a *bad* idea!" the first voice said with a loud guffaw. "The softwood that made this up is probably three months old at the most, and the plywood ... well, that was probably not around in the eighteenth century!!"

There was a loud ripple of laughter from all three men, and Petru wondered what the significance was.

"Okay then, last push," the second voice said. "*One ... two ... three*!!"

Taking his chance, Petru went nimbly up the steps, hugging the walls to keep out of view. He knew that their angle of sight might reveal his feet, even if he couldn't see them. He stopped at the second floor.

Here the full derelict state of the house became apparent. Nothing seemed to be restored, and it had the appearance of a building site. Old doors were propped against the walls, paper hung in great swathes from the ceilings, and the floors were bare. It looked like there were no habitable parts here.

The voices were suddenly louder now, and he looked nervously around. He had to be careful. Quickly deciding that the disused section would be his best escape in an emergency, he decided to check it out. Gingerly making his way down the landing, he entered the chaos that time wreaks on neglected spaces.

The first room that branched off this passage proved to be

symptomatic of all the rest. The window frames were rotten, the shutters were hanging on rusted hinges, and the trees and shrubs outside were piling in through the openings where the windows were broken. Nature was doing her best to return the chateau to the wild, and here she seemed to be getting the upper hand. In the second room on the right there was a ponderous wardrobe on one side of an open sash window; its once exquisitely carved cornice now had a tangle of climbing shoots and foliage bunched on one side. To Petru it looked like a lopsided shock of hair, cheekily added to undermine the grandeur of the design.

He pushed the sash upwards; it slid reluctantly up a few inches and then jammed. He pushed his chest through and leaned out. He was high, somewhere around fourteen meters. Beyond the window, the branches of a yew tree were forcing themselves against the masonry and twisting into weird shapes. At this level, they were relatively thin, but a bit farther down, a heavy branch offered a bridge from the house to the garden.

He figured that in an emergency he could slide out of the window feet first and put his weight on the slim masonry ledge which ran along four feet below. Then he'd have to overcome his fear, let go of the cill, and somehow leap onto the branch below, hoping it would take his weight. Moving farther along the corridor, he came to a lavatory. He could barely enter this room, it was so full of greenery. Climbing plants clung to the walls, to the ornate cornice around the ceiling, to the picture rail, the light fittings, and wound their way around every pipe to be seen. Plump cushions of moss coated the backs of the basin and taps whilst fernlike plants were growing rampantly out of the plugholes. The whole room had the atmosphere of a greenhouse.

He returned quietly to the staircase and to the reassuring sounds above. They were moving from the third floor upwards now. He knew he could hide now, but he would have to be quick. Someone coming down the stairs would provide little time. Putting a foot gingerly on the first step, he inched his way upwards. Suddenly he felt his mobile shivering in his breast pocket. It was a message from Constanta.

"*What the fuck's happening?*"

He quickly tapped out a reply. "*Very close to them. Give me 30 mins.*"

The sounds of heavy exertion from above carried on as he moved ever closer, now using his hands as well as his feet in order to keep his head and eyes low. Then he saw one of them about twenty feet above him. His shirt sleeves were rolled up and his forearms were straining as he heaved a large object in front of him.

"*Nearly … nearly … one last push!*" a voice encouraged. There was a heavy thud. "*There, we've done it!*"

"Phew. Well done, everyone, what an achievement!!" another voice said, gasping for breath. "Let's go down for a cuppa!"

"*Bloody good idea, Oliver!*" another voice said, equally breathlessly. "*At last we can relax a little!*"

Petru, from his position towards the third floor, quickly began to retreat. The footsteps above him, released of their load, were at once lighter, more agile and dangerous. Back on the second floor, he now glided silently back down the landing and disappeared into his self-appointed refuge in the room with the wardrobe. He could hear his heart thumping as he stood just inside the door peering along the landing towards the stairs.

They ambled down chatting, at first out of sight and then turning the corner and coming fully into view. They were dabbing their sweaty faces with shirt sleeves and hankies; the crate must have been heavy, Petru figured. He recognized them … the same three guys from the car park—two older men and the young one who came on the train.

The car park rendezvous seemed like years ago, not just yesterday, as he felt a surge of tiredness go through his body. Suddenly one of the older men stopped and pointed towards him. He pulled his head back, panicking.

"What sort of state is it in down there, Fabien?" Oliver said, looking quizzically down the landing. "Terrible, Oliver! That is where we really need to start when we bring the workmen in. We must get the windows sorted out and then completely gut the rooms. The rain just comes straight in!"

"Hmm ... mind if I take a look?" Oliver said, taking a few steps in that direction.

Petru froze. He heard Oliver very clearly. He scanned the room for a hiding place. There wasn't much. A chest of drawers on its side with the drawers scattered around the room. The wardrobe ... a door propped against the wall. The wardrobe would be dangerous, a trap.

"Sure, if you want ... but don't you want a rest first?" Fabien said.

There was a pause during which Petru had grabbed the door and was carrying it towards the shadow side of the wardrobe to be propped up so he could get behind it and be hidden.

Oliver was looking around him with interest.

"Yuh ... guess you're right," he said at last. "I am feeling a bit buggered. I'll take a look tomorrow."

Petru let the air hiss between his lips as he crouched behind the door. He looked at his watch; it was three forty-five. Moving back to the door of the room, he listened. The three men were on the steps nearly at the ground floor. Whilst keeping a sharp eye on the stairs, he now called Constanta.

"What the fuck's going on?" she said before he could utter a word.

"I haven't seen the cabinet yet!" he whispered. "I'm about to go and look now. The men have gone down to the kitchen, and I'm on the second floor. I've taken some pictures and gonna take some more now. The cabinet is still in its casing at the top of the stairs, I think. They've been carrying it up for the last hours."

"You haven't seen it yet? You've been in there for an hour and half, Petru!" she said irritably.

"Look, I don't know any more than you what the fuck is happening ... be patient! I saw another chest thing downstairs which looked like it was being repaired but ... but it is not clear what it is. Call you in a bit later when I've looked at big box at the top of stairs." He closed off.

Moving along the landing to the stairwell, he listened. He

could just about hear voices far away. He sprinted up the stairs past the third floor and on up to the garret. There was the crate. It was big, not far short of his outstretched arms and nearly up to his midriff. He gave it a nudge, but it resisted him.

Taking out his camera, he took several shots and put it away again. He then turned his attention to his surroundings. This really was a very different floor. There were no rooms up here, at least not like below.

The landing section up here looked very different, like it had been decorated long ago, but now … well, it was like a farm building. Huge structural timbers and no attempt at disguising them. This floor displayed the real bones of the house, the raw architecture. He looked around for an appropriate hiding place should he get caught up here. There looked to be plenty. But he must be able to see the crate … see what was going to happen to this mysterious thing. He scanned for a good viewpoint.

Then he noticed the three dormer windows. Light flooded in from these and lit up the space, but beyond, at the other side of the floor, it was dark. He could disappear in there, but he would not get a view of the crate. There was a wall blocking his view. He had to hide towards the windows. Listening down the stairs again, he satisfied himself they were still on the ground floor. He quickly pulled his camera out and took more shots of the garret showing the dormer windows, the roof with its rough timbers and the staircase. He then switched to flash and took some more of the dark interior of the floor away from the windows. He needed a record of these, he figured.

Moving quickly, he went to the first of the windows and crouched down to allow his eyes to accustom to the gloom below. There was a boarded section which formed a low vertical wall just beneath the windows. This formed the edge of the floor, as the pitch of the roof made the space behind unusable.

But just to the right of the first window there had been a leak; the vertical wall and the floor were stained. Several of the vertical boards had been removed and replaced with new wood. But the timber to the right of these was now rotten. Rummaging in his rucksack, Petru pulled out an ancient-looking cold chisel wrapped in a cloth. Carefully, he pushed it between the first two boards. They almost fell off. The next ones proved more stubborn and creaked alarmingly as he pried them free.

He stopped and listened intently again, like a rummaging rodent on the forest floor. He stuck his head inside the space. Light came through various cracks in the roof tiles giving him an impression of size. It was tight, but it would afford him a hiding place and hopefully a chance to view the crate. But he would have to crawl behind this wainscoting under the window boxing and farther towards the staircase if he was to get photos of the crate. But were there enough cracks or holes for this?

His ears pricked. He moved past the window to the point where he would be when inside. There were definitely no apertures big enough; he would be hidden inside, blind to what was happening. Without hesitation, he glanced over his shoulder at the crate, made a snap judgment, and chose a spot. Pressing his hand against the lower part of the thin board to stop it splintering the whole way down, he levered off a section with a loud crack. He stopped dead and listened. Nothing. But the splintered edge looked somehow too fresh for comfort. Moving back to the opening he'd made, he reached inside and took a handful of dark sooty dust and smeared it onto the jagged edge, blowing away the excess. It helped, but not enough to disguise it. He spat onto his hand, took some more dust and thoroughly smeared it into the sharp fibres. Perfect.

Standing up and wiping his hands on his trousers, he again listened. All was quiet. Moving back to the staircase, he took a last look down. It was now or never. Taking out a bottle of water, he took several long gulps and smacked his lips. What had he got himself into, he thought as he stretched his back and arms with a loud sigh. Moving back into the main space, he noticed his footmarks showing prominently in the dust where he'd been prying the boards off. He picked up an old cloth and flapped it randomly across the dusty boards, as he backed towards the opening. Then with reptilian agility, he slid in sideways, his head cocked to one side to avoid the beam above.

Once inside he pulled his rucksack in and then started placing the tongue and groove boards back into place as far as possible. The final one was half wedged and half propped. He was inside now, completely hidden … but he still had to crawl underneath the window boxing to get to the right position to view the crate.

Chapter 30

Constanta moved lithely through the dense twisted branches to the place that she and Tarquin had chosen as their lair for the duration of the afternoon. Lying down next to him on the thick layer of old dry leaves, she scrunched her coat into a pillow and then thumped her head onto it. They were completely hidden to the outside world apart from a narrow view to the west through a gap in the foliage. It was as though they were underwater. Light stabbed erratically through the restless canopy around them, dancing chaotically on their faces and arms, playing with the contours of their bodies and turning them into weird speckled creatures of no definite shape.

"Anything happening out there?" Tarquin said, feeling a faint tinge of uneasiness at her close proximity.

"No. Van doors are still open … no one's around," she said listlessly. "We're just gonna have to wait for Petru to find out what the fuck's going on."

"Yuh … looks like it. I was imagining he'd have rung by now and revealed the master plan … you know, a sort of 'eureka' moment and explained everything to us!" Tarquin said.

"A reeka moment?" she said, turning her head towards him for an explanation.

"Oh … I meant a moment of … realization … understanding. You know, 'the penny dropping' sort of thing," he said, stretching out and putting a hand behind his head.

"Can you speak in plain English, Tarquin?" she said, giggling at the irony. "What is a 'Reeka' moment, for fuck's sake?"

"You've never heard of this?" he said, casting a wary glance at her.

"No, I fucking haven't."

"It's what you say when you suddenly understand something. It's 'Eureka' not 'Reeka.' From what I can remember, it was a Greek guy—a mathematician called Archimedes—who sat in the bath one day and, so the story goes, suddenly realized that the amount of water his body displaced was the same volume as his submerged body. He went on to work out that that's how a boat floats. The displaced water is equal to its weight."

"Wow. You are *so* clever, Tarquin!" Constanta said, giggling and flashing her white teeth. "If only I had been to your 'smart school' for upper class English boys."

Tarquin smiled self-consciously.

"Well, from what you say, you were taught pretty well in Romania," he said.

"Oh my, you are *so* tactful as well! Were there separate lessons in 'manners'?" she said, turning her body towards him slightly.

"No, actually. That … well, those you just pick up, I suppose."

"From your terribly well-bred parents … in their well-bred circle of friends!"

"Possibly," Tarquin said, feeling a wave of heat. "It's just common sense to me. You want to put people at their ease."

"I don't," Constanta challenged. "I like to make people feel uncomfortable!"

"Well, that's a bit sad, isn't it? A bit pointless?"

"Not at all. It's a game. You're too concerned about other peoples' feelings, darling. Fuck their feelings! Loosen up and pull their toes, as you English like to say."

"Their legs."

"Okay, legs then. Have some fun. Play with them. Back home that's how we are. We're always taking the piss out of our friends. But you English like heavy, serious conversation and always play it very polite in case you offend somebody. So boring. But then you suddenly go the other way and … boom! You go off like a nuclear weapon and turn really nasty. All that pent-up politeness explodes out!"

Tarquin looked at her, incapable of a reply. She burst into quiet spurts of muffled laughter at his expression and wriggled even closer, so she was touching him. Reaching up, she broke off a fleshy leaf and began to run its stem slowly across his forehead, then down over the bridge of his nose and across his lips … sensuously, from side to side.

Tarquin smiled and rubbed his forehead. He was anything but relaxed.

"You're an enigma, Constanta," he said, staring up through the leaves at glimpses of blue sky. "I can't make you out."

"Now that's a surprise … you being so smart!" she teased, digging her elbow into his ribs.

Tarquin rolled over to face her and rested his head on his hand. Her marbled eyes watched him defiantly, her lips parted slightly, revealing the sparkle of moisture on her teeth. There was a challenge in those blue green eyes … a dare. To Tarquin she looked absurdly beautiful in that theatre of dancing light—other worldly, beckoning, but infinitely dangerous.

With a mixture of fear and primal lust, he leant down and allowed his lips to brush gently onto hers with a rhythmic movement of his head. She sighed and put a hand around the back of his head, pulling him closer. Her mouth was like warm velvet, her tongue delicate, searching, needy … the shy representative of another hidden Constanta, the child in her, freed of the armouring Tarquin had come to fear. The real Constanta needed love, craved for it … he could feel that. Her defences were down; she was naked. They kissed amongst the leaves in that sun-spangled paradise for a length of time unknown to either of them, but presently, and without any warning, the old Constanta returned.

"Don't get any ideas," she announced, suddenly sitting up. "It ain't gonna happen."

Tarquin pulled away from her. Her voice was harsh, almost

hostile. It splintered the pure crystal of the moment like a musket ball.

"I'm sorry?"

"It ain't gonna happen, Tarquin. I'm not going to fuck you in here."

"Well … I … er … didn't expect you would," he said, perplexed by the sudden change.

"Just didn't want you getting carried away, that's all. I know what you men are like," she said sternly.

"Constanta," he said, staring at her. "Calm down. I'm not going to try anything, do anything; we're in the middle of some bushes waiting for another person to arrive any moment. I'm not insane, for God's sake!"

"Good, then that's fine!" she said, running her fingers through her tangled hair. "What time is it, anyway?"

He squinted at his wrist. "It's twenty to five."

"Okay, let's hope Petru gets some more information soon. We still don't have a fucking clue what's going on! It's getting late, and they'll be closing the shutters and windows soon," she said.

"True. He needs to get a move on or he'll be locked in for the night!" Tarquin said, reaching over and disentangling a small twig from her hair. "And then what do we do? We can't stay here in the bushes all night!"

Constanta succumbed again into quiet spurts of laughter.

"What the hell is so funny?" he said perplexed.

"You make me laugh; you're a fucking joke!" she said, staring at him affectionately.

He looked at her for a few moments.

"You know, you're really good for me, Constanta. Somehow you loosen me up. I can be a bit pompous …"

"Too bloody right, darling, you've got an iron bar up your arse!" she said, chuckling.

"But I like you, Tarquin. Don't get me wrong. You're honest; you're not full of shit like so many of my men friends—trying to big themselves up all the time to impress me. I like this about you. Plus you're old fashioned, as well. I mean, look at those fucking shoes!" she said, pointing at his heavy leather lace-ups. "You *are* Sherlock bloody Holmes!"

He looked at her briefly, before grabbing her head in his hands and kissing her hard on the mouth again.

Thomas Charrington

Chapter 31

"There it is ... Marston Meysey!" Sammy said, peering at a white sign pointing chirpily from an overgrown hedge. "Four and a half miles ... take a left!"

The black Sprinter turned sharply, throwing Bob against Sammy and Sammy against Gus.

"Slow down, G!" Bob said, straightening himself. "We've got all bloody night ... what's the big rush!"

"I don't want to be arriving at the 'ouse too late, okay ... it'll look a bit queer," Gus said. "We're supposed to be delivering a parcel."

"Okay. Okay. But cool the speed, for fuck's sake. If something comes round one of these corners we're gonna wipe 'em out!"

"Don't excite me, B," Gus said with a leer. "Look, I just want to arrive. These narrow lanes are doing me head in. Like I told yer it would, the sat nav threw in the towel way back. Look at it now ... it's saying turn around. The box of shit!"

"Yeah, it's a bit confused, that's for sure," Sammy said, looking at the screen. "Keeps trying to reroute itself."

"Right, Sammy, it's time for you to duck into the back, my friend," Gus said. "We're gonna be there soon. As I remember, the house is about half a mile before Marston. There's like two low walls on either side of the entrance and then a line of trees on both sides of the road to the house. Quite impressive, if yer know what I mean. Like straight out of some film."

"Can't wait!" Sammy said, elbowing Bob surreptitiously.

"Strupe Hall," Bob said jauntily. "Come on, show yourself, girl!"

They passed a small crossroads, and suddenly Gus hit the brakes hard.

"That's it! We take a right here!"

He reversed and headed onto an even smaller road. Here the swollen summer hedges of brambles, hawthorn, and hazel scratched and clawed at the dark skin of the van with horrible screeches, whilst the wing mirrors choked up with white umbrellas of cow parsley.

Gus cursed and winced at the cacophony surrounding them whilst Sammy threw his arms around like a mock conductor, laughing. Abruptly the noise stopped, as the hedges fell away from the road and they reached the edge of a small copse. Gus slapped his hands on the steering wheel.

"There she blows! See that line of trees over there … well, that's Strupe Hall," he said triumphantly. "Get ready to take a gander through the 'eyes,' Sammy, we'll be there in a few minutes."

Mary had just let Titus out of his kennel when she saw a large black van coming along the drive. She felt a small ripple of nervousness at this unexpected arrival and walked hesitantly across the gravel to meet it.

Titus yapped excitedly around the tyres of the vehicle as it drew alongside her. The window lowered to reveal a pair of men inside dressed in some form of uniform. She did not like the look of them.

"Evening, love," the driver said with an unconvincing smile. "Sign this, will yer, we have a parcel for Mr Smythe … sorry we're a bit late. The roads around here are a bloody nightmare! We could hardly fit the van down the final stretch, to be honest!"

"Mr Smythe?" Mary said looking puzzled. "There is no Mr Smythe down here … this is Strupe Hall. Are you sure you have the right address?"

Gus picked a parcel from the seat to his left and pretended to scrutinize it.

"Right … Mr Robert Smythe … Peacocks, Marston Meysey …"

"Well, this isn't Peacocks … it's Strupe Hall," Mary said matter-of-factly. "You've come to the wrong place, I'm afraid. I would try and help, but I've never heard of Peacocks. Can I see the parcel?"

Gus held it up with the address for her to see. She looked at it and shrugged, whilst noticing the livid bruise on the other side of Gus's face.

"No, never heard of the place. I know this area quite well, so I'm doubtful that it's around here," she said.

"Bloody hell!" Gus said with mock frustration. "Oh sorry, excuse me, love. Just it's our last delivery of the day and I was hoping to finish. Now we've got to go on a wild goose chase!"

"Sorry I can't help you," Mary offered politely.

"Who does live here then?" Gus asked, conjuring up an innocent expression. "It's a lovely house."

Mary immediately thought the question was odd from a man who was keen to finish his shift.

"Oliver Clasper," she said quietly, with a sense of reluctance.

"Oh right … well, that certainly isn't Smythe, is it!" Gus said with a grin.

"No, it isn't," she said, looking over her shoulder toward Titus.

"Is the gentleman here at the moment, he might be able to help with …"

"No, he's in France," Mary said, and immediately regretted it.

"Yeah, of course," Gus blurted.

"I'm sorry?"

"I meant … er … so when's he back?"

Bob coughed loudly.

"Is that of any relevance?" Mary said, giving Gus a sharp look.

"Oh … so I suppose you have to look after the place in his absence," Gus said casually, his eyes roving over the house.

"Must be huge inside … look at all those windows!"

Mary thought fast. This line of questioning was unnerving her.

"Well, obviously. My husband and our own dogs … er … German shepherds … are in the house. Titus here doesn't get on with them."

"Mmm …," Gus murmured as though thinking about something. "Right, well, sorry to disturb you and … er … thanks, love."

He put the van into gear and, after doing a loop on the gravel, headed back down the drive. Mary watched them go until they were out of sight. Something about those people made her uneasy, but without wanting to dwell on silly feelings, she attended to the task of taking Titus for his evening walk.

Sammy stuck his head through the curtain and climbed into the front seat.

"Guys, I'm gonna be perfectly honest with you, this isn't looking good. I heard all that conversation, and I reckon that woman was suspicious."

"You do?" Gus said, surprised.

"Yes, I do. Your questions, Gus, with due respect, weren't exactly smart."

"No?"

"No! You seemed just a bit too inquisitive, if yer know what I mean! I may be wrong, but that's what I think."

"But we had to find out what the situation was," Gus said defensively.

"True, we did. For whatever reason, I still say she was suspicious. Either way, we have a problem. If she isn't in the house with her husband, i.e. she told us a porky, she may well put a call through to the coppers and explain what happened. That might make them sweep by unexpectedly, like when I'm there later on. If she is in the house with her husband and her bloody Alsatians, then I don't think I want to be there with them!"

Bob burst out laughing.

"Why ever not, Sammy?" he said, guffawing.

"Shut it, Bob," Gus said sternly. "This isn't funny! We have to make a decision."

"Cool down, for Christ's sake," Bob said, looking out of his own window. "I was only trying to lighten things up a bit."

"My advice to you, mate, is abort this job now. I've done plenty of jobs like this, and if you smell trouble at the start, get the hell out of there. It isn't worth it. Even the big man himself said, don't take any risks. We know the geezer is coming back to his London gaff at some point; you just nail him then in your own territory. We did our job and got down here. We've established Oliver is away. We've been professional, okay?"

"The man's right, G," Bob said. "She was suspicious. We can't afford to get nailed a second time."

"A second time?" Sammy said, puzzled.

"Yeah … well …as we was sayin' earlier about the bruises on…"

"What he means, Sam," Gus interjected quickly, "is we can't afford to get our arses kicked a second time. Once by Oliver's henchmen, and then again by his local coppers."

"Oh right … sure … that makes sense," Sammy agreed, whilst scrutinizing the livid marks on Gus's face with interest.

"I mean, what are yer going to achieve sneaking around that house, anyway?" Bob added, "We know the geezer's up to something."

"It's *what* he's up to that Viktor and Zoltan want to know; they reckon he's making some sort of furniture. Yer know, really old stuff worth a shitload of wonga."

"S'pose so," Bob said disinterestedly.

They sat in silence for a few minutes whilst Gus sucked heavily on a cigarette.

"Right," he said eventually. "We're gonna head back to town."

*   *   *

Petru peered through the small hole he'd made in the wainscot as the men came up the final steps. They were panting heavily and carrying something between them. They stopped for a few moments at the top to catch their breath.

"Good God … those stairs never get any easier!" the fatter of the two said.

"It's good for you, Oliver," the other said. "Strengthens up your heart."

"Where there's pain, there's gain, I suppose," he replied, still panting.

Petru scrutinized the object they'd brought up and realized it was the chest he'd seen earlier on the ground floor. Pulling away from the hole slightly, he brought his camera up and took a couple of shots. He sank back down on his knees and waited, intrigued to see what was going to happen.

"Okay, let's get on with it," Oliver said. "We don't have a load of daylight left."

"True," the other man said. "But enough, I think."

"Where the hell's Fabien with the lid?" Oliver said.

"Oh, don't worry, it's not important at the moment. Cecile is probably bending his ear about this and that … you know what women are like. Also, he's going around closing the windows and shutters before the air gets damp," the second man said.

Petru felt a wave of fear flow through him. Close the windows … cut off his escape route? Having to open shutters and windows on his way out was going to slow him down and possibly attract attention.

The second man pulled out a pair of screwdrivers and handed one of them to Oliver.

"Okay, if you can just start taking the eight main screws out of the front panel, Oliver, but leave the corner ones, okay, or it'll fall apart! I'll do the top. When they're out you can start on the right side."

"You're the boss, Melvyn," Oliver said, squatting down.

They started working on the crate they'd brought up earlier, unaware that a pair of eyes was watching their every move from behind the wainscoting, twelve feet away.

"Blimey, Mel, I'm getting cramps in my fingers!" Oliver said after a few minutes. "All this bloody twisting!"

Melvyn laughed. "Yeah, it is tough when you're not used to it, I suppose!"

After twenty minutes of muttering and swearing, Oliver stood up, flexing his fingers.

"God, that was painful, you must have hands like claws, Mel!" he said, chuckling.

"Grab the other side of the lid, Oliver," Melvyn said. They eased it gently off and put it to one side.

"You know what, Mel, you're one clever bugger!" he said, looking at the faux pine shell which disguised the real cabinet. "This looks like cheap rubbish!"

"Well, that's the idea, Oliver. Just wait till the sides and front come off. Okay, now take the two screws on your side out of the front panel and I'll do my end," Melvyn said. "But keep hold of the panel!"

They removed the screws and then very carefully pulled the panel away. Chunks of foam fell away with it.

Another scuffed pine frame with a pair of recessed panels revealed itself.

Petru looked on in a state of puzzlement. What exactly was going on? The cabinet didn't look impressive at all.

"Okay, Oliver," Melvyn said, standing up. "Very gently put your fingers around the edges of the panel, like me, and pull upwards. They're only dowels but quite firm."

They slowly worked the panel up until it was free of the side frames. Melvyn put it to the side.

"Now do the same with the front panel. Very gently … gently … here she comes."

Oliver chuckled and peered at it in awe. "Oh my God, what a heavenly sight!" he said affectionately. "I get such a thrill just looking at it."

Petru gasped quietly inside his chamber; he knew at once he was looking at the "cabinet." Even to his untrained eye he could see the magnificence of the piece in front of him.

Without hesitation, he lifted his camera and took several more shots. He then pulled out his mobile and sent a text to Constanta.

> *"They just unpacked cabinet. is f.. amazing. Cannot talk very close to them. Got photos call u asap."*

A text came back within seconds.

> *"F. great! Any idea whats going on?"*
> *"No, still don't know yet."*
> *"Ok, remember getting late now and windows r shut."*
> *"Ok."*

He closed the phone and peered out as Fabien appeared at the top of the stairs with the chest lid under his arm.

"Wow! Shit! She is so wonderful," he gasped in amazement.

"She looks good, eh?" Oliver said smugly.

"More than good, Oliver … she is a masterpiece!" Fabien said, moving around the cabinet.

"Right, we're going to remove the two sides now," Melvyn said, trying to keep the momentum rolling.

After a further fifteen minutes, the cabinet stood gloriously naked and utterly out of place in the dilapidated rustic surroundings of the garret.

Oliver burst out laughing at the sight.

"Have you ever seen such a ridiculous spectacle in all your lives!" he said grinning. "One of the most exquisite pieces of the eighteenth century standing in this barn!"

"It does look blooming odd, I must admit!" Melvyn agreed, smiling.

"But this will make its discovery all the sweeter … all the more plausible!" Fabien said.

"True. Yes, that's very true, Fabien," Oliver agreed.

Petru lowered his camera again. What were they saying? Something about eighteenth century and a discovery being sweet. He struggled to understand.

"Right, time is six forty-five, we need to get a move on," Oliver said, glancing at his watch.

"Oliver," Melvyn said suddenly, rather sternly. "I can tell you right now; this will not be finished tonight."

"Oh?"

"I've been thinking," he continued. "The light is dropping quite seriously. I didn't realize how gloomy it would get up here, and I need light … a lot of light … daylight."

"Okay, Mel," Oliver said. "If that's the case, so be it. We don't want to jeopardise this for the sake of an extra half a day. It is getting gloomy up here, I quite agree. What shall we do?"

"I reckon we should place the cabinet inside the chest for the night for safekeeping."

"What, in case some squirrel takes a fancy to it!" Fabien said with a chuckle.

"Something like that," Melvyn said, pulling on a pair of gloves. "Here, put these on, please," he said, handing each of them similar gloves. "We don't want our fingerprints all over the cabinet. They've got strands of rubber sewn into the fabric so you'll get a hell of a grip!"

"Smart thinking, Melvyn, hadn't thought of that," Fabien said.

They moved the remains of the crate away to the side, so the cabinet and the chest stood facing each other.

Petru was looking from an angle behind the chest but face on to the cabinet. He quickly took some more shots from his hideaway. He was beginning to feel cramped and uncomfortable and could feel things crawling around his ankles. The light was fading, and he began to worry about getting out of the house.

"Right," Melvyn said. "As you can see, I've removed the front panel of the chest so all we have to do is take the weight of the cabinet and move it straight across and onto the base of the chest, okay?"

"Sure, no problem," Fabien said, getting underneath one corner whilst Oliver took the other.

"On the count of three … very gently, please," Melvyn said.

The cabinet slid gently across and into its new home without a hitch. Melvyn then squatted down and fixed the front panel of the chest temporarily into place. Finally he laid the lid loosely on the top.

"Voila!" Fabien said with a sigh. "Bon nuit, mon cherie!"

Petru took some final shots and popped his camera away. He stretched one leg out and then the other to keep the blood flowing. All he wanted was for them to disappear downstairs so he could get out of his hellhole.

"Okay, I think we can say that's a good job done," Oliver said with a yawn. Wiping his handkerchief across his face, he suddenly made his way towards the closest dormer window. Petru saw the fabric of Oliver's trousers very clearly as he passed within a foot of the hole and stopped. He crouched low and put his head between his knees trying to diminish himself.

"God, what a stupendous view!" Oliver said, gazing out on the parkland below, now bathed in a soft pinkish light. "This truly is paradise. I can just imagine some dusky maiden cantering across those meadows on a white charger."

"You can, Oliver?" Fabien said with a snort. "I'm sure it can be arranged!"

"I think we both know that's a lie, Fabien!" Oliver said, turning away from the window.

"C'mon, let's go down and have a drink. God knows we've earned it! Ready, Mel?"

"Give me a few minutes … I'll follow you down," Melvyn said.

"Okay. See you down there, Mel," Fabien said, moving towards the stairs.

"Sure," he replied vaguely. Their voices slowly receded. It was suddenly very quiet.

Melvyn gathered up his tools and popped them in a bag. He then stood very quietly scrutinising the chest. There was dead silence in the garret now, and Petru knew this was the most dangerous moment so far. He froze and watched Melvyn through a smaller crack lower down which afforded him a more discreet view. After standing motionless for a full two minutes staring at the chest, Melvyn then started scanning the garret itself.

His eyes flickered over the floor boards at the top of the stairs and then began probing the architecture towards the windows. He stared at the wainscoting where Petru was crouching, hidden and fearful in the darkness. He prayed Constanta wouldn't call now, as even the muffled vibration might be picked up in this heightened situation.

Suddenly Melvyn ambled purposefully towards him and then beyond his field of vision. Like Oliver, he gazed out of the window onto the parkland below whilst his strong fingers, like scouts on a battlefield, moved restlessly over the wood surfaces around his midriff, sniffing for information on texture and density. Petru couldn't see him now, but he heard him turn. He seemed to be staring into the darkness of the main garret where the light was losing its fight with the shadows. Again he stood like a statue, so that Petru felt his heartbeat must betray him.

Then, without warning, he was off. With a final glance at the chest, he made his way down the stairs to join the others.

Petru waited a further five minutes in case one of them had forgotten something. He let himself stiffly out of his lair, and then carefully replaced the wooden boards back in place.

He stretched for a minute or two, allowing the blood to filter back into his numb muscles. What an ordeal! Now he had to get out of here. Flapping the cloth across the floorboards to erase his latest footmarks, he went over to the staircase and listened; voices a long way down. He pulled out his mobile and phoned Constanta.

"Okay, I'm out of here," he said. "I've done all I can."

"Well? Are things clearer now, darling?" Constanta said with a small chuckle.

"Yes. A bit better. I'll tell you when I come out. Where are you?"

"Where you left us, but a bit farther in … you know, towards the other side of those bushes, away from the courtyard. Just call me when you're out; you may have to take a different route. Be very careful, darling."

"Okay."

"Well?" Tarquin said, in the gloom of the bushes.

"He's coming out," Constanta replied.

"Has he discovered what's going on in that madhouse?"

"I'm not sure, he couldn't really talk. Said he would explain when he sees us."

"Sod it!" Tarquin said in frustration.

"What's the problem?" she said. "Give him a chance … he has to get out of there now, and all the windows are shut."

"I know. It just doesn't sound like he's cracked it. He would have said something more positive."

"Tarquin," Constanta said firmly. "Just wait and see what he comes out with. Stop being so negative. He's got loads of photos, and he says he's seen the cabinet, which is fucking amazing!"

"Well, that's brilliant … but we still don't—"

"Tarquin, you're beginning to annoy me now," she said, raising her eyebrows. "Give him a fucking chance!"

"Okay. I'm sorry. Just want this whole trip to have been worth the effort," he said solemnly.

She threaded her fingers through his and pecked him on the mouth.

"Be patient. It's all gonna work out. He'll be out shortly, and then we have to do some serious detective work."

Tarquin slumped back down and gazed through the leaves at the deepening lilac sky.

"The bats will be out soon," he said with a sigh.

"You fucking nutcase, Tarquin," she said, nuzzling up to him and laughing in suppressed spurts.

Petru listened from the shadows of the garret to the distinctive notes of a piano far below him. They skipped joyfully up the stairs accompanied by laughing voices, beckoning him to join in the new frivolous mood of the house. But they did nothing to lighten his surge of despondency and worry. He knew only too well that the piano was tucked in the curl of the main staircase on the ground floor, and that this meant his route was blocked … at least for the moment. He cursed. Pulling his camera out for the final time, he took more photos of the chest and the remains of the crate which it had arrived in. He also took some of the pine panels that were propped against the wall.

He knew these had some relevance but wasn't sure what, at this stage. He was tempted to open the lid of the chest to take more photos of the cabinet, but this might be risky, and he had many shots of the cabinet from before. It was getting dark and he had to use a flash, but that was risky; anyone in the garden would see. True, someone was playing the piano, but the man, Melvyn, had a habit of wandering off alone; perhaps he was out in the garden right now.

Zipping up his rucksack and scanning around for anything he may have left, he headed down the stairs. The sounds of merriment from below grew in tempo as he descended, but he was keenly alert. Perhaps only Oliver and Fabien were at the piano, with Melvyn somewhere else … like on the first floor. Reaching the second landing, he looked over the banister down the stairwell to the ground floor. He could see one person far below, holding a glass and agitating to the music, but who it was he couldn't see. Certainly there was no light coming from the first floor, so this suggested they were all at the bottom.

He crept down, step by step … a ghostly figure with shadows for eyes, clinging to the wall to avoid the light. The sharp smell of tobacco smoke and wine grew in intensity as he descended. Moving onto the first landing, he stopped and peered gingerly down.

Fabien was on the piano stool, flanked by the other two men. Oliver was completely immersed in the moment, laughing and cajoling, whilst Melvyn stood by like a statue, awkward and stiff, unable to let himself go. Petru feared the sixth sense in Melvyn. He knew he only had to glance up to see his face illuminated as though on stage.

Cursing again, he moved away from the stairwell and tried to figure out a plan. What the hell was he to do? Wait until they went into the kitchen for supper? That could be some time away, and what's to say they would all go in there, anyway? Perhaps Fabien would cook, and leave the other two in the main hall.

Should he climb out of the window? He glanced outside. It was dark. That would be impossible. Suddenly his mobile shivered.

"*Where the fuck are u?*" Constanta wrote.

"*Trapped inside. cannot get past them on ground floor.*"

"*Why, the house is huge?*"

"*They blocking stairs.*"

"*Only one stairs?*" she wrote.

Petru stopped and thought. There were other stairs; he'd seen them when he first entered the house … in that first passage.

"*Let me check. Give me 10 mins,*" he wrote.

He moved away from the stairs and into the deep twilight of the first landing. There were no other stairs accessible from here, he suddenly remembered; the landings were blocked by huge partitions.

Quickly he moved up to the second floor again. He peered into the gloom beyond and felt a shiver go down his back. The house seemed to be holding him prisoner. Very carefully, he moved along the second landing into space he hadn't searched earlier. It was dead dark. No windows to shed even the faintest glimmer from outside. He held his mobile up for light as he moved forward, cursing that he had no torch.

Doorways passed on either side; he tried some of them, but they were locked or had no handle. He desperately wanted the landing to open up into a new stairwell or at least a back staircase, but the utter blackness crushed in on him and breathed its ancient breath down his neck. He had to be in the centre of the house now … it was as silent as a tomb.

Without warning, his foot sank downwards and a floorboard whipped up and struck his temple. Yelling in panic, he yanked his foot out of the cavity and fell on his side. The board fell back with a thud. He clambered up and stood listening, as a warm trickle threaded its way through his hair and down his cheek. He dabbed it with his sleeve, his hand shaking uncontrollably. He strained his ears for noise below. Suddenly the floor vibrated noisily and made him jump in terror. The fucking mobile! He picked it up … another message.

"*Well?*" she wrote.

Petru took several deep shaky breaths and tapped out a reply. "*Leaving now. No contact.*" He texted back.

He moved back down the long landing, crouching very low to the floor for fear of another loose board. He stopped at the stairwell listening. The voices and piano notes were still there, oblivious to his trauma. He took a left towards the rooms he was familiar with and headed carefully down that landing. It was brighter here; he could get a sense of space and distance.

Without hesitation, he entered the room with the wardrobe and went straight to the window. He gasped in amazement; it was quite light outside. There was a bright moon dipping in and out of some fast high clouds. It threw wild branch shadows onto the walls and floor and over his bloodied face. He remembered Constanta's words about the house being haunted; he shivered. Rubbing his hands on his trousers very thoroughly, he pushed the sash up those few inches. He mustn't leave blood; he mustn't leave any signature of his existence here. Next he removed his small rucksack.

The moon came out again as though on cue and illuminated his escape route. Leaning out, he scrutinized the sill, the ledge, and the branch of the tree below very carefully. There would be no second chance. They glittered with an eerie light, but were well defined. Then everything dissolved into inky shadow as the moon dived into the clouds once again. He had to time this right. If he jumped at the wrong moment, he'd be jumping blind.

With a final dab of his temple, he manoeuvred himself out of the window backwards, snatching his rucksack as he did so. As his centre of gravity moved ever outwards, he felt a surge of fear. Down … down … he slid, his chin scraping the stony surface, the rough clinging lichens … his toes searching for that life-saving platform. Then he was there and he could let his feet take the weight. He stopped for a few moments in relief, and glanced at the bright impassive moon and its hustling cohorts.

His hands were wrapped like claws around the window ledge, and he had to relinquish these precious anchors in order to proceed. His rucksack hung from his right wrist. With extreme care, he let go with this hand and allowed the sack to wriggle up to his shoulder. Taking hold of the sill once again with his right hand, he then twisted outwards and managed to get his left hand through the strap and the sack up onto his shoulders. This was it … he had to time it perfectly.

He now studied the racing clouds impatiently with a sense of intense danger in the pit of his stomach. In quick succession he was plunged from brightness to inky dark, to brightness again. And then, after a few interminable minutes, there it was … the patch of clear sky he'd been waiting for. A further half minute dragged by in the hellish gloom before, once again, he was bathed in silver light. Then, looking over his shoulder at the branch below one final time, he took a deep breath and released his hands. He started falling backwards, but as he did so, he twisted his body outwards, bending his knees to propel himself away from the building.

With his eyes fixed like lasers on the dark arm of the branch below, he accelerated rapidly before hitting it with a heavy slap and continuing downwards with a tremendous whoosh of leaves and branches. His arms locked around it and he felt his chin grind against the rough bark with excruciating pain. The branch sank down dramatically and then recovered itself, as though appalled by the insolence of this primate. From the moment he got a hold of the branch, he wasted no time in moving farther down the gnarled spiny surface to relieve the strain on the limb and save it from breaking. By the time it had stopped its thrashing, he was already at the trunk … cut all over but still clinging on.

The main trunk was solid as iron, but the countless branches which sprouted from it slowed his progress and snagged his rucksack at every opportunity. Down the last eight metres he slid and twisted, until finally he swung from the lowest limb and landed in the soft deep shadow beneath. There was no moonlight here, nor plants … just the smell of dank earth and the silence of the garden. He was alive!

Thomas Charrington

Chapter 32

Gus heard the phone being picked up and stiffened.

"Yes, Gus, I'm listening," Zoltan said coolly into his mobile.

"Er, hi, Z. Sorry to call yer so late, but … er … I thought yer should know that we've aborted the assignment."

"You have? Why?"

"Well … er … we made …"

"Is Sammy with you?" Zoltan interrupted.

"Yes. Yes, he is. I know that Viktor has him on a flight tomorrow night, and that …"

"Good … carry on," Zoltan said impatiently.

"Well, as I was saying, we get down to the Hall, yer know, Strupe Hall, at about five this afternoon. I remembered it quite well as it happens … that line of trees is like a …"

"Yes, yes, and?" Zoltan said, cutting him off.

"Well, we arrived at the 'ouse at about five, and there was a lady on like the gravel at the front watching us as we drove in. So I stopped and told her we 'ad a delivery for a geezer called Mr Smythe. Anyway, we was chatting away, and Sammy was in the back giving the 'ouse a good eyeballing through the lenses. Bob was in the front with me. Anyway, we chatted for a bit … yer know, I was trying to buy time … and suddenly she got a bit foxy with me, if yer know what I mean."

"Foxy? You mean she took shine to you?" Zoltan said incredulously.

"No, no, that's not what I mean at all!" Gus said with a snort. "She turned a bit odd like, sort of a bit standoffish, for no reason at all."

"And?" Zoltan said.

"Well, I tried to be friendly, but she wasn't having none of it and made it clear that we should leave," Gus said, feeling a sense of failure as he recalled it.

"Look, Gus," Zoltan said sternly. "You were not there to make friends ... you were there to get an understanding of what security the house has, and whether there was anyone there! For the love of Lenin, what's got into you that you abort a job because you're not liked!"

"No, no, Z. I'm not explaining myself proper," Gus said, feeling embarrassed. "The woman was suspicious of us ... yer know ... she didn't trust us. And when we left, we all chatted about it, and Sammy was adamant that she might call the police and get us checked out, or send the cops over later when he was inside."

"I don't understand," Zoltan said peevishly. "Why was she suspicious? You were authentic delivery people in uniform. What is there not to trust ... unless, of course, you said something to arouse her suspicions."

"No, nothing," Gus said sheepishly. "I ... I just think it was the fact she was there on her own with us, and she felt a bit nervous about a van suddenly appearing out of nowhere at that time in the afternoon. Some people are paranoid. Anyways, she said her 'usband and two German shepherds were resident in the house whilst Oliver was away, so it didn't look great."

"Oh, I see," Zoltan said softening. "Well, that does change the scenario. Guess you probably did the right thing, in that case. Viktor will understand you made correct decision."

"That's what I thought," Gus resumed. "What's the point in taking a risk when Oliver's going be back in a day or two? We can take him out when he's back in Battersea."

"But how do we know he's going to be back in a day or two? We don't, do we," Zoltan persisted. "He could be away for a month."

"Look, Z," Gus said, feeling suddenly more in charge. "We're going to get Oliver one way or the other … he's got too much going on to disappear for long. I bet yer he's back within the week, and then we'll have him!"

"Okay, let's speak tomorrow," Zoltan said resignedly.

"Sure thing … cheers, mate," Gus said, and then waited for his boss to close off.

Thomas Charrington

Chapter 33

The next morning, Petru came self-consciously into the breakfast room holding his rucksack and meandered through the tables to join Tarquin and Constanta in their corner. There were cuts and livid blotches all over his face and neck which caused a couple of late breakfasters to gaze at him in astonishment. He managed a small smile as he arrived.

"You look a mess, darling!" Constanta said, standing up and giving him a hug. "I'm so sorry."

"If you want to eat, old fellow, you better order now," Tarquin said, folding his newspaper.

"We told them you'd had an accident and needed some rest! How are you?"

"Painful ... all over my body, Mr Tarquin. Scratches, bruises, cuts; the shower was really bad ... had to turn the water to cool!"

"I'm sure," Tarquin said, scrutinizing him.

"Did you sleep okay, darling? You were soo fucked last night. I never seen you so hungry. Had your own pizza and then half of mine!" Constanta said with a small giggle.

"I know ... I was very hungry by the end," Petru said. "I guess I burnt a lot of energy in that place; it was so weird."

"Creepy?" she said.

"Sure! Just ... just not like anything I seen before. It was like the place was alive ... like it knew me and them were not together. It wanted my respect ... but it also helped me to get out alive."

"Odd," Tarquin said, picking up the menu. "Look ... choose

something, and I'll order it; we need to be fast."

"Sausages, mushrooms, cheese omelette … toast?" Constanta said, pointing.

"Yes, looks good, thanks," Petru said, leaning back and gulping down a glass of orange juice.

Tarquin went and ordered.

Half an hour later, Petru pushed his plate away and reached into his sack.

"Right, I think I'm ready to try and explain what went on in there yesterday and to show you the photos," he said, flicking the camera on. "Go easy with me. I'm not really awake properly … feeling cloudy in my head."

"Don't worry, old fellow," Tarquin said, putting a hand briefly on his shoulder. "You had a hell of a night, and I think you did brilliantly. We were just biding our time in the bushes."

Constanta threw him a fleeting scowl.

"Okay, sweetheart, let's see the show," she said, moving her chair next to Petru.

"This is the big hall I was talking about, with the broken table, the piano, and the stairs."

"Fuck me, it's huge!" Constanta exclaimed. "So that's where they were last night … at that piano?"

"Exactly!" Petru said. "Blocking my way."

"Mmm … that did pose a problem," Tarquin agreed as he eyeballed the screen. "God! What a beautiful place. What grandeur. That's the home of true French aristocracy!"

"Okay, Tarquin, we get the message; you're impressed!" Constanta said.

"I am … it's positively stately. Look at that marble floor!"

"This is the kitchen, and this is the small room with the chest … you know, where I told you there were tools and stuff."

"Okay," Constanta said, staring at the image.

After some more shots of the ground floor, they suddenly jumped to the garret.

"Okay, so you see the big crate there at the top of the stairs, well, here's them unpacking it … and there's some panels they took off which look like shit. I thought these were the chest at first, and I was thinking, this can't be right … that doesn't look worth fifty pounds! And then … just look at that!"

He moved back to let them both see the screen.

"Fucking hell! That's our baby!" Constanta said with a huge grin. "What a beauty!"

"Good God!" Tarquin gasped. "What an exquisite piece!"

"When I saw that thing, I knew straight away it was the cabinet," Petru said triumphantly.

"It just oozes money."

"Sure does, darling, and we're gonna get some of it, even if it kills me!" she said, raising her voice and causing the waiter to glare at her.

"Okay. So now we have some shots of the chest they brought up from downstairs … you see there," Petru said, pointing with a fork, "that's what was being put together downstairs. They put the cabinet into this last night."

"Right … so they took it out of the crate it travelled in, and then put it in this thing," Constanta said, frowning.

"Interesting," Tarquin said, pretending to grasp what was going on.

"Well, Sherlock?" Constanta said, calling Tarquin's bluff.

"Well … well, it would seem that there's a reason for this manoeuvre," Tarquin said with a grave expression.

"You don't say, darling … what powers of deduction you have!" she said with a giggle.

Tarquin reddened.

"Well, there's got to be a reason for doing this!" Tarquin said indignantly.

"Of course there's a fucking reason, Tarquin … but *what is it,* for Christ's sake. Why have they taken it out of one box and put it in another?"

"Well, the chest they put it in looks old," Tarquin said, without quite knowing why.

"And? So? Who gives a shit if it looks old or new? There's no one to see it apart from the guys who put it in there," Constanta said forcefully.

"Perhaps they will take it somewhere else afterwards," Petru said.

"That's just plain crazy," Constanta said. "You lift a heavy box to the top of the house with a cabinet in it and take another box to the top of the house, and you change them over and bring them back down?"

"True, it doesn't make any sense," Petru said. "There must be a reason for it being up there."

"Perhaps they needed the exercise!" Tarquin said with a snort. "Look … I'm completely flummoxed."

"Yes, that sounds like you, Tarquin. Now, c'mon guys … think! We need to work this out!" Constanta said in exasperation.

There was a pause in the conversation for a minute or so, during which Petru tapped the fork on the table like a drum.

"Right, I think it is something like this," Constanta said eventually. "I think the cabinet is being hidden in the house out of the way for some reason, and at some point in the future, say in a couple of months or something, some other guys are going to come here and collect it. I don't have a fucking clue why. It must be hidden or it could be stolen, so it is taken right up to the top in that old place."

"But why not just put it in a storage place with security cameras if there's risk of being stolen?" Petru said. "Why the big house in middle of countryside?"

"Because it must not be clocked by anyone, that's why, Petru. No one must know about it," Constanta replied.

"But who will know … it is just a box like many other boxes?" Petru persisted.

"No," Tarquin interjected. "The house is important. There's a reason it's being there. Possibly there's a very rich individual who's going to buy the place, do it up and … and …"

"Yes, we're waiting," Constanta coaxed.

"And … well … the cabinet will be waiting for him."

"I don't understand," she said, searching Tarquin's face.

"What I mean is … the cabinet had to be brought here now

… for some unknown reason; perhaps the police were sniffing around Oliver's house and it needed to be brought here prematurely," Tarquin stammered.

"Hang on!" Constanta said excitedly. "Or perhaps Oliver uses the house as his storage place for valuable fake cabinets; you know, somewhere out of the way. There may be more cabinets in that place."

"Yes … he makes them in UK and gets them across here for storage before he sells them. It's just a way to avoid police. They raid his house and nothing … nada!" Petru said enthusiastically.

"Exactly! Sometime soon a dealer with rich clients will appear at the house and make him an offer. The house is his showroom. Guys, I think we may have worked out his little game!" Constanta said, giving Petru a high five. "The chateau is Oliver's French showroom … his hideaway!"

"Could be, I suppose," Tarquin said, twisting his mouth down. "Seems a very laborious way to sell fake goods; crossing the channel every time and driving into the middle of nowhere. And why all the changing of boxes at the top of the house?"

"Tarquin, he's not coming over here *all the time,* for Christ's sake, these things take time to build … he's perhaps making one a year!"

"Possibly to order?" Petru said.

"Exactly!" she said.

"Bloody hell," Tarquin said, gazing out of the window. "I suppose you could be right. He's probably well known in the trade and wants these pieces away from his English operations as fast as possible."

"Exactly!" Constanta said eagerly. "Now do you agree with us?"

There was a pause.

"Yes … possibly," Tarquin said, looking at her. "You could have cracked it!"

"Well, are we three clever motherfuckers or what!" Constanta said, grinning.

Tarquin stood up and put his jacket on.

"So what do we do?" Petru said. "Go back up there and tell them we know what they're doing and demand money?"

"No! Definitely not … not yet," Constanta said forcefully. "We have to think. Like we discussed yesterday, we don't want them to remove the fucking chest and … and … leave us looking stupid!"

"Look, we don't know there are other pieces of fake furniture in there," Tarquin interrupted. "Perhaps this is the only piece, and by the time the police arrive it would have gone missing."

"Exactly! But we're not going to tell the police, Tarquin!" Constanta said with exasperation. "That's the last thing we do."

"Okay … good."

"Guess you're right, they would somehow make us look stupid and we lose everything," Petru suggested.

"It's exactly the same as the situation in Battersea, when you wanted to confront Oliver, darling. It wouldn't work! They'd come out with some bullshit to the police. So we do not go to the house and threaten them … definitely not!"

There was a pause for a few moments.

"Yes … yes," she said, gazing out of the window. "That's the only way. We have to make contact with the Russian guys and tell them we know where the cabinet is and … and we want a payoff for the information!"

"Are you crazy, Constanta?" Tarquin said, raising his eyebrows. "Those guys have unfinished business with us, and next time they're going to kill us!"

"For Christ's sake, Tarquin, the only reason they want to kill us is because they think we are someone else … Oliver!"

"It doesn't bloody matter what they think or don't think … they still want to kill us," Tarquin persisted.

"So Tarquin, we have to somehow get across to them that we are *not* the people they want!"

"And how the hell do we do that? We don't have any phone numbers, addresses … and we certainly don't have a clue who is hiring these guys," Tarquin said, frowning.

"Tarquin," Constanta said sternly. "Those guys do not want

us dead."

"Well, it bloody looked like it!" Tarquin retaliated. "And you said they did."

"That was to shake you up … they don't want us dead … it doesn't make sense. They want the bloody cabinet!"

"Okay, then … how in the hell are we going to explain to these two nice guys, waiting outside my house when we get back, that we are innocent? They want revenge! You humiliated them, Constanta!"

"Are you complaining?" she said, grinning.

"No … I was impressed, to be frank, but—"

"Thank you," she said.

"But, can't you see this is going to be difficult to do? If they get hold of me and threaten me, I could just be talking nonsense to save my skin. People who are being physically threatened say anything. These guys are used to this, I'm sure. They won't believe a word I bloody utter!"

"True, Mr Tarquin," Petru said solemnly. "Be very careful with them."

"This is where we have to be very clever, darling. Like the male spider moving towards the female … step by careful step. One foot wrong and … *zap*! We're eaten for breakfast!"

"God help us," Tarquin muttered.

She stood up.

"Shall we take a stroll around the square?" Tarquin said, looking at his watch. "I feel like a bit of exercise, and there may be a museum or something over there which could be worth a visit. Besides, I'm sure poor old Percy wants a walk."

"You and your fucking culture, Tarquin!" Constanta said with mock annoyance. "C'mon, let's go and see … there might be some nice shops. Go and get Percy."

Tarquin disappeared upstairs.

"I'm gonna take it easy, if you don't mind … catch some more sleep," Petru said quietly, zipping up his rucksack.

"Sure, no problem, darling … you've earned it," she said affectionately. "You're gonna rest today. See you later. Oh, help yourself to antiseptic creams and stuff in my bag. Some of those cuts look nasty."

She slumped back in a chair and waited until Tarquin reappeared with Percy. Then they went out onto the street and took a left towards the square. Constanta threaded her arm through Tarquin's.

"Poor fellow looks in quite a bad way. That house really gave him hell … and as for jumping into that yew tree …"

"Yes, he could have lost an eye … just imagine how we'd have felt," she said.

"He probably should have waited till they went to bed and then just climbed out of the window," Tarquin said.

"Sounds simple, darling, but he had no torch, he'd been whacked on the head by a piece of wood, he had no idea how long he would have to wait, he was starving hungry, and he was worried about us! I think he was getting scared as well … he wanted to get out!"

"Yuh, guess you're right. I was forgetting he was in the dark … can't have been easy."

"Hey! It's all happening here," she said, as they entered the square and were suddenly being jostled by shoals of excited children. "C'mon, old man, let's take a ride on those horses!" she said, suddenly speeding up.

"Carrousel de Tempes Modernes," Tarquin muttered, looking at the sign on the gaudy merry-go-round as it careered around with its shrieking occupants. A pair of painted horses swung into view, followed by a balloon and basket, a tram, a tea cup, and a particularly luxurious curved chair with rich gold carving.

"Come on, Tarquin. Let's get on the next ride!" Constanta said, scooping up Percy as the carousel came to a halt. She jumped into the red padded interior of the golden chair, "Hurry!"

Tarquin climbed in hesitantly, his large hand gripping the curved roof which curled over them like a seashell.

"Cheer up, darling. This thing won't eat you!" she said,

wriggling close to him and gripping an overexcited Percy.

A long-haired attendant with a bulging leather pouch, like a sporran, appeared in front of them. Tarquin handed him some coins.

Suddenly they were off. The children shrieked and Constanta yelled out as well, as the grand buildings of the square revolved around them, making Tarquin feel both dizzy and exhilarated. He wasn't used to spontaneous bursts of enthusiasm and settled his face into a fixed grin, which after several more revolutions evolved into a grimace.

"Loosen up, for Christ's sake, Tarquin, and kiss me," she demanded.

He was pondering as to how passionate this kiss should be, when the carrousel slowed down and stopped. He made to get up but she stopped him.

"Where are you going? I said I want a kiss."

"Oh … sorry," he said sheepishly.

He leant towards her and gave her his best tender (but in a public place) kiss, and made sure not to hurry. Suddenly there was a whistling behind him and the man with the pouch was back, looking surly.

"Fuck him," she whispered as she pulled the back of Tarquin's head towards her more forcefully, before releasing him. Tarquin clambered out and thanked the man, whilst wiping the back of his hand across his mouth. The attendant regarded him with mild disgust.

They moved across the square to an older-looking building, one that seemed to hold authority over the others—probably the town hall. It was baroque looking, heavy and stained by the onslaught of centuries. There was a distinct, carved inscription above the arched, blue doors. Tarquin moved closer, squinting.

"UNITe INDIVISIBILITE DE LA REPUBLIQUE, LIBERTE, EGALITE, FRATERNITE, OU LA MORT"

"Does that say 'death' at the end, Tarquin?" Constanta said at his shoulder.

"Yes … yes it does. The revolution was a very bloody business," he said, staring up.

"But of course you know all about that … you had your own," he added.

"True … sometimes the people at the top take the piss. Fancy a coffee … there's a café over there and I could kill a hot chocolate," she said, moving off, pulled by a snuffling Percy. Tarquin caught her up.

"Tarquin," she said slipping her arm through his.

"Yuh?" he said, turning to look at her.

"I wondered if … if we could go home via Paris? You know … spend a night there on the way back. I just really always wanted to see Paris."

"You mean all those wonderful shops in Paris, darling!" he said with a small snort, aware he'd suddenly addressed her differently.

"No!" she wriggled against him like a puppy. "The Eiffel tower … Notre Dame."

"The Palace of Versailles," he interjected.

"Yes, the Palace of Versace … Chanel … Hermes …," she said giggling.

They both erupted in laughter and he slapped her playfully on the shoulders.

"Not so hard, you clumsy ape!" she said with a sharp frown. "I'm not one of your public school boyfriends."

*   *   *

Oliver came into the kitchen to see Fabien studying a map of the house and garden, spread out on the table.

"Morning, Oliver!" he said, rising. "Coffee?"

"Morning, Fabien. Sorry, seemed to have slept in again. I find this house increasingly relaxing," Oliver said.

"No bad dreams this time?" Fabien said.

"No, not last night; slept like a baby. Must admit, I feel

slightly thick in the head though ... how many bottles did we get through?"

"Two—and a 'alf! Not too bad, eh ... between three?" Fabien said with a chortle.

"Well ... erm .... it wasn't really between three, was it. Mel hardly drank very much and you're fairly sensible, so it follows that I'm the culprit!" Oliver said with an embarrassed chuckle. "If you *will* play jaunty tunes on the piano, what do you expect!"

"Come on! You're on 'oliday!" Fabien said heartily. "'Ow about some eggs and bacon?"

Oliver hesitated.

"Erm ... okay. Bloody good idea! Love some. It's the only cure," he said, slumping down at the table. "What's this?" he said, gazing at the drawings. "Doing something for Cecile at long last?"

"Well ... I've got to give some thought to the garden, or I'll be in the dog 'ouse, as you English say!" he said, folding the map. "Would you like to come and see the 'Folly' after breakfast? I'm having it repaired, if I can ... it was once beautiful ... a place my grandmother adored when she was young. It 'as a similarity to Le Temple de L'Amour at Versailles ... a smaller, simpler version. Do you know it?"

"No, I can't say I do, Fabien ... would be intrigued," Oliver said, trying to muster up some enthusiasm. "Is Melvyn upstairs already?"

"He went to the garret hours ago, before I got up. There was no sign of 'im down here, so I went up and there he was. Felt he didn't really want me around, though, so I came back down," Fabien said, taking a packet of bacon from the fridge.

Oliver chuckled.

"I can imagine! It's the one time when Mel really wants to be alone. You can sort of see his point. He's really concentrating up there."

"Ah ... it's not a problem. I appreciate his talent ... his expertise. He 'as to get it absolutely perfect."

"We'll have to help him move the chest into place, of course, but I doubt that's for a while yet," Oliver said. "Oh, by the way, I was thinking we'd leave tomorrow, early afternoon, and catch a night ferry across again. Is that okay?"

"Sure, no problem, that means there's no rush."

After breakfast, and after Oliver had made a short trip upstairs to see Melvyn, he and Fabien stepped from the musty air of the chateau into the bright sunshine. In a split second he was engulfed by a strange new mood, as an elixir of divine fragrances wafted up his nostrils. Huge expanses of flower-strewn meadows stretched out to the south, swirling around the bases of the stately beeches, and between the islands of colourful shrubs. To the west, a line of poplars guarded the way to Troyes.

The air throbbed with the low hum of countless flying insects … insanely busy, crisscrossing each other's flight paths in chaotic synchronicity. The sun warmed the back of his neck as he followed Fabien through the knee-high grass, and for a few inexplicable moments, the high excitement surrounding the cabinet dissolved into a feeling of intense emptiness. It was as though the raw beauty of the garden was imposing its own values and perspectives on him, and subtly undermining the trivial focus of his ambitions.

Presently they emerged from a cluster of tall shrubs and were confronted by a sort of miniature temple, with a semicircle of Greek columns.

"Voila!" Fabien said with a flourish.

"Golly. this is a find," Oliver said in awe, gazing up at the columns.

"This is my 'idden mistress!" Fabien said grinning.

"You mean Cecile doesn't know about this?" Oliver said, perplexed.

"Of course she knows. She knows the garden much better than me," he said. "What I mean is that I'm going to get this renovated and made into a real folly where Cecile can come and read and …"

"Write poetry?" Oliver said with a smile.

"Exactly! Where she can write love poems to me!" the young man said with a chuckle.

"Lovely idea, Fabien. It's an elegant little building, but it needs its roof repaired."

"Of course. Come on, let's take a closer look," he said enthusiastically.

They made their way over and stepped through the columns and onto its cool marble floor.

"The columns are in good condition!" Oliver said, rubbing his hand over the round surfaces like he was caressing the flank of a horse. "Doric, if I remember rightly … but you must get this ivy out of the way. It's terrible for stone surfaces; you don't want to let them get too pitted."

"I know. Bernard will deal with that. As I mentioned, it's like a small copy of the one at Versailles. Also, the one there doesn't 'ave this weird little room at the back," Fabien said, pushing an impenetrable cascade of creepers to one side and peering into a dark space. "Perhaps it was one of those ice storage places. There seem to be some steps going down, but with this tree growing across the entrance and the thick undergrowth, I can't really see.

"It's dry, as well, thanks to this low roof. I've never gone inside … well, it's impossible as it is; you'd need a chainsaw. And to be honest, when I was a child I remember being told a serpent with six eyes lived 'ere and it's always made me scared. There's a pair of slit windows at the top, though, and you get these beautiful shafts of light. It was obviously used for some purpose … but what? A changing room for musicians?"

"Hmm, wouldn't know about that," Oliver said, staring at the semicircular floor. "I love it. It's quirky. I'm sure the historical records in Troyes will tell you. Can you see it from the house, or do those shrubs hide it?"

"In the winter you can make out the roof and the tops of four columns, but at this time of year, no chance. Cecile will be so happy if I get this done; it looks terribly neglected."

"You have a lot on your plate, Fabien," Oliver said, stepping back through the columns. "One thing at a time. Get the windows and roof sorted out in the main house first, and then you can consider the way forward."

"True. The only problem is that we can't touch the main 'ouse for a year, as you know. We can't have tradesmen climbing around in the place until the chest has been discovered."

"Well, that's right … it's out of the question. I guess you're just going to have to hold back on all major activity here until that time," Oliver conceded.

"Oliver, I can wait! It just makes me so 'appy to be able to repair this whole place. It's a dream beyond anything I ever thought possible!" the young Frenchman said with passion.

"You're a talented young man, Fabien. It's time your true worth was rewarded," Oliver said with a small smile. "Let's hope and pray our project doesn't hit any glitches."

Back in the house, Oliver went up to join Melvyn whilst Fabien put a call through to Cecile.

"How's she coming along, Mel?" Oliver said breathlessly at the top of the stairs.

"Good timing, Oliver. We're ready to take it through to its resting place," Melvyn said, standing up and stretching himself. "Bloody hell, that took it out of me, Feel exhausted! The part that really hurts is powdering the blooming cabinet."

"Sorry, Mel?" Oliver said, lifting his brows.

"Powdering the cabinet. You know … blowing dust on the appropriate surfaces to age it. It's been in there for two hundred years, don't forget, so it's going to have grown a coat of dust particles, that's for sure. Even popped a few spiders in there for good measure!"

"What will they eat, Mel? No flies can get in, can they?" Oliver said, genuinely concerned.

"Oh yeah. There are cracks here and there, for sure. Besides, they quite enjoy eating each other when times are hard," Melvyn said without humour. "I want loads of webs in there."

"Good God!" Oliver said, patting his shoulder lightly. "Are

you quite certain there's nothing you could have overlooked?" he said, giving Melvyn a searching look.

"Like what?" Melvyn said.

"Look, I'm sure not," Oliver said quickly. "Just want it to be one hundred percent, that's all. But you've never let me down before, so I'm sure it's fine. Come down and have some tea and a break, even lunch, if you want; you must be famished."

"I am, to be honest," Melvyn said with a sigh. "Would you help take some of these bits down, like the crate and panels?"

"Absolutely. It's all going to be burnt; well, apart from the fake panels, of course," Oliver said, picking up a bundle. "They'll be useful in the future."

"Blooming right there, Oliver," Melvyn said, picking some pieces up.

"Fabien's cleared a spot at the back of the house for the fire, so I think we'll get on and do that whilst you're having a break," Oliver said, leading the way downstairs. "We've been looking at the folly in the garden … very elegant little building."

"Oh?" Melvyn said absently.

"I'll take you over to look at it before we go. You'll probably find it rather interesting," Oliver said.

"Good, I'd like that," Melvyn said, brushing some dust from his trousers.

"Oh, by the way, Mel, we're going to head home early afternoon tomorrow. Does that suit?"

"Yep, that's fine."

"Bernard and his wife are arriving on Wednesday afternoon and will be taking up residence in the rooms at the back of the house; you know, along that passage by the kitchen and up those stairs. Cecile has made it as nice as possible. They're going to be responsible for housekeeping and all sorts of other duties around the house until Fabien moves in," Oliver said.

"And gardening. I think Fabien mentioned that Bernard was very keen on his plants."

"Yes. I think you're right. The main thing, Mel, is that there are people here to look after the place when Fabien and Cecile can't be here. We can't have the cabinet here without some protection. He's got a pet carpenter to come over to put up a temporary partition over the entrance to the garret on Tuesday; you know, at the bottom of the staircase. He and his son have done quite a bit of work in the house already, apparently, and know the ropes. I think Fabien's told them that there may well be children running around; you know, Cecile's nephews and nieces or something along those lines. Just to give some reason for blocking it off."

"Good. He's got it all worked out, hasn't he!" Melvyn said with a chortle. "But he'd better be careful that this carpenter doesn't go snooping around up there before it's closed off. The cabinet will be at its most conspicuous at the beginning … you know, before the spiders weave their magic and blend it into the surroundings."

"Very true, but he has already told them that they're forbidden to go up there, because the floors are very weak; he's also going to put on some old clothes and do some clearing, until the route is blocked. They probably won't want him there, but it means he can keep an eye on them."

"Good. That makes me feel a bit easier," Melvyn said.

"Yuh, we've both given it a lot of thought, to be frank. Besides, the carpenter has a load of other work, apparently, and won't want to hang around. And Bernard's got a couple of those big farm dogs, so the place will be well protected."

"Fantastic!" Melvyn said with approval.

They wandered into the kitchen, and Melvyn made a beeline for the kettle.

"Right. I'll let you help yourself," Oliver said. "I'm going back upstairs to get the rest of the stuff, and you'll find us out at the back. Just follow the smoke!"

He disappeared out of the door and left Melvyn to yawn in peace.

*   *   *

Viktor was discussing the aborted trip to Strupe Hall with Zoltan.

"On this occasion, I have to agree with Gus," he said down the telephone to his son. "I think Oliver *will* be back soon. The hire vehicle tells me this is a short-term trip. Better we abort a job than take stupid risks. If the woman was suspicious, who knows what could have happened if she contacted police with those idiots in charge."

"Sure, Father. When Sammy smells trouble, we have to listen."

"So we wait," Viktor resumed. "Get them to keep watch on his house in Battersea, and when he returns, we'll pay him a little visit … simple as that. But not straight away. He'll be expecting something to happen after that piece of madness on way to Dover, but he won't know when."

"Sure thing. The son of a bitch knows we're hunting him now. Perhaps he'll come to his mind and call us."

"Mmm, I'm not so sure. In his mind he won that round," Viktor said. "We have to wait and see. Whatever that bastard is doing, we're going to find out. We're going to make him sing like canary. He's making shed loads on the back of our ideas, boy, and he's going to pay a heavy price! How many letters you sent him? Two? And that's after that phone call, and still he ignores us like we don't exist!"

"Yes, that's right. He's had plenty of warning," Zoltan said. "I'll tell them to start sweeping by tomorrow and to watch in the evenings. When we've got him, how do you want to proceed? Give him the usual treatment?"

"No!" Viktor said emphatically. "We need to be careful with him. We need to frighten him, yes, but no serious physical damage yet. We need to find out what he's doing, what he's got up his sleeve. If you're right, and he actually is making one of those cabinets or *has* already made one, then we need to know if he's sold it yet, and if not, where it is now. He's no good to us in hospital with the police involved.

"We want his money, Zoltan. Keep focused. Our game is

blackmail, not revenge, and for that to work we need to let his bird come home to roost … if it hasn't already."

"I think the bird is coming back to roost now, Papa. He will return from his French trip with heavy pockets," Zoltan said.

"Hang on, Zoltan. I've got Vladimir on the other line," Viktor said suddenly.

There was a pause as he gave the other man a quick instruction.

"Right," Viktor resumed twenty seconds later.

"It's busy over there!" his son said tentatively. "You seem … er … less stressed, Father."

"It's moving in the right direction at last, shall we say."

"So, as I was saying, Oliver will return with heavy pockets," Zoltan offered.

"Yes, exactly. In which case we will find this out, won't we, when we tie him to his favourite chair and present him with various scenarios," Viktor said with a rasping chuckle. "We will suggest to him politely that it might be good idea if he *shares* his money with us, fifty-fifty, to save himself from imprisonment or castration!"

"Mmm … that sounds good," Zoltan agreed with a sadistic smirk.

"But don't presume too much … yet. We simply do not know the full picture. We could be wrong. We can't let the son of Stalin wriggle free and bring the heat on ourselves!" Viktor said emphatically.

"That won't happen, Father, I assure you," Zoltan said. "I will be there."

"Good, keep me in the loop, boy," Viktor said, closing off.

*   *   *

Oliver arrived at the top of the stairs behind the other two, panting heavily.

"Okay," Melvyn said, putting on a pair of gloves and handing a pair to each of the others. "This is going to be heavy, so go easy. We'll take it through the gap here and then on into the other section. The difficult part is lifting it off the deck and putting it down again, so the more we can do in one stretch the better.

"Okay, Mel, we'll do our best to keep going," Oliver said, still slightly breathlessly. "But we'll need a couple of breaks, I think."

"No problem, Oliver," Fabien said politely.

They all bent down and Melvyn counted, "One … two … three … up she goes!"

They wavered and then steadied.

"Christ, this is heavy!" Oliver hissed through a tight windpipe. "Let's go!"

The trio moved like an ungainly six-legged animal, its feet shuffling drunkenly, from the small landing into the deepening shadows of the garret. Fabien and Oliver took the front and Melvyn took up the rear, so he could instruct them where to go.

"Keep going … keep going!" Melvyn said to the increasingly loud moans and expletives coming from Oliver. "All right, let her down!"

"Good God!" Oliver said, straightening up. "That was hellish!"

"You did well, Oliver. We're halfway there!" Fabien said, smiling.

They stood around for a few minutes, during which Oliver took the opportunity to gaze down on the landscape below.

"We're so close now," he said, wiping a handkerchief across the back of his neck. "Our baby will soon be put to bed! Then we can sit back and relax for a year …"

A minute or two passed.

"Right!" Melvyn said, squatting down once again. "One … two … three … up!"

Once again they staggered briefly and then moved forward and into the gloom at the back of the garret. On reaching their destination, Melvyn began barking orders.

"Steady now … steady!" he said, peering ahead. "Okay, move sideways a bit … a bit more. Let her down gently … there! Well done!"

He straightened up and pulled a torch from his pocket which he perched on one of the rickety steps to the platform. It shone a beam into the recess where the chest had to be gently shuffled.

"Jeepers! Thank God that's over with!" Oliver said with a hysterical laugh. "Almost killed me!"

"Don't have a heart attack, Oliver!" Fabien said, chuckling.

"Okay, we just have to manoeuvre it back into the recess now," Melvyn said, kneeling down. "Just need to put these strips down first so the chest feet don't scuff the floorboards. Can you guys lift each end in turn so I can slip them under?"

"Sure," Fabien said, getting a grip with Oliver. They lifted the ends and Melvyn put the strips in. They then slid the cabinet back into place, and Melvyn removed them.

"All done! Thanks, everyone," Melvyn said triumphantly.

Suddenly Oliver's voice changed cadence and boomed out solemnly.

"We are now observing a chest which was placed in the garret of this magnificent chateau in the year seventeen hundred eighty-nine," he said, patting it gently with his gloved hand, "at the outset of the French Revolution. May it rest in peace!"

"And grow many a cobweb!" Fabien added with a grin.

"Phew … we've made it!" Melvyn said quietly, almost to himself.

Oliver shook Melvyn's hand and then Fabien's.

"Well done, fellows. This is a hell of an achievement. What do you say to a celebratory glass of champagne?"

"Not just yet, Oliver," Melvyn said, standing in the torch beam. "I've still got about an hour's work up here to get it all right. Need to remove all our footprints and make the floor look untouched again. Besides, it's only four thirty!"

"Oh, okay, Mel. No hurry. We'll wait for you downstairs," Oliver said, making his way towards the staircase. "We'll go and check on the fire."

As the sound of their footsteps receded, Melvyn stood motionless for a few minutes and allowed the true nature of that space to descend on him again. Apart from the erratic murmur of the summer breeze over the roof tiles, there was only dust, oak beams, crumbling masonry, and silence.

Thomas Charrington

Chapter 34

Oliver stepped stiffly from the van onto the gravel at Strupe Hall, and was nearly bowled over by the ecstatic attentions of Titus. Against all previous instruction, he jumped up at his master repeatedly in paroxysms of excitement. The trip back from France had been uneventful. Leaving the chateau at around one o'clock on Monday afternoon, they had made a straight run to St Malo in time for the overnight ferry to Portsmouth.

"Down, boy!" Oliver said gruffly, turning sideways to protect himself from the onslaught. "Down will you …!"

"He's been waiting for you for hours, Oliver," Mary said. "They always know, do dogs … they've got a sixth sense."

"How are you, Mary?" Oliver said formally, as she went to the driver's side to give Melvyn a simple squeeze of his shoulder. He was rooted to the driving seat and made no attempt to get out.

"Very well, as it happens," she continued. "Everything's been fine … no problems. Well, apart from Friday evening when me mum locked herself in her bedroom and needed me to get her out! Cor blimey, what a carry on. Door handle came off. Luckily I met one of your lady friends in the village shop … Lily … and she was happy to take Titus out for his evening walk, which was very fortunate. Nice lady."

"Lily?" Oliver said, startled. "She came over and took Titus out for a walk?"

"Yes," Mary said, looking embarrassed, "I'm sorry if …"

"Oh no... no! I couldn't care less about her coming over. I …

er … just was surprised that you two should have bumped into each other, that's all," Oliver said, peddling backwards.

"Well, it was damn handy," Mary continued. "He likes his evening walk, and I would have felt terrible to keep him in all that time; dog would 'ave gone crazy!"

"No, absolutely, Mary, that was a perfect solution. I must ring her and thank her. You said that was on Friday?"

"Yeah. Friday evening. Shop was about to close and I needed some milk, so …"

"Well, thank God for serendipity," Oliver interrupted.

"Whatever that should mean," Mary said with a chuckle. "It would seem my husband 'as lost his voice," she said, casting a matronly glance at Melvyn who was still stuck in the driving seat. "What's 'appened … forgotten how to speak English, Mel?"

"No. Just waiting. My right leg feels a bit stiff so I'll wait till we get back, if you don't mind," he said, looking drawn.

"Look, you better be going," Oliver said, opening the sliding door and grabbing his suitcase and briefcase. "Poor old Mel has been driving all the way from Portsmouth, and he needs a soak in a hot bath."

"That's about the gist of it," Melvyn said with a good-humoured chuckle as he started the engine. "I did volunteer."

"Thanks again, Mary, and we'll get you sorted out tomorrow, if that's all right. You've been a saviour," he said, helping her into the cab.

"I'll call you in the morning, Mel … not too early!" Oliver said, bending down to get a final glimpse of his companion. "Have a good couple of days' rest … you deserve it!"

"Cheers, mate," Melvyn said quietly.

"Oh, Titus has had dinner, by the way," Mary shouted through her open window, "but he'll pretend he hasn't!"

"Don't I know it!" Oliver shouted as the van pulled away.

The Toyota did an arc on the gravel and then disappeared off down the drive.

Oliver turned to see Titus, his body low to the ground, eyes bulging, tearing around the flower beds in a mad display of energy and excitement, to a chorus of noisy blackbirds.

*   *   *

Tarquin, Constanta, and Petru sat in the departure lounge at Charles de Gaulle Airport waiting for Petru's flight to Bucharest.

"Spending the night in Paris … isn't that cool!" Constanta said with a small giggle. "I would have killed you, Tarquin, if you'd refused to come. We got a busy day tomorrow!"

"We're going to miss you, Petru," Tarquin said in a voice tinged with sadness. "You've been an invaluable asset to our little expedition. In actual fact, without you we would never have got this far."

"Well, thank you for paying for my flight, Mr Tarquin … this was very kind," Petru said with sincerity.

"Not at all, Petru … it's the very least I can do for all the hard work you've done."

"It's true, darling," Constanta said, curling her hand round Petru's neck. "You been ace … an honour to Romania!"

"When we get back to the UK, we'll sort you out with more," Tarquin added. "I've got limited reserves out here."

"I understand. It's not problem, Mr Tarquin," Petru said, smiling. "Please don't lose the memory stick … you've got all the information you need on that. I have a copy, though, like I said, if something happens."

"Thanks, I appreciate it. Did you make that at the hotel in Troyes?"

"Yes, Andre the barman let me use his laptop for a bit."

"All this technology," Tarquin muttered. "It's quite beyond me."

"And be very careful, Mr Tarquin … when you get home, they'll be waiting. In my opinion, this is the most dangerous time for you. I feel bad not to be around to help, but—"

"Petru, you're needed at home. I'll be okay," Tarquin interjected quickly.

"No, you won't, Tarquin," Constanta said forcefully. "I need to keep a sharp eye on you, or you'll end up at the bottom of River Thames."

Tarquin made a grimace which was mirrored by Petru.

"She's right to be concerned," he said. "The problem is, you have no way of contacting those people except through those guys … and they want to kill you!"

"No, not kill, darling, scare shitless," Constanta said firmly. "They want to know about the cabinet, that's all, because they want the money."

"We'll find a way, Petru," Tarquin said with a thin smile. "Just need to get at the people in charge. It won't be easy, but there must be a way."

"Okay, they're on time for once," Constanta said, looking up. "You got to go to your gate now, darling."

Petru glanced at the screen and then stood up, shouldering his rucksack.

"Well, thank you again, Mr Tarquin," he said, extending his hand shyly.

"No! Thank *you,* Petru!" Tarquin said, standing over him like a benevolent school master. "Let's hope you can turn things around at home … happy flight."

Constanta embraced Petru and stroked his back affectionately.

"Take care, darling … we'll talk soon. Give my kisses to Natalia."

Then he turned and disappeared into the marching lines of people.

*   *   *

Fabien stood on the second landing, looking at the hefty partition which now blocked the entrance to the garret. He'd instructed the carpenters to be careful not to damage the woodwork and to make the fixings as discreet as possible. This wasn't meant as a permanent barrier. Ostensibly, it was just to stop inquisitive children. They'd done a good job; the garret was now sealed from prying eyes, and the cabinet in its protective chest could now incubate for the next year. Gradually, the spiderwebs and dust would soften its contours and allow it to melt into temporary obscurity.

In the gathering dusk, the chateau seemed empty without the other two men, and now that the carpenters had gone, he felt increasingly isolated. It had been fine the previous day after Oliver had left. He'd busied himself studying plans of the garden and trying to work out the best way forward for Cecile's big surprise. But he now felt an increasing sense of pressure. When he got back to Paris, she would be assailing him with countless questions about what the architect had said, what his suggestions were, what he thought about a water garden, and so on. And there had been no architect; it had just been a ruse to keep her away. He would have to be on his toes. He decided to take a wander round the floor before it got too dark, in order to see the garden from some different perspectives and possibly get some new ideas.

He headed to the once grand north-south landing which he hadn't visited in months. Avoiding odd chunks of furniture, rolls of old carpet, and broken floorboards, he gingerly picked his way towards a huge arched window at the far end. It was in a terrible state, and he felt a surge of despondency at the enormity of the task before him. Once the cabinet was found, he'd bring an army of artisans into this place and return the chateau to its former glory, but in the meantime he had to wait.

He stopped suddenly and gazed at the floor, perplexed. The hairs on the back of his neck bristled. There were footprints … unmistakable footprints in the dust, which had the sharp definition of having been planted recently. He stared at them and felt the presence of an unseen stranger; they exuded energy and purpose … a hidden agenda. Whose were they? The prints were bold with harsh ridges … certainly not from the shoes of Oliver or Melvyn, both of whom wore old-fashioned country shoes. No, these were from those running shoes … trainers … that so many people wore these days, including arthritic old women.

Suddenly his furrowed face softened. Of course! They must be from the carpenter's son! He probably wore trainers. He wondered what prick of curiosity had lured the boy along here … but there again, it wasn't so odd. The chateau was a wonder to see despite its state, and perhaps the carpenters thought that the restoration work would land at their table; which it probably would.

Henri had probably told his son to go and take a peek at the rest of the floor, once the partition had been finished, and leave him to finish off. Fabien wouldn't challenge them. They'd done a good job; what would be the point? But he was thankful that he'd stayed with them until the staircase to the garret was blocked; those curious feet might have taken that boy on a tour up there, and possibly even to the chest.

After studying the garden from a variety of viewpoints on the second floor and having an imaginary conversation with Cecile, Fabien made his way downstairs. He poured himself a cold glass of sauvignon blanc from the fridge, and then strolled out into the scented evening air.

Bernard and his wife were arriving the following afternoon with their dogs, so this was his last evening of solitude. He slumped down on one of the stone benches under the columns and watched the undulating meadows turn from pink to a deep violet, all the while aware of the priceless guest which sat quietly in the shadows of the garret.

Chapter 35

Tarquin had been back two days. He and Constanta had arrived at number nine Warriner Gardens in the midafternoon of Thursday, and it was now Saturday. Because of the situation, she'd agreed to stay with him for the time being in case of trouble, and to try and bring things to a head. They were lovers, but not in any format that Tarquin understood; their relationship was tacit, discreet, barely recognizable in the daylight hours. It seemed that tenderness was not an emotion which chimed with Constanta … she refused to be tethered in mind or body.

"You okay, darling?" she said breezily as she came down the stairs with Percy.

"Yes, thanks, fine. Just trying to catch up on some news," Tarquin said, lowering his newspaper.

"Good. Okay. I'm going up to the Clapham Junction to get those medicines Petru wanted. Do not answer the door, Tarquin, unless you're absolutely sure who it is, okay. The last thing we want is for those guys to corner us in here; it must be on the street, where they will be forced to control their violence. Then we have a chance to talk to them; you know, make them realize their mistake, before they get us."

"Yuh, you're right," he said, his brow furrowed with anxiety. "How long will you be?"

"Perhaps an hour. Shall I get something for lunch?" she asked.

"Would you mind?" he said, pulling a note from his pocket and handing it to her.

"Thanks, darling, I'll see you soon then."

She disappeared onto the street, and he noticed her glancing up and down the pavement through the window.

Fifteen minutes later, Tarquin got to his feet, slapped his paper down, and grabbed Percy's lead from a chair. Constanta wouldn't approve, but he would not be held hostage by a pair of thugs; Percy lived for his walks. He pulled his tweed cap tightly down on his head, put on a pair of dark glasses, and for that "house occupied" quality, he switched the radio on loudly. His dog would be the give away, but he felt strangely remote, like a man watching a lion charging towards him through the lens of a camera. He locked the door thoroughly and stood on the pavement hesitantly for a few moments, as though summoning the courage to go. Then he was off, his eyes flickering nervously around him as he strode purposefully along Warriner Avenue, across Prince of Wales Drive, and into the park.

It was strange being back in London; everything seemed different, even foreign. It wasn't home at the moment; it was a place where trouble was slowly tracking him down … a place where he felt the constant presence of adrenaline in his bloodstream. Although they'd only been away for a week, and back in London a couple of days, it seemed like a month. He had changed. He was half in love and half in fear for his life. The very ground beneath his feet had transformed to quicksand. Even Percy looked at him as a stranger.

The park was busy for August, awash with noisy, happy families enjoying a break from the constricting routines of the week. He kept to the trees and watched for pairs of men through suspicious eyes as Percy snuffled around the tree trunks and bushes. After half an hour, he was back on the street again, taking an unusual back route to his house for fear of some sort of ambush. This was just plain crazy, but he was compelled to do it.

Back at home, he shut the door with relief and double-locked it. So this was how it felt to be on the run—edgy and claustrophobic. The worst thing was that the encounter with these men was essential. Without it he would always be on the run. He was like a man who'd been diagnosed with a brain tumour. It had to be removed, but the thought of the operation filled him with foreboding; it could all go so horribly wrong.

He pondered as to whether a Bloody Mary was a good idea, but decided to wait and resumed his perusal of the newspaper to the reassuring sounds of Radio 4. Twenty minutes later, Constanta rapped impatiently on the door. Tarquin unbolted and let her in. She had a couple of plastic bags with her and marched past him to the kitchen like a purposeful housewife.

"Taken up smoking, have we, darling?" she said casually, as she started to unpack the bags.

"Smoking?" Tarquin replied from the sitting room. "I'm not with you?"

"There's a smell of tobacco in here, Tarquin. Are you hiding something?" she said with a small giggle.

"No!" he said, wandering into the kitchen clutching the newspaper. He did some loud theatrical sniffs which made her burst out laughing.

"You fucking idiot!" she said happily. "If only you could see yourself. You're meant to be an upstanding member of the upper class, and here you are sniffing the air like a—"

Suddenly there was an unmistakable creak on the ceiling above them. They both looked at each other.

"Where's Percy?" she said sharply.

Tarquin glanced round the corner into the sitting room.

"He's on the sofa fast asleep," he said over his shoulder.

"Have you been out, Tarquin?" Constanta said in a low voice, a shadow of fear crossing her face.

"Well … just a short walk. Percy really needed—"

"Oh my fucking God! Get out of here!" she yelled.

She raced past him and into the sitting room as a man plunged down the stairs followed by another. With two rapid strides, the first man threw his full weight on Constanta before she could react, and they fell, she screaming, in a heap of arms and legs on the floor.

Tarquin flew towards the struggling bodies but was trounced by a heavy blow to his side from the knee of the second man, who came at him viciously. Tarquin yelled in rage as he hit the floor, kicking out at the bulk looming over him, catching him in the stomach. Bob groaned with the force of the kick and staggered back, whilst groping in his pocket. Then he brought it out … a grey handgun. He waved it angrily at Tarquin.

"If this is what yer want, yer fucking bastard, then it's coming your way!" he screamed, kicking Tarquin hard. "I'll make Swiss cheese of you yet, you piece of shit."

Tarquin froze. The gun mesmerized him and triggered a rationality to his behaviour.

Constanta had also gone quiet, and Tarquin saw in horror that she had a knife to her throat.

There was suddenly a silence amongst the human beings in the room—a sort of tacit realization that the game was up—but this didn't extend to the dog. No, Percy was barking hysterically from the arm of the sofa, darting in to nip Bob's leg at every opportunity. Bob swung his foot angrily at the terrier, but his focus was firmly on Tarquin. He moved towards him with hatred in his eyes.

"Get up, Oliver! Any funny business and it's curtains for you, my friend!" he jeered, swinging the gun menacingly in front of him and kicking him again. "I said *get up*!"

Tarquin got shakily to his feet.

"Go and sit in that chair … *now*!" Bob yelled, pointing to one placed against the wall.

Tarquin went and sat down, his eyes glazed.

Gus, who'd been whispering obscenities into Constanta's ear as he lay on top of her, slowly gathered himself to his feet whilst holding her tightly by her hair. The blade lay flat against her neck, but with the point pressed into the soft skin.

"Such a pretty girl," he snarled. "But we really shouldn't go kicking strangers in the 'ead, should we? No! That's just plain nasty. It's so sad that this has to 'appen, but we have to learn our lessons the hard way, don't we, my pretty Russian tart?"

He sliced through a chunk of her hair and it fell to the floor.

"And this," he chuckled, slicing another chunk off and throwing it down. Then another … and another. Suddenly she looked misshapen … punkish. Her character was changing before Tarquin's very eyes. Constanta was ebbing away and a street urchin was replacing her. Her eyes blazed like a snared eagle.

"Now, girl," he said, gazing at her new look with some pride. "You go and sit in that chair. Yeah, the comfy one with the cushions. Yer know, I didn't have to jump on yer. Could have just waved the bloody gun, but *no*! I wanted to squash you, you Russian bitch. I wanted to show you that yer not the Kung Fu princess yer think yer fucking are, okay?"

She walked silently over and sat down.

"Now, you need to do some explaining, don't you? But not to us. Oh no, you have to have a little chat with the boss! And you better have some fuckin' good reasons … oh yeah! But first we need to make sure you're not gonna do something silly, okay, so Bob 'ere is going to tie your hands and legs together, all right?"

Bob handed Gus the revolver and then brought out a bundle of nylon ties from his jacket pocket.

"These make life so easy," Gus smirked, waving the barrel first at Tarquin and then at Constanta. "No messy tape, just a simple tighten and you're caught! Now no funny stuff, or I'll fucking shoot you, okay?"

Bob crouched down and tied Tarquin's ankles together with a forceful wrench.

"Right, cross your hands in front of yer … palms down."

He did the same with his hands, and even though the plastic tie dug into Tarquin's flesh, he refused to acknowledge any pain.

Then it was Constanta's turn. She didn't flinch.

"Right, you're trussed up like a pair of Christmas turkeys, so it's time to call the big man," Gus said, pulling out his mobile and wandering back into the kitchen. "For fuck's sake, B, turn off the bloody radio, will yer … it's doin' me head in," he shouted back.

Bob yanked the lead out and threw it on the floor.

"Yes, Z, they're ready and waiting for your arrival," Gus said in the background. "Yeah … yeah … okay twenty-five minutes is great. See you then."

He sauntered back into the sitting room.

"I am not Oliver Clasper," Tarquin said in a voice which was aiming at authoritative but ended up as a quavering croak.

"Sure you're not!" Gus sneered. "You're Bill Smith!"

"My name is Tarquin Stanhope," Tarquin resumed.

"Oh my Gawd!" Gus said with a loud snort. "I've 'eard some goodens, but that … that's a fuckin' cracker!"

"Why not just go for Marmaduke, mate," Bob added with a spiteful grin. "Go the whole hog! It'll give the boss a reason to kick yer even 'arder!" He laughed loudly at his own joke.

"Look at my post … it's all over there," Tarquin said, pointing with his chin.

"Please, please, Oliver, do not take us for a pair of assholes," Gus said with a warped smile. "Even if yer had a truck load of post with this Mr Tarquin guy's name, it wouldn't wash with me. For all we know, yer probably have loads of aliases. We're grown-ups, Oliver. We know these little tricks. Don't waste yer breath, mate."

The room fell silent, Percy included. The fact that his master and Constanta were no longer struggling made him assume things were getting back to normal. But when Gus crouched down to stroke him, he snarled and bared a set of impressive teeth.

"Yer got a good dog there," Gus said, straightening up. "That little animal's got guts, and I admire that." He went on wistfully, "Yer know what, I can't wait to hear what you people are up to. I mean, we just do our job, but it's always fun to hear the story unravel. I've 'eard that you're into furniture, and that you've been making a copy of something important in your little workshop, Oliver."

Tarquin and Constanta, with their hands tied in front of

them, didn't say a word.

"Your mistake was to use Zoltan's idea," Gus continued. "And that's why he's going to kick the shit out of yer. He gets right bitchy, he does, when he thinks he's not getting respect. And oh my … yer both have taken the piss big time. Not calling him when he asked yer to. Not replying to his letters, which we personally have dropped through yer door."

"If I don't know who sent the letters, how can I reply?" Tarquin said, looking straight at Gus.

"Yer know, mate, I really feel like walloping yer right now," Gus said angrily. "Yer sit there with yer posh fucking accent and innocent face, spewing this bullshit. I tell yer, yer got it coming, mate! B, take this and shoot them if they try it on, okay. I'm going outside for a puff in the garden. He's winding me up."

Bob went over to the sofa and sat down whilst keeping a wary eye on the other two.

Fifteen minutes later, Gus came into the room looking flustered.

"Yer can't be, Z. We're right here in the sitting room and no one's knocked or rung," he said, looking out of the window. "Keep watching them, B," he said sharply to Bob.

"Yeah, yeah … number nine … what? Five? No, it's number nine. I don't understand, Z," Gus said, getting more and more agitated. "We've got 'em ready for yer, but it's number nine, not number five!"

Gus looked down at his screen which now showed "call ended."

"What's up, G?" Bob said.

"Erm … er … he's confused, talking about number bloody five," Gus said, his face a mask of worry. Twenty seconds later, there was a loud rap on the door.

"Watch them, Bob," Gus said as he strode to the door.

A young blond man came into the house followed by another huge man. Percy started barking again.

"Why are you here?" Zoltan said icily to Gus.

"'Cos … 'cos this is where Oliver lives … number nine,"

Gus answered nervously.

"Gus, this is not Oliver's house. Oliver lives at number five," Zoltan said, giving him a piercing look.

"Well … well, why is he here then?" Gus said, without understanding.

Zoltan pushed past him and into the room where he saw Tarquin and Constanta tied up.

"Who is this man?" Zoltan demanded, looking at Tarquin.

"Oliver," Gus muttered behind him, but with rapidly diminishing confidence.

"This is not Oliver, you crazy idiot!" Zoltan yelled. *"You've got the wrong man! I don't know this person!"*

There was a pause.

"Bob," he said, shaking uncontrollably. "Watch these people; they mustn't move. Gus, come with me."

The three of them left the house and went out onto the street.

"For the love of Lenin," Zoltan shouted uncontrollably, once they were out of earshot. "We're in a heap of trouble here, *a heap of fucking trouble, Gus!. Have you been … yes, you've been tracking the wrong man all this time. Oh Christ, no!"*

"Keep voice down!" the huge man accompanying Zoltan ordered.

Zoltan steadied himself and tried to marshal his thoughts.

"This must … must *not* get back to Viktor, okay, or we're all dead," he stammered, his eyes fixed intensely on Gus.

"The thing is, Z, from the beginning we thought it was number nine … yer said numba nine!"

"No, Gus! I said number five!" Zoltan roared.

"Voice down!" the big man demanded again.

"Well, we both 'eard nine, and the guy had a dog. It all seemed to fit in nice," Gus said with an apologetic flavour.

"We'll go over this later," Zoltan resumed, shaking with fury. "We … we now have the problem of what to do with these … these two people."

"Well, it's obvious, innit, without being funny or nothing, we have to … well … we have no choice," Gus said solemnly.

Zoltan went silent and marched ahead of the other two. The man accompanying Zoltan was six-seven and massively built. Gus looked diminished next to him. They walked along the side streets that form a network between Battersea Park Road and Prince of Wales Drive, until Zoltan steered them back to the house. He pressed the bell, and Bob let them in.

"Gus, I want you and Bob to go and wait in the van so I can speak to these two alone. Well, almost alone. Sergei will stay with me."

"Does he want this?" Bob said, proffering the revolver.

"No, he's armed."

Gus and Bob hurried outside, and Sergei closed the door behind them.

"Okay," Zoltan began, turning to the captives, "we need to … er … have a discussion."

Sergei pulled the curtains shut and settled himself onto the sofa with his own revolver on blatant display. Tarquin felt a shiver go down his spine. Was this how it was going to end? A clinical shot through each of their heads. Zoltan strode over and stood in front of them.

"You people have been mistaken for another … unfortunately," he continued. "We have an issue with a neighbour of yours."

"Oliver Clasper," Constanta said crisply.

"Oh? You know him?" Zoltan said, surprised.

"We know a lot about Oliver Clasper," Constanta resumed. "We had to make it our business to find out, because we realized early on that you thought he lived here."

"*No*! I certainly did not think he lived here," Zoltan snapped. "There has been … er … misunderstanding."

"Whatever the reason, this man," she gestured toward Tarquin, "has been wrongly targeted by your men. He's been attacked by them on three separate occasions: once in Covent Garden, once on the way to France, and then an hour ago here."

"Well, this is true, and I extend my …"

"We don't need your apologies," Constanta riposted fiercely. "We want payment."

"You want what?" Zoltan spat back, "You are in no position to demand anything!"

"In that case, you will never know where is the cabinet," she retaliated.

"The what?" he said, raising his eyebrows.

"You heard me … the cabinet," she continued boldly. "You mentioned it in one of your letters to Oliver … which, of course, we received."

Zoltan paused for a few moments. This discussion was taking an unexpected turn.

"So … so you realize we want … er … there is a cabinet involved?" he said.

"Yes, we do. And we also know where it is," she said sourly.

Zoltan looked at her quizzically. She seemed sharp and had a manner he was familiar with.

"Where are you from, your accent is not English," he said.

"Romania," she answered, looking at him defiantly.

"Romania … mmmm. Yes. That figures." He looked at her … a long hard look.

"Okay … let's get talking. You've made some claims … I am listening."

Constanta took a deep breath.

"Tarquin is a friend of mine," she began. "We were out at a show in the west end a month ago, and went for a drink afterwards. At a certain time he wanted to leave and I wanted to stay, because we had met other friends. He left, and after say half an hour, I left too … to meet with these friends. But we found him beaten up on the street. He was dazed and said he'd been robbed. But nothing was missing, which was strange. I made sure I got him home and he showed me the letter … the letter presumably from you."

"Okay," Zoltan said, listening intently.

"As you know, that letter mentioned a cabinet. We didn't understand what this meant. We were not even sure if you were chasing a real cabinet or an idea of a cabinet or a design of a cabinet. But I figured out that Tarquin was not who you were looking for … for a start, he is not called Oliver! So who was this man? We couldn't contact you—there was no number or address on the letter—so what could we do? I noticed the next morning before I left, a card on the board in the kitchen—it was from an antique dealer called Oliver Clasper, who just happened to live at number five in this street. This people deal in furniture—in cabinets—so I mentioned it to him."

She gestured toward Tarquin.

"He wasn't interested … like all English people, he pretended it wasn't happening."

Tarquin looked across at her without saying a word.

"Then another friend of mine, who is also Romanian, pointed out that nine and five can sound quite similar on a bad line, and we figured that it was possible your operators had misheard your …"

"Very good," Zoltan said, feeling vindicated, but instantly frustrated that he'd let it show.

"And this turned out to be the case … as you have just shown us. You see, I worked out pretty quickly that Tarquin was last guy on the planet to be involved in funny business. You know, he's just not the type. So there had to be a mistake."

"Okaaaay …," Zoltan said, slowly drawing the word out. "But this doesn't really explain how you came to know where the cabinet is."

"So Tarquin here is thinking that I am talking nonsense, and goes about his life as normal. This is until you push another letter through his door. Then he wakes up and realizes this is serious, and I am not so stupid. So he agrees to let me put someone into Oliver's house to take a look around and … and perhaps find some stuff that might give us some clues."

"You got someone into his house?" Zoltan said incredulously.

"It's not so hard for some people. I'm Romanian, don't forget, but it wasn't me, it was my friend. That is when we realized that he was your man. He left some information on a notepad, which we took. It mentioned a cabinet. It had the itiner …" she hesitated. "The schedule of a trip to France. So we had no choice but to follow Oliver to France to discover what he was doing; what else could we do? Wait for your guys to kill us? And that is what we did. And, as you know, your idiot guys attacked us on the way to Dover."

"By the crazy wolves of Khrushchev, it's making sense now!" Zoltan said, now fully realizing that he was talking to two allies, not potential corpses.

"So in France, we tracked Oliver to a certain destination where his … schedule said he would be, and we followed him to this huge house. This is where the cabinet is now."

"The cabinet is in France in a huge house? Did you see it?" Zoltan said, trying hard to mask his excitement.

"Sure, we have loads of photos of it, and of Oliver and his helpers and of the house. But not here. They are in Romania with my friend, because we figured that it was only a matter of time before you came for us."

"Mmm …" Zoltan said, rubbing his chin thoughtfully. "Can I see some of these pictures?"

"Of course," Constanta said, "but once you believe this is the cabinet, we want a payment. You have made this man's life hell for the last months, and I have suffered as well—had to give up my job to help him—and look at my hair, all over the floor!"

"Okay … okay …" Zoltan said, studying her. "But be very careful of smart tricks with us; my father is ruthless and has many people at his disposal. You would not last long."

"I hate the police," Constanta said with feeling. "I look after myself, thank you, and I stick to my word."

Tarquin, who'd been almost silent until now, lifted his head and addressed Zoltan.

"I … er … have listened to everything that's been said," he said hesitantly, "and let her do all the talking—she's much better at this than me … but, erm … I want to make it clear to you that I will not be in contact with the police either. At the beginning I was sure this was the best way forward … but she," he nodded at Constanta, "she told me it would be useless, and would backfire on me. She's right. They would start digging into my affairs … asking questions … wasting precious time. I was frightened, and to be frank, I just want this over with."

Zoltan stared at Tarquin as though making a series of judgements.

"Yes, you've been caught up in something you shouldn't," he said with a hint of apology. "But if what you're telling me is true, then there may be a better ending. I want to see photos; photos of the cabinet, of the house, of Oliver. Then we can be certain. I'm going to send you my contact details, or should I say, contact details specific to you. This will be an email address and mobile number. I will need your email address and a mobile number to send them to. I will send the password to your mobile. You will transmit this password to your Romanian friend and he can load the photos, save the draft, and we can open it here. Are you familiar with this technique?"

"Yes … I think so," Constanta said, whilst Tarquin looked on bemused.

"But I reiterate what I just said. If it turns out you have the police involved, you will shortly be dead … that is a promise. You only have to look in the newspapers to see how we Russians operate; surgically."

He turned towards the front of the house.

"Sergei!" he shouted at the imposing bulk on the sofa. "Release these people, please."

To Tarquin's surprise, as Sergei stood up, he noticed that Percy had been nuzzled against him on the far side. He now stretched briefly before slumping back down against a large cushion.

Sergei came over and did his duty with the adept use of a flick knife. Even Tarquin appeared small against him. Both he and Constanta flexed their fingers repeatedly once released, and stood shakily to their feet.

Tarquin shuffled stiffly into the kitchen and picked up a pen.

He jotted down the details. He handed the note paper to Zoltan, who repeated it all before folding it and putting it in his jacket pocket.

"Could I have your … er … name please," Tarquin stammered, "or a contact name?"

"Yes, call me David. You will receive an email from us in the next twenty-four hours." He then hesitated for a few moments before asking a final question.

"Can I ask if … if you have discovered what Oliver intends to do with this cabinet?" he said, looking at Constanta.

"We think he sells to important clients from that house … it's like his French showroom for international dealers," Constanta said quietly.

"Is this a guess, or did you find information suggesting this?" he enquired.

"No … there was no information in his house about that. We just figured it out," she said confidently.

Zoltan gave her a long hard look.

"It's possible," he said with an enigmatic smile. "But things are not always what they seem."

With that, Sergei swung open the door, and the two men left the house and disappeared down the street to join the others.

After the door had slammed shut and the sound of their footsteps had retreated, Constanta sank to her knees and held her head in her hands. Tears began to flow freely down her cheeks. She was a sad sight. Her once luxuriant blond hair, now hacked off in ugly clumps, left her looking like a scarecrow in a cornfield. Percy trotted over wagging his tail and licked her face, imagining this was a new game for his benefit. Tarquin squatted down awkwardly next to her.

"I'm so sorry, Constanta," he said softly, whilst gently caressing her shoulders with his large hand. "I know I shouldn't have gone out. I … I just felt I owed it to Percy to …"

"Don't kick yourself," she said, trying to control her voice. "It wasn't your fault. I felt bad about Percy as well. They were going to get us somehow. I don't know why this has affected me like this …"

Tarquin got up and collected a paper roll from the kitchen.

"Thanks. I think … I think having that guy lying on me … so aggressive … I think it reminded me of my father … he used to drink and would get close to me. Used to terrify all of us when we were young; we were powerless. My mother couldn't protect us either; she would be beaten."

"Blimey," Tarquin mumbled, struggling to process what she was saying. "Well, it's over now. You're safe, and those two guys are going to get a lashing. They really buggered up! Did you see the anger on that Russian; he was ready to explode. But sweetheart, you were absolutely brilliant! So cool. I was astounded. You told the story brilliantly in the circumstances … and with some attitude!" he said with a small chuckle, whilst kissing her head.

"Thank you," she replied. "I was fired up as well. It wasn't difficult."

"And now we have contact … at last. Well, that's assuming he sends us the email."

"He will. Did you not see the look on his face when I said we knew where was the cabinet!" Constanta said, beginning to gain control. "His eyes … they were full of excitement. I knew we had him then!"

"Yes … smart of you to say the photos were in Romania," he said, stroking the back of her neck affectionately. Suddenly she twisted her head and kissed him long and hard on the mouth. The emotional turmoil of the last hour had somehow released her.

He was completely taken aback. Her kisses were usually so shy, reticent, almost reluctant, and here she was, utterly different in appearance and metamorphasised in character. Without hesitation, he gave himself to the moment and pushed her back on the rich Persian carpet where her face was framed by smoky reds, ochres, and French blues. He kissed her again, more passionately, until she pushed him roughly aside. Rocking back, she adroitly unfastened her shorts, pulled her knees to her chest, and wriggled free of her under clothing. She then unbuttoned her small chemise and removed her bra.

He stared for a moment at the impeccable contours of her naked body. The muscular lines of her calves, the long powerful thighs, the small impudent thatch, beckoning at the apex. She giggled, a white-toothed girly giggle, as she watched him devouring her resplendent nakedness with an expression of such awe.

"Kiss me, you big oaf!" she said unbuckling his trousers and lying back down. "Kiss me, crush me … do it now!"

Obediently, he crouched down and planted a series of soft kisses onto her navel and across the soft blond down of her flat stomach; then, moving slowly up over her pouting nipples to her face, he kissed the long damp lashes that lay like tiny wet feathers below her closed eyes. He carefully lay down on her, and pressing his mouth gently onto her soft parted lips, he kissed her deeply and passionately. She moaned as he gently pushed himself forward, giving himself to the moment. But suddenly he felt a series of sharp tugs at his ankles. He whipped round irritably.

"Percy, bugger off!" he hissed forcefully. "Basket!"

"Oh, don't be nasty; he's feeling left out," Constanta murmured dreamily, whilst twisting to see the small dog. "Come to Mama, Percy."

Percy came self-consciously over, wagging his tail. He licked Constanta's grinning face affectionately, leaving Tarquin and his white naked buttocks feeling vulnerable and distinctly foolish.

Presently he climbed back onto the sofa and lay down with his back turned towards them, sighing loudly. After a certain amount of convulsive giggling from Constanta, Tarquin succumbed once again to her magnetism, and fell head over heals into the beguiling well of her sexuality.

By the time he was lying on his back staring at the ceiling, with her soft sleeping skin pressed intimately to his, he knew he was utterly and hopelessly in love.

Half an hour later, she yawned, sprang to her feet, and

wandered over to the gilt-framed mirror hanging above the fireplace.

"Oh my God!" she exclaimed in horror. "I'm a fucking mess! I need a hairdresser, Tarquin … and fast!"

"Well, there's a few at the junction, I think," he said helpfully.

"No, Tarquin. In Chelsea, for fuck's sake! I want someone good."

"Oh, right, of course. Kings Road; bound to be some along there. Do you want me to drive you?"

"I can't just walk in off the street," she said, moving back into a familiar gear. "In the land of women, Tarquin … we have to book. I'm going up to have a bath, and I'll look for a place on the Internet. Hopefully I can get a booking for later … I'll say it's an emergency."

"Okay. Machine's on standby, I think. I'll make us up some lunch," he shouted.

There was no reply … she was already upstairs.

Thomas Charrington

Chapter 36

Zoltan stood alone in Sasha's flat, staring out on Beauchamp Place. As his eyes idly watched the bustling people on the pavement opposite, his mind worked through the conversation he was about to have with his father. He had to be careful. If Viktor realized that Gus and Bob had been trailing the wrong target for the past month … well … he, Zoltan, would feel the crushing force of his father's rage. He had to lie. Honesty in this situation would be suicidal. He turned up the radio so the clarity of his voice was diminished and picked up the phone. Drawing a deep breath, he pressed the appropriate speed dial.

"Yes, Zoltan … I've been waiting for an update," Viktor said thickly.

"Sorry, Father," Zoltan said nervously. "Things have been busy here … really busy. How are things over there? Are the new machines up to the mark?"

"Get to the point, Zol, what's been happening?" his father replied petulantly. Zoltan swallowed hard.

"Well, I think I … er … have some very good news for you," he began hesitantly. "But I wanted to wait until I was absolutely certain though."

"Yuh?"

"Have you got a few minutes so we can talk?"

"We *are* talking, aren't we?"

"I meant … uninterrupted by your people," Zoltan said, his stomach tightening.

"Just speak, Zoltan. I'm listening," came the intolerant reply.

"I … er … felt I'd let you down, Father … over the Dover debacle," Zoltan said apologetically. "I felt I needed to try a different approach … use my initiative … to sort out this mess."

"Mmm. So have you?"

"Yes … I think I have. I am about to find out exactly what Oliver's game is. I am also about to receive photographs of the piece of furniture, with incriminating pictures of Oliver and his helpers," he said, forcing a jaunty twang into his voice.

There was a pause.

"And how in hell have you achieved this, boy?" Viktor said, with a mixture of interest and suspicion.

"Because, Father, I … I … er … used someone to track Oliver in France. This is a woman; a Romanian woman whom I trust completely and who specializes in this sort of thing."

There was another pause.

"What are you talking about? Where did you find this woman, Zoltan? How do you know she's safe?" Viktor said with an edge to his voice.

"She came through Sergei … he has connections in Romania," Zoltan said, bracing himself.

"Oh? So if Sergei says she's clean, then that's fine, is it? For the fucking love of Lenin, Zoltan, have I taught you nothing?" Viktor exploded.

Zoltan held his cool.

"He's known her a long time, knows her mother and sister. He swears she's completely safe," Zoltan said, trying to balance a deferential tone with an assertive one.

"I have never heard him speak of Romanian connections," Viktor retaliated.

"With respect, Father, you have not had many conversations with him … ever," Zoltan said candidly. "You complain you cannot understand what he's saying."

"True, the man speaks gibberish, his accent is so thick. So, you had Oliver followed, eh?"

"It's even better than that," Zoltan replied, feeling a first wave of relief that a major hurdle was being overcome. "We found information in Oliver's London house indicating where he was going with the item, and when. We didn't need to follow him … we knew where he was going!"

"You've been into Oliver's house? You have been busy!" Viktor said, this time with a trace of humour.

"You have a lot on your plate, Father. Why should I bother you all the time," Zoltan continued skilfully. "We also found his hideaway."

"His hideaway? What do you mean?" Viktor asked, suddenly with more enthusiasm.

"A place he goes to in France, where he thinks he's safe."

"Where is this place, Zol?"

"I cannot tell you this now … it's coming by email shortly, along with the photographs," Zoltan said with growing confidence.

"You mean you both have access to the same account, I presume?" Viktor said, concerned.

"Of course, Father. We never *send* emails with this type of information. The photographs will be attached to an email in Bucharest, saved as a draft, and then opened in London. Nothing will be sent."

"This is good, Zoltan. You're an idiot sometimes … but I'm impressed by your initiative on this occasion. You're showing leadership, boy. Well done. Who is this girl? What's her name?" he asked as an afterthought.

Zoltan was momentarily paralysed. What *was* her name? He hadn't a clue.

"We call her … we call her … erm … Anya," he stammered.

"Anya? You sounded unsure. A code name, yuh?" Viktor said.

"Yes, of course. My memory was playing tricks for a moment. I should mention that I haven't agreed a fee for her work yet," he continued quickly. "It was difficult to assess the time it would take. I need to discuss this with you when we know what we're dealing with."

"Mmmm, later we can discuss," Viktor said.

"The photographs will tell me what Oliver has up his sleeve. If this piece is the copy I think it is, from the Wallace, then we're playing for very high stakes. But that would seem an impossible task. I cannot believe he could pull that off; it's one step too far," Zoltan said, mumbling the last sentence as though speaking to himself.

"Right. I'm through," Viktor said brusquely, sensing distractions in his son. "Keep in touch … well done, boy." The line went dead.

Zoltan slumped back on the sofa and let out a huge sigh. He noticed the back of his shirt was wet as he called his technical man.

"Well, Ivor … did you do it?"

"Yes. The email address, as you instructed, is 'oliver2gulag' on our regular network. I sent it over to you twenty minutes ago. I'm sending you the password by mobile now."

"Good, I'll forward it to my two contacts in the same format. Thank you."

"No problem," Ivor said, closing off.

*   *   *

"Petru?" Constanta said on Tarquin's landline.

"Yes. Hi, Constanta. How are you?"

"Good, darling. Things have been happening here!"

"Oh? Like what?"

"They got us … the bastards got us in Tarquin's house!" she said, her eyes filling with tears at recalling the ghastly moment when she realized they were caught.

"*Shit! Fucking hell!* Are you okay? What happened?" Petru said, instantly more alert.

Constanta went through the details of that scary experience, to the horror of Petru, who listened intently.

"Jesus, Constanta!" he said at the end. "You must been terrified."

"I was, darling!" she said with a hollow chuckle. "I really

thought we were finished."

"I think so."

"So look … he really wants to see these photos. Can you do this … like now?" she said.

"No problem. I'll use Natalia's PC; it's always running. The memory stick is in my rucksack; I don't go anywhere without it," he said.

"Cool. I'll send you the password now from my mobile and send the email address from Tarquin's PC in a few minutes. His name is David—at least that's the name he gave us—but he's a Russian bastard!"

"Okay. But you do know you can do this yourself, Constanta? You have the memory stick as well," he said.

"I know. It sounds crazy, but I just want to do it like I told him … you know, from Bucharest … in case … he …,"

"He works it out? That you did it in London? That's impossible," Petru said, chuckling.

"Whatever. Anyway, you'll be better at selecting than me. I'm a bit fucked at the moment, darling, and I wouldn't trust Tarquin!" she said with a small snort.

"Sure. No problem."

"But be very selective what you send him. No outside pictures of the house; well, none that would show the place completely. We don't want him working out where it is by going through lists of big French houses or something crazy. And be careful about details in the background; you know, like a road sign, a name, or something like this."

"A road sign? It's not near any roads!"

"You know what I mean," she said.

"Sure. How many photos should I send?" he said.

"As many as you have to. You need to show one of Oliver and the other two guys, together if possible. You need to show the cabinet … from different angles and some details, the crate it went into, the stairs, the place it was put in that dusty room … perhaps the room itself and … and then possibly a shot at the bottom of the stairs at ground level, to give impression of the sort of place it is. Oh … and a shot of the outside of the house … but only a part, if you can?"

"Sure, okay. But I think you better take a look at them first, so I will text you when they're loaded so you can check them out."

"Good idea," she agreed.

"May have to be three separate emails with all these photos; there's a limit," he said.

"Sure. Anyway, he can always get more. He just needs to smell the meat at this stage!" she said with a giggle.

Petru laughed.

"He's a hungry dog, is he?"

"Woof woof!" she said. "I'm going to send you a picture of my new hair style; it's so fucking cool."

"Okay. But go careful, Constanta."

"Bye, darling."

"Bye."

*   *   *

Oliver pushed open the door to Melvyn's workshop.

"Morning, Mel. How you feeling?"

"Oh, not so bad. To be honest, though, it seems really empty in here. I'm so used to that bloody great cabinet in here, that it's left a real hole. I can't seem to settle!"

"Yuh. I quite understand … with me too," Oliver agreed. "It's like our whole lives were taken up by the damn thing, and suddenly it's … well … flown the nest! I hope it's feeling homesick!"

"Some hope of that," Melvyn said. "I reckon it's settled into its new home with barely a thought for us, its creators. I hope those spiders are giving it the itches, though. I must've put seven or eight in there. We want that thing nicely webbed up when it comes to opening the lid in a year's time."

"Good God! What a crazy game we play, Mel," Oliver said. "Beats a nine to five, I suppose. Are you enjoying *Drawn to Trouble*?"

"What?"

"That book I gave you by Eric Hebborn. *Drawn to Trouble*."

"Oh yeah ... well, I've only skimmed the first few pages; haven't had it long. That guy had some cheek, though! Fancy copying all those masterpieces; you know. Rembrandts, Gainsboroughs, Rubens ... he even did a Michelangelo. The bloody nerve of the man!"

"It's absolutely outrageous!" Oliver said, bursting out laughing at Melvyn's irony.

"Yer, well ... at least we're not printing them off like bank notes!" he said sheepishly.

"That wouldn't be easy, Mel," Oliver said, still chuckling. "Knocking out high-end 'one-offs' is bloody impossible!"

"That's why they're 'one-offs,' Oliver. No machine could be set to create that cabinet; there are too many fine judgements to make throughout the process."

"True, Mel, too many indeed. It would take a very complex series of machines to knock those out! Music ... books ... pictures, can all be funnelled down wires and through the air, but solid oak cabinets ... I don't think so!"

"They do in *Star Trek*," Melvyn offered with a grin.

"And guess what, Mel ... then they'd be worth nothing! Like a song you just suck from the web."

Suddenly Oliver's mobile squealed in his pocket. He looked at the screen and strolled outside.

"You took your time, darling! Must have called on Tuesday evening," he said.

"I'm sorry, Olly. I was terribly tied up earlier in the week, doing Lord knows what. So many silly things that always need doing," Lily said.

"I know," Oliver said, wandering farther away from the workshop. "When are you around for, um ... a catch up? I've got a few bottles for you; think you'll enjoy them!"

"Oh, how sweet of you. Well ... er ... where are we ... Sunday ... shall we say Tuesday? Giles will be in London ... always is for the first three days of the week, and I'll be on my lonesome. I'll need some company. You can join me by the pool."

"Sounds alluring."

"Come for twelve-ish. I'll throw a salad together."

"Lovely, darling. Well, until Tuesday. Oh, I nearly forgot! Thanks so much for taking Titus out that Friday. That was beyond the call of duty, but my word, was it appreciated. What a chance meeting that was … in the village shop!"

"No problem, Olly. I like Mary … and it was rather nice to have a snoop at the Hall when you weren't there!"

"Well, thank you very much!" Oliver said theatrically.

Lily sighed.

"Oh, it's lovely to hear your voice, Oliver," she said quietly. "Seems I haven't seen you in ages … see you soon."

"Okay, darling," he murmured, closing off.

Oliver put the mobile back in his pocket and stood thinking for a few moments. He then wandered back into the workshop.

"Now, Mel, as we discussed, we're going to take a few weeks off. I suggest you and Mary hire that caravan thing, that motor cruiser, and go on a tour of grand English houses. You've always talked about it, so this is your chance."

"Could do, I suppose," Melvyn said, without a glimmer of enthusiasm.

"Does anything really excite you, Mel?" Oliver said with a wry smile.

"Yeah … it's just I don't jump up and down," he replied with a grin. "I really would enjoy a tour like that."

"Good … well, start organizing it. As for me … I'll have to give it some thought. A bit of fishing would be fun; yes, a trip to Scotland."

They carried on in this lazy whimsical vein for the rest of the morning, discussing their individual ambitions and the various pieces that were in the pipeline for restoration. Eventually Oliver glanced at his watch, slapped Melvyn fondly on the shoulder, and returned to the Hall.

*   *   *

Tarquin reached for his mobile; it showed "number unknown."

"Hello," he said tentatively.

"Hi. It is David," came the clipped Russian voice.

"Oh, hi, David … er … did you get the email?"

"Yes, I did. As I thought, Oliver has copied a high-value piece. We need to meet and discuss our options. Where is your girlfriend? It's important she is at this meeting."

"One moment, I'll get her."

Tarquin held his hand over the mouthpiece and started up the stairs, yelling.

"What the fuck is it?" Constanta said, looking over the banisters two floors up.

"It's David. He wants to meet."

"Tell him I'm coming down."

"Sorry, David. She's just coming," Tarquin said, as though his mobile had transformed into a scorpion. "I'll hand you over."

She bounced down the final steps and snatched the phone.

"David, hi. You've received the photos?"

"Yes, I have … impressive. We need to meet. Can you do tomorrow at three?"

"Where?"

"At the Buddhist Temple … by the river in Battersea Park."

"At the Buddhist Temple in Battersea Park at three?" she repeated, for Tarquin's affirmation.

He put his thumb up.

"Sure … three o'clock … we'll be there."

"Good. Bring your mobile."

"Sure."

The phone went dead.

Constanta looked at Tarquin and smiled.

"See? That guy is so hooked. Now we just got to be really cool. He's seen the cabinet and he wants it. Oh God, he wants it!"

"Well, let's just wait and see what he's going to come up

with," Tarquin said sternly.

"I reckon I'm right," she said confidently. "Oliver makes the cabinets in Gloucestershire and gets them over to that house in France as quickly as possible."

"You wonder why he doesn't make them over there," Tarquin said lazily, whilst inwardly thinking there was more to Oliver's strange actions in that house.

"Well, first of all he'd have to be in France most of the time, which may not suit him," she said. "Since he's meant to be running his English antique business."

"Suppose so," Tarquin said doubtfully.

"I mean, there could be a heap of reasons, darling, just don't worry your little head over it," she said, slumping down on the sofa and throwing her legs over his.

He ran his fingers up the back of her neck and chuckled.

"It's all bristly there! Rather sexy, actually," he said, stroking the short hairs repeatedly.

"Remind you of your school days, darling?" she said mischievously, allowing her head to rest against his cheek.

"Please, Constanta ... don't spoil the moment," he said tenderly. "Now, about our meeting with this guy tomorrow ... we need to think it through."

Chapter 37

Bernard stood by the folly in the garden at Chateau Clery, studying the tree growing around the rear of the structure.

"It's well and truly dug in around the masonry, Jeanne," he said to his wife, slapping the rough trunk. "And it's completely blocking off the entrance to that pit, or whatever it is down those steps."

"Well, Bernard, you should know!" his wife said mockingly. "After all, you did work here all those years ago."

"Yeah, when I was fifteen, Jeanne! That's forty years back."

"Well, can't you remember anything about it? The tree and all this undergrowth wouldn't have been here then," she said.

"No, I can't, Jeanne! It doesn't look anything like it did … the whole place has gone to rack and ruin. They built all sorts of weird things then for these big houses … just for the hell of it. I mean, look at this building, for Christ's sake … what's its purpose? Nothing!" Bernard said with a loud snort, gazing up at the rows of columns.

"They did it because it was pretty, Bernard, and when you have lots of money, that's what you do. Build things that have no real purpose, but look nice when you look out of your bedroom window," she continued, like a school mistress.

"True, Jeanne. Anyway, this wasn't even a part of the garden I was concerned with. They had loads of gardeners, and they all had their patch. We weren't allowed to wander around sticking our noses where they weren't wanted … we had a job to do and we did it. Things weren't so casual then!"

"Well, it doesn't matter, he doesn't want us to do major stuff, like cutting trees down, until next spring. When it's all stripped bare, it'll probably all come back to you."

"Might do," Bernard conceded. "I reckon we'd start by stripping the branches off the thing first, and when it's cleared, rope up the trunk and make sure it falls down the hill and out of harm's way."

"You make it sound so easy, Bernard, but you know as well as me that trees have a habit of falling oddly when you're involved," his wife said in bossy tones. "You tend to go hammer and tongs at these things and then regret it after."

"I know, I know," he said irritably. "Of course, we have to be careful … and we will be careful. But why are we discussing something that's not happening for ages?"

"Well, we don't want to be wiping out his folly, do we?" she said with a cackle.

"Jeanne, for Christ's sake, we're not going to damage the bloody building, just stop worrying," he said, removing his cap and running his hand back over his brown scalp.

"Any normal person would want to get the inside of the house in order first and then start on the garden," Jeanne said, cupping a bunch of yellow blooms in the palm of her hand. "But he seems adamant that we mustn't touch the inside … well, apart from superficial stuff on the ground floor."

"There's enough to do, Jeanne, on the ground floor, don't you worry," Bernard said. "Varnishing the window sills and panels, mending the shutters … the floorboards, skirtings … oh yes, it'll keep us occupied, all right. You've got to understand, he's trying to get a grant, and for that to happen the inspector needs to see it looking rough. He's forbidden us to do *anything* on the upper floors, and he meant it! He had a look in his eye when he said that, so be careful!"

"Bernard, I don't need you to lecture me on where we can go and what we do here," Jeanne said sharply. "As long as he's paying us, I don't give a fig!"

"Exactly, my lovely. Just enjoy the place; the peace, the space.

He just wants us here, I think, to keep an eye. Where are the dogs, by the way?"

"Oh … up at the top in the rhododendrons. They've cornered a rabbit, I think," Jeanne said, glancing up the hill towards the house.

"When's he next coming down, by the way?" Bernard said.

"Do you ever listen, Bernard?"

"No, I don't, you hussy!" Bernard said, lunging forward and slapping his wife's bottom.

"Bernard, stop being childish," she replied shrilly, swivelling round to face him. "He's not down this weekend, but the one after. Then he's going to try and come down every other weekend. And by the way, he has a girlfriend called Cecile, in case you'd forgotten."

"Very funny, Jeanne. You know when I speak about him I mean them both," he said with a twinkle in his eye.

"If you say so. Come on. Let's go and list the things we need to get in town tomorrow; it's going to be a *big* shopping day."

With that, they started up the hill towards the house, calling the dogs.

•

Thomas Charrington

Chapter 38

At two forty-five on Monday, Tarquin and Constanta arrived at the cream-stoned Buddhist temple known as the Peace Pagoda in Battersea Park. They were early and the place was deserted apart from a pair of Japanese tourists on the steps taking photographs. The air felt heavy, hot … aching to unleash a summer downpour. They gazed up and down the walkway by the river wall and then scanned the nearby benches, but there seemed to be no sign of the Russians yet. Tarquin nervously checked his mobile, making sure he had a signal.

"Take it easy, darling," Constanta said, scrutinizing him. "We just got to see what he says. We have the trump card. We know where the cabinet is, he doesn't. Without that information, they can't do very much, and David knows it."

"I know, I know," Tarquin said tensely. "It's just this is such foreign territory to me."

"Leave it to me, Tarquin. You know I'm good when it comes to thinking on my feet. Everything's going to be fine. The best thing you did was research the cabinet and find out what it is. Now that was cool; that nearly blew my mind! You got to admit it, Oliver's got some style to try and pull that one off."

"I know. I still feel we're going to realize we've all made a terrible mistake and he's completely innocent!" Tarquin said with a furrowed brow.

"For fuck's sake, darling, stop being so *naïve*!" she said, and then paused before adding, "Hey, my English is getting better, isn't it! That's not a word I ever used before … must be catching it from you!"

"Thanks," Tarquin said with a tight smile, whilst gazing over her shoulder towards Albert Bridge. "This guy gives me a bad feeling."

"Why? It's all working out now. We got those assholes off our backs; you should be happy. Should be doing somersaults and …"

She stopped suddenly. "Shit. Here they are!" she said, looking past Tarquin and down the river.

Tarquin spun round and saw the unmistakable silhouettes of the two men strolling from the direction of Chelsea Bridge. Sergei towered over Zoltan, who was engrossed in his mobile, whilst a third person seemed to be lurking a few strides behind them. Constanta figured they were taking no risks. As they approached, the third man peeled off and stood by a tree, a pair of binoculars hanging from his neck.

"Hello," Zoltan said, extending his hand as he arrived at the top of the steps. Tarquin shook it, followed by Constanta.

Sergei perched himself on the wall opposite and watched them with cool indifference. He seemed to be squeezed into a bomber jacket one size too small, and Constanta made a split-second guess that he was probably a boxer. Zoltan, on the other hand, was dressed in a white linen jacket over a blue silk shirt with Armani jeans. His sport shoes looked expensive.

"Okay, this doesn't need to take so long … we just need to know that we're all on the same page," Zoltan said in a friendly manner. "Firstly, though, I need to confirm your names. You are 'Tarquin' by your email?"

"Yes, that's right," Tarquin replied sternly.

"And you are …?"

"Constanta," she said.

"Constanta. Good. Now, I want you to remember that in my company, you will have a new name. You will be known as 'Anya,' okay?"

"Anya? Why?" she asked.

"For security. You don't need to ask why," he said decisively.

"It is your code name ... remember it. Also remember that Sergei," he pointed with his chin, "has been known to your parents in Romania for long time. You have old family ties. It may seem confusing to you, but you're probably going to meet other members of our network. When you do, this is your connection to us, okay?"

"I don't understand ... but yes, sure," Constanta said, bemused.

"You don't need to say any more than this. It is for your own benefit. If anyone starts asking awkward questions about Sergei, just say you're sorry, but you cannot discuss it. This will underline your professionalism."

"Professionalism?" she repeated.

"Yes. You hunt people down. This is your profession ... your training. If you want to be paid, then follow my instructions carefully. You do not discuss it with anyone! Are we understanding each other?" he said, staring at her.

Constanta looked at him and nodded.

"Okay," he continued. "Firstly, as I mentioned on the phone, Oliver has made a copy of a piece of extremely valuable furniture. Royal furniture, to be precise; French royal furniture. Commissioned from one of the best German cabinetmakers of the eighteenth century."

"Wow!" Constanta said, feigning surprise. "He has a cheek!"

"Yes, he does," Zoltan said, his pale blue eyes burrowing into hers. "He has cheek and good dose of stupidity."

"Why?" she said innocently.

"Because such a strategy was my idea, not his!" he said forcefully. He looked out over the river and allowed his eyes to focus on a passing barge.

"But this is irrelevant now," he resumed after a few moments. "What we want is our rightful rewards. I shall now explain to you what his game is, because it is not what you think."

"Oh?" Constanta said, genuinely surprised.

"No, it is not Oliver's French showroom; not at all. Oliver

has placed the cabinet in this house for one reason only. *In order to give it a false history … and an entirely plausible one!*"

"I'm sorry, I'm not with you," Tarquin said, craning forward.

"Oliver is creating the illusion that this cabinet was always at the chateau … hidden … forgotten … and then rediscovered." Zoltan said, looking at Constanta and Tarquin in turn.

Constanta's eyes narrowed, but she said nothing.

"This is why you saw it being put in old scruffy chest in roof of the house. He is creating the illusion that the cabinet is lost twin of its sister at the Wallace Collection. How, we don't know yet, but there must be a connection with this house or the family that it once belonged to, and the cabinet. A connection that lends credibility to its being there. It was secreted away for reasons only known to Oliver at the moment; fictitious reasons, but ones which I can assure you will be very convincing. I know Oliver well. He will have done his research, and he's seen an opportunity."

Constanta gazed at Zoltan whilst her mind worked through the information.

"Okaaay," she said, trying to formulate her question. "So he's playing this trick, which I have to say makes a lot of sense, but … but surely the owner of the house will be the lucky guy, not Oliver?"

"Of course. This is exactly right. And this makes me think the owner of the house is part of the plot. He knows the game," Zoltan said, enjoying watching the penny drop. "It could be that Oliver now owns this house … but I doubt it; that would work against him."

"Fucking hell!" Constanta blurted. "The smart bastard!"

"Well, not so clever, because you watched him doing it," Zoltan said, allowing his guard to slip and smiling.

"And what now?" she probed.

"Well, now we have waiting game on our hands. Because Oliver has gone for such high-profile piece—such a magnificent artefact—he's had to be extra careful as to how he presents it to the world. He would normally try and sell such a piece privately, through appropriate dealers who would approach institutions, rich private collectors and so on. But I think with this piece, he's going to shout about it from the rooftops and act like silly school boy who's discovered a Roman coin or a Saxon sword!"

"You mean, this would make it less suspect ... more authentic?" Tarquin interjected.

"Of course. It will appear more genuine. Every dealer knows that big auction houses like Hardy's charge large commissions on sales, and that someone 'in the business' would seek a different method to sell. But this implies sophistication, and this is last impression he wants to project. Don't forget, it is not Oliver who's at centre of the wheel here, it is the owner of the house. Oliver will be gone, out of the frame. *But giving instructions from his command post.*"

"So you think this person will sell more publicly ... like at an auction?" she said.

"Yes, I do. He's going to throw it at the world and say, look what I've discovered! The cabinet will be forbidden for export outside France—again it depresses its value—*but again, it adds to its authenticity!* It will be in the papers, on news. This piece has a twin at the Wallace Collection here in London; it was commissioned by Marie Antoinette."

"How long, David, do you think the cabinet will remain at the chateau before Oliver plays his hand, as it were?" Tarquin asked stiffly.

"Who knows, it cannot be less than a certain time ... say six months ... but it could be lot longer. But I think not longer than say two or three years at most; it depends on many things. You must understand, the cabinet has to blend into house to look real ... and this takes time."

Zoltan glanced at his watch and caught the eye of Sergei.

"Okay, so we need to round this up, my friends," he continued. "We need to know the way forward. On our part, we will be watching those websites which monitor valuable French artefacts. We will be watching all the auction houses and, of course, we will be keeping sharp eye on directory of 'monumentes nationale,' which is where the cabinet will be listed. My guess is that in six to eighteen months we will be hearing about it. I will then be in contact with you. I could call Oliver right now and tell him the game's up. But what would be point of that? We need him to proceed as though it's all fine … and then we strike. When the money is in his bank!"

Constanta's eyes glinted. Zoltan resumed.

"After the sale and after funds have exchanged hands, I will call Oliver, tell him what I know, and suggest a meeting. He will have no option. Then we agree my percentage—which will include a slice for you both—and the deal will be done."

"But how can we trust you to give us anything?" Constanta challenged.

"You can't," he replied sharply. "The exact whereabouts of the cabinet is not really of much importance any more. By showing Oliver the photos you sent me, he will assume that we've been to that place."

Constanta looked bereft.

"But luckily for you, this is not way I work," Zoltan continued. "You did the ground work, you took some hits, you've shown initiative. You will be rewarded!"

"But how much?" she persisted.

"He can't answer that, Constanta, the cabinet hasn't sold yet, things can still go wrong," Tarquin interrupted.

"Thank you," Zoltan said, turning to Tarquin. "This is precisely right. We have to wait and see. Once the piece has passed through the hands of the experts and been sold at auction, then I can answer you."

Constanta looked at him, the wheels of her mind whirring. He saw her conundrum.

"I regret to say, you can do nothing to put pressure on me," he said. "Our organization is powerful … you just have to trust."

He looked toward Sergei and made a "come here" gesture with his fingers. The big man came over whilst doing a quick scan of the immediate locality. He handed Zoltan a fat leather wallet, which he'd been concealing inside his jacket.

"Now, we decided to give you something for your achievements to date, which are considerable. This contains twenty-five thousand pounds in cash."

Constanta took a sharp intake of breath and her eyes started watering.

"Fuck me!" she blurted, unable to stop a huge grin sweeping across her face. "Fucking bloody hell!"

Zoltan handed the wallet to Tarquin. "She seems happy, I think."

Tarquin took the wallet and his fingers tightened around the handle.

"Thank you, I … don't know quite what to say," he said, looking Zoltan in the eye.

Constanta kicked him surreptitiously.

"You do not have to say anything, my friend, you play fair with me, and I play fair with you."

He pulled a slim diary from his pocket and opened it at a back page. There were some words in Russian and the figure of £25,000.

"Sign here, please."

Tarquin hesitated for a split second, realizing he hadn't counted anything, but then scribbled his signature.

"Thank you, David," he said.

"My pleasure," Zoltan replied cordially, slipping the diary back into his jacket. "We will be in contact as soon as we have some news."

"Multumesc David," Constanta blurted in her mother tongue, momentarily phased by the enormity of events.

"My pleasure, Anya, and remember what I told you. Sergei is an old family friend and you are a professional man hunter."

"Yes …yes of course," she said, grinning stupidly.

Zoltan looked at her for a few moments, as though about to add something. Then he gestured to Sergei with his eyes, and the two men walked casually back down the steps and rejoined the third man.

$*$ $*$ $*$

The Gloucestershire sun beat down on Oliver with a rare intensity as he emerged from the glittering water and sauntered, dripping, across the hot paving stones and into the pool house. A minute or two later, a pair of brown feminine feet followed him, stepping silently and purposefully along the steaming trail of water he had left in his wake. Then they stopped.

Oliver had just removed his trunks when the light in the musty sweltering room dimmed suddenly. He turned in surprise to see Lily's sylphlike figure silhouetted in the doorway. Her smouldering eyes locked onto his, blocking the vacuous words he was about to utter and rendering him speechless. She stood in that classic feminine pose, with one knee slightly bent, her head tilted to one side, her lips parted suggestively. There was no smile. Then very deliberately, her eyes still fixed to his, she adroitly unfastened her bikini top and let it fall in a flash of lilac to the floor.

Oliver suddenly found himself looking at Lily as though for the first time. Her naked breasts, so primal, beckoning and excitingly white against her tanned skin, caused a great welling of animal desire to plume up inside him. Before he had time to think about his nakedness, he became unashamedly aroused, and like a raw beast, moved quickly towards her.

Taking her temples in his hands, he kissed her passionately on the mouth, feeling the heat of her sun-kissed torso acutely against his cool flesh. Consumed with desire, he buried his head hungrily into her breasts, drawing in the warm scent of her skin and teasing the pink nipples to stiffen as he brushed them repeatedly with his nose and lips. She moaned as though in a dream, as his kisses moved down across her soft stomach, forcing him to his knees. Without hesitation, he yanked her bikini briefs down, ignoring her murmured protests.

"Do it, Oliver … do it now!" she groaned a few moments later, as though in pain. "I adore you…I always have…"

"I will … I will," he said in a voice he didn't recognize. "I bloody will!"

Stumbling to his feet, he curled his forearms under her thighs and hoisted her carefully up. She locked her legs around his waist and then sank onto him with a piercing shriek, driving her fingernails into his shoulders fiercely. Moaning uncontrollably, she then buried her face in his chest and started undulating in an aggressive animal rhythm … ever more feverishly … as he thrust her hard and breathlessly against the pine wall of the pool house.

Thomas Charrington

Chapter 39

The Auction (one year later)

The suited official stood illuminated at the rostrum studying his notes, whilst above him the big hand of the clock clicked forward to ten fifty-five. The auction room buzzed with tension. For once, every seat was taken, and it soon became apparent that the crowd was split into tight parcels of representatives from various institutions vying to lay claim to the magnificent piece of the day—the Freiburg Cabinet.

They whispered excitedly amongst themselves whilst casting furtive glances at their competition. And, of course, there were the more sinister characters who preferred to stand at the fringes; those who hid behind dark glasses in Armani suits, telephones to hand.

Situated in a grand building on the Avenue Matignon in Paris, Hardy's was well aware that this would be one of those electrifying days of high theatre. A day when the big beasts of the art world would unsheathe their weapons and duel for a prize which eight weeks earlier was never thought to exist.

Tarquin and Constanta sat towards the back, trying to remain aloof and unaffected. But the atmosphere demanded compliance; they were wired into the crowd as into a circuit board … its current pulsing through them, making their stomachs flutter with an ungovernable anxiety.

Suddenly Tarquin felt the sharp jab of Constanta's elbow in his ribs and jumped involuntarily.

"What?" he said, looking at her furiously.

"Calm down, darling, take it easy!" she whispered to him. "I think I seen the guy from the house … in Troyes."

"Which guy?" Tarquin said, confused.

"The young guy from the chateau … who was with Oliver; it's him over there, I think," she said, pointing with her eyes.

Tarquin looked along her line of sight between various heads and saw him … yes, definitely him … with a pretty, dark-haired girl. They were about four rows forward and more towards the edge. He was studying his catalogue intently, morosely even, whilst she glanced around the room happily, soaking up the drama, enjoying herself. Their moods seemed incongruous, and Tarquin wondered if she knew, or whether this was his secret.

"I can't see Oliver," Tarquin whispered.

"Don't be crazy, he won't be here … that would be way too risky," she whispered forcefully. "Don't forget, he's meant to be in the background. I guess Zoltan wants to keep a low profile as well, but I bet you he's got someone here to see how it goes."

Suddenly, the baritone voice of the man at the rostrum burst into the room from every direction, giving him a stature way beyond his physical size.

"Ladies and gentlemen," he said, gazing around the assembled faces with an experienced eye. "Today is one those special days when something quite exceptional has become available for purchase. Something which was thought to have burned at the outset of the French Revolution … over two hundred years ago!"

A wave of excitement rippled through the room, and Constanta turned to Tarquin with a twisted smile, whilst putting her hand on his lap. The auctioneer gave a short talk on the history of the cabinet; of its commission by Marie Antoinette in the year 1786, of its twin at the Wallace Collection in London, of its unbelievable discovery at a chateau near Troyes. As he concluded, the atmosphere crackled with tension.

Then, it began. The auctioneer's voice moved up an octave and the figures rolled from his tongue, injecting an urgency into the room and causing the assembled faces to stare at him, mesmerized by his mantra.

Beginning at the opening value of £500,000, he rose in increments of £100,000 in a professional delivery, staccato and precise. At first he struggled with the sea of subtle gestures in front of him, but as the bidding soared past £3,000,000, the number of participants rapidly diminished, until at £6,500,000 there remained only three.

Constanta's hand, which had closed round Tarquin's knee, was steadily tightening as the bidding continued, but now it reached an unbearable level. He pushed it away roughly; she hardly noticed.

Two men and a woman were fighting for the prize of the decade. A heavy, slick-haired man on the front row, a middle-aged woman in a scarlet jacket to the right, and at the back, a tall, lean man hidden behind dark shades. All three had telephones to their ears and were part of small groups.

"Eight million six hundred thousand pounds ... £8,700,000," the auctioneer barked hotly.

"Eight million eight hundred thousand pounds ... £8,900,000 ... £9,000,000," he continued. The man at the front dropped out and a communal gasp rippled through the room. The figures continued to roll.

"Nine million five hundred thousand pounds to the lady," the auctioneer continued. "Nine million six hundred thousand pounds to the gentleman at the back ... £9,700,000 to the lady ... £9,800,000 to the gentleman ... £9,900,000 to the lady." The lean man at the back pulled out suddenly.

"Any other offers?" the auctioneer said, scanning the sea of faces whilst allowing the gavel to hover threateningly over the block.

"Nine million, nine hundred thousand pounds to the lady here," he said, gesturing to the scarlet woman. "Any further offers, ladies and gentlemen?"

He delayed tantalizingly ... the room was dead silent.

"Going once ... going twice ... GONE!"

He dropped the gavel with a sharp "thock."

"The Freiburg Cabinet twin is sold to the lady for nine million, nine hundred thousand pounds!" he boomed across the room.

Constanta turned to Tarquin with a look of absolute shock.

"My God! My fucking God!" she said, staring at him … but without seeing.

*   *   *

A few weeks later, they were driving down the Embankment in London.

"Your mobile's ringing," she said, as they took a left turn onto Albert Bridge.

"Well, can you answer it then," he said, swivelling the steering wheel. "It's in that pocket."

She pulled it out.

"Hello?"

"Hello, it's David," came the Russian reply.

"Oh, hi," she said, suddenly focused.

"Is this Anya?"

"Erm … yes. Yes, it is," she said quickly.

"Good. We have to meet. As I said in my email after the sale in Paris, money transfers for these amounts take time … that's why you haven't heard from me for six weeks. But now everything is in place. I've spoken with Oliver."

"Okay … so where and when?" she said.

"Thursday … in the evening at seven o'clock … Chelsea Harbour. My father is bringing his cruiser into the Thames; he has mooring there. I will send you precise instructions by email. Are you absolutely sure you can make that time?"

"Thursday, seven o'clock at Chelsea Harbour," she said loudly, looking at Tarquin. He nodded.

"Yes, that's fine. Do we need to bring anything?"

"It is not 'we,' it is 'you' only! Are you crazy? My father must never meet or see Tarquin or our cover will be blown! He lives next door to Oliver, for love of Lenin!"

"Oh … er, sure … I'm sorry," she said, feeling foolish, "I wasn't thinking clearly."

"Just don't be late."

"Okay, see you then,"

The phone went dead.

"Shit …I'm so dumb sometimes!" she said, sliding her hand under Tarquin's thigh.

"Of course his father can't meet you! That would be crazy. But you can still drop me at the harbour . Those weirdos may try and play some funny game and then you can come and rescue me, yuh?"

"But of course my angel. Your wish is my command," Tarquin said with a grimace.

*   *   *

Oliver sat on one of Melvyn's scruffy chairs pulling heavily on a cigar.

He looked haggard. His face had lost the florid plumpness of a few months earlier and deep lines were etched into the grey skin. He looked like he hadn't slept properly in weeks.

"So I had no choice, Mel, it was that or full exposure. They knew *everything*!"

"I just can't get my head around them being in the house watching us!" Melvyn said, looking at Oliver in horror. "Taking those photos and listening to our conversations … *so bloody close*! I've been getting panic attacks just thinking about it," he said, tumbling a peg through his fingers nervously.

"I know, I know," Oliver agreed. "There we were, thinking they were out of the frame, not really interested … going about their other business, and then this! I think I very nearly had a heart attack when I opened that envelope…"

"I bet. To be honest, I reckon I *would* have had a heart attack," Melvyn said with feeling. "I understand why you couldn't face coming over; you've been in shock, you poor sod. Seeing those photos of us all on the stairs, moving the cabinet;

it's just too terrible to think about. I mean, how in the hell did they get into the place and not be seen? It's … it's just unbelievable!"

"I know, Mel," Oliver agreed.

"Nearly ten million quid … ten million pounds … and he takes half! And he even has the fucking nerve to let you pay the commission from your half," Melvyn said in exasperated tones.

"What could I do, Melvyn? What the hell could I do? I couldn't pretend it sold for less; it was out there for all to see. It was Fabien that I really dreaded telling, Mel. You *know* Zoltan … the Russian lot, his father. You know the setup. We know each other very well … but Fabien … he was an outsider. I'd assured him it was safe, that the project was bulletproof, that he could trust me … us … to deliver. And then this."

"Exactly," Melvyn said gravely.

"I've already leant him a couple of hundred thousand on the back of this, for Christ's sake, before the cabinet was finished, to help him get his life back together with Cecile and push them into the chateau. It worked beautifully. She changed overnight and looked at the place with fresh eyes. But now … well, you know the position. You know what building costs are. And the cabinet … well what's left has to be split between you two after I've taken back what I paid out in material costs.

"He's got all sorts of commitments on that place which is going to cost a pretty fortune … how can I pull the plug on that now that he's moved in? By announcing I made a cock up in my planning. How? She'd probably leave him for good. And then there's you, Melvyn. You've broken your back to get this thing airborne, and you've had a fair few people in the trade to pay as well. You need your cut. It should be more, for God's sake, but … well, there's nothing we can do. I really don't want to go to prison, Melvyn, I really don't," Oliver said, looking with tired eyes through the window onto Melvyn's walled garden. "That would kill me."

"You're not going to prison, Oliver," Melvyn said quietly. "You've paid the money, they're off your case now. Zoltan has a sense of rules in that Russian head of his, if I know him at all. I think you're off his hook now."

"I bloody hope so. You hear about blackmail—you read about it in detective novels—but to experience it is something else. It's always there; a pair of hands around your throat."

"As I said, Oliver, I think it's behind you. Look forward. Look at what we achieved. We really scaled the heights this time!"

Oliver stayed silent for a few moments, lost in his own thoughts. Then he replied quietly, as though half asleep.

"We did, Mel. We certainly did."

Thomas Charrington

Chapter 40

Bernard sat eating breakfast in an outbuilding off the courtyard at Chateau Clery, which was now his and Jeanne's permanent dwelling. He was surrounded by plates of cheese, salami, and chunks of bread. His dogs lay sprawled on the flagstone floor on either side of his chair, their eyes watching his hands moving from the plate to his mouth with hypnotic intensity. Suddenly, one of them leapt to its feet, growling, its ears pricked, quickly followed by the other.

"That'll be Marc," Jeanne said, wandering into the room with a pair of towels over her arm.

"Yeah, guess so," Bernard said, standing up, draining his coffee cup and wiping his mouth. "I'm quite looking forward to this."

The sound of a distant tractor outside on the drive became steadily louder and eventually stopped nearby.

"As I said, Bernard, just be careful with that tree. I've grown fond of this place. I don't want you destroying his precious folly and getting us kicked out!" Jeanne said with a cackle.

"You worry too much, Jeanne," he said, putting his cap on and heading out of the door. "We've got it all planned out. You coming to watch the thing fall?"

"Yeah, I'll be down in three-quarters of an hour," she said, tidying the table.

"Reckon it'll take an hour to get it all roped up, so don't hurry," he shouted over his shoulder.

Down at the folly, Bernard and Marc began clearing the

dense undergrowth around the tree trunk, revealing the old lichen-mottled masonry that lay in its shadow.

"What a place," Marc said, wielding his hook on the tangle of brambles, bindweed, and other creeping plants. "I'm keen to see what's going on down those steps …. it's so blooming dark down there. Perhaps the monster is waiting for us!"

"Don't get too excited, Marc. I reckon it's an old ice vault or something like that. Could even have been a sort of changing room for those events they had down here," Bernard said, grabbing a bunch of greenery in his gloved hands.

"What sort of events?"

"I reckon they had musical evenings, shows … that sort of thing," Bernard said, breathing heavily from the exertion. "This was once a very important chateau, you know. They had royalty to stay on certain occasions, so it had to have some outside entertainment, or the king would have got pissed off!"

"Well, it makes sense, doesn't it? I mean, why else would they have found that cabinet here last year?" Marc said. "I've heard that they had the exact same one at Versailles."

"Cor, we do know our history," Bernard said with a hint of sarcasm.

"I'm interested, Bernard, that's all, and it was splashed all over the papers. Nothing much exciting happens in these parts, so of course we're all listening for tidbits."

"True," Bernard conceded, as he yanked a length of creeper from the nettles.

"Life's so bloody unfair," Marc continued. "Why couldn't I discover some piece of treasure in my roof, Bernard!"

"Well, because you live in a cottage, Marc, which royalty probably didn't have a lot to do with," Bernard said, throwing a branch onto the trailer.

"Did you meet the roofer?" Marc said, stopping.

"You mean the guy who discovered the cabinet?" Bernard said, looking up. "Yes, of course I did. That was a day to remember! Fabien had the roofer coming around at ten o'clock, and then some official from the university in Troyes coming in a bit later to give him a historical tour of the house. I remember Cecile was very excited about the tour."

"Okay."

"So the roofer arrived … on a Saturday morning, I think—yes, must have been, because they were both here, Fabien and Cecile, summer last year. So the three of them, the roofer, his mate, and Fabien, went upstairs to check out what needed doing up there. The roof was quite bad in places … tiles missing, leaks, and so on. I remember Fabien had a big torch with him so they could really see what was going on up there.

They had been gone for about half an hour when Fabien came rushing down the stairs in a right state and told Cecile she had to go back up with him because they had discovered something in a box up there. He was really excited; I've never seen him like that! His eyes were bulging out of his head!"

"Oh?"

"Yes. He told me later what happened. They were up there in the roof, you know, measuring, taking a look at the state of the place and, and they suddenly spotted this wooden box hidden in a recess in the wall. It was really old, covered in dust. Fabien asked the roofer to help him pull it out, but it was bloody heavy and wouldn't budge! Roofer said it was gold! Anyways, they did drag it out in the end by yanking its feet. But then they couldn't open it! So he had to come back down to his truck and get a tool. Anyway, they did open the bloody thing, and there it was!"

"What?"

"The cabinet you, fool … the thing you've seen in the bloody newspapers!" Bernard said with feeling.

"Wow!" Marc said.

"And then half an hour after that, the university guy arrives and he takes a look at it as well. He couldn't believe his luck!"

"Shit, that is incredible … what a find!" Marc said, agog.

"It certainly was incredible … and as you know, it sold for an incredible price in Paris … millions I think."

"Shit! Lucky bastard!"

"It's the way of the world, my friend," Bernard said, lifting his cap to scratch his forehead.

"So why did this place get so bad over the years?"

"Money. The family ran out of it, I think. You know, the revolution, it destroyed a lot of the big families back then. A lot of them were guillotined."

"Jesus!" Marc said, rubbing the back of his neck. "Those were rough times. Hope the blade was sharp! So the guy who's coming down tomorrow … he owns the place, does he?"

"Yes, Fabien. It was his grandmother who was living here all those years. You know, the recluse everyone used to speak about. Used to live in a hell of a state, apparently; dirty as hell in the house. She didn't have much help, said she couldn't afford it, but I guess she was a bit cuckoo, to be honest. Anyway, she died four years ago or so, and he took over. Didn't do much to start with, but then suddenly got interested and began to ask tradesmen in to do things. It was such a mess. It's been cleared up now, though, thanks to me and Jeanne. Quite presentable, really. Bloody cold in the winter, though. We had to live in a small room near the kitchen with a bloody great fire!"

"Wow!" Marc said, removing a thorn from his glove. "Bit of a change from the cottage, wasn't it?"

"Yes, it was. Took some getting used to. Dogs bloody love it, though … so much space and a stack of rabbits."

"Bet they do," Marc said, beginning to lose focus as he fiddled with some rope. "Okay, I'm heading up the tree now to take out some of the branches. I've roped up the chainsaw, so when I give you the word, I want you to steady it as I yank it up."

"Okay, son."

For the next half hour, the quietness of the garden was shattered by the angry growls of the chainsaw as it sliced off branch after branch, showering the ground with wood chippings and eventually leaving the trunk solitary and exposed. Back on the ground, the two men roped the trunk around a neighbouring tree in order to control its fall. On cue, Jeanne appeared.

"Seems I came at just the right moment, boys," she said with a grin.

"Too right, ma cherie," Bernard said with a chuckle. "Come and stand with me, Jeanne, he's going to start sawing through the main trunk now, and I need all the weight I can get on this rope."

"Are you being cheeky, Bernard?" she said, chuckling.

The motor fired up and they were soon drowned in the tortured screams of the saw at high revs. The blade slowly sliced passed the halfway point, and Marc watched carefully for the first signs of the trunk breaking. Suddenly, he pulled the saw away and shouted at Bernard to pull. As predicted, the pillar of wood fell away from the folly with a loud cracking sound followed by a heavy thud.

"Perfect!" Bernard shouted. "You see, Jeanne, it's nowhere near the building!"

"Well done, boys!" she exclaimed,. "Now get the rest of that undergrowth away from the steps and let's see what's going on down there."

Thomas Charrington

Chapter 41

Tarquin and Constanta walked tentatively along a planked pontoon in Chelsea Harbour, following instructions on a printed email. Impossibly white seagulls hung on an easterly breeze above them, shrieking at each other through bright cartoon beaks. The air smelt salty; somehow not quite London.

"It says turn right here," Tarquin said, looking over Constanta's shoulder.

"No it doesn't."

"Yes, look. We're here," he said emphatically.

"Oh, okay," she conceded, striding ahead.

She arrived at another junction and stopped.

"Left here," Tarquin said, walking ahead.

"Fuck's sake, Tarquin … slow down!" she muttered behind him.

"The berth was number forty-four, wasn't it?" he said over his shoulder.

"Yes. I can see it. Shit, look at the size of that thing!" she said, gazing in awe at a huge prussian blue motor cruiser with a gently revolving radar scanner.

The name *Pushkin* stood out in large elegant lettering on the bow, where polished steel rails parted company and glided back on either side of the deck. A line of ropes with large rubber defenders hung from these like obedient servants.

"Right that's me done for now," Tarquin said, giving her shoulder a squeeze, "good luck and be careful, Angel."

He turned and headed back out of sight as she continued;

eventually she approached the two men standing at the base of the boarding ramp.

"Hi, I'm here to meet Zoltan," she said firmly.

One of the men shouted to another on deck. A couple of minutes later, Zoltan appeared above, silhouetted against the evening sky, and beckoned her aboard. She nervously ascended the ramp and arrived on a bleached teak deck where he shook her hand formally.

"Welcome on board," he said without smiling. "You found us okay?"

"Yes, not a problem," she answered breezily. "This is fantastic. It is your boat?"

"Yes, Anya," he said pointedly. "It is." He looked at her as though waiting for another question, but Constanta unhooked from his gaze.

"I never seen the river from this position," she said, sweeping her eyes around the restless cluster of boats surrounding them. "It's a different world down here."

"It is, a very different world," he replied tightly. "Right … so let's get down to business; come and meet my father."

Constanta felt the first pang of fear and wondered if she was being led into a trap. She followed Zoltan forward under a huge white awning which contained the wheel of the vessel with its accompanying host of levers, dials, and screens. A pair of high seats bolted to the floor on an elevated tier, were obviously the navigation positions for the pilots and afforded unimpeded views to the bow of the boat. As she passed underneath, Constanta looked up in awe at the dazzling array of technology and felt the full power of the organization Zoltan belonged to.

They descended some steps and entered a luxurious cabin with polished teak panelling and white leather couchettes. A large, heavy-boned man lounged on one of these, reading a newspaper. At the far end of the cabin, another man sat facing them with an intolerant expression; he was a similar build to Sergei.

"Father," Zoltan said, moving over to Viktor. "Anya's here."

"Ah!" he said, closing the paper and swivelling round to face Constanta.

He shook her hand, and gazed curiously at her for a few moments.

"So, you are the clever person who tracked down Oliver?" he said with an avuncular smile on his thick mouth. "We have to thank you for winning where others failed!"

Constanta looked at him and smiled awkwardly.

"Well, we did our best," she said, keeping it unspecific.

"Your best is good. You cornered our squirrel and found his stash of nuts without him realizing!" Viktor said, smiling.

"True," Constanta said.

"Followed him to France and then to a beautiful chateau?"

"Well, I am not sure so beautiful," she said. "It was falling to pieces!"

"Ah! You gave yourself away then, Anya," Viktor said smiling. "You cannot see the beauty in old things; it's too reminiscent of home, where 'old' means poverty and squalor. I was like you once; everything had to be new and shiny to be worth anything. But now I've spent time here in Western Europe, you begin to see old, not as squalid, but as vintage world, romantic, and often very valuable! Do you follow me?"

"Sort of," she said, feeling out of her depth.

"Zoltan says you are an acquaintance of Sergei?" he said suddenly, giving her a penetrating look. Zoltan moved uneasily on her left.

"Oh, he's more a friend of the family. He knows my parents better than me," she said guardedly, following Zoltan's instructions. "I'm not really sure of the full story, but we are in contact every so often."

"We don't worry about the 'hows,' Anya," he said, gazing out of one of the long side windows and across the water. "The less you say the better. Privacy is a very valuable commodity in these times, when everyone likes to crow from the rooftops about their boring lives. Wasn't it Winston Churchill who said 'loose lips sink ships'?"

"Sounds familiar," she said, lying.

"Good, you have initiative and that Romanian determination. You are very focused, I can see that." He stopped and studied her for a moment. "In actual fact, you could be very useful to us."

"Okay," she said, wondering where this was leading.

"This is very true," Zoltan agreed, with a small laugh to relieve the tension.

"Right, Anya, it is time to talk business," Viktor said, lighting a cigarette. "You've done some excellent detective work and emphasized the stupidity of some of my men. So Zoltan and I have decided to pay you over the odds on this particular assignment. It is one off, so don't expect the same level next time; that is, if you—and I hope you will—decide to become a more fixed member of the organization."

Constanta regarded him with a mixture of horror, greed, and excitement.

"I … I think I must give some thought to this, and then we can discuss," she blurted.

"Of course, that goes without saying, but we will be making you an offer," Viktor continued.

"Okay."

"Now, with regards to this French trip, we have decided to give you £250,000. As you know, there were very large sums involved."

Constanta looked at him in absolute disbelief whilst also struggling to conceal it.

"I … er … we … you said two hundred fifty thousand pounds?" she stammered, her eyes watering.

"Yes, that's right," Viktor said, puzzled by her reaction. "You have a problem?"

"Yes, I mean no! It's just … it is more than I was expecting," she said, cursing herself for allowing her shield to melt so publicly. "It is … er … a generous figure."

Viktor smiled. He could see she was overwhelmed and angry to let it show.

"You deserve it," he said, stretching over and gripping her arm forcefully. "You did well! We are going to give you a further £50,000 now in cash, and the balance of £175,000 will be delivered to Battersea tomorrow."

Zoltan stood up and went over to a locker. He opened it with a key and plucked a small black holdall from the interior. He handed it to his father.

"Sign here, Anya," Viktor said, proffering an open cash book to her with a string of entries.

She momentarily panicked; how should he sign? Taking the pen, she hesitated for a second or two. Then she wrote "Anya," whilst being sure to give the final "a" an extra twist.

"I see you are discreet," Viktor said, closing the book. "This is good sign." He handed her the black bag.

"Thank you," she said, clutching it to her chest like a baby. "Thank you very much."

"Good ... We will be in contact with you in due course."

Zoltan put his hand gently on her shoulder to usher her out, but Viktor interrupted with one final question.

"Anya, why did you get your hair cut so short? I can see it was done recently."

Constanta felt a stab of panic.

"Well … it was … was getting in the way," she blurted, "and …"

"Grow it! You're too pretty for such a short cut," he said, slumping down onto the couchette with a grunt.

Back on deck, the dusk was gathering and the lights up and down the river glittered more fiercely.

"Okay, Anya," Zoltan said, looking relieved, bordering on happy, "thank you for coming over. I'll send you a message tomorrow morning with a time for the drop-off."

With that, Constanta went back down the ramp and started walking briskly along the pontoon. After a few minutes, she reached Tarquin. On seeing him, she fell to her knees laughing and crying hysterically.

"What on earth's going on?" Tarquin said, looking down at

her in astonishment.

"Tarquin, do you know what they fucking gave us?" she said, peering up through moist eyes.

"What?"

"Two hundred fifty fucking thousand pounds!"

"What are you talking about?" he said frowning.

"I just told you … two hundred fifty thousand pounds … that's what they are giving us for finding the cabinet!" she said, staring at him defiantly through watery eyes.

"*What?*" he said, pulling her upright. "Are you being serious?"

"Yes, Tarquin, I am being serious," she said defiantly. "He gave me another fifty thousand now in this bag, and … and the rest, the one hundred seventy-five thousand, is coming tomorrow!"

Tarquin stared at her for a few seconds, and then flung his arms around her, in a gigantic bear hug. "Good God!" he muttered. "That's just incredible.. you're a genius!"

Back in Tarquin's car, the air crackled with an unbridled energy. Percy jumped from the back to the front repeatedly, trying to offload his pent up emotions. Giggling deliriously, Constanta demanded a tour of central London to see the best clubs, the celebrity restaurants, the most fashionable shops.

So they cruised up Knightsbridge past Harvey Nichols and Harrods with her venting a constant stream of chatter about the fashions in the window displays; how ghastly some were … how beautiful others, and how she was going to come on a buying extravaganza and refit her wardrobe.

As they passed Apsley House, Tarquin told her to shut up and pay homage to the ultimate address in the world … Number One, London, to which she accused him of being "full of shit." He called her an ignorant peasant, and they took the corner into Park Lane at pace. Suddenly, the Stranglers burst from the speakers with "No More Heroes," so Tarquin flicked the volume up and put his foot down in an outpouring of pure pleasure.

She laughed at his crazy antics, and wedging her bare feet

against the windshield, she clutched Percy tightly whilst leaning out into the rushing wind. His ears flapped madly as they weaved dangerously among the lanes, the majestic plane trees of Hyde Park flicking by on their left. Then, as they swooped around Marble Arch, she shouted at him above the noise of the music.

"I'm hungry, Tarquin!"

He turned his head.

"Okay, McDonalds, it is!" he shouted, throwing her a wicked grin.

"No! Take me to the bloody Ritz, you bastard, wherever the fuck that is!"

Thomas Charrington

Chapter 42

Oliver, pale, unshaven, and reclusive, stood gazing out of the open drawing room sash, towards the copper beeches lining the drive. Over a year had passed since that fateful day when his world had collapsed, along with his self-esteem and ambition. Nothing really mattered anymore; a terrible listlessness had infected his every waking hour, and he struggled to keep track of time.

Autumn had arrived, and a gusty southerly wind taunted the big trees, showering rusty leaves across the unkempt lawns and the overgrown flower beds. A line of swallows clung to a swinging telephone wire in readiness for their long flight south.

In front of him, a bee wobbled drunkenly over the window ledge and toppled onto the scuffed parquet floor at his feet. He gazed down at it for a few moments through glazed eyes and felt a surge of empathy; it was disorientated, lost, a reflection of himself and his own life. Plucking an old card from a table, he squatted down and presented it to the struggling insect. After a moment or two, it clambered on board and he heaved himself up with a groan.

Holding it close to his face, he studied the little creature with something akin to affection; those dark eyes, the agitated whiskery body, the exquisite gossamer wings … it was a kindred spirit in a hostile world. Presently, and with great care, he extended his arm through the open window and flicked it into the wind.

Suddenly the phone leapt into life and made him jump. He

ambled slowly over and picked it up.

"Hello?" he said tentatively, gripping the old-fashioned black receiver.

"Oliver?" a voice said.

"Yes, speaking. Is that you, Fabien?"

"Oh, it is you, Oliver!" Fabien said from Chateau Clery. "You sounded different; not quite yourself!"

"Oh, sorry, must be the line," he said flatly.

There was a pause.

"Oliver," Fabien said in a strangely formal way.

"Yes," Oliver said, sensing trouble.

"I have some quite extraordinary news for you."

"You do?" Oliver replied, guessing it was something to do with Cecile.

"You know the Folly ... in the garden?"

"Of course."

"Well, yesterday morning we cleared away the last of the undergrowth and debris at the bottom of those steps; there was half a meter of dirt down there."

"Okay."

"Well, there was a sort of recessed door at the bottom, tucked under a lintel; solid oak, very rotten lower down because of the wet. It took us a long time, but we eventually levered it open on some huge rusty hinges; that's me, Bernard, and his friend Marc. It opened into a sort of cave-like room, a cellar; quite clean with a cobblestone floor."

"Oh?" Oliver said, waiting.

"It had shelving in there; crude shelving, with loads of old pots, plates, glasses, and things, including some small tables and quite a stack of chairs, decorative chairs which obviously used to have upholstery on them. Very rotten, as you can imagine."

"Well, we always did think that the folly was more than just a visual delight, didn't we, Fabien," Oliver said, dropping his guard. "How intriguing. I look forward to taking a look when—"

"No, Oliver! This is not why I've called you. Just ... just let me speak."

Oliver stopped dead. He could hear the emotion in Fabien's voice; he was struggling.

"Inside the cellar there was a wood panelled wall at the far side opposite the door. It was also rotten, especially towards the floor. The whole thing was covered in mildew and fungus. We began to remove it, and it just fell away in chunks. And behind this was a stone wall, as you would expect."

Oliver grunted.

"But then we noticed a part of the wall behind this panelling—vaguely the shape of a door that looked different, like it had been filled in at a later date," Fabien said, swallowing. There was another pause.

"We all thought this was a bit strange, so I told Bernard to get a pick axe and see if he could knock it down. I actually wondered if it was a tomb or something crazy like that. When he came back, he gave the axe to Marc—he being younger—and he started swinging at it. We were all laughing a bit nervously as something seemed about to happen. Well, it did, Oliver. Something did happen."

Fabien stopped for a few moments to gather himself and heard a muffled grunt from Oliver.

"The false wall crumbled quite easily, and suddenly we … we shone the torch through and found ourselves looking into another room with a number of marble statues and these bundles … linen bundles, some small, some huge propped up in an open box. A few of them were lying on this massive oak chest in the centre of the space. It was raised off the floor on a rotten wooden platform. I was shocked; we all were. It was like we 'ad found some hidden treasure! So I climbed through this broken hole, and walked really carefully across the platform to look. Marc was right behind me."

"And what was ….was …in the …." Oliver mumbled, before trailing off as Fabien resumed.

"Very carefully we lifted these flat bundles off the chest and put them on the floor. Then between us we lifted the heavy lid and put it to one side. There was loads more linen lying on something big inside. Well…..we started pulling this old stained cloth away, piece by piece, and …and…. mon dieu, *there it was Oliver*!"

"What …*what* was there?" Oliver said pressing the phone hard to his ear.

"The *original* Freiburg Cabinet my friend!"

There was no response from Oliver for at least five seconds. Then he said in a low irritated voice.

"What are you talking about Fabien?"

"As I just said, there it was … The Freiburg Cabinet twin."

"Fabien…please,"

"Oliver you have to *believe*!"

"No …NO! This canNOT be true!" Oliver exploded down the phone, "You're … you're …yes, you're bloody joking with me! What the *hell* are you talking about?"

"Oliver I am telling you the *truth*….it is here …*it always has been here*!"

"No … No … I can't take this …you must be mistaken …it's *impossible!*"

"Believe me Oliver. The Freiburg Cabinet original twin is here in the Folly at Chateau Clery – I've seen it with my very own eyes! *I know what I'm talking about*!"

Oliver clutched his hair and squeezed it into a painful fist at the back of his head.

"But ….but this means there are now *three* cabinets for *Christ's sake* – what in the hell are we to do?"

"I 'ave thought about this already Oliver. There is only one answer. *Absolutely nothing*! We reveal this to the authorities and it becomes obvious that the one we just sold is a fraud. This cabinet must *never* see the light of day again. This is why when I realised what it was, I pretended to Marc that it was nothing of any great importance. Just …just a nice piece that we needed to cover up quickly again to save it from the damp. But Oliver ….there is some other news which …which is going to make you smile."

"What now?"

"You know the linen bundles I mentioned?"

"Yes."

"Well later …when the men had left ..I began to unwrap them. I suggest you sit down to hear this!"

"Jesus *wept*, Fabien …what's happening this afternoon! Go on …let's hear it!"

"Oliver …they are paintings! Mon dieu, beautiful paintings … valuable paintings, some in massively ornate gold frames. These must have been the most valuable paintings in the house, and they had the sense to hide them at the outset of the revolution! Among them, there are two Fragonards, a Watteau, a pair of Bouchers, and a Rubens!"

There was a long silence as Oliver once again stood dumbstruck, trying to take in the enormity of the news.

"Rubens … Fragonard? *No!*" he muttered, a great heat welling up inside him. "*This cannot be true!* How can you tell?"

"Because they are all labelled on the back…..all of them!"

"Are you absolutely sure, Fabien?"

"Yes, Oliver, *I am*, absolutely!" Fabien said emphatically. "I know the signature of Rubens; it's plain to see! There's a huge van Dyke, as well. I mean really massive. It must have been a nightmare to get it into that room!"

"But … but … are they damaged?"

"This is the whole point, Oliver. They are perfect. We are sitting on some masterpieces here … a fortune. Just believe me … and I can …"

But Oliver had gone, dropping the phone as he went. He half wriggled and half fell out of the sash window, landing like a plump bear in the flower bed three feet below. Titus catapulted through the window above him like a stag, eager to join in this new crazy game.

With tears rolling down his face, he staggered to his feet and, laughing like a madman, ran towards the big trees, only to fall flat on his face having caught his foot on the shallow curb of the path.

He lay on the ground convulsing as Titus tore round him in

circles, barking hysterically, his claws sending clods of earth and grass flying. Again Oliver hauled himself up, laughing louder than ever, and staggered on and under the copper beeches where he flopped down on his back, his limbs akimbo like a starfish. As the salty tears rolled down his face, the thick fleshy tongue of Titus darted in and slapped his cheeks and eyes, whilst the wind mixed his manic laughter with the leaves and carried it across the lawns.

The End

Note from the Author:

If you enjoyed reading this novel, it would be so appreciated if you could pen a short review on Amazon. It's really easy - whether you bought it online or have a hardback copy instead – just as long as you have an Amazon account. (Go on... do it now!)

Like this I will get an understanding of the book's strengths and weaknesses.

With my sincere thanks.

Author page: https://www.amazon.com/author/thomascharrington

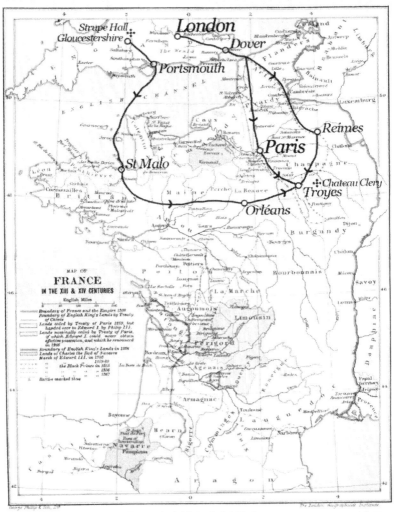

Printed in Great Britain
by Amazon

84245675R00223